Call of Kythshire

By Missy Sheldrake

First published by Missy Sheldrake March 2015
Printed by CreateSpace, An Amazon.com Company

Second publishing, September 2016: This version has been edited for errors and reformatted to justified paragraphs. Due to these changes, the novel page count is much lower than previous versions, but the content is the same.

Illustrations for this story were created using the Procreate iPad App and Prismacolor Markers.

www.missysheldrake.com

For

James, Wes, and Mom

Contents

MAPS

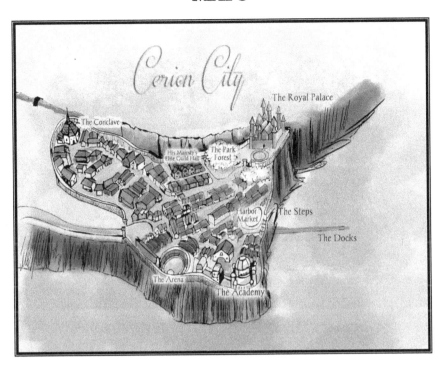

Chapter One

CERION DAY

"Azaeli Hammerfel. Sponsor: His Majesty's Elite!" The crier announces my name, and a cheer erupts from the overfilled stands as I march into the arena and take my place on the pitch beside the other Squire hopefuls.

"Hammerfel. Wretchedsmell," Jord, the boy beside me, guffaws at his own brilliance. The rest of the competitors on the line chuckle, their amusement easily missed by the noisy crowd of spectators above. I ignore him and focus on our shadows stretched across the grass. My own seems quite out of place beside the others, so much shorter than those cast by the boys in the line.

"Dacva Archomyn. Sponsor: Redemption!" The crier calls.

I square my shoulders and stare ahead at attention as the name is called. Of course it has to be him next, I think to myself. Master Ragnor probably made the list order himself. A small part of me truly believes he enjoys seeing boys torment me. As the only girl in swordplay training. I'm used to being a target. After eight years dealing with it, I've learned to brush it off. Dacva's reception from the crowd as he comes to stand beside me is loud enough and long enough to mask his flung insult so only those close by can hear it.

"Hammerfel. Corpse's shell." He snorts, standing in perfect formation.

"Fishbait," offers Jord from my right. He rocks back on his heels, obviously pleased with himself. This one bothers me more than the last two. It conjures the memory of a group of them dangling me by the ankles over Cerion's high sea wall when we were younger. I can still hear their cruel laughter, see the angry white waves crashing into the jagged rocks of the cliff face far below, and smell the salty spray in my face. Another player is announced, and another cheer sounds from the crowd as that one files in next to Dacva.

"Good one, Jord," Dacva murmurs. "Wormsmeal."

"Heel-grind," Jord says with exaggerated menace.

"Royal pup," growls Dacva.

"Wench."

"Braggart."

I turn a deaf ear and occupy myself by searching the colorful stands for our guild's gold and blue until I finally spot my father. Bryse, our shield master, towers beside him. The giant of a man takes up three seats on the bench, but his size is not overly remarkable among the diversity of the crowd. Cerion is a place that welcomes all types, and that lends itself to a very interesting mix of people among the throngs. All races are welcome within the city's walls, and the colorful blend of guild banners and allies sitting side by side makes me beam with pride for my country. Da and Bryse catch me watching and wave, and as the mocking continues I know what Bryse would say: *Use it. Let it fuel you.*

"You know today is your death day, right, Fishmeal?" Dacva jeers.

I don't give him the satisfaction of an answer. He's told me the same nearly every day for the past year: *Cerion Day will be your last.* I'm not afraid of him, though. I've bested him in practice many times. What bothers me most is that he's done more than his share to make me dread this day that I've dreamed of for so long. Cerion Day is a festival that I look forward to every year at midsummer, a celebration to honor our king and the peace that his family's reign has kept for nearly two hundred years now. The squire trials are just a small part of the festival, but a very popular event nonetheless.

There are sixteen of us when the list is done, each of us sixteen years old. We'll be paired up and pitted against each other in a quick game of skill. Eight will come out victors, earning the title of squire. My heart races at the thought. When I'm named squire, my duties will lie with my guild, and my training will be their responsibility. I'll be through with these wretched boys for good. I'll never have to go back to Ragnor's arms training again.

In the distance the bells of the Conclave ring, pealing out the royal wedding song. I try not to think about the hundreds of eyes on me, waiting to see what I can do. The games today are in the Prince's honor to celebrate his wedding day, and so the stands are packed twice as full as usual with masses from all over the known world, hoping to catch a glimpse of him and his new bride at their first public appearance. The trumpets sound and Master Ragnor rides down the line to take his place at the end. As the cheers rise again, Jord sways and bumps my shoulder.

"High strung blood, blood wretch..." He stumbles and falls

forward, landing on his face with a thud. I'm not surprised. The blazing sun of midsummer is brutal, and with all of us decked in padded gambesons, full chain mail, and the surcoats of our sponsoring guilds, it was only a matter of time before the heat claimed some. The vigil itself is part of the trial. Jord is only the first to go down. As we stand at attention waiting through the afternoon for the royal procession, three more hopefuls fall and are carried off.

Finally, the trumpets sound again and the crowd erupts with a deafening cheer. My attention snaps to the royal box, and I stand rail-straight as His Majesty King Tirnon mounts the steps hand in hand with Queen Naelle. A simple gold circlet rests on his silver-blonde hair, and beside him Her Majesty is stunning as always as she smiles and waves at the crowd. Even on a day such as this, their clothes are fine but not too bold, an echo of the city's sentiment.

The king and queen are followed by Prince Eron, who is an exact younger version of his father, though his hair is cropped shorter and his face clean-shaven. Beside him is his new bride, Princess Amei, who is both exquisite and exotic. She comes from a small island nation to the south called the Stepstone Isles; a new ally and an important marriage for Cerion. Her azure wedding gown complements her dark brown complexion perfectly, and the bright amethyst jewels of her tiara are dazzling against her midnight black curls. The newlywed couple kisses each other tenderly, and a fresh wave of cheers washes over the arena.

They take their seats, and behind them the two princesses climb up to join their family. Sarabel is my age, but so ladylike in her deep purple gown that I barely recognize her as she holds her little sister's hand. Margary, the tiniest royal, is dressed all in lace and ruffles. She's the portrait of a princess with a dainty sparkling circlet perched on her dark curls. As the princesses greet the crowd, Margy scans the row and her eyes stop at me. She points and hops and tugs at Sarabel, and they both favor me with an excited wave. I want to return the gesture, but I show discipline by giving just the slightest nod instead.

The trumpets sound again and my heart pounds in time with the rumbling of hooves that approach the line. I try to keep my eyes forward but I can't help but slide them to the side as the riders approach. Twelve riders, all decked in gleaming armor and bearing the flags of their guilds, thunder the circuit of the ring. Clumps of earth are churned up just within arm's reach of us as each rider passes, but I remain as still as stone, steady and strong.

My sponsor, high atop a massive horse draped to the hooves in blue and gold livery, comes to a halt facing the royal box. I march forward with the remaining hopefuls to the great relief of my stiff muscles, and take my place beside my knight's towering steed. In perfect unison, we all snap to salute. The king rises to speak, and the arena goes so silent that I can hear my knight's chain-mailed boot ringing softly just beside my ear.

"My dear subjects, allies, and guests, I present to you the hopefuls of Cerion's Festival of Peace. As is our tradition, these houses and guilds have volunteered to demonstrate their skills and present to us the future squires of Cerion. The victors of these games shall win our favor and be honored with the title of Squire, and one day, Knight. Hopefuls, I invite you now to show us the fruits of your years of training. May you fight honorably for Cerion!"

"For Cerion!" the crowd roars as His Majesty settles back onto his throne. I hold my salute while a wiry man in purple livery readies to announce the matches. He unfurls a scroll and waits for the crowd to settle, but they don't show him the same silent respect as they did the king.

"Hopefuls of the first match," he shouts as he reads from the scroll, "Dacva Archomyn, Redemption," a roar erupts from the crowd, and I notice Prince Eron applaud enthusiastically, "versus Azaeli Hammerfel, His Majesty's Elite!" It's fitting that our knights would be paired here on the field. Our guilds have been rivals since mine gained His Majesty's favor, and it's obvious the tension is famous with the crowd, which thunders its approval of the match with such enthusiasm that my ears ring from the din.

"Their challenge," the crier continues, "the rings!"

The rings. It's one of my favorites. Rings of various colors are thrown to the field by spectators and hung by ribbons from the walls. Each color accounts for a certain number of points, the most valuable being the purple ones tossed by the royal family. The object is for the squires to collect the rings as quickly as they can and fasten them to hooks on the livery of their knight's horse. Points are tallied when the sands of the hourglass run out. It would be a simple game, if not for the risk of being trampled by a war horse or caught in the midst of the knights' fierce battle.

My knight turns back to our place and I follow, glancing across the field at our opponents. Redemption's knight, who I recognize as Dacva's cousin Dar, is huge. His shoulders are as broad as two strong men. My knight is half his size, but carries twice the skill. I'm confident in our victory.

The trumpet sounds again and Dacva presents his knight with an enormous broad ax as he flashes me a taunting grin. *Let it fuel you,* I think to myself. I turn for my own knight's weapon and smile as its familiar presence bolsters me. The great sword is nearly as tall as I am and etched with an intricate design that glows blue as I heft it up to my knight.

"Yeah, Azi!" Bryse shouts. Others cheer my name as the two horses ride to meet each other at the center. The knights give the ready signal, and the crier turns the hourglass.

"Begin!"

Instantly I'm pelted with rings from the excited crowd. As the knights clash together furiously, the larger man's red and orange cape snaps around him like flames licking at char. The battle is as fierce and entertaining as it's meant to be. Though Dacva's knight has power, mine has speed. The powerful clash of their weapons sends sparks scattering around them. I tear my attention from the fray and crouch to scoop up a handful of rings strewn across the grass.

As I stand up I'm aware that Dacva is charging me. His sword is raised, his teeth are bared ferociously, his battle cry lost among the roaring crowd. I'm caught off guard and barely have time to shove the rings into my surcoat and slide my sword from its scabbard before he's upon me, slashing furiously. He means to keep his promise, that much is clear. I know his style so the counters are easy, but I'm unprepared in my footing and I fall back into the grass as I raise my sword to parry.

In training, the spar would pause now and I would have time to get up while the fight resets. But the bloodlust in his eyes assures me that training is over. He isn't stopping, he means to kill.

"Foul!" an indignant voice hollers above the crowd, possibly my father's.

"You're through, Cur!" Dacva sneers as he drives his sword at me and I raise my own to block it. I kick his stomach hard and he doubles over and falls back. *Let it fuel you.* With a rage that has been bottled up for years, I jump to my feet and swing with all of my strength, hitting him hard in the side with the flat of my blade. I feel the blow crack his ribs beneath his chain mail and he falls to his knees, breathless. I lunge at him again, but he recovers quickly and our swords clash as we press each other back and forth along the wall.

In the center of the field, my knight and his are locked in a similarly ruthless battle. It's impossible to tell who has the upper hand. Dacva and I fight on, circling each other until I'm sure the hourglass must be half empty. The rings are forgotten. Sure in my footing now, I swing another heavy blow to his side as he raises his sword arm, and meet the same cracked ribs. Furious, he stabs at me with a grimace of pain and his sword finds the gap in the armor at my collar and slices into my shoulder.

I shove him away, ignoring the pain that sears through the wound. Enraged, I charge him, raising my sword, ready to end this once and for all, but I'm suddenly blocked by a wall of blue and yellow livery. The horse rears up and strong hooves thunder down inches from Dacva's head as he sprawls back.

"The rings!" my knight commands.

On the other side of the steed, the blue sword arcs and meets with Dacva's, and Redemption's knight thunders across to bear down on us. I quickly sheath my sword and fumble into my coat for the rings, ignoring the pain that shoots from my shoulder into my arm. I grasp a hook just behind my knight's knee and try to fasten the rings there, but my glove gets caught. The rings scatter to the ground, and I'm dragged as the fight moves across the field toward the royal box. I struggle to free myself, but now I'm pinned between the beast and the wall with Dacva charging us as the battle rages between axe and sword above me.

Slowly I'm aware of a sensation radiating from my knight. Calm. I push away the pain and steady my shaking hands to work the buckle which cinches my glove to my wrist. The feeling gradually pulses stronger until it washes over me with a comforting peace. My desperate fumbling fingers become sure. The pain in my wounded shoulder disappears. The horses stand still. The clashing of weapons slows, quiets. Dacva looms nearby, his mouth open, his expression vacant. The crowd nearby hushes. As my hand finally comes free, I glance at the nearly empty hourglass.

"Azi!" A tiny voice breaks the strange tranquility. Princess Margy leans over the wall above me, grinning. A purple ring tied to a pink ribbon bobs from her delicate fingers. Half-dazed, I reach up and take it and hang it onto the hook where my glove is still caught.

"Time!" calls the crier. The crowd seems to find its voice again, cheering as officials rush onto the field to inspect the horses and count rings.

My knight slips from her horse hastily, her golden braid tumbling to her shoulder as she pulls her barrel helm free. She rushes to me and takes me by the shoulders. Her panicked blue eyes mirror my own and then search me, pulling my armor away from my skin to examine the injury, looking frantically for the source of the blood that has soaked the front of my livery.

"I'm okay, Mum," I whisper, slightly embarrassed as I brush her hand away. "You healed it already." Over her shoulder, I watch Dar throw his helm down in a fury and slide from his own horse. He shoves a still-stupefied Dacva roughly aside with the butt of his axe as he storms toward us. Dacva blinks and shakes his head, only just now starting to realize the game is done.

"Filthy Paladin tricks!" With his helmet off, Dar is even more intimidating. He stalks up to us with his nostrils flaring like a bull, his grimace baring two missing teeth as his nose bleeds into his beard. He spits blood at my mother's feet and shoves her shoulder. She turns to face him, placing herself between us.

"Your boy was out to kill," she says with a measured tone.

"Damn right."

Dar's eyes flash with cruel hatred. In the face of his rage, my mother's peaceful demeanor makes him look a bit ridiculous. I shift my stance so she and I are shoulder-to-shoulder. When Dar glances past us at the king, his words are low and secret.

"Put her in her place," he growls. "In the ground, with the lot of you beside her."

Behind us in the royal box, an argument between the prince and His Majesty draws my attention. Two officials stand before the throne, each bearing a pillow. The red and orange one is empty, and upon the blue and gold one rests a single purple ring tied with a bloodstained pink ribbon. Prince Eron is contesting my mother's calming pulse as an unfair advantage.

"Under the circumstances," His Majesty the King declares firmly, "we rule that the use of magical force was justified." He raises his voice to the crowd as Eron crosses his arms and looks away.

"The victor with one ring," he declares, "is Azaeli Hammerfel, Squire of His Majesty's Elite." With a roar that is quickly drowned out by the crowd, Dar stomps to Dacva and grabs him by the back of his collar. He screams and cuffs the boy hard across the face with his metal gaunted fist. Dacva tries to struggle free and walk off with dignity, but Dar grips him by the back of his vest and drags him from the field in a ruthless fury.

My victory is dampened as I watch the two of them disappear through the dark exit at the edge of the arena. Redemption takes their station seriously. Their reputation is more important to them than friendship or family. They are ranked second in the king's favor, right behind our own guild. Where I have been brought up with encouragement to succeed and patience for my failures, Dacva obviously has not.

"Come, Azi," Mum says, slightly shaken as she tears her gaze from them. The horses and rings have been cleared off of the field and the second tournament is announced, pairing two guilds from the harbor borough. She guides me to the long empty bench just beside the royal booth where the rest of the winning squires and their sponsors will eventually be seated.

I think of Dacva and Dar as I stow my helm and gloves beneath the bench and scratch at my sweaty scalp. Perhaps it might have been better to let him win just to spare him the wrath of his family. Then I realize letting him win would have meant my own death. I try to push those thoughts away as I shift closer to my mother, whose attention is not on the game, but on the doors exiting the arena. Her eyes are narrowed, and in her lap her hands are clenched into fists.

"Mum?" I watch her for a moment and then follow her gaze to where Dacva's form is crumpled against the wall of the exit tunnel. My father stands between him and Dar, who is obviously still enraged and inviting a fight. Da points deeper into the doorway apparently telling Dar to leave, and Dar kicks dust at Da and shoves him, but the attack doesn't move him. My father is slightly smaller than the beast of a man, but not intimidated. He stands firm, strong and brave.

The scuffle catches the attention of the guards, who move in cautiously. My father points again and Dar waves a furious, dismissive hand at Dacva before stomping away into the darkness. As soon as he's gone, the guards return to their stations and my father stoops beside Dacva and gestures to another man nearby: Brother Donal, our guild's cleric. He and my father lift Dacva up and carry him off. My mother's eyes are tear-filled as she turns to look at me. She starts to speak, but the words catch and she shakes her head.

"I'm proud of you," she says on her second try. I know she wants to go and help, but it would be unheard of for either of us to leave the box until after our accolades are given. Instead I loop my arm into hers and squeeze it. The crowd roars again. The second game is finished and victors file in beside us as the next group is announced. Suddenly, I'm attacked by a flurry of brown curls and ruffles as Princess Margary bounces onto the bench beside me and dangles the winning purple ring in my face.

"This is for you." She grins as she lowers it into my open palm. "Squire Azi! You can keep it. Mother said!"

"Thank you, Your Highness." I tuck the ring into my surcoat. "And thank you for helping me win. Without your favor, I'd have to wait another year for my chance."

"I know," she says with a bob of her head, and goes back to watching the players on the field.

"You'd better go back up now, before one of us gets into trouble," I say, feeling a little awkward with her sitting there. *Royal pup*, I think, and push the words away. I won't ever have to hear them again now that I'm a squire.

"Father said I could sit with you." She bounces up and down beside me as the crowd cheers at the games that have failed to capture my attention. "And tomorrow, you can come to the palace and show me how to play at swords." I glance up at the throne and His Majesty gives me a friendly wave. I smile and bow my head respectfully.

Normally I would welcome an invitation to the palace, but the timing is troublesome. Tomorrow, the guild will be readying to set off on the King's Quest, which is traditionally declared on sunset the day after the festival. My duties to run messages, inventory supplies and provisions for the trip, and to polish weapons and armor are too important to put off.

The bench slowly fills with new Squires and their proud Knights, and we are presented with the ribbons and medals of our new station. I wish I could be present in the moment, but my thoughts are already on tomorrow's obligations. As I bid farewell to little Margary, I wonder how I'll manage it all.

Chapter Two

HIS MAJESTY'S ELITE

I'm half-starved and exhausted as Mum and I make our way slowly through the throngs leaving the arena. It takes us three times longer than usual to weave through the main streets, and eventually we break away to the lesser-traveled route which leads to our guild hall. The white stone spires of the palace gleam coral-pink us above the rooftops to the east, washed in the light of the setting sun. Mum and I avoid the road along the gardens that separate our street from the palace, knowing the crowds will be thick with sightseers along the park promenade, eager to catch a glimpse of the royal family returning from the games.

Though our hall is only a fraction of the size of the palace, it takes up a modest block of the city on the other side of the forest park. The compound is made up of a row of three two-story houses at the façade, and then another row beside it to form an L-shape. Ours is the first house we reach coming from the west, and the closest to the market square.

As soon as we step through our front door, all of the tension of the crowds and the games falls away. Our home is the perfect size for us, with two armchairs and a small couch surrounding the hearth, and a writing table against the front window. A cozy dining nook in the kitchen at the back of the main floor serves us well for breakfast and lunch. We usually take our supper in the meeting hall. Over the wooden counter, a window overlooks the back courtyard and my father's forge.

"It wasn't a bad hit," I say over my shoulder as we make our way upstairs. Here, in the safety of our house, the fight with Dacva seems trivial. "I barely felt it. I've had worse in training." *Usually by his hand,* I think to myself as we reach the small dressing room which connects our bedrooms. "I'm used to it, Mum." She strokes a sticky strand of hair from my forehead and hugs me tightly.

"I know," she says, sighing. "It still doesn't make it easy for a mother to see her child bleed." She steps back and brushes my shoulder with her hand as if to clean the bloodstain away. "It was well-fought, though, and Bryse is sure to be impressed by the amount of blood." She rolls her eyes and musses my hair with her fingers. "Perhaps you should wear that to dinner." We laugh and chat together as we help each other out of our armor, wash up, and change into comfortable, clean clothes. Mum chooses a soft gown and I decide on simple blue trousers and an undershirt. After a bit of thought I pull the bloodied tunic back on, a mark of my first real battle. Mum is right, if nothing else it will make for good conversation.

"Brace yourself. They're not going to go easy on you, squire," she says with a grin as she hands me my sheathed sword and picks up her own, and I lead the way downstairs and out of the kitchen door. In passage to the hall, my stomach growls at the aroma of roasted pheasant hanging thick in the air.

As we approach the open doors, I catch snippets of our guild mates' gathering. Mya is playing a lazy tune on her lute, and there's a constant underlying snoring as Cort and Bryse argue boisterously about some wager. Two others discuss something in hushed tones. As we near, I catch a hint of the conversation.

"...going too far," my father says. "They've never outright threatened us before. Not like this."

"Keep your head, Benen," Brother Donal warns. "A brash act is a dead man's last folly. There is another solution. We yield to them. Relinquish..." The lute-playing stops as Donal's voice trails off, and the rest of the room goes silent. The awkward pause continues for just a moment as my mother and I appear together in the doorway, and then chaos erupts.

"Azi!" Cort and Bryse whoop as they leap from the table and lunge at me, swords ready. Behind them Rian and Uncle Gaethon rise and lift their hands toward me, fists closed. My father and Donal jump to their feet and charge me, too. In the chaos I hear a screeching that makes me want to clap my hands over my ears: Mya's warfare song. Thanks to Mum, I was expecting this welcome. I keep my wits and pull my sword free from its sheath.

Bryse reaches me first. I parry a high blow from his sword as he clashes into me. The muscles in his grey arms bulge, as thick as my waist, as he swings his shield in an attempt to stun me with a blow. I turn my shoulder to him, duck around the shield, and dive beneath his wide stance. Behind him, I roll and jump quickly to my feet, turn, and catch his sword around my own with a twist. It clatters to the floor.

I spin again to face Cort who's been waiting behind him, flourishing a slender curved blade in each hand. As an opponent, he's a stark contrast to Bryse with his slender build and deep brown skin. His long braids whip around his face as he flourishes his swords in an intricate dance. The weapons move so quickly they whistle and blur before my eyes, threatening to entrance me. His style is the most difficult for me to defeat with my own sword, which requires two hands and a slower swing. Still, I relieve him of one sword and then the other after a quick bout.

There's no reprieve. Spells crackle and boom from Uncle Gaethon across the room, arcing flashes of light which burst before my eyes leaving spots of blue obscuring my vision. Brother Donal comes next with his staff. He battles me halfheartedly, a twinkle in his kind eye, and our short session ends when I send the long stick flying across the room where it only just misses the fireplace. He settles onto the bench nearby, breathless but smiling. Finally, my father approaches with his hammer. He goes easy on me with a very familiar three point combination I parry with ease before sending his weapon clattering to the floor, and then he jumps at me and curls his arm around my neck, laughing. Everyone cheers and embraces me. They clap me on the shoulder and hug me and congratulate me. I laugh and squeal as Bryse lifts me far up over his shoulder and hefts me across the room to drop me into an overstuffed armchair.

"If we're quite finished!" Mouli appears in the doorway beside my mother and clicks her tongue disapprovingly. Tufts of grey hair peek out from beneath her hat. I blink the magic-induced spots from my eyes as my stomach growls again at the sight of the pheasant on the tray.

"Mouli!" Bryse jumps to grab his sword and mockingly charge at her, playing at recreating my greeting.

"Really, flashing your swords in the dining hall. Someone's liable to get killed." She ducks her head and bats Bryse away.

"Nah, Donal would heal us up in no time." Bryse eyes the pheasant hungrily and tries to steal a taste as Mum helps Mouli with the tray. I laugh. This place is my refuge from the outside. Here there are no airs and graces. We've been a guild together for so long we're as comfortable as family.

The meeting hall is a great square room. Its rich stone walls are decorated with several generations' worth of tokens, trophies, and tapestries. In the center of the room is a long table lined with benches, which is used for both dining and planning. The great hearth, just inside the door, is encircled with an array of comfortable mismatched stuffed arm chairs. At the far end of the hall beyond the long table, the walls are lined with shelves of books, scrolls, and maps. There are several writing desks there as well, for studying and drafting letters and plans.

Everything here in the guild hall is shared between its members. I've played as a toddler on its plush carpets as my parents planned their routes, and I've sat for hours practicing my writing as Uncle watched over my shoulder. I've fallen asleep in the comfortable chairs when meetings ran too long, and I've crawled along the floor beside Rian as we made a game of tracking down the source of ants in springtime. This is my home, and my family, and with my induction as Squire I'm finally a true and official member of its company.

As I begin to drowse beside the low embers of the fire, I'm aware of the steady snoring which has been constant since we were in the passage. I turn to the chair beside me. How anyone could have slept through the chaos of my welcome is beyond me, but there Elliot lies, his legs draped over the chair's arm, sound asleep. Now his nose twitches beneath a shaggy fringe of red hair as the smell of pheasant and pie and so many other wonderful things fills the room. Very slowly, he raises his head. His eyes, which have always struck me as an exotic shade of gold, take a moment to focus on me. In an instant he leaps up onto the cushion and his loaded bow appears pointed at my forehead faster than I can blink.

"Azi!" he shouts, and I'm too exhausted to do anything but shrink back into the chair and curl my knees up to guard myself. I let out a tiny squeal of surrender and cross my arms over my face.

"Too late." Bryse says from the table, where he's already heaping his dish with potatoes and both pheasant legs.

"Missed it." Cort smirks and grabs a leg from Bryse, who growls and threatens a stab with his fork.

"Aw." Elliot stretches, tosses his bow onto the chair cushion, and saunters to the table. "This looks amazing, Mouli."

Wearily, I push myself up from the chair and join the meal. Dining at the guild hall is informal. There is no head of the table, everyone sits where they are most comfortable. I slide in next to Rian, who is a bit taller than me and rail thin. His slightly pointed ears peek out from his short cropped auburn hair. He grins at me as I sit, and leans to bump my shoulder with his. His mother, Mya, sits beside him. Her build is heartier and it is obvious Rian gets his height from her. It's strange to see her dressed for a performance. Her usually spiked red hair is smoothed back with a sparkling band, and she wears a revealing sleeveless gown with long slits revealing her bare legs. Beside Mya, Elliot is unremarkable aside from the wood elf's point to his ears and the soft deer leathers he wears, dyed green.

Across the table, my parents greet each other with a kiss. Smiling, she smooths back my father's sandy gray hair and serves him a plate before taking her own. Beside them, Uncle Gaethon, her brother, straightens a stack of pages beside his dish. I pile my own plate with meat and root vegetables and bread and cheese. When everyone has a full plate before them, we bow our heads, clasp hands, and speak the blessing together.

Mouli, who has been bustling around the table filling mugs and serving bread, stops beside me and fusses at my tunic.

"Oughtn't you have changed your shirt, Azi? Look at all that blood." She clicks her tongue again.

"Bah, looks good on her. Makes her look tough." Bryse winks at me across the table. "Was a good fight." He shoves some potatoes into his mouth.

"It was a dirty fight." Cort's tone is distasteful. "Never should have happened. It's supposed to be a game. They ruined it."

"Azi came out the victor. Good was served." Brother Donal nods and takes a gulp from his mug.

"It should have come as no surprise you'd be pitted against

Redemption." Mya's soothing voice is steady, but there is an underlying note of anger. "I'm glad it's over."

"Over?" My father's blue eyes flash across the table at Mya, and he stabs a chunk of meat with his fork. "How can you say it's over? You didn't see—"

"Benen." My mother's hand on his arm calms my father instantly. "I'm sure Mya only meant the arena. All of us here know it isn't over as far as Redemption is concerned." I look past Rian at Mya, who nods.

"As I was saying to Benen just before," Donal brushes crumbs from the front of his brown robes, "it might be wise to relinquish our standing—"

"The coward's way!" Bryse booms and his fists slam the table, and out of habit most of us reach to catch our mugs before they spill. "Give them our titles, our glory? Then what?" He leans across the table, looming over Donal. "You think that'll fix it all? Giving them what we've earned by the sweat of our own brows? If they want it, they've got to earn it!" Donal folds his hands on the table and calmly meets Bryse's furious gaze.

"I'm sure it wasn't your intention to accuse me of being cowardly. I take no offense, of course."

"Bah, don't pull that with me." Bryse drops to the bench and rips a loaf of bread in half. "You know it's not what I meant."

"It was a brazen act." Cort shakes his head. "They're out for blood. If they would be so brash right in front of everyone, in front of the king…"

"They'll stop at nothing." Elliot finishes his thought.

"Perhaps if we looked at the situation differently," Mya offers, and she gives everyone a moment to settle into the suggestion before she continuing. "Perhaps the boy just got swept up in the excitement. Maybe Dar's abuse toward him at the end of the bout, as you described it Benen, was a punishment for Dacva's behavior toward Azi."

"You weren't there. The boy had it out for her from the start. Has for a long time and you know it. And Dar wasn't going easy on Lis, either." Bryse tears at the bread with his teeth and then sits brooding.

"Still, the game is done. Azi fought well, and we have no evidence they are threatening us directly."

Mya has always tried to be the voice of reason. Her level head and ability to look at a problem from every angle is how she rose to leadership. Still, I remember the fury in Dar's eyes as he towered over my mother in the arena. I remember his words. *Put her in her place. In the ground. The lot of you beside her.*

"Until we do," Mya continues, "it's best to just act as we always have. Keep ourselves in His Majesty's favor by serving him and the kingdom, and watch our backs."

"A wise beetle respects the spider's web," Donal proclaims. My mother catches my eye from across the table, and I can tell Dar's threat is also on her mind. She chooses not to mention it, though, and I respect her silence. There's a moment of quiet as everyone eats and drinks thoughtfully.

"Will Luca be joining the feast?" Elliot leans forward addressing Mouli, who had slid onto the bench beside me silently during the discussion.

"No, no. He's tending to our guest in Donal's house. Making sure he stays asleep. I'll take them both a plate when we're through."

"I didn't know we had a guest. Are we hosting someone for the festival?" I ask, looking across the table at my Uncle. He looks away, and Brother Donal clears his throat uncomfortably.

"He could be useful. We could ask him some questions." Rian suggests from beside me, startling me. He's been so unusually quiet, I had almost forgotten he was here. Uncle Gaethon throws a warning look from across the table and Rian nods and turns his attention back to his plate.

"Maybe he talks in his sleep," Elliot offers hopefully. "I could sit in there with him…"

"Filthy whelp." Bryse sneers. "I still say we should ransom him back to them."

"Because *that* would be honorable," Cort rolls his eyes.

"Don't see," Bryse says around a mouthful, "why he should be our problem."

"We couldn't leave him there to die. He's just a boy, after all." My father's gaze meets mine. "I hope you understand, Azi." It takes me a moment to realize what he means, but then the scene after the arena fight comes to mind. I remember my father and Brother Donal carrying Dacva's lifeless form off into the shadows of the hallway, and

I realize the boy who tried to kill me just hours ago is here, under our care, resting soundly in Donal's bed.

"I can only imagine what his life has been like until now," my mother says quietly. "Was he badly injured?" Her serene tone only serves to annoy me. Still, I try to keep my composure as I set down my fork and clench my hands in my lap.

Mum has spent many hours trying to teach me the art of meditation. As a paladin, she has perfected the skill of peace to such a degree she's able to radiate her serenity to affect everyone around her. She's mastered it so well she's able to do it in the heat of battle, as she did in the arena. The power of peace, she's told me so many times, can bring down the fiercest foe. It's a skill not many can master, and she's very careful to use it sparingly. People should be allowed to feel their own true emotions. Forcing calmness on anyone for too long or to further your own agenda is an abuse of power. I recognize it now, though, the gentle feeling reaching across to me, telling me to be calm. Not to let my anger take hold. Somehow that small push from her makes me even angrier.

"Broken ribs, broken nose, black eye, fractured cheek, bruised neck, punctured lung." Brother Donal ticks down Dacva's list of injuries casually. "I healed him up but the sleeping draught will do him good." I look at my shaking hands and blood stained sleeve, and close my eyes to see Dacva bearing down on me. The memory of his blade as it slices my neck is like a fresh wound. Deep down, I know it's right to show our enemies mercy and kindness. Bubbling on the surface, though, I can't help but feel betrayed. I set my hands on the table to keep them from shaking. I can't meet my father's eyes as I slowly rise from my place.

"Please excuse me," I manage around the lump in my throat.

"Azi…" My father stands as I turn away from them and walk out the door.

"Let her go, Benen." My mother's tone is hushed. "She'll work it out." I shake my head just slightly as I storm into the corridor. Behind me I can hear Bryse's raised voice, then Mya's calmer one, but I don't care what they're saying. I've been attacked and bloodied and threatened, and my tormentor lies comfortably sleeping, tended by people who are supposedly on my side. Family whose duty it is to look after me and keep me safe. I realize I'm not walking home, but toward Brother Donal's, toward Dacva. My heart pounds as I push open the back door and let myself in.

I don't know why I'm here or what I plan to do, but my feet carry me through the kitchen and up the stairs without thinking. I push open the bedroom door cautiously to find Luca dozing in a chair on one side of the room. The boy in the bed against the opposite wall is barely recognizable with his swollen eyes and lip and his face mostly black with bruises. I step closer, cautiously, my heart racing. I think of the years of torment he's caused me and the threats his guild has made against mine and it makes me want to hurt him more, to show him I'm stronger than he is, and we'll always win.

"He looks a bit better now." Luca pushes himself up with a groan and comes to stand beside me. "I thought you'd be celebrating!" He hugs me and I pat his arm halfheartedly.

"We're done. Mouli says you should come down and eat. I'll stay with him." The lie formulates in my mind and escapes my lips and I'm instantly ashamed of it. Still, I want Luca gone so I can be alone with my enemy.

"Ah, thank you, dear." Luca pats my back. "He shouldn't wake up. If he does, just give him another sip." He gestures to the bottle at the bedside and I nod. I listen to his footsteps move through the house. I hear the door close.

"Shouldn't wake up," I murmur and step closer. "What if you didn't?"

I imagine taking the pillow and pressing it to his face. I think of what would happen after. His guild would declare war. They'd come after us, full out. It would be the perfect excuse for them to get rid of us once and for all and take what they feel is their rightful place. I lean over him so my knees rest against the edge of the mattress. He's my age, but much bigger. Lying there in bed, he looks so different than the sneering boy who flung secret insults in the arena.

Still, I think about what it must be like to be him. It's always been obvious swordplay doesn't come as naturally to him. He's had to work much harder at it than I have. For the first time, I see him not as my rival or my sworn enemy, but as a boy with an unhappy life. A bullied child who's constantly forced to reach for something which will most likely always be out of his grasp. The whipping post for his family's twisted frustration, a constant second place. As I begin to feel sorry for him, my mother's words to my father ring in my ears: *She'll work it out.* I huff and drop into the chair beside the bed. Why does she always have to be right?

"Should've killed me," Dacva murmurs, and I sit up and lean toward him. His blackened eyes are open just a sliver, and he's watching me. "Self-righteous—" He coughs and winces as he lifts his head. "Perfect little...Fishbait." His eyes close. "Couldn't just let me die, could you?" He reaches up to touch his face and groans. I uncork the bottle on the table hold it out to him.

"Sip it. You'll go to sleep," I say, surprised by how much the bottle is shaking in my hand. "You'll feel better when you wake up."

"You're trying to poison me." He could be glaring, it's hard to tell. I shrug.

"So what if I am? You want to die anyway, right?"

He stares at me for a long time as though debating with himself. After a while, he grabs the bottle and tips it into his mouth, emptying it. His hand falls to the bed and his eyes close slowly. Trembling, I pick the bottle up and hold it to the light. It's empty. I wonder if it'll kill him to have drunk the whole thing. I'm only a little ashamed when I realize a part of me hopes it does.

Chapter Three

THE PALACE

I wake in the morning to a soft tapping on my bedroom wall. Slowly I open my eyes and shield them from the morning sun which filters through the cracks in the shutters at my window. The tapping comes again and I push myself out of bed with a yawn of protest. Yesterday's hours of standing at attention have made my muscles stiff overnight, and I groan as I stretch my arms and legs. The polished wood feels cool and welcome on my sore bare feet as I pad across my bedroom. I gaze sleepily into the small circular mirror on the wall, turning my head and pulling the yellow fabric of my nightgown from my neck. The scar from Dacva's attack yesterday is nearly gone now, healed by my mother's magic on the field. I rub my finger across it and I can barely feel it at all. I push my knotted hair away from my face and the tapping comes again from the other side of the mirror.

The row of houses that makes up the front side of the guild hall are directly connected by several secret little trapdoors. Some are close to the floor and large enough to crawl through, but the one that connects my room to Mya and Elliot's house is a tiny circular hatch disguised as a mirror. I lift the latch and pull it open and the reflection of my sleepy blue eyes is instantly replaced by a pair of hazel ones, pressed right up against the opening. I yelp and jump back.

"Rian! I wish you wouldn't!"

"Got you," he says, chuckling. "Really, who else were you expecting?" Admittedly, he's right. Our morning ritual of meeting at the hatch has been going on every day since we were tall enough to reach the latch on tiptoes. He steps away from the wall and pulls on a long vest which hangs from his lanky frame, and when he turns back again I stare. Just peeking out behind the laces of his shirt, right over his heart, is a swirling black design almost like a tattoo. Mage Mark. He cinches the lacing at his collar quickly to hide it, but it's too late.

"What did you do, Rian?" I ask in a hushed tone, stepping closer to the hatch. Mage Mark is a blemish that comes as a result of chaotic magic. I've been told outside of Cerion, more ruthless Mages wear the marks proudly, and some have dabbled so much into the arcane arts their entire bodies are covered with the swirling blue-black lines. Here within Cerion, though, anyone bearing the Mark is considered dangerous, unpredictable, and untrustworthy. Rian ties the sash of his blue vest and rakes a hand through his hair.

"I got a little carried away yesterday in Rumination. Viala was showing me something." He leans against the wall and smiles sheepishly. "Master Gaethon was furious, you should have seen."

"I can imagine." I lean, too, so if the wall wasn't there, we'd be shoulder to shoulder. "What did he do?"

"Well, first he tore me out." Rian closes his eyes and presses his fingertips to his brow. I'm fairly unfamiliar with the concept, but I do know being torn out of a deep meditation can be jarring, depending on how deeply the Mage has gone in. It's best to transition slowly, to allow your mind to acclimate. My mother has told me this. The meditations she uses for Calm are similar to a Mage's rumination, but more pure. I don't really understand it, or care to, but being torn out definitely hurts.

"Ow." I wince. Rian nods.

"Then he swore me to Silence for the night."

"That's why you were so quiet at dinner." I remember the previous evening, when he barely spoke a word through the heated discussion at the table.

"Mmhmm," he shrugs. "Not quiet enough. According to Master Gaethon, I've earned myself another day of it." His voice changes to a deep impersonation of Uncle as he scolds me through the hatch. "To think about your indiscretions."

"We shouldn't be talking then," I say, and reach to slide the mirror closed. Rian rests his hand on the sill to stop me. "Really, Rian. If he catches you, it'll be a week before we can talk again." He may be my uncle, but he scares me.

"I'm sure he has better things to do than spy into my bedroom and stop me from talking to you." He scowls. "Besides, don't you want to hear what happened after you left last night?" I pause. I know the conversation would have shifted to other topics after I left. Interesting topics. I wonder if they ever came to a decision about Dacva. Perhaps they started planning for the upcoming quest. But a sworn silence is important. Rian is too flippant about his training. Magic must be heavily disciplined. The more he rebels against his teachers, the more he risks endangering himself and those around him. I stare at the white of his shirt and imagine the tendrils of Mage Mark one day swirling and peeking up above the collar.

"No," I say firmly, and slide the door into his fingers. He doesn't move his hand or even flinch.

"Not even that they were talking about the King's Quest? They think they know what it'll be."

"I can wait and hear it later, when it's proclaimed." Honestly, I'm dying to know what they think it'll be, but I won't risk my best friend's conscience and training. If he wants to defy his master, he can do it without my involvement.

"Fine," Rian concedes, but he keeps his hand in the door, blocking it. "Tell me what happened with Dacva. I won't say a word."

"You promise?" I drop my hand from the latch. He nods.

I know I can tell Rian anything and he'll understand, and so I share everything that happened in Donal's room, even the part where I contemplated using the pillow to suffocate Dacva. He reacts as I knew he would, not with judgment but with a bemused shake of his head. I recount Dacva's accusations that our guild was too righteous to kill him, and his seeming desire to die. When I get to the part when he drank the entire draught, Rian lets out an astonished gasp and starts to speak, but I flash him a look and he closes his mouth.

"After Dacva drank the draught, Brother Donal showed up. He said Dacva would probably be violently sick, but he'd live through it. He also said they'd decided to heal him thoroughly and send him home. Then he sent me away. I thought about going back to the hall but I don't know..." I shrug, remembering my confusion after that. Honestly, I'm still not sure how I feel about what happened. Is it wrong to hate someone even after you begin to understand the source of their pain? Mum tells me hate is a strong emotion fed by ignorance. But the more I learn about Dacva and all of Redemption, the harder I find it to sympathize with them. "I'm not angry at Mum and Da anymore, though. I understand why Da helped."

Rian reaches through the hatch and takes my hand to squeeze it reassuringly. His hand is warm and soft in mine, and I'm suddenly aware of how much my own is sweating, and how rough the calluses from my training must feel to him. I'm also aware of his eyes on me, watching me with a mix of concern and something else, an intensity I've started to notice more and more from him lately. I find myself wishing the wall would disappear so we could be closer, and I look away from the hatch in the direction of my window. The feeling is new, and I'm not sure about it.

Outside in the courtyard just below my window, a ring of steel on steel announces my father has started his day at the forge. The steady clang as he hammers is calming and familiar. I think about how angry I was with him last night and I feel a little guilty. It takes a strong person to stand up to adversity and offer kindness to someone you don't even like. Stronger than I am.

"I'd better get to breakfast," I say after a stretch of awkward silence.

"Mm," he agrees wordlessly, drawing his hand back through to his own side.

"I'll see you later?" I ask. He ducks away for a moment and I hear a scratching. I peek through to find him writing something on a page. "That's cheating!" I say, but he rolls his eyes at me, pushes the parchment through the hatch, and waves before closing up the door. I catch the sheet as it drifts to the floor. His handwriting is hard to decipher. I imagine how it must infuriate my uncle, who constantly impresses on me the importance of legible handwriting. For a moment I wonder if Rian does it just to annoy him. I wouldn't put it past him. I chuckle to myself as I smooth the note and read what he has scrawled:

You're too nice. I would have used the pillow. By the way, they think it'll be Kythshire.

Kythshire. Land of Fae. I wonder why they would think that. It seems a little farfetched that the king would send his best guild off to chase after fairies when everyone knows they no longer exist. Actually, it's a ridiculous notion. No one can even find the land let alone enter it. I wouldn't put it past Rian to tell me such a thing just to see if I'd believe him. Then he would laugh when I bring it up to the rest of the guild.

I shake my head and toss the note onto the shelf holding my helm and boots. It's just the kind of trick he'd try to pull, and he's not getting me this time. I'm not saying anything to anyone until I know for sure what the quest is. The pages will deliver the declaration at sunset tonight, and then we'll have one day to plan and ready ourselves before heading out. My pulse quickens as I imagine riding through the gates on my first true quest alongside my parents, holding the guild's banner high as the crowds cheer farewell. It's been my dream for so long, and finally, now that I'm a squire, it's coming true.

I'm still smiling as I dress in trousers and a light tunic and go downstairs barefooted. In the kitchen I grab an apple and crunch into it as I step outside into the courtyard where my father is working. My mother sits under the shade of a canopy beside him, and my previously bloodied chain tunic sparkles beneath the surface of a pail of water at her feet.

"I should be doing that." I gesture to the bucket as I lean in to kiss her cheek. "Good morning."

"Good morning. You have more important things." She smiles and holds Margy's purple ring up to me, looped over one finger. "The official invitation is inside on the table." I take the ring by the ribbon and turn it in my hand, remembering the panic I felt being dragged by horse, trapped by my own glove, and the triumph as I hooked the ring into place.

"But I have so much to do..." I tap Da on the shoulder as he hammers out a dent from the inside of Mum's helm, most likely dealt by Dar yesterday. I fight back a scowl as Da leans his cheek down to me for a kiss.

"We'll manage," he says as he holds up the helm and turns it one way and another to check for imperfections. It looks perfect to me, but he sets it down again and strikes it gently with the rounded peen of the hammer. "So I'm forgiven, then?"

"I suppose," I say as I hop up to perch on the stone wall along the side of the forge where the coals have cooled to black. Mum bends again to scrub the red from my mail and Da works diligently at the dent I can no longer see. "I wish I could stay here, though." I take another bite of my apple.

"Azi. You can't ignore a royal summons. Not even from the

youngest member of the family." Da is right, I know. I finish my apple and slide from my seat to return to the kitchen where the tiny folded note rests on the table. The purple wax seal is pressed with the little princess's crest: a tiny winged lady dancing on a daisy. It's so pretty I hate to break it, so I peel the wax away from the paper carefully and slip the hardened disc into the pocket of my trousers. The note inside is a colorful child's drawing of a girl with blonde hair in a blue and yellow tunic raising an enormous sword over her head. The sword has been gold leafed, and flakes of it glitter as they drift to the table like snow when I raise it to read the inscription. Written in a page's impeccable hand, it says:

Her Royal Highness Princess Margary and Her Royal Highness Princess Sarabel request the presence of Squire Azaeli Hammerfel at court this morning. Please present this invitation to the gateman upon arrival at the palace.

I find myself walking a little taller as I pass other girls my age who are escorted by their housemaids as they rush here and there along the city streets. My new title of Squire affords me a freedom I've never had, and I grin and bob my head at those who greet me as I make my way to the palace. At the portcullis, I hand my invitation to the gateman and when he grants me entry a young page bows to me respectfully. I follow him deep into the palace to an area I haven't been before, an alcove off a side hall lined with plush, comfortable chairs. I'm asked to stay here, and he rushes off to announce me.

As I wait, I'm entranced by the artistry of the tapestries on the walls which tell various stories of Cerion's history and the Plethore family's rise to the throne. A particularly dark tapestry catches my interest, and I find myself drawn into it. Woven masterfully into the tapestry, an ominous sky looms over a craggy black mountain, pelting the range with sharp white streaks of lightning. Glimpses of creatures lurk in the shadows at its rocky base, barely visible except for a hand here and a boot there. As I move closer, the shapes change and I can make out eyes looking at me and hands reaching toward me.

I'm so absorbed by the tiny figures I don't realize someone has come to stand behind me until I feel a hand on my shoulder. I start to turn, but a second hand catches my waist and slides to my hip. The touch is too firm, too assuming. It sends a chill through me, and suddenly I feel vulnerable without my sword.

"The Fall of Diovicus." The whisper is hot and breathy in my ear. The hand on my shoulder slides down my back and around to my stomach, holding me. Yet something about the voice is familiar, and my instinct tells me to be still. "The mysteries of Kythshire, so compelling, so..." He brushes my cheek with his, grazes my hair. "Forbidden." I feel the stubble of his chin on my neck, just where Dacva's blade had sliced me. A lump rises in my throat as my heart begins to race. Thinking back, I realize this hall, so tucked away, had no posted guards. I wonder if that was on purpose. I don't like feeling this way, vulnerable. Powerless.

No, I tell myself. Not powerless. I'm a fighter. I could take him by surprise, throw my elbow up behind me into his chin and smash his jaw. Gouge my heel into his foot and turn and punch his stomach. Run. Scenarios of escape race through my mind and then it clicks. I know who it is, and I know fighting would have serious consequences. Instead I stand rooted in place, carefully masking my shock at his appalling behavior. At attention. Disciplined, just like yesterday in the field.

As he circles to face me, he slides a finger along the line of the sash tied at my waist. I feel my cheeks go warm with humiliation as I fight to keep my gaze locked ahead. Why is he acting this way? I watch until his rich boots come into view, then his deep purple doublet, the glint of gold at his neck. He strokes my chin and raises it up, and I look into Prince Eron's face.

"You did well yesterday," he whispers as his fingers trace down my throat and along my collar bone. I hold my breath, grateful I listened to my instincts rather than attack him. "Such skill, such grace, such restraint." I remain stoic, keeping my eyes fixed on the eyes of a dark creature before me, praying he can't hear my heart pounding. He pulls me closer, his hand on the back of my neck, his face tipped to mine.

"Azi!"

Footsteps patter around the corner and the prince and I jump apart as Margary emerges. Sarabel follows close behind, laughing as her little sister dances around me and takes my hand. Both seem completely oblivious to the tension between Eron and me, and before the prince can do anything to protest, Margy takes my hand and pulls me away. We run together through the winding corridors and into the sunny royal gardens, and by the time the sun brushes my cheeks I'm laughing along with Margy, infected by her bubbly excitement.

"Come see what we made!" She leads me to a corner of the garden where we stop in the shade of a copse of well-pruned trees. Her nurse settles on a nearby bench and I find myself reminded of the girls accompanied by their maids outside. This time, though, I'm comforted by her watchful eye. Eron wouldn't approach us here.

Margary pulls me to the edge of the row of hedges and crouches, careful not to soil her dress. I kneel between her and Sarabel and peek into the hedge. In the space between two gnarled trunks, on a carpet of bright green moss is a tarnished silver jewel box standing on its side. A little path of smooth colorful seashells and pebbles leads up to it, and inside is a tiny bed draped with a canopy of fine lace.

"What a fine little house," I say, hoping my cheeks aren't as red as they feel.

"It's a fairy house," says Margary. She takes a cube of sugar from a fold in her dress and places it carefully on the edge of the box. "They love sweets."

"Do they?" I ask, leaning in for a closer look.

"Oh, yes." Margy's brown curls bounce as she nods. "Twig loves sugar cubes, they're his favorite." She looks up and around as though expecting something. I turn to Sarabel, who is covering a smile with her hand.

"Twig?" I ask.

"Twig is Margy's special friend." Sarabel's nod tells me I should play along. "Perhaps we should give the fairies a little room," she suggests as she stands and brushes a bit of grass from her cream colored skirt. Margary shakes her head and adjusts the sugar cube. "I thought you wanted Azi to teach you sword fighting?" Sarabel coaxes.

"After he comes, she can," she says. "He's still very shy." Her tone tells us her answer is final.

"She and I will take a walk, then," Sarabel links her arm through mine. "I think he might be frightened with too many of us watching." Margary nods, her eyes locked on the house with determination.

"Every day, it's something new," Sarabel laughs softly as we stroll away. "Yesterday she wanted to be a knight like you. Today, she invents fairy friends to play with." We walk together and she guides me deeper into the gardens, where the park grows wild on the other side of the palace wall. Sunlight sparkles through the canopy, casting shadows that dance with the breeze over the carpet of grass below.

"Do you remember when we were her age?" I ask. "We were just the same."

"Except we were the fairies," Sarabel laughs. "I think I still have the wings we made from Gaethon's parchment tucked away."

"Oh, I had forgotten all about that!" I laugh. "He was so furious!" All those years ago, Sara and I had decided we needed proper wings to become fairies. I stole a sheaf of Uncle's parchment from the table in the guild hall and tore it into pieces that were perfectly wing shaped. Sara had been delighted, and we ran through this very garden holding our wings out and flapping them and pretending to fly. It didn't occur to us I had sacrificed a particularly difficult bit of my uncle's research for our game until he found some of the discarded fragments of paper lying about the hall the next day. Uncle had been terrifyingly incensed with me. Thoughts of my uncle and his ruined parchment remind me of Rian and the hastily scrawled note he passed to me earlier. I remember what he wrote and I think of how odd it is to be reminded such an obscure legend as the fairies twice in one day.

"What do you suppose got her thinking of them?" I ask as we settle on a bench beside the wall. I can barely see Margary in the distance where she continues to kneel at the hedge, seemingly in conversation with her own hand.

"Eron read to her from a story book that Princess Amei brought from the Isles," she replies. "It's a rather old one with stories I've never heard before."

I press my palms flat against the surface of the bench at the mention of the prince to stop my hands from shaking.

"Ah." I manage. I'm not quick enough to hide my discomfort. Sara notices.

"Azi, did Eron...?" She trails off.

"No," I say. I'm not really sure why I feel the need to defend him.

"Good," she replies. "He's been acting so strangely lately." Margy pops up beside us before I can ask what she means.

"Twig said he's not meeting you. Not yet," she says. "Let's go battle."

Sara grins at me over Margy's shoulder.

"All right," I laugh.

We spend the rest of the day happily diverted. We explore the gardens and have a picnic lunch under the trees. A page brings us some light training weapons made of wood and I play at swords with Margy. Sarabel even joins in, ignoring the disapproving gaze of their nurse, who obviously believes the princess is too grown to do anything remotely amusing. The sun hangs low in the sky when I'm finally sent on my way with hugs and a gift of a fairy house of my own which Margary has made for me from a dented silver pitcher.

Chapter Four

RECONCILIATION OF GRUDGES

Rian greets me at the corner where the palace street meets the park promenade. His expression is shadowed as he offers me his hand. I take it as I tuck the bundle containing the princess's gift under my arm, and he leads me into the forest park which stretches between the palace and the guild hall.

"Why are we avoiding the road?" I ask. He turns slightly and taps his lips with one finger, reminding me of his earlier promise to keep silent. Our meeting at the bedroom wall feels like it was days ago with all that has happened since this morning. I want to tell him about Eron, but his decision to route through the forest distracts me. He quickens his pace and I grip his hand more tightly. When I peer through the passing trees, I catch glimpses of a crowd outside of the main door of our hall and I realize they must have made the proclamation for the quest already. It isn't unusual for a crowd to gather to hear what the quest will be. My pulse quickens with excitement.

"Is it Kythshire, like they thought?" I ask, but Rian keeps his silence. I'll get no answers from him; he's taking his promise to me very seriously. We manage to go unnoticed as we make a wide berth around those milling by the main doors. Their voices are meshed together, and we're too far away to make out any details of the conversation. Rian leads me through the back door past the kitchens, where Mouli is shucking beans.

"Hello, dear," she says to me with a hint of pity. Before she or I can say anything else, Rian whisks me through to the corridor beyond.

"Really, Rian! What is going on?" I jog to keep up with him. The hall is just ahead. I can hear the guild talking in hushed voices. When we reach the door, the conversation around the table stops abruptly.

Everyone is here: Mya and Elliot, Mum and Dad, Brother Donal, Cort, Bryse, Uncle Gaethon. "What's going on?" I ask again. Bryse clears his throat and looks away. My father meets my eyes apologetically and picks up a scroll from the table beside a box containing a glittering gold amulet. He hands the scroll to me, and I'm vaguely aware of my mother's hand on my shoulder as I accept it and read it over. The parchment is so crisp and fresh when I unroll it I have to hold it smoothed onto the flat surface of the table to keep it from curling up again.

THE KING'S QUEST
RECONCILIATION OF GRUDGES
IN HONOR OF THE MARRIAGE OF HIS ROYAL HIGHNESS
PRINCE ERON
TO HER ROYAL HIGHNESS PRINCESS AMEI

It is the declaration of his Royal Majesty King Tirnon that select members of His Majesty's Elite shall forge an alliance with select members of Redemption in order to strengthen and honor the kinship of the leading guilds of the Kingdom of Cerion. This newly allied company shall travel to Kythshire, where they will return a lost treasure, thereby Reconciling a Grudge trespassed upon its lands by the former King Diovicus before the Age of Peace.

These members shall include:
Sir Benen Hammerfel, His Majesty's Elite
Sir Lisabella Hammerfel, His Majesty's Elite
Lady Mya Eldinae, His Majesty's Elite
Elliot Eldinae of the Wood, His Majesty's Elite
Sir Darvonax Archomyn, Redemption
Master Rikstarn Archomyn, Redemption
Sister Maewyn of the First Order, Redemption
Squire Hopeful Dacva Archomyn, Redemption

Let the public announcement decree only that these members shall unite in solidarity to support the Throne of Cerion in a Quest of great risk and honor. The precise manner of the Quest shall be kept secret with the exception of guild members, so as to honor the high secrets of the Land of Kythshire. The new alliance shall make its plans and preparations in anticipation of the farewell procession in two days' time.

By Order of the King
His Royal Majesty
Tirnon Plethore

I read it twice, three times, and four. I turn the page over but the back is blank. I read it again with a mix of understanding and disbelief. I'm not on the list. I'm not, and Dacva is. It isn't supposed to be this way.

"I don't understand," I whisper. This is supposed to be my first quest as a Squire. I should be riding out beside my guild and my family, off to risk myself on an adventure in the name of the king. I have been looking forward to this from the moment I first picked up a sword. I look to my mother and she shakes her head and looks down at the page. One glance at her somber expression is enough to show me she's just as disappointed to be leaving me behind. "I don't understand." I say again but this time my voice is thick with emotion.

"His Majesty has ordered us to ally with Redemption and travel to Kythshire. We're to return a lost treasure to them that was stolen by King Diovicus before the Age of Peace starting with the Plethore dynasty. But the fact that we're being sent to Kythshire is meant to be kept secret from the—" Mya is interrupted by Bryse.

"Crack the stone, Mya!" he curses. "She understands that part! Why's she not on the list? Why are half of us off it for that matter?" Bryse slams the tabletop with his fist, causing half the guild to grab their cups.

"I'm sure King Tirnon has his reasons," my father interjects. "It's not our place to question him. We must trust in His Majesty's judgment." We all know he's right. We don't need to agree or even understand. Our duty is to trust and to do as we're bidden.

"We can use the opportunity to mend our differences," Mya says. "Perhaps it will help us to understand each other's motives."

"Yes. Perhaps it will carry out as His Majesty hopes, and bring our guilds closer," Master Gaethon presses his fingertips together thoughtfully. "But I must impress upon all of you who are going on this journey to remain cautious. Do not let down your guard. And under no circumstances should you cross the border uninvited."

"That considered," Mya rises and reaches for the proclamation, "if anyone who is on the list wishes to decline, I can write out a formal petition to remove you." She looks up from the page, making eye contact first with my mother, then my father, and then her own husband, Elliot. Each one shakes his or her head in turn. They have a choice, and their choice is to do as the king bids them.

"The ride to the border of Kythshire is at least a week, so pack accordingly." Mya ticks down a list.

Silent beside me, Rian watches his mother lead the meeting. When he slips his hand into mine and squeezes it, I know what he's thinking. In two days, we'll both watch as our parents ride off alongside the only few people in the kingdom we all know can't be trusted. I'm thankful, at least, he'll be staying here with me.

***

They left a week ago, and I've had little sleep. I kneel at my window, shivering from the damp morning breeze and my mind races constantly. I think about the hungry look in the eyes of Redemption's members as they waved farewell to the crowds with our blue and gold banners flapping beside their red ones. I worry for my parents as I imagine them sleeping out in a dark forest camp along their journey, with Dar or Dacva sitting guard. I hope they're not so trusting to allow themselves to sleep while Redemption takes watch.

When I try to force my musings along another path, my thoughts almost always wander to my encounter with Prince Eron. I feel his rough hands on me and his hot breath in my ear, and that's usually when I finally give up on the notion of sleep and slip out of bed to find some way to distract myself. This morning, I spend some time setting the Princess's fairy pitcher on my windowsill and fixing the tiny bed she made from scraps of lace and feathers. When the first glow of dawn finally reaches my room, I stand up, stretch, and cross to the hatch to tap on the wall and wake Rian.

Our parents' questing has been a part of our lives since we were young children, and the routine of their absence is normal for us. When we were much younger, Mouli and Luca would stay with us, but now that we're older and can take care of ourselves, the caretakers keep to their duties of cooking and caring for the grounds while Rian and I spend our days at the Academy and training. I try to comfort myself that this time is no different than all of those other ones, but I'm too unsettled by Redemption to believe it.

I tap a little louder. Elliot always sends a bird with progress messages in the morning, and Rian and I have promised each other not to check the hall for it unless we go together. I'm anxious to read the note today. I need to know Mum and Da are safe. I rap again impatiently, and finally the latch rattles softly as it's lifted and the door slides open. I peek inside and can just make out a bristle of auburn hair over the nest of blankets on Rian's bed across the room. One slender finger creeps up over a rumpled fold, pointing in my direction.

"Hey," I say, leaning in to squint through the dim morning light. He flicks his finger and the door wriggles on its own, threatening to slide closed, but I block it with my hand. "Doing magic with your eyes closed," I say. "Impressive."

"Why are you not sleeping?" Rian's groan is muffled by his pillow.

"How can you?" I ask as I drum my fingers. "Come on, it's morning." He groans again and shoves the blankets away. I glance at his chest to see whether the Mark has grown, but the shirt he's slept in is laced too tightly for me to tell. He yawns and stretches and rubs his eyes, and makes a great show of being annoyed I've woken him so early. I'm used to it. He's like this every morning. When he finally comes to the hatch ruffling his short-cropped hair, he leans dramatically against it and glances past me toward my windowsill.

"What's that?" He points over my shoulder and I turn to look.

"Oh, a fairy house." I say, feeling my cheeks go red. "Princess Margary made it for me. I'm supposed to put a sugar cube inside."

"A fairy house?" His lips curve into a half smile. "It won't work," he says. "They're repelled by metal, you know." I tear my gaze away from his lips to his sleepy hazel eyes to see if he's joking, but his expression is as grave and serious as I've ever seen it. We stare at each other for a long silent stretch, and then he bursts out laughing. "It's just too easy to get you," he says, shaking his head. "I'll meet you downstairs." He slides the door closed and I grumble to myself as I make my way through the dark house and out the kitchen door.

Rian steps into the outside corridor the same time I do, and having just seen the chaotic state of his room I wonder how he can look so impeccably neat in his deep blue apprentice robes. I could swear I had seen them tangled in the nest of blankets on his bed. I suspect magic had a play. We fall into stride together and walk in comfortable silence to the guild hall. The table is laid with a simple breakfast spread of fresh rolls, cheeses and fruit. The message is already smoothed out on the table beside a map and two dishes containing the remainder of someone else's meal. Rian picks up the note and reads aloud as I help myself to a warm roll.

"Excellent pace yesterday, uneventful night. Believe we have found the boundary. Will reach by midday today. All is well." Rian gives the note to me and takes a handful of berries for himself. "See? Nothing to worry about. They'll return the treasure today and ride hard for home. If all goes well, they'll be back in a week. Maybe less." He leans across me over the map and points to where it seems they should be now, based on the updates they've been sending.

Ceras'Lain, where the elves live, is to the southwest of Cerion. Kythshire is rumored to border it in the far west, but its whereabouts are a well-guarded secret. The land is sacred. Legend and children's stories say it is the home of the fae, but nobody has claimed to see a fairy for centuries aside from the occasional madman or imaginative child. Most everyone believes they were wiped out. I agree with them. If fairies were real, then why would they hide themselves away?

"And if it doesn't go well?" I ask as I reread the note, which is smaller than the palm of my hand. The writing on it is tiny, and I wonder how Elliot manages it. I turn it over to see Bryse and Cort's freshly scrawled initials on the back. That would explain the empty plates. They must have finished their own breakfast and moved on to the sparring square next door already.

"You worry too much." Rian sighs and holds his hand out. "It's going to go well." I press the note into it. One of our duties when a note comes to the hall is to make sure every member has seen and initialed it, and then deliver it to the palace so they can be informed of the progress of the quest. Rian tucks the paper into the pocket of his robes.

"I can do it today," I say as we finish our quick breakfast and I follow him to the sparring square. Through the wall I can hear the faint rhythmic clang of metal on metal and occasional shouts. Rian pauses with his hand on the door.

"I don't mind," he says. Ever since I told him about what

happened with Prince Eron, he has insisted on delivering the notes to the palace himself. "I wish you would tell someone what happened," he says quietly, tipping his head toward the door.

"Tell them what, the prince breathed on me?" I roll my eyes, trying hard to make the incident out to be less than it was.

"Don't try to play it down, Azi." He scowls. "He put his hands on you."

I want to tell him it was nothing, that I'm not bothered by it, but I can't. Not when I've spent countless hours going over every moment in my mind in an effort to figure out exactly what the prince was trying to lead up to. What might have happened if he hadn't been interrupted by the princesses? What did Sara mean when she said he's been acting strangely? I feel Rian's eyes on me and I look up into them. Instantly I feel safe.

"Just think about it, okay?" he says. "They ought to know." He slides the door open and we step through, and I press my knuckles to my lips to keep from laughing at the scene that greets us.

Cort stands in the center of the ring, his deep brown skin already shining with sweat. He has attached Bryse's massive shield to one arm, and it's so huge he has to rest the edge of it on the dirt floor to keep it upright. In his other hand, he wields Bryse's enormous sword, which is comically larger than the graceful dual blades he normally favors. He whips his long braids over his shoulder and braces himself behind the shield unsteadily. The tip of the heavy sword lowers ever so slightly as he stands at the ready. Opposite, Bryse charges him. Clenched in Bryse's giant fists, Cort's delicate swords could be toothpicks.

The much larger man's thick biceps ripple beneath his stony gray skin, and he snarls and brandishes the small weapons in a poor attempt at Cort's swashbuckling style. They clatter fervently against the shield behind which Cort barely has to duck to stay protected. Occasionally Cort peeks to gauge the attack while Bryse moves slowly around him, slashing. Then, catching an opening, the smaller man reaches around the shield with the great sword and taps Bryse on the knee.

"Touch!" Cort cries and pops up, letting the shield fall forward. He shakes out his arm, loosening it up.

"Bah!" Bryse catches the shield before it crashes to the dusty floor. "You got lucky," he says. Rian and I clap. Cort offers a bow with a flourish, and Bryse taps him on the top of the head with the flat of his fist. "Showoff."

Rian approaches them and checks to be sure they have both seen the note, and then he heads off to find Brother Donal and Gaethon to collect their signatures on his way to the Academy. I cross the room to the weapon stand, pick up a random sword and a whetstone, and sit at the bench.

"You going to sharpen that one again?" Bryse causes a tremor which rattles my teeth as he drops down onto the bench beside me. "S'been sharpened by you three times this week. You could probably split the last hair on Donal's head with that one, you could. Keep sharpening it and there'll be nothing left." He chuckles.

I look down at the pristine blade in my lap. He's right. I've sharpened every sword, axe, and dagger in the hall in the past week, more than once. I'm meant to be shadowing my knight, but she isn't here, and I can't be with her. Instead, I've polished armor and groomed horses and oiled tack and scrubbed floors and organized maps and split wood. It's hard work, but at least I don't have to spend any more days at the arms guild with Ragnor. Bryse pats my shoulder with his enormous hand and when I look up at him, his smile is kind and understanding.

"Go get your chainmail on," he says as he takes the sword and stone from my hands. "The two of us are bored out of our skulls. We could use some fresh meat to practice with."

We spar together through the morning hours. I hold my own fairly well; it's refreshing to have partners who are so skilled but don't want to murder me. They certainly don't go easy, though. It isn't the first time we've had bouts together, but after a couple of hours it's obvious to me they were being cautious in the past, when I was just a child with a sword.

Today, they're far more relentless. Cort uses all of the tricks I know against me, and then dozens of new ones I've never seen him perform before. Bryse doesn't let up after a few good hits, but instead tenaciously forces me to keep up my guard as we circle the training square, swords clashing. I hold my own, and we are all grinning and laughing as they face me two against one. By the time Mouli comes to scold me for missing lunch, I'm soaking with sweat and every muscle in my body aches, but my heart is swelled up and I'm grinning like a fool.

"Y'know Az," Bryse says around a mouthful of cold roast as he sits beside me, "there's nothing that says you have to wait around for Lis. A squire's a squire. A knight's a knight." I take an enormous bite of leftover turkey sandwiched inside a sliced breakfast roll and look up at him as I chew. Bryse would be a terrifying-looking man to a stranger, but his heavily scarred face and strong brow are so familiar to me that I have never been afraid of him.

"Aha, and here it comes." Cort chuckles on the other side of me and takes a bite of cheese. At my questioning look, he winks. "He's trying to steal you away from your lady knight."

The mention of my mother casts a shadow on my mood, and I take a long time to swallow. Bryse is also a knight, and he's right. As a squire I'm not tied to any single knight.

"Why not? Just until she returns, of course." I agree. I catch the two exchanging a glance, but they quickly look away from each other.

"Here, I'll show you a trick with the shield." Bryse brushes crumbs from his lap and strides to the center of the ring. I set down my roll and reach for my sword, and as my hand closes around the hilt, a sharp pain jolts through it and up my arm. Specks of darkness form at the edge of my vision. The room starts to spin, and my ears are flooded with blood-curdling screams.

I throw the sword down in pain and it all goes away. Cort leans to pick it up for me and offers it hilt-first. He looks concerned. He says something and claps me on the back, but my ears are still ringing from the screams and I can't hear what he's saying. I grasp the hilt and the pain comes again, up my arm, into my neck, jolting my body. I keep my grip and the room starts spinning, spinning. The darkness closes in on me. The screaming thunders into my skull. I loosen my grip and my sword slips away and all of it stops abruptly. I drop to my knees. My stomach churns, and my lunch revisits me, and then everything goes black.

Chapter Five

HOMECOMING

A cool breeze, rich with the scent of ripening wheat, washes over me as I'm cradled on a soft bed of grass. Above me golden fronds wave gently, brushing at the perfect blue sky. The breeze sends flakes of gold leaf glittering across the blue, wafting and dancing and dazzling my eyes. I am washed over with serenity as I watch the way the light plays blue, gold, and white. The colors bring me comfort, and I lie in silence among the grass and the wind. I watch the flecks move and swirl and imagine being carried off with them, way up into the deep blue sky. This place is my peace, it is all that matters to me. Time stretches slowly as the warm sun passes across the sky. I listen to the soft rustling of wheat mixed with the distant song of birds, the tapping of a woodpecker, the hum of a cricket playing like a symphony. Slowly, sky blue transitions to pink and orange and lavender.

The light wanes and the stars arrive one by one, winking onto the black night sky in a spray of sparkling diamonds. A smiling sliver of the moon shines down over me, washing everything in blue and white and gray. All around me, the golden fronds sparkle with dew. I feel the cool drops kissing my hair and my face and my arms and legs. The moon is high, and the crickets' song blended with the peeping frogs stills to an eerie quiet. A soft rustling tells me someone approaches, but I'm not afraid. The wheat and the dew, the breeze and the moon will protect me. Rian's smile eclipses the moon, and he comes closer and closer and presses his lips to mine. I close my eyes, and when I open them again it isn't Rian, but Prince Eron. I try to move, but my body doesn't respond. I feel the roots of myself dug deep into the earth. I have lain here for so long that I am one with the wheat and the grass and the soil. The Prince hovers over me and my eyes drift to his bare chest, where blue-black lines swirl and undulate and grow. They crawl up to his neck and across his arms. His hands graze my shoulders and the Mage Mark blackens his fingers and twists them into roots which wind and grow and twine around me. It doesn't occur to me to fight it. I am safe, just an observer as the prince's blackened body is swallowed up by the coiling form of a tree trunk, and the roots encase me and burst upwards, stretching knobby fingers, reaching wiry branches to touch the diamonds in the sky.

My roots are strong and calm, my branches sway among the stars. The sun rises and sets and rises again so many times I lose track of the days and the nights. The crickets' song comforts me; the woodpecker taps a soft rhythm. In the quiet of a cool autumn night, I'm visited by a tiny creature dressed in white gossamer and down. Her rainbow wings cast prisms of light over the bark of my tree and I am reminded of the dancing flecks of gold leaf and the wafting fronds of wheat against a crisp blue sky. She resembles my mother with her delicate nose, the soft curve of her cheek, and the constant kind glint of a smile in her blue eyes. Her blond hair shimmers as her wings carry her up to look into my face. She rests a miniature hand on the bridge of my nose and peers deep into my eyes, tilting her head this way and that as if looking for something hidden deep within me. We smile at each other and then she gestures to a bright star which streaks overhead, twinkling with thousands of colors. I reach out a hand to catch it and it settles gently in my palm. It is a diamond, beautiful and pure, a match to all of the thousands I have watched twinkling above me for so many nights. The fairy flutters down and closes my fingers around the sparkling gem. Then she opens her mouth to speak.

"Azaeli Hammerfel, enough of this! You wake up right now!" Mouli's voice startles me. I'm shaken by the shoulder and torn away from my tree and my wheat and my stars. Suddenly I'm painfully aware of the deep hollow feeling in my stomach. My head is pounding. My arms and legs are heavy. My mouth feels as if it's full of sand. I try to push my eyes open but my lids only barely flutter in response. "Oh!" Mouli's voice pounds in my ears, driving daggers through my aching head. "Oh! She's up!" She fusses at my blankets and pats my face with a damp cloth.

"Luca!" she calls and my ears ring with each syllable. I hear her rush from the room and I let my eyes shut again. I try to conjure the beautiful place again, but it's too distant now, an ancient memory.

"Ow," I whisper as I squint at the blur that is Mouli. Any more noise like that and I swear my head will split wide open. She drops a bundle on the chair beside my bed and comes to my side again.

"Let's sit you up slowly, dear, and get you changed. You're soaking wet from fever." She unties the laces of my nightgown and falls back with a cry, her hands clapped over her mouth. "Azi! Explain this!" My thoughts are jumbled, torn between two places. Dazed, I follow her scandalized glare to the bare skin over my heart, where a very small blue-black tendril swirls and twines in contrast against my pale white skin.

"I don't..." My mouth is too dry, my voice too hoarse. My bedroom is too enclosed, too crowded even with just the two of us in it. I close my eyes. I think of the tree. I wriggle my toes, imagining the roots which felt so real, so strong and protective. Beneath the blankets, I clench my fists and feel something hard and unyielding press into my palm. I roll it between my fingers, trying to figure out what it is. It is smooth and cool, and when I focus on it, I'm reminded of the stars against the midnight blue sky. The fairy. The shooting star. The diamond.

"Luca! Send for Gaethon!" Mouli shouts, and I groan again as she rushes back downstairs. When I'm sure she's a safe distance away, I pull my hand free of the blanket with great effort, feeling as if I haven't moved in a week. The jewel is the size of my thumb, and when I hold it to the beam of sunlight that streams across my bed from the open window, it catches the light in colorful prisms that remind me of the fairy's wings in my dream. I watch it dance and gleam for a long time, thinking about what it could have meant. I've never had a dream so real before, never longed to go back to it as much as I long to now. It was so beautiful.

Mouli returns and helps me change out of my damp nightgown and into a dry shift. I clench my hand around the diamond, careful not to drop it or to let her see it. Something in my heart tells me it's meant to be a secret. She helps me to my bedside chair and presses a cup of water to my lips, which I take and drink gratefully. I close my eyes again while she changes the bedclothes. I'm shaking and weak, which seems strange. "Mouli?" I ask. "How long was I asleep?"

"Six days, poor dear." She slides into the small space between me and the foot of my bed to tuck the ends in.

"Six days?" I groan. With any luck, my parents will have finished their quest and be home soon. I glance at the hatch to Rian's room. "What word have they sent? Are they coming home?" Mouli pauses in her work and I open my eyes and watch her.

"Never you mind about that," she says. "You need your strength back. I'll fetch you something to nibble on while you wait for your uncle." She finishes the bed and bustles out of the room again. I rest my head back against the chair. It's no use trying to get anything out of Mouli. I've had too much experience with that in the past. She tells me what she thinks it's good for me to know, and not much more, no matter how hard I try to get it out of her. She takes her duties seriously, and those duties sometimes involve keeping a tight lip.

My heart is racing, thumping against my chest as I sit slumped in my chair. She sent for Uncle. He's coming here. He'll see the Mark over my heart and what will he think? That I've been dabbling in forbidden magic? My stomach flips and I tuck the diamond under the covers of Margy's fairy bed before Mouli returns with a tray and silently helps me back to bed. She watches to make sure I take a bite, and then pats me kindly on the shoulder. With a quick concerned glance at the Mark on my chest, she rushes out again, leaving me to wait alone in fear of my uncle's wrath.

Once, when I was only seven years old and Rian was seven and a half, we were studying alone together in the guild hall. I set aside my dull writing to watch him as he practiced a simple movement spell. He would wave his hand and wiggle his fingers in an intricate pattern and speak strange words, and the button on the table would slide this way and that. It was fascinating to watch, and he taught me the incantation in secret whispers. He held my hands in his and showed me how to move them to perform the spell. The feel of the magic flowing through me as I made the button move was thrilling, and made me feel wonderfully lightheaded. It wasn't long before we were nearly collapsed in a fit of giggles together as the button zoomed back and forth between us.

It was then Uncle Gaethon discovered us, casting and laughing as the button skidded across the table and struck the far wall. His fury was like none I had ever seen. His blue eyes seemed to glow with a white heat as he raged at us. Rian was at the time a Mage of First Circle. The spell he was practicing had been Third Circle. Uncle raged that no spell is harmless. It was too powerful for Rian. It could upset Cerion's delicate balance. On top of that, it is strictly prohibited for an apprentice to teach anyone magic without the express permission of the Headmaster. He told us we were careless, and threatened to cease Rian's training then and there. Rian swore he'd never share magic with me again, and we were both forced to Silence for a week.

I did get a bit of the Mark then, but it faded quickly. Uncle's fury left me terrified and confused, and with a healthy respect for the strict rules that govern magic. I understand now it requires a certain balance, which can be upset by even the smallest indiscretion. The childish fear is fresh in my memory as his footsteps sound softly on the stairs outside of my room.

"Come in," I say before he reaches the door. As Uncle enters, his eyes flash with a hint of the same furious white heat they showed all of those years ago. When he looms over me at the bedside, his nostrils are flared and his lips pressed tightly together, framed by the high collar of his deep blue robes.

"Show me," he commands in a terrifyingly steady voice, and I pull the neckline of my gown down to show him the Mark at my chest. It's rather small, about the size of a hen's egg, with a beautiful curling pattern of tendrils. They remind me so much of the roots of my tree that tears prick my eyes. Or perhaps it's the fear of his fury that causes it. I shrink away from him as he inspects the lines.

He turns abruptly and paces the floor and I fight the strong urge to defend myself. I know enough not to say a word until I'm spoken to, with him. When he turns to face me again I'm puzzled by his softening expression at first, but then I realize it's because I'm crying. I brush the tears away, embarrassed, as he takes a seat in the chair by the window.

"You collapsed in the training square. Mouli suspects from overwork and heat. Yet you slept for several days, which is not in keeping with heat exhaustion." His eyes flick over Margy's pitcher and back to me again. "According to her, you did not have the Mark when you were put to bed. Interesting." He reaches over and turns the pitcher to peek inside of it. I force my breathing to slow, and pray he doesn't see the secret I've hidden inside. "Where did you get this?" he asks, momentarily distracted from his train of thought.

"The Princess." My response comes as a whisper, and I swallow the lump in my throat.

"Explain to me what happened in the training square," he says. To my relief, he turns away from the pitcher and folds his hands in his lap.

"I'm not sure," I say. I force myself back through the dream to focus again on the moments before. "We had just had lunch, and Bryse wanted to show me something with his shield. I went to pick up my sword and everything started spinning. I heard screaming and I felt like the ground beneath me was slipping away. Everything went black, and when I woke up, I was here in bed." Uncle taps his lips thoughtfully with a slender fingertip.

"Which sword was it?" he asks. "I will have it inspected."

"My own. The long sword. My name is etched on the hand guard." He nods and stands, but then pauses as his eyes rest on the hatch.

"Have you and Rian been experimenting again?"

"No! I swear it, Uncle. Rian has kept his promise."

"Then how do you explain the Mark, Azi?" He spins, and his eyes bore into mine as if he can see every thread of thought in my mind. I think of the dream I had and how wonderful it was and how real. I glance at the little fairy bed hiding the diamond which was once a star in my sky. I wonder if anyone has gotten marked simply by dreaming, but the question catches in my throat. I shouldn't tell anyone about it, not even Uncle, who is trying to help me. I shake my head.

"I can't." I say, looking down at my lap. I snap a cracker and scoop up a bit of soft cheese with it, grateful to have something to do with my hands to hide their shaking. Uncle pauses at the door. In the distance, I can hear trumpets sounding and people shouting.

"Is there anything else..." His voice trails off as the shouting grows closer, mixed with the quick beat of horses' hooves. He goes to my window and looks out. "Get dressed," he throws over his shoulder as he rushes out of my room and down the stairs.

I'm still a little shaky as I push the tray from my lap and cross to look out the window, jarred by Uncle's sudden departure. A single rider approaches our front door and Uncle meets him in the street. They talk too quietly for me to hear, and then the rider goes off again toward the center of the city. I hear the thundering gallop of several horses a distance away and I know it can only mean one thing. They're home, and early. I rush to the dressing room and pull out a long, easy blue dress which I slip on hastily. I still feel weak, and I have to stop and rest against the wall a few times as I make my way downstairs. The horses are closer now and their quick pace makes me nervous, as does the general quiet in the streets. The sounding of horns generally draws a crowd. I lean heavily in the front door frame, tired from my short trek down the stairs. My eyes fix on the street corner where I know they'll emerge, and I reach up and smooth my sticky hair back from my face. I wish I'd had more notice, to make myself more presentable for my parents' arrival.

The soft sound of Mya's voice is carried on the breeze to me, surprisingly clear above the pounding of the horses. She sings a song of calm healing, its words ancient and melodic. They round the corner at full speed, four horses and three riders. Mya leads the charge with my mother's empty-saddled horse tethered to her own. Behind her, Elliot rides with my father's horse close beside him. As they near, I realize my father's form is slumped over the neck of his horse, his hands bound to the reins. At first I think he's unconscious, but as they near he raises his head slightly and I gasp. His face is a solid, swollen bruise. Blood is caked over his right eye. The side of his helm, which is tied to his saddle, is badly dented; he has obviously been bludgeoned in the head.

Bryse emerges from his house to meet them as they skid to a stop. The horses dance in place as Elliot works deftly to free my father's hands and legs from the bindings that served to keep him steady on the journey, and then Luca leads the horses away to the stable. Mya's voice melds perfectly with her lute as the men heft my father, and as her healing song washes over us all I can feel my own strength returning. My father's form is limp, and I grab his hand as Bryse rushes him past me into the house. We stumble up the stairs together and Bryse lays him in bed. Mya's singing helps me feel better. I know it's helping Da, too. His eyes are closed now. He lies unmoving and I when I squeeze his hand, it's cool and still in mine.

"Brother Donal is on his way," Elliot says softly, resting a hand on my shoulder. I reach and brush a blood-crusted strand of hair from my father's brow.

"What happened to him?" I whisper. In my mind I see my mother's empty saddle and I go numb. I won't ask. My father is here. He needs me now.

"We don't know for certain." Mya answers softly. "He and your mother crossed the border ahead of us into Kythshire. He returned raving mad, struck by his own hammer. Lis…" She clears her throat. "Elliot went to find her but only met with the empty boundary."

"We know exactly which path they took," Elliot's tone is apologetic, "but there was no sign of their passing, in or out of the border. It was as though she disappeared."

"Redemption stayed to search for her. We didn't realize the extent of Benen's injuries at the time or we would have had their cleric come with us. We thought to keep him with us, but in the end we agreed he'd be better off here, with the Conclave to tend to him."

"So we decided to ride hard for home," Elliot finishes for her. Brother Donal's arrival is announced by the soft rustling of robes, and he tries to move me aside to get to my father, but I refuse to budge. I know they're talking around me, but I'm unable to focus on what they're saying.

Finally, Bryse's strong hands scoop under my arms and Donal pries my fingers away, and I watch my father's hand fall limply to the bed. I'm vaguely aware I'm being carried down the stairs and tucked into our worn sofa with a soft blanket. Bryse and Mouli whisper in hushed tones. A mug of something warm is pressed into my hands. Mya's healing song continues to fill the house. The cushion beside me sinks under Bryse's weight as he sits.

"Why are you sitting here?" I turn to him suddenly, surprised by my own fury. "Why are you just sitting here when my father is up there dying and my mother is lost who knows where, maybe even--?" I can't say it. Bryse turns to me sadly and I realize Cort is here, too, and Uncle and Rian are behind them, crowded in the kitchen with Mouli.

"He'll be okay, Azi. Donal will heal him up," Bryse offers.

"What about Mum?" I shout and jump up, throwing down the mug, which shatters at my feet. "We have to go! We have to find her!" My rant is interrupted by a knock at the door. Enraged, I stalk to it and throw it open.

A page in royal livery stands perfectly erect, his gloved hand offering an envelope stamped with the royal seal. He bows when I take it from him, and then turns and trots off in the direction of the palace. My hands are shaking so much I have difficulty opening it. Rian comes to my side and takes it gently. He cracks the seal and pulls out a quickly scrawled note.

"His Royal Highness Prince Eron requests the presence of Lady Mya Eldinae and Elliot Eldinae to recount the details of their quest at their earliest convenience."

"He must have gotten word of our return," Elliot says from the bottom of the stairs. His low voice does little to calm me. "I'll tell Mya." Rian hands the note to his father and then folds me into his arms. At first I feel like fighting him away, but it's so comfortable I rest against him and bury my face into his shoulder. He smells sweet, like the spicy smoke of the incense I know is used to aid in Rumination. Suddenly, I wish we were alone together.

"I'm glad you finally decided to wake up," he murmurs as the others converse quietly in the kitchen. I nod into his shoulder. I want to tell him about everything, even the dream, but it will have to wait. Upstairs, Mya has stopped playing to talk with Elliot, and I can hear Brother Donal at prayer over my father. I hear the couple come down the stairs, and I feel Mya's arms around the two of us. She kisses Rian on the cheek and tells him to take care of me, and then she and Elliot slip off into the darkening streets to the castle.

Chapter Six:

THE SEARCH

Curled in the crook of my father's strong arm, I lie staring out his window at the cloud-covered sky. I imagine the moon dancing behind the clouds, smiling as it did in my dream. Sleep won't come for me tonight. I'm afraid if I let it take me, I might be out for days again and miss something important. I have a feeling even if I wanted to doze, I wouldn't be able to. My head is too filled with thoughts darting in and out, making me dizzy.

After Mya and Elliot left for the palace, Brother Donal called me up to my father's room. He told me Da's physical wounds were grave, and had Mya and Elliot not raced him home so quickly, he would be in much worse shape. But his healing took well, and with luck and good care Da should be up and about within a day or two. I'm so grateful. Too many times tonight I've imagined life without him and it was too painful to bear. I turn away from the window to look at him. The bruises on his face are faded to a yellow-gray ghost of what they had been earlier this afternoon. There is a scar across his brow where he took the worst of the blow, but after the healing and with the blood cleaned away it isn't so frightening to look at now.

After a while I hear the door downstairs open and close, and the soft shuffle of Rian's footsteps as he makes his way upstairs. He peeks his head into the room.

"They're ready for us," he whispers. I sit up and turn and stroke my father's stubbly cheek, and then pull the blankets up to his shoulders and smooth them tenderly.

"Sleep sweet, Da," I whisper as Rian's warm hand encloses around mine and he leads me down the stairs.

"What did the prince say to your parents?" I ask him once we're downstairs. He pauses in the dark sitting room.

"He wanted a full report of the Quest." He scowls. "He told them they're to go back and find your mother at all costs. But he said they must keep it a secret. Their Majesties don't want anyone to catch wind the quest might have failed. He said it's a bad omen for his marriage. It was supposed to be a simple task."

"A simple task?" I shake my head in disbelief. "They were sent to a land that isn't supposed to exist on a mysterious quest to return some lost treasure and to whom? Kythshire has no people! It's only spoken of in legends and storybooks. How is that a simple task?" Rian shakes his head.

"I don't know. My mother seemed to feel the same way, though she'd never say it." He reaches up and rubs his eyes. He looks exhausted. "It seems to me she agreed with everything the prince said just to get through the meeting quickly. Her greatest concern is to find your mother. She wants to ride at dawn, as soon as she's able to talk to us and make arrangements."

I'm comforted by Mya's urgency to start the search. It means she believes there's hope my mother is still alive. Not for the first time tonight, the thought of being orphaned at sixteen pushes into the edge of my mind. I shove it away.

"Do you think we'll be able to go this time?" I ask. I would hate to leave my father behind, but I can't imagine the agony of sitting here in an empty guild hall while everyone else goes off to search.

"That's what they were discussing when I was sent out to get you," he says, shaking his head. "It's hard to say which way the conversation was tipping. Mum, Bryse, and Cort were for it. Gaethon and Donal seemed to be against."

"And your father?" I ask. If Elliot was for it too, that would help.

"Sleeping," he says with a bemused shake of his head.

"Always sleeping," I sigh. "Well, we shouldn't keep them waiting."

There is no fanfare or royal proclamation, no crowd at the door of this guild meeting. When we arrive at the hall, everyone is slouched in armchairs around the great hearth. The air is thick with a sense of tedium and fatigue. Mya looks especially exhausted but determined. There's a fire in her eyes that matches the bright red shock of her spiked hair. Beside her, Elliot is curled up in his own chair, his eyes closed, sound asleep just as Rian had said. Across from him, Bryse, Cort, and Brother Donal are bent together in quiet conversation. Master Gaethon sits rail-straight on the edge of his cushion. When Rian and I enter the room, he eyes us thoughtfully and gestures to two chairs between himself and Mya. They exchange looks and Mya nods to him. She closes her eyes as he addresses us.

"It has been decided that the two of you are to remain here." He raises his voice as Rian and I start to protest, and holds his hand up impatiently to silence us. I bite my tongue hard and slump back into the chair, crossing my arms. Being left off of the quest list was bad enough, but being made to stay home through this is unthinkable.

"Azaeli, you are to care for your father." Uncle says. "When he is well enough to ride, you may accompany him to meet us." He presses his fingertips together and turns to Rian. "Rian, I will take a temporary leave of my position at the Academy and join in the search. Mistress Viala," he pauses and meets Rian's eye meaningfully, "will oversee your studies while I am away. You will show her the same respect you show me. Understood?" His eyes burn into Rian's and I find myself looking away uncomfortably.

"Yes, Sir," Rian says, his tone careful and disciplined. I can't help but be impressed by his restraint. Viala is Rian's rival, his own version of Dacva. Though she's only a couple of years older than him, she has far surpassed him in her studies during her short time at the Academy. I know for a fact he both admires and resents her for it.

"I have begun research on the source of Azaeli's affliction." Uncle hands Rian a thick roll of notes. "The sword itself showed no sign of magical tampering. I have suggested other causes in my notes, and it is important you explore them together. You will write a report of your findings and send it on to me. You are to share this information with no one else. If you complete this task by the time Sir Benen is able to ride, then you may join him and Azaeli to meet us."

"Yes, sir," Rian says again as he unrolls the scroll and looks it over with interest. I crane my neck and he leans closer so we can read it together.

"Azi, if you're feeling up to it, I'm sure your help is needed with the preparations for our departure. Luca could use a hand in the stables." Mya stretches and rises with the grace of a dancer despite her obvious exhaustion. She leans down to her sleeping husband and tickles his cheek. "If no one has anything else, I'm going to try to steal an hour or two of rest before we set out."

There is a collective noise of dismissal from the group as those gathered agree she should rest. Elliot blinks slowly and slides to his feet a bit reluctantly, and the two of them step out of the room together hand in hand. Watching their tenderness reminds me of my own parents and sends an ache through my chest. I swallow hard and push myself up. The others are too involved in their own conversations to acknowledge my leaving.

On the step between the guild hall and the training square, I hesitate, remembering my last moments in this room, when I gripped my sword and passed out. I take a deep breath and steel myself before I step down onto the packed dirt floor. Nothing happens. I glance over my shoulder and bend to pick up my sword, which has been returned to the rack. Pain shoots through my fingertips as they graze the hilt and I bite my lip to keep from crying out. Furious and confused, I storm off to the stable and lose myself in my work.

Eventually Luca joins me and we spend the morning repacking the saddlebags and grooming and checking the horses for injuries. Ollie, My mother's enormous white draft horse, nuzzles me and we lean against each other as I brush his mud-crusted haunch. In the quiet solitude of the stable with my mother's horse beside me, I succumb to my fear and cry into his soft, warm shoulder.

Through my tears, I catch a glimmer of multi-colored light outside of the stable. When I snap my head toward it, I'm met with only the dark curve of a tree trunk and rustling leaves washed gray in the light of the dull, foggy dawn. My hand slides over Ollie's strong leg to my mother's saddlebags. Unthinking, I open one of them, and my fingers graze a sheet of parchment. I pull it out and crouch in the straw, holding it up to the lamp light of the stable. I blink my tears rapidly away so I can read:

> *My Dear Azi,*
>
> *It is with a heavy heart that I write this, imagining you alone, reading it. We know the risks of our profession, but each time it seems to get more*

difficult to say goodbye and leave you behind. This time, especially so. If I should not return, I want you to know how proud I am of the young woman you've become. I know in my heart you will one day be a knight and honor the values we have taught you. Always remember the values our family stands for: Integrity, kindness, justice, charity, and loyalty.

With that in mind, I leave you with a warning. Listen to your heart, my Sweeting. Pay attention to your dreams. If you must venture, never do so alone. Have faith in the Elite, but be wary of others who you've grown to trust. Be cautious. That is all I dare say here. I love you always and forever, no matter where I am, my darling girl. Be strong.

As ever, it is my prayer you never have a reason to find or read this note.

With all of my love,
Mum

I read it three times, committing it to memory, and then I tuck it back inside the bag. When my mother returns, I'll keep her believing that her prayer was heard, and I never saw it.

"All right, Sunshine?" Luca asks, peering around Ollie at me. I nod and wipe my eyes as I push myself to my feet. "Atta girl. Give me a hand with this, here." He nods at the saddle girth around Mya's horse and I go over to help him. His long, knobby fingers work to pull the cinch tight, but they slip off. "Argh, these old hands," he grumbles, and I take the billet strap from him and buckle it snug under the horse's belly. "That's it, thank you." Luca says, patting me on the shoulder. I give him a weak smile and check the rest of the tack.

As I tie Mya's cantle bags to the back of the saddle, I'm aware of the approach of clomping hoof beats. I look out into the soft light of sunrise to see Rian leading a horse I immediately recognize as Thunder.

"Good lad," Bryse calls from inside the passage that runs to the guild hall. He strides up to his horse and strokes his gleaming neck. "Hey, beaut," he murmurs affectionately before throwing his own bags up and fixing them to the saddle with ease.

Rian barely has time to greet me as the others filter in. There's a flurry of activity as they make last moment preparations, and Rian and I are sent running for this and that. Then they're gone, and we're left alone in the quiet.

"It seems strange to send them off that way," Rian says as he leans into my shoulder. "No banners, no trumpets…"

No Mum or Da, I think to myself. He turns to me and picks a bit of straw from my hair. He gazes into my eyes and I feel my cheeks warm. Here, so close to him, all of my pain and fear seem to fade away. I find my gaze trailing to his lips again.

"Wow," he whispers, drawing my attention back to his eyes. His brow furrows. "You look awful," he says with exaggerated gravity.

"Oh! Such a charmer you are!" Mouli bats at him with her kitchen towel. "Course she does with no bath for almost a week and no sleep all night and all morning in the stables mucking about. Look at yourself, little sir! You're not all blossoms and blooms, either."

"Ah, Mouli," Rian winks. "I love it when you call me little sir." He takes her by the waist and spins her around and she yelps in protest and beats him away playfully. I can't help but laugh at the scene of the two of them sending straw dust swirling in the sunbeams that filter through the thatched roof of the stable. This is why I'm so glad he's here. Rian can always make me laugh, no matter how dark things might seem. Mouli eventually fights him off and takes me gently by the elbow.

"Come on, Dear. I have a bath ready for you." I catch Rian's eye and he wriggles his brows up and down. I bite my lip and shake my head.

"Don't worry about me, Mouli," Rian says, dejected. "I guess I can find my own bath."

"Get out of here!" Mouli shoos him off and Rian skirts out of the stable, flashing a mischievous wink over his shoulder.

"Knock after you're all cleaned up, Azi," he calls with a wave as Mouli leads me back inside.

Later, alone in my room, my thoughts wander to the dream I had and how real it was. The memory of the diamond's hard edge against my palm entices me. The pitcher where I stashed it yesterday gleams in the sunlight, and I reach in and take away the coverlet fashioned from scraps of lace. The facets of the stone send glittering beams dancing all across the walls of the tiny house. I nudge it with my finger and the droplets of light wiggle and flash and mesmerize me. They remind me of the glimmer I thought I saw earlier, outside of the stable. Rian knocks on the hatch and I nearly jump out of my skin. The pitcher falls with a clatter to the floor and the diamond skids across it and rolls under my bed. I swear I hear a sound, something like a sneeze, as the knock comes again and I jump up to slide the hatch open.

"What are you doing in there, throwing things?" He cranes his neck to look into my room.

"You startled me!" I pick up the pitcher and set it upright on the shelf beneath my window. I'll retrieve the diamond later.

"Jumpy," he says as he rests his chin on the edge of the opening. "I like you better this way than sleeping beauty, though."

"Me too," I say honestly.

"At least you smell better now." He wrinkles his nose.

"Thanks." I roll my eyes.

"Are you ready?" he asks. "We have work to do."

"I just want to check on Da. I'll meet you downstairs."

We slide our hatches closed and I crouch to lift up my bed skirt and look for the diamond. It winks brightly at me from beside a ball of dust and I retrieve it and drop it back into the pitcher, covering it again with the lace. As I turn to leave I hear it again, a faint and squeaky sneeze. When I look over my shoulder in the direction it came from, I think I see a flutter of light but I blink and shake my head. Certainly it was just the way the sunlight waved through the rustle of my window curtain, reflecting off of the rim of the pitcher.

My father is sleeping when I check on him, and he's attended by a healer assigned by Brother Donal. I recognize her as Emme. She has ministered to our guild before in Donal's absence.

"Azaeli, child!" she whispers. Her smile is slightly pitying as she sets down her knitting and crosses to hug me. She holds me at arms' length and looks me over. "My, but you've grown!" I feel my cheeks grow warm at her appraising look, and I manage a smile. Behind her, my father is sleeping soundly just as I left him hours ago. She follows my gaze and turns to guide me to the bed. "He's resting now, exactly what he needs," she whispers. I sit on the edge of the bed and stroke his arm gently.

"How long will he sleep?" I ask, noticing the bottle on his bedside table.

"Oh, as long as he needs to." She settles into her chair again. "Another day, most likely."

Without warning, Da bolts upright and grabs me by the throat. His eyes are wild and frantic as he pulls me close to him. I try to pry his hands away, to escape, but his grip is too strong. His fingers are closing off my air. His lips curl into a sneer and his eyes bulge feverishly, darting back and forth.

"Two steps in, I only took two steps!" he growls. "You can't have her!" I choke and kick away from him as Emme dives for the bed. He screams piteously as she wrestles him away from me, prying his hands from my throat. I fall back to the floor and gasp for breath, my lungs burning, vaguely aware of someone else in the room as I try to recover my senses. Emme calls for the sleeping draught. I look up to see Rian uncorking the bottle. My father gurgles as they force it on him.

"Leave him alone," I croak. My neck throbs where he squeezed it. The struggle at the bed subsides and Rian sinks down next to me. He tries to put an arm around me but I move away from him. I don't understand what just happened. My father attacked me. He has never raised a finger to me in all of my life. He's one of the kindest, gentlest people I know. Emme finishes settling him in and smoothing the coverlet over him, and then comes to crouch beside me.

"Oh, child, I'm so sorry," she whispers. "It comes with a blow to the head, sometimes. The fits. I ought to have warned you. It'll pass in time." She raises my chin to look at my throat, which I'm sure has already started bruising. I pull away and push myself to my feet.

"I'm fine," I lie, smoothing my trousers. I stare at my father, lying so peacefully again. I want to kiss him, to tell him it's okay, but I'm too afraid it might happen again. Disturbed by own fear, I spin around and leave the room. I need to put space between us, to gather my thoughts and calm myself.

"Azi…" Rian calls after me.

My feet carry me unthinking through the house, out the door and into the familiar city streets. Dazed, I wander all the way to the low cliff wall near the docks, to let the sea air wash over me. All around, the people of Cerion bustle about their every day jobs, pulling in traps of shellfish, checking lists and collecting tariffs. Labor men work at cranking the lifts, hauling barrels on pulleys up and down the cliff side, loading and unloading the tall-masted ships lining the harbor below. I disappear into everyone else's routine. Nobody recognizes me as Azaeli Hammerfel, the young new squire who won the Princess's favor in the arena just weeks ago. Here, I'm simply a girl in plainclothes staring off into the vastness of the sparkling blue ocean.

A gentle hand rests on my shoulder and I know at once Rian has tracked me down. We watch the gulls swooping down and up and down again, catching morsels that tumble from the traps into the crashing waves below for what feels like hours. The sea breeze has long since dried my tears. After a while, he wraps an arm around my shoulders and leans close.

"We have work to do," he says quietly. I nod, and we walk together back to the guild hall.

Chapter Seven

THE CURSE

On the way back to the hall, Rian diverts my attention to his studies regarding my affliction. He thinks we should recreate the moments leading up to my passing out, which he and Uncle believe was probably caused by some strong magical effect. In the training hall, Rian takes detailed notes as I go over the events of that afternoon. I try to remember even the smallest bit of information I think might be helpful, from where I sat to what I ate for lunch. I finish with my conversation with Bryse.

"Then he got up and said he wanted to show me something with the shield, and I reached for my sword." I reach out for the hilt of my sword which Rian placed there for me. As my fingers close around the hilt, a rush of darkness washes over my vision. The ground spins beneath my feet. Ear splitting screams ring in my ears, melding with my own until I throw the sword down with a clatter. Rian is at my side in an instant, reassuring me.

"Breathe, Azi," he says, and takes a long, deep breath himself to guide me. It's not until after I mimic him that I realize I have in fact been holding my breath. He watches me with concern as I take a few deep breaths and finally nod for him to continue.

"Now," he says, his sharpened stick of graphite poised over his notes. "Tell me what you felt." I describe to him in detail all of the sensations, from the spinning, to the darkness, to the screaming. "And it starts when you take your sword?" He asks. I nod. He thinks for a moment, then crosses to the weapon stand and takes a dagger. He comes back and offers it to me. "Try this." I take it cautiously. The pain comes, the room spins, the blackness threatens, and the screaming drowns out his voice. As he tugs the weapon from my hand, I lean away from him and vomit into the bucket he had the foresight to set up at my side. I drop sideways to lie on the bench and wipe my mouth with a groan. Rian pats my arm absently while his other hand scratches notes. He leaves and comes back shortly, offering me a cup of water, which I take gratefully.

"Can you go on?" he asks, distracted by his notes. His serious tone makes me feel like the inanimate subject of some study. Still, I nod. He goes around the room, collecting an array of weapons of all types which he brings back to the bench. One by one I grasp them and succumb to the darkness, the screaming, and the spinning. When the stash of weapons has all been tried, I rest my aching head against the wall and close my eyes, thankful that I managed to get through them all without getting sick again.

"The weapon doesn't matter," he murmurs, tapping his lip with the stick of graphite. He looks at it thoughtfully and then offers it to me. I peer down at the writing instrument warily, bracing myself before reaching up to close my fingers around it. Nothing happens. I sigh with relief and hand it back to him.

"Well, I'll be sure to carry a writing stick at all times in case I ever need to defend myself," I say dryly as I close my eyes and rub my face.

"Whatever the cause, it covered all possibilities," he says, looking down his list. "Even a bow and arrows."

"That was hardly necessary." I scowl at the bow long ago discarded at his feet. "Shooting was never my strength, anyway." I sigh and tuck my knees under my chin, gazing at my beloved sword lying in the dust at my feet, buried under a pile of everything from knives to cleavers to clubs. "I don't understand."

"It seems like," Rian makes another note, "something or someone is trying very hard to keep you from fighting."

"But who?" I ask. "And why?" He shakes his head, poring over the page, searching for some clue.

"Rian, what if it's like this forever? What if I can never fight again?" I press my forehead into my knees. It's all too much. I've lost my mother, my father is a madman, and now even my own abilities have failed me. At this point, I'm beyond tears. Rian seems to sense the despair creeping in on me.

"No curse is unbreakable, Azi," he says softly.

"Do you think that's what this is?" I ask, looking up at him. "A curse?" His hazel eyes burn with something I've never seen before in him, something dark and angry. He doesn't look away until I do.

"That's what I think this is, and I promise you we'll find a way to break it." I lean against his shoulder as he scours his notes, and eventually I fall into a dreamless doze. When he taps me awake, the sun is already dipping down to touch the rooftops outside.

"I need to go to the library," he says. "I've read all of Master Gaethon's notes and my own and I have some questions." I slide away from him and stretch. My muscles are stiff and sore. Usually by this time of day, I've had several hours of swordplay and training. I wonder to myself how long it will take to lose the strength I've worked so hard to build up over the years. Rian stands up. His hair is disheveled and his usually bright eyes are framed with dark circles.

"Have you had any sleep?" I ask him. He bends to roll up the notes and tuck them into a scroll case so that his long side locks obscure his face. "Rian, you need to rest."

"I will," he says. "When I finish this."

"Why don't you just take a quick nap now? It can wait." I pick up the bucket I'd gotten sick in earlier. I won't leave that for Mouli, it's too disgusting.

"It can't," Rian says. "Your father's going to be ready to ride out when he wakes up, Azi. With or without us. If I don't figure this out, then we're stuck here. Again." I sigh. I know he's right. As soon as my father is well, nothing will keep him from joining the search. I'd be allowed to go, but what could I contribute? If anything, I'd be a hindrance with no way to defend myself on the road.

"I'm keeping you here," I say. "I'm so sorry, Rian."

"Azi…" he shakes his head and steps close to me, circling his arms around me. He strokes my hair and my back as I rest my cheek on his shoulder. Too soon, he drops his arms and steps away. "I promise I'll be back with answers as soon as I have them."

"Can I do anything to help?" I ask. He shakes his head.

"I wish you could, but you're not permitted." I know he's right. There is a strict law governing who is allowed within the walls of the Academy. Only students and teachers of magic may enter the compound. Even the fact that I'm related to the Headmaster won't grant me entry. "Don't worry." He flashes me a grin that melts away the anger and exhaustion that was there just moments before. "Take care of your Da. I'll see you soon." He turns, and I watch until his slender form disappears around the bend beyond the park promenade, leaving me alone.

The bucket is easily emptied, but when I return to the training square my next task seems insurmountable. The scatter of weapons lying dusty and discarded by our experiment is my responsibility. One of my first duties, even before I was able to start training, was to tend to polishing, storing, and organizing the guild's cache. I take pride in the fact that they are always on gleaming display in the racks around the square. The state of them now is a disgrace. I nudge the butt of a hammer with the toe of my boot. Nothing happens. I crouch and wrap the loose hem of my trouser leg around my hand, and then grasp the handle of the weapon. Screaming, blackness, spinning, and I toss the weapon down with a growl of frustration.

Determined not to give up on the simple chore of putting the weapons away, I go to my father's forge and find his pickup tongs. With them I'm able to line the weapons along the training bench and wipe each one down. I find that avoiding the hilt prevents me from any effects of the curse, so I am careful not to touch any handles even with the barrier of oiled cloth in my hand. I'm halfway through the task when Mouli finds me kneeling in the dust, polishing the blade of a scimitar that rests on the bench. I secretly slide my father's tongs between my knees before she notices them. I don't want to worry her with the curse.

"Always working, you." Her tone is soft and affectionate. She steps down from the hall door, and with her she carries the sweet scent of fresh, warm bread. My stomach growls. "Skipped lunch today, I expect?" I think back and realize that I haven't actually eaten at all since yesterday. This information, I know, would incite her wrath, and so I keep it to myself. "I'm starving now," I admit truthfully enough as I carefully slide my fingers under the blade and flip the sword over to work the other side. "Something smells amazing."

"Well, it's your favorite for dinner. Sea crab stuffed rolls." My mouth waters as she dusts some flour from her skirt. "Will you take it in the hall, or perhaps with your father in his room?" I've avoided thinking of my father for most of the day. Our earlier encounter still rattles me. But I know that wasn't really him, and I know he should be getting better. Suddenly I feel guilty that I haven't checked in on him all day.

"Has he woken up yet?" I ask.

"Now and again," she replies. "He had some broth at midday." My heart skips.

"How was he?" I search her face. She looks to the side, and I can tell she's deciding how to word her reply.

"Not quite himself, yet." She offers me a sympathetic smile. "But think of how he's improved since yesterday. He'll be up and about in no time." I look down at my work and then along the bench at the dozen weapons waiting for their shine.

"I'll finish up here and then eat upstairs," I say. It'll take at least an hour to get through the task, and I hate to leave it half-finished.

"Luca'll finish up for you," Mouli offers. "He's been sitting up there with your Da all afternoon. He'll be glad of the work. Go on and wash up. I'll bring you a tray."

Da is asleep when I arrive a little while later. I whisper my greeting to Luca, who gladly hurries off to finish my work in the training square. He's not much different than I am in that respect. We both hate to sit idle when there's work that needs doing. When he's gone, I approach Da's bedside with caution. Just like this morning, he's tucked perfectly into bed, resting on his back. His shirt has been changed, and the yellow fabric against his skin makes him look sallow. I sink to sit on the edge of the bed, and I slip my hand into his. His skin is rough and calloused, but his hand is warm and his fingers close gently around mine. Slowly he turns his head and his eyes flutter open. They take a moment to focus, and I feel my muscles tensing, ready to jump up and run away if I need to. I'm relieved, though, when his lips stretch into a weak smile.

"Azi, my Azi," he whispers. His eyes rest on my throat and I reach up quickly with my free hand to cover the bruises that I'm sure are there. His hand tightens around mine and a tear brims in the corner of his eye and rolls down his cheek. I wipe it away before it gets too far. "I didn't know." He closes his eyes.

"It's okay, Da. It's okay." I smooth a curl behind his ear and stroke his hair until he falls asleep again.

When Mouli comes with my supper, I finish two rolls the size of Bryse's fist and delight her by asking for more. My father's recognition of me and his apology have lifted my spirits. The warm glow of candlelight dancing over his sleeping form comforts me. He knows me. At least I have him. At least we're together. With a full belly and an exhausting day behind me, it isn't long before I find myself dozing curled up in the soft cushions of the bedside chair. I don't know how long I've been sleeping before I'm roused by a single thump in my room. When I open my eyes they're drawn to the hallway, where an odd cast of light dances on the wall. It melds with the waning lamplight, but its pattern is a dapple of every color of the rainbow, and its flicker is brighter.

In a sleepy daze, I glance at my father before I push myself up and tiptoe to the door. The light reminds me of the diamond in my pitcher, and its source is somewhere in my bedroom. Curious, I creep through the hall as quietly as I can and peer into my room. The pitcher on my windowsill lays on its side again, though I distinctly remember setting it upright in my haste this morning. Sparkling light glimmers from inside of it, casting colorful prisms across the walls. The pitcher wriggles a little, and the ribbons and lace adorning it flutter. I stand fixed in the doorway and rub the sleep from my eyes as I watch the odd spectacle. I've just about convinced myself that some outside source must be shining on the diamond inside to cause such an effect when I hear a tiny whisper.

"You can stay, just be quiet—"

"What?" I cross the room in two strides and pick up the little house. The light goes out instantly, leaving me blind in the sudden darkness. When my eyes adjust, I pull out the little bed and the scraps of lace and silk to discover my diamond rolling around beside a small black cricket. I stare at it for a moment. "Did you…" I realize that it's mad to be addressing a bug and I shake my head. With impeccable timing as always, the hatch slides open and Rian peers in at me. I imagine how I must look, standing at my window, talking to a pitcher. Maybe I am going mad.

"Catch any fairies yet?" He jests. I set the pitcher on its side. At this point, I'm not sure how to answer him. The whispering was clear as day, but already I'm doubting it. I had been sleeping. It was probably just a lingering dream.

"None yet." I force a laugh and tuck the makeshift bed back inside, careful not to crush the cricket. "Did you find anything?"

"Nothing. But an interesting nothing. Can I come over?" I nod. The wall between us shimmers and shifts, and Rian steps right through it to stand beside me. As the wall solidifies again behind him, he gestures to it dramatically and turns to grin at me.

"How...?" I gape at him.

"I found a tome about borders and territory. It was fascinating. The theory is that with permission, one can cross any border, ethereal or physical, no matter how impossible it may seem." The cricket's chirp emanates from the pitcher, followed quickly by a "Shh!" I look at Rian, who has heard it too, and is staring at the source of the sound. He shakes his head dismissively and turns back to me. "It's a fairly simple spell once you get the hang of it."

"How does it relate to the curse?" I ask, trying my best not to let my eyes stray to the windowsill where the cricket has started up again.

"That's where the interesting nothing comes in," he says. "I was halfway through a book of known curses when I found a page torn out. The page before that described something similar to what you're experiencing. I found several tomes with similar pages gone, but I was able to piece a bit of information together nonetheless. One of them mentioned an affliction that was caused by crossing into unwelcome territory, which led me to the book with that spell." He reaches up and slides his fingertips through his hair sheepishly. "I got a little distracted after that. I really wanted to learn it."

"Typical." The whisper from the pitcher is faintly audible alongside the cricket's song, which stops abruptly. Again, Rian's eyes snap to the source. He looks from it to me and I'm finally certain that he's heard it, too. He brushes past, reaches for the pitcher, and starts to cast something, but then he stops and looks back at me.

"May I?" he asks. I nod, though I'm unsure what exactly he's asking for permission to do. He picks it up and looks inside. I come to his side and peer in, too. The cricket and diamond are hidden behind the pile of fine scraps. Rian murmurs something in the scholar's tongue and sudden pinpoints of light burst forth from the pitcher. A light, larger than the cricket but smaller than my palm shoots over my shoulder and lands on my bed with a soft "oof!" Rian and I exchange glances and I rush to the bed to get a closer look.

A tiny girl with beautiful iridescent wings at her back looks up at me, her arms crossed. Her skin is so light that it's nearly translucent, and it shimmers beautifully. Her hair is done up in many pony tails across the crown of her head, each one a different color of the rainbow. The scowling narrow slits of her eyes are unlike anything I've seen before. They shift constantly from gold to green, from purple to pink. She's dressed in a tiny skirt pieced together with shimmering bits of ribbon, some of which I recognize from Margary's pitcher. At her waist is a belt weighed down with several tiny pouches. Her corset, like her eyes, shifts in color according to the way the light plays on it. As she scowls up at us, everything about her reminds me of my diamond.

FLIT

"Rude!" she squeaks, pointing across the room at Rian. "So rude!"

His wide eyes are fixed on her in disbelief as he stands holding the pitcher. He looks at me and snaps his mouth shut. When I kneel down beside the bed to get a closer look, she stands up and flutters her wings until her toes are barely grazing the coverlet. Her lips are pressed tightly together and she brushes at her clothing and bare arms as if trying to clear something away. After a moment, she thrusts her finger back in Rian's direction. "Take it off, you! It's not nice!"

"Uh…" Rian leans away slightly, his mouth hanging open again. He looks at me with wide eyes and his shoulders slowly slide up to his ears. I look back at the fairy, who is now hovering at eye level with me, her nostrils flared in annoyance.

"Um…" I croak, barely able to muster any words through my utter disbelief. I clear my throat and my voice comes a little stronger. "Take what off?" Her light dazzles my eyes and I raise a hand to my brow to shade them. She scoots back in midair and rests a fist on her hip, the other hand still thrust at Rian. She jabs her pointer again.

"Revealer! He put a Revealer on me and I wasn't ready yet! Take it off!" She darts across the room at him and stabs the tip of his nose with her finger. "Take it off right now!" Rian drops the pitcher and it rolls away from him as he claps a hand over his nose.

"Ow, cut it out." He ducks away and she chases after him, catching his auburn side lock and tugging it with fury.

"Take it off!" she squeals.

"I don't know how!" He yanks his hair away, sending her tumbling through the air. She rights herself just beside my head and hovers behind me.

"Typical!" she squeaks, "So typical!" She ducks behind my shoulder and I turn my head slowly to look at her. She's absolutely smoldering with anger but when Rian takes a step closer, she darts away. "Don't you come near me, you, you, Mage!" She spits the last word out with distaste.

"You're real," I whisper, staring at her. "A real fairy."

"Well of course I'm a real fairy. I've only been sitting in that tin pot of yours for two days now waiting for you to notice me. Which, by the way, stinks of metal. This whole place stinks of metal and smoke and I don't even know what. Did you know that? The ribbons are nice, though. I wonder how long I'd have stayed in there before you really believed in me. Maybe it's better he put that spell on me, isn't it? I mean it could have taken weeks! You're a little thick, aren't you?"

"Hey!" Rian warns, and she creeps around to hide behind my other shoulder.

"Well, really. Really, I've heard all sorts of things about your kind but I honestly didn't believe half of it. And now that I'm here I realize it's mostly true. Especially the part about Mages. I didn't realize there'd be one so close by. I kind of wish I hadn't agreed to come after all." She wrinkles her nose at Rian.

"Well, since no one's invited you, maybe you should just go!" He rubs his nose and the roots of his tugged hair simultaneously, scowling.

"Well I can't do that, can I? I just now got back here. I'd have to wait for sunrise to go again. That'd be a waste anyway. Nothing to report. Unless you count utter disregard for my privacy! But they'd already expect that from your kind." I look between them, trying to focus. There is a fairy in my room. A real one. They exist. I am not crazy, Rian sees her, too. We're having a conversation with an actual fairy. I think of the dream, and the diamond.

"How long did you say you've been here?" I ask her.

"Well, I got here yesterday. So I guess it's really just a day. But still." I stoop to collect the pitcher that Rian dropped. The diamond clinks around inside, and I scoop it out to show her.

"Is this from you?" I ask.

"Hmph!" She crosses her arms and turns her shoulder toward me, "I'm not telling you anything with *him* in here."

"Rian's my best friend," I say. "I'm going to tell him everything you tell me, anyway." She immediately presses her lips together and shakes her head firmly. I sigh and look at Rian, who all at once seems bemused and insulted. On top of that, his eyes are framed with deep circles. He's exhausted.

"Ah, I guess I'll go to bed, then…" his voice trails off as he backs away to the door, his palms open and up. I'm grateful that he decides to use the stairs rather than slip through the wall again, for the fairy's sake.

"So, Azi, what do you want to know?" She grins and bats her eyes sweetly, completely amiable once she's sure Rian is gone.

"I…" I sit with my back resting against the bed. This is all so strange. "How do you know my name?" I ask. She comes to hover at my knee, her pretty wings almost invisible as they flutter to keep her aloft.

"Well, your mother told me." She answers casually, her eyes fading from blue to lavender. She glances up at the hatch, which I've left open, and she flies up to slide it closed. It's a struggle for her at first and I start to get up to help her, but she manages it on her own and eventually clicks the latch over the bar.

"My mother? When? Do you know where she is?"

"Ah, ah, ah," she raises a hand to stop me as she drifts back down. "That's not how we play." She points at me. "You ask a question," she points to herself, "and then I ask a question. Then, you. Then, me. Then, you. Then, me. You, me, you, me, you, me. Got it?" She nods sagely and folds her arms. I bite my lip. This is a game to her, but not to me. She's spoken to my mother. She might know where she is. Still, I doubt she'll tell me anything unless I play by her rules.

"Fine," I say, "Your turn."

"Why are you friends with that stinky Mage?" She wrinkles her nose and rolls her eyes in the direction of Rian's room.

"He isn't stinky. I think he smells wonderful. Like old books and incense." I smile, and she blinks at me.

"Old books are dead trees. And incense is burnt plants. And you didn't answer the question." She scowls. I sigh.

"Rian is my friend because we grew up side by side. We've been together through everything for as long as I can remember. He cares about me, and I care about him. He's a good person." I glance up at the hatch. I really am lucky to have him in my life.

"Your turn!" She drifts down to stand on my bent knee.

"When did you see my mother?" I ask, barely feeling her there.

"Yesterday. My turn! What's your favorite color?"

"Blue. Where did you see her?"

"In Kythshire." She sniffs at the fabric of my trousers and wrinkles her nose, then hovers up again, "Who made the pretty little house for me?"

"Princess Margary." I pause, thinking, "Is she safe?"

"Is who safe? Princess Margary? How should I know? I haven't met her. She makes a lovely house though. It really is sweet, with all of the ribbons. Do you think she minds that I've taken a few of them?"

"No, she wouldn't mind," I say. It occurs to me that she's broken her own rule by asking several questions at once, but I don't want to anger her by pointing it out. I think of how delighted little Margy would be to see a fairy here, a real fairy. I'd love to introduce the two of them. They'd get on well. "What's your name?" I ask.

"Well, you can call me Flit." She darts across the room and back again. "I flit here, I flit there. Do you have any sugar cubes or fruit juice?" she asks. I think of the little cubes in Margy's fairy house and Sarabel's handful in the garden. My thoughts meander through that afternoon that seems so long ago now. The sun was so beautiful that day, glittering through the summer leaves overhead. It was such a perfect afternoon. I sigh and smile, and rest my head back against my soft mattress remembering Margary's sweet laughter. "Ahem!" Flit coughs and flies up to look into my face.

"Sorry…" I think for a moment. "Was it my turn?" I had something important I wanted to ask, but the question escapes me now.

"No, I asked you if you had some juice or sugar, but you didn't answer me."

"Oh, right. I think I do. I'll go check." I get all the way to the kitchen before I blink back to my senses. I was trying to find out about my mother, but the conversation got unhinged. I don't know who to be angrier with, Flit for leading it astray or myself for allowing her to. I grab a handful of sugar and take the stairs back up two at a time. Flit is waiting for me on the edge of her pitcher, where the cricket is singing softly again. "Here," I say. "Please don't do that again." She looks up at me and studies my face for a moment, then breaks into laughter.

"I'm just playing the game," she grins, "Games are supposed to be fun, you know." She takes a cube and crunches into it, chewing happily. "Your turn," she says around a mouthful. I take a deep breath and tick down the mental list of what I need to know about. My mother, and my father, too, and then the diamond. I'm sure she can answer everything I need to know. Maybe even tell me about the curse.

"Is my mother safe?" I ask.

"I imagine so. Is your hair always just yellow, or does it change?" She licks her lips and takes another bite, humming happily to herself.

"It's always yellow…" I press my fingertips to my eyes and try to focus. She isn't giving me very thorough answers, and it's beginning to annoy me. "Flit, please. My mother is very dear to me. All that I know right now is that she's missing and we don't know why or how or whether she's safe. I just need to know what's going on. Please."

"Well, that isn't really a proper question." She shakes her head and licks her fingers.

"Well, 'I imagine so' isn't really a proper answer, is it?" I snap. "Tell me what's going on!"

"Really, it's an easy game, and fun if you know how to ask your questions." She dips into the pitcher and lies on her stomach on the bed of silk and lace with her chin in her hands. The cricket comes up to settle beside her and she pats him sweetly on the head. I think for a while. What she's told me already is that my mother is in Kythshire, and she saw her yesterday, and that she imagines she's safe. What I want to know is why she stayed, and didn't come out with my father. And why my father came out so broken.

"My mother and her friends were sent to return a lost treasure to your land. Do you know if she returned it?"

"Yes, I know." She grins. "Do you know why she was sent to return it?"

"Well, the king sent her. It was to repay a debt, he said." I chew my lip. She didn't answer properly. I think carefully on how to form the question to get the answer that I want.

"Was my mother successful in returning the lost treasure?" I ask.

"Good job! See? You're getting better. Yes, she returned it." She holds up one of the sugar cubes, "Do you want one?"

"No, thank you." I wait a moment for her to ask her question and I realize she's counting that as one. "Why didn't she come back?"

"She promised she'd help us. She's very sweet, your mum." I nod. That sounds right. "Did you mean it when you said you'd tell the stinky Mage everything I say?"

"Everything," I say, "You said before that you wish you hadn't agreed to come. What was it you agreed to?"

"I agreed to watch over you and let your mother know how you're doing here at home in exchange for her staying to help us." She stretches and yawns, "I'm bored of the game now. I'm going to sleep. Goodnight." She scoots around so her feet are all I can see poking out of the edge of the pitcher. Before I can protest, she's sound asleep. Her feet flicker for a moment and disappear. I lean close to listen and can hear her breathing very softly, masked by the cricket's soft chirp. Feeling defeated, I slip out of my trousers and crawl into my own bed. Though my mind is racing with all of the questions I ought to have asked, sleep finds me quickly.

It isn't long before the dreams come again. I'm standing in a lush golden field of wheat which brushes gently at my legs and fingertips as it bends and flows in the cool, sweet breeze. Overhead, the midday sun shines brightly in a cool, impossibly blue sky. I have been here before, I know. But last time, I was lying in the grass and couldn't see all around me. Now I can see that the wheat stretches far and wide. A thin strip of black on the horizon is the only thing that separates gold from blue. I watch the breeze blow the fronds in beautiful waves that remind me of a vast, golden ocean. Slowly I turn and take in my surroundings. Behind me, on the horizon opposite the black strip of mountain, a lush green forest towers over the field. I can make out many different types of trees: firs, elm, and willow. They are such a long way away but so immense in size that I imagine they must be centuries old. I turn back to the mountains again and see a storm brewing. A massive black cloud flashes violently over the mountain, and a gray smudge of rain falls between them.

Behind me, the wheat comes to life. I hear the chatter of small creatures, and the song of birds and frogs and katydids and crickets in beautiful harmony. The music is beautiful and enticing. I am about to turn toward it when a flicker of ruby catches my eye in the direction of the storm. I look closer and I realize that the wheat in the distance ends, and the stretch between field and mountain is heaped with endless treasure. Gold and silver, emerald and ruby spill out onto the wheat in great piles. I feel myself pulled in two directions at once. The treasure entices me. It could buy all of a small kingdom such as Cerion, but it's right in the path of the storm. It also doesn't belong to me. I'm not a thief.

The sounds of the forest call me, promising friendship and shelter. I turn away from the riches and start to make the long walk to the safety of the woods. I long to see how large the trees truly are. I wonder if my tree is still there, waiting for me. As I walk, the wheat grows taller and taller until it stretches high above my head. Far in the distance behind me, a rumble of thunder causes the earth beneath my feet to tremble. I quicken my pace. The wheat is as tall as treetops now, and I can see the first bit of leafy canopy stretching higher than two times the tallest tower in Cerion.

The edge of the wheat is lined with the thickest, most plush carpet of green moss I have ever seen. When I reach it, I kneel and brush it with my fingers, marveling in its velvety softness. The thunder rumbles closer and I look over my shoulder. In the distance, the wheat is moving erratically. Something large is tunneling through it. I step backwards into the nook of an enormous elm root that's thicker than my torso. It's then that I realize I'm tiny. Fairy sized.

The tunneling creature moves with terrifying speed, almost as though it is flashing forward in bursts. I crouch behind a knob of roots, shaking. I'm certain if it finds me, it will kill me. A troupe of fairies darts out of the forest. I try to call to them to warn them, but my voice fails me. The creature in the wheat bursts forth. It reminds me of a shadow, but it gives off a much more ominous energy. It is formless, a shimmer of gray streaked with black, and transparent. Within it, I'm disturbed to catch glimpses of tiny forms spinning and churning. A hand here, a leg there. A face. The creature twists like a cyclone and the fairies from the forest charge to drive it away. They zoom around it in the opposite direction of its spin, confusing it. A tendril of black snaps out and grabs one of them, pulling him in. I cry out in disbelief as he becomes a part of it, swallowed up to join with the other pitiful figures in the churning black shadow.

The ground beneath me trembles again, this time caused by heavy footsteps. A woman in gleaming plate armor steps out from the shelter of the trees. Her blond braid sways behind her as she draws her glowing blue sword and charges the shadowy spinning creature. "Mum!" I try to call out to her, but again my voice is mute. She doesn't see me, she is focused on her foe. One swing is all she needs. She slices sideways through the shadow's middle and it bursts apart with a deafening thunderous rumble.

Lying in a heap where it once twisted and swirled are nearly a dozen tiny bodies. Their wings are limp, their clothes disheveled. Mum kneels and carefully scoops the battered and bloodied little creatures into her arms. When she turns to carry them into the woods, she looks at me. The face is familiar, but it's wrong. It isn't my mother's; it's as if I'm looking into a mirror. It's me. She presses a finger to her lips and nods at me, and then she disappears between the tree trunks into the depths of the forest.

I wake with a lingering feeling of wonder and optimism. It feels like a festival day, like I know I have something exciting to look forward to. Warm morning sun splashes over my bed and a cool, autumn-like breeze drifts in from the window to brush my cheeks. I smile and stretch and snuggle deeper into my blankets to savor the warmth and comfort of my bed. The gentle, rhythmic swish of a file on metal outside my window soothes me. It is such a lovely familiar sound: the sound of burrs being filed away, of a blade being made new. I can almost see the thin, freshly polished sword edge in my mind's eye as I listen to my father work. Then I realize it's wrong. My father...

I stumble out of bed and pull on my filthy, rumpled trousers from the day before. I run barefooted to his room. His bed is unmade and abandoned. So is the chair. Why is no one here to watch him? I curse under my breath as I realize that that task was supposed to be mine. I was so distracted by Flit last night that I left him unattended. My feet barely touch the stairs as I speed through the house and skid to a stop at the back door. There he stands in the bright morning sun, working at repairing a sword held by a clamp at his bench. He slides the file along the blade with a perfect stroke and leans down to assess it, one eye closed.

"Good morning, my dear," he says in a singsong voice. I stand, mouth agape, watching him.

"Good…" I blink and shake my head. I'm dreaming. I must still be dreaming. If Da was really awake, he wouldn't be casually sharpening swords. He'd be packing his horse. Readying to go and find my mother. But the pebbles pressing into the soft soles of my bare feet feel real enough, and the wood of the door frame is as rough as it ever has been when I graze my fingers over it. I clear my throat. "Feeling all right?" I manage in my confusion. He turns to me and winks.

"Never better." He slides the file over the blade once more and takes a strip of oiled leather to start the polish. One hand loosens the clamp and the other closes over the sword's hilt. Then it happens. He falls to his knees, his free hand flying up to his ear as the other grips the hilt tighter. His eyes roll back into his head and he starts to scream. I'm at his side instantly, desperate to pry his fingers free from the hilt, but his grip is too strong. He's lying on the ground now, his body shaking and convulsing.

"Let go, Da!" I cry, grabbing the sword by its ornate guard with both hands. I clamp my feet around his wrist and pull, and my hands slip to the newly sharpened blade which slices into my skin so cleanly that I barely feel it. The sword finally comes free and I fling it away. My father groans and turns to his side. I clench my bleeding hands into fists to slow the flow of blood and kneel beside him.

"Breathe, just breathe," I whisper into his ear, rubbing his shoulder with my bloody fist, leaving a smear of red against the soft blue. He rolls onto his back, panting, and I help him to sit up. "Just rest for a moment," I say as he hunches forward, his pale brow beaded with sweat. My thoughts are clouded with rage. Da is cursed, too. I want to find out who did this to us and make them hurt. I want them to feel just as helpless. Whoever it is, I want to make them beg. The dark thoughts jar me. I know it isn't right to think this way.

It's bad enough that I'm cursed, but I can take up a new skill if I need to. I'm young. But my father has worked at this his whole life. His livelihood is at stake. He's renowned all over the city for his artistry at forging weapons. Everyone knows the pride he takes in his work and the love he puts into even the smallest job. People come from other kingdoms to seek him out. If anyone finds out he's been cursed, he'll be ruined.

"Hello?" Mouli's voice calls as I hear our front door open and close. She bustles about the kitchen and I pat Da on the back with the flat of my fist.

"Da, can you stand?" I think about the aftereffects of the curse on me. He'll be dizzy and tired, but he should be able to get up. He nods weakly and I help him to a stool. I have just enough time to kick the sword under the bench and shove my bloody hands into my pockets before Mouli appears in the doorway.

"Benen! You're up and about? How wonderful." My father grunts and gives a halfhearted wave. He looks a little green and I'm sure he's trying hard to hold the contents of his stomach.

"I thought he could use a bit of sun," the lie is bitter on my tongue. What am I becoming?

"Wonderful. I'll set the breakfast out, oh and Azi, this came for you this morning from the palace." She holds up an envelope with a tassel and a purple seal. I groan inwardly, but I force a smile.

"Thanks, Mouli. I'll read it at the table." She ducks back inside and I lean close to Da's ear to whisper. "Da, don't say anything to Mouli. We'll talk about it after breakfast, okay?" He nods weakly and I help him up from the stool with my hands still balled into fists. I have to do something about them. After I help Da to the table, I jog to the stairs. "I just have to run upstairs for a moment," I try to sound casual, grateful that Mouli's too distracted by the morning meal to notice the blood. The last thing I need right now is her fussing over me.

"Mm," Mouli slices up a melon. "Best change those filthy clothes while you're at it." She clucks her tongue with disapproval.

In my room I dunk my hands into my washbowl and work the red-brown crust from my fingers. When I'm able to open them, I clean my palms, careful not to reopen the wounds. Thankfully, the cuts across each palm are clean and not too deep. They don't need stitching, and they should heal well if I get them bandaged. If I have time later, I'll go to the conclave. In the meantime, I wrap them with a stash of gauze I keep in my dresser and change into a simple frock to appease Mouli.

The silver pitcher glints in the corner of my vision as I'm lacing the ties at the side of the bodice, and I hear the tiniest sneeze. I take a moment to listen to my father and Mouli talking downstairs. Mouli is telling him about a new stall at the market. It seems a safe enough conversation to buy me a little time. I step to the windowsill and peer inside the pitcher.

"Flit?" I whisper. There's a rustling of fabric scraps and then her face appears, blinking up at me.

"It stinks like blood and metal," She pinches her nose. "Did you kill someone?"

"No!" I whisper adamantly.

"Oh, good," she says, rubbing her eyes. "What is it, why did you wake me up?"

"I just wanted to see if you were still here."

"Typical," she says, and burrows back into the silk and lace. I peek inside and see the glint of the diamond flash back at me from beneath her makeshift pillow. The cricket has gone. I have so many questions for her, but I don't think I'm ready for another game just yet. I glance at Rian's hatch and decide to let him sleep. Right now, my concern is for my father.

Chapter Nine

MADNESS

Mouli gives me an appraising look as I return to the kitchen and sit beside my father. Her eyes linger on my bandaged hands but she simply shakes her head and lays a bowl of boiled eggs down beside me. She's used to me being bandaged and bruised. Next to me Da is frowning, and I can tell his thoughts are racing behind his eyes. We let Mouli go on and on about the latest gossip in town while we fill our plates. It takes me a moment as I chew my breakfast to realize she's talking about a ball. My eyes slide to the official-looking envelope tucked beside my plate. I take it and break the seal, which I recognize to be Sarabel's: a rose crossed over a fleur-de-lis.

A ROYAL INVITATION

Sq. Azaeli Hammerfel
is Requested to Attend the Ball
In Celebration of the Sixteenth Birthday
Of Her Majesty Princess Sarabel
Beginning Sunset on the Twenty-First of Autumnsdawn, Year 37 of the Age of Peace
Present This Invitation for Entry into the Palace
Please Respond Yes or No as Soon as Possible

I sit reading the invitation over and over for so long that my father and Mouli both come to look over my shoulder. It seems preposterous to me, getting an invitation to go to a ball in the midst of everything else that's happening. How can anyone celebrate at a time like this? Then I remember that these crises are my own. Everyone else is going on with their everyday lives. Most people don't even realize that my mother is missing, and my father and I are cursed. All they know is that our guild is on the King's Quest. I set the paper down beside my plate.

"Well, I'm glad to have an excuse to decline," I say quietly. It's true. Even if nothing else was going on, I don't care much for dressing in fine gowns and dancing at court.

"Nonsense!" Mouli bats my shoulder with a towel, "That, my dear, is just the medicine you need. Something to lift you up and brush you off. You've had a bad time of it these couple of weeks. We all need to forget our troubles once in a while."

"Forget my troubles?" Is she honestly suggesting I just set aside the fact that I might never see my mother again? That my family might be ruined?

"Mouli's right, my dear," Da says, his attention back on his breakfast, "It'd do you good to get your mind off things for a night." I look at him in disbelief and he slides a glance at me that tells me to go along with him.

"I'm glad you're talking sense, Benen," Mouli nods and starts clearing plates, "Listen to your father, Azi. Good man." I read the invitation again and then get up to clear my plate, but Mouli takes it from my hands to do it herself.

"It's just a few days from now," I say. "I don't even have a dress."

"Never you mind that," says Mouli, and I know she's already planning everything from jewels to shoes and in between. She hums with delight as she cleans up the breakfast, and Da and I sit in silence as she goes on now and then about the color, and the style, and the weight of the dress. "So much to think about! I've got to get to market. I'll be back for midday meal." She takes off her apron, tucks it into her basket, and rushes out the front door.

"Well, that got her out of the way," Da shakes his head. "Poor Mouli, she's so predictable. Heart of gold, though, that one." I slide closer to my father and hug him tight. He might be cursed as I am, but at least his mind seems whole again. I was worried he'd never be the same. He pats my arm absently.

"How did you know to make me let go of the sword?" He asks, and I pull away to look up at him. His gray eyes are the sort that always look as though they're smiling, even when the rest of him isn't.

"It happens to me, too," I say. I recount everything to him, from the afternoon in the training hall with Cort and Bryse, to my days of sleep, to the experiments yesterday with Rian. I leave out Flit and the dreams. I don't want him to worry that I've lost my mind. By the time I've finished, he's leaning forward over the table, his clenched fists supporting his forehead. I let him sit for a moment in silence, as long as I can stand to be quiet. I have questions to ask him. I need to know.

"Da, what happened that day? To you? To Mum?" I watch his back rise and fall. He's going through it in his thoughts, I can tell. His body tenses, the muscles of his arms ripple. The front door opens and I turn. Rian stands on the threshold, his arms weighed down with books, and his scroll case stuffed to overflowing. His eyes are half-wild, but when they stop at me and he sees my father sitting beside me he smoothes his expression so it's nearly unreadable. When he crosses into the light, I notice that he looks even worse now than he did last night. The dark circles under his bloodshot eyes are prominent against his pale skin. His robes are disheveled and wrinkled, his hair limp and oily. I wonder if he's gotten any sleep at all. He certainly doesn't look it. His collar is pulled up high, but not quite high enough to cover the thin inky tendril that has curled up to his jawline. My father sits upright and turns to look at him. His expression darkens. Rian shrinks like a mouse caught under the cat's paw.

"Hall. Now." His chair slides back, and he disappears into the covered walkway that leads to the guild hall. As I follow him through to the corridor, my eyes fix on the streak of blood I'd left on his back earlier, which has since darkened to a rusty brown. Behind me I can hear Rian's nearly silent steps along with the swish of his robes. Then I hear something else, so quiet that it might just be a thought in my head.

"Is that your Da, out of bed? He's a little scary." Flit. I look to one side and then the other, but I don't see her. Rian doesn't notice. His attention is fixed on the smooth floorboards as he walks. He has the look of a judged man on the way to sentencing.

"Not now," I whisper as quietly as I can, unnerved by the fact that I can't see her, and that I can hear her all too well in my mind. This could get annoying, fast.

"He's not as tall as I thought he'd be, though. And he has nice hair. But he stinks worse than the stinky Mage." I shake my head. "Go away, Flit." I whisper, a little louder. I turn to Rian, but he is so deep in his thoughts

that he doesn't notice. Or if he does, he doesn't react.

We follow my father into the hall, where he crosses to the door that connects it to the training hall and slides it closed and locks it. He comes back around Rian and myself and closes and bars the main door as well. It's an odd thing to do. We never lock the hall doors. The thought of it makes me uneasy as I watch him.

Rian dumps the armload of books onto a chair by the hearth and shakes his arms out, then sinks into the chair beside it. He closes his eyes, preparing for the onslaught. Da is muttering to himself now, and I can't make out what he's saying. I have never seen him so agitated. He is usually one of the more patient members of the guild, the voice of reason. Not now, though. Now, he lets out an anguished growl and drives his fist into the stone wall with all his strength. I wince as I hear the crack of his knuckle bones on the unyielding stone, and rush I to stop him but he pushes past me and stalks to Rian.

"Da, stop!" I cry, but he's already half-lifted Rian out of his chair by the front of his collar.

"You," he snarls, "and your never ending secrets!" Rian's feet graze the floor as my father lifts him so they're eye to eye. The contrast between the two men is frightening. Rian has always been tall for his age, but his body is lean, almost too lean. Mouli is constantly trying to fatten him up, but he has always had the build of a sapling tree. When it comes to physical fighting, he avoids it at all costs. So when Da draws his fist back to threaten him, Rian screws his eyes shut and tries to press his face into his own shoulder to brace for the blow. His hands are occupied trying to free Da's choke hold.

"DA!" I run behind him and grab his hand, pulling it down to keep him from swinging. He doesn't relent.

"I never should have listened to you. I should have listened to my gut! You knew what you were sending her into, didn't you?" He violently shakes Rian, who struggles weakly, fighting to breathe.

"Didn't you, Gaethon?" *Gaethon*, I think. He doesn't even know who he's talking to.

"Da please, that's not Uncle, it's not! Look at him! It's Rian! He can't breathe!" I pull his free arm with all of my might, but it isn't enough. My father has years of training and heavy labor on me. He's just too strong.

"You knew what would happen. You knew she'd have to stay there, you knew because it's in your blood, too! You should have stopped her! Forced her to stay! Now she's lost!" He drops Rian into a heap on the floor and falls to his own knees, sobbing. "She's gone, gone..."

"Are you okay?" I rush to Rian who is on his hands and knees gasping for air. He nods and I throw my arms around him. "I'm so sorry," I whisper. My father's sobbing slowly subsides as Rian catches his breath. I feel his eyes on us as we look up at him. His eyes are filled with hatred as he watches us kneeling close together, holding each other.

"And I trusted you, Lisabella. You swore you'd never go back." He starts to sob. Beside me, Rian whispers something and casts an arm out, and I yelp in surprise as my father is suddenly flung away from us. He lands with a thud against the far wall and slides down it. Rian gets to his feet unsteadily and weaves his fingers in an intricate pattern. He murmurs some incantation and a soft pink glow hovers in the air over my father and then settles over him, fading until it disappears into his prone form. Da's eyes slowly close as he fades into a deep sleep.

"What was that?" I ask, clinging to Rian.

"Sleep spell," Rian murmurs.

"How long will it last?" My heart breaks when I realize the gravity of what's just happened. Rian drops to his knees and leans over until his head is resting in my lap. I stroke his hair back with shaking fingers as I stare blankly at my sleeping father.

"Until I wake him," Rian croaks. He coughs softly and rubs his throat.

"Are you okay?" I ask again, smoothing the fabric at his shoulder as he lays there. When turns away to cough, I notice that the inky tendril peeking up over his collar has thickened slightly.

"Oh, just fine," he forces a laugh and I realize that it was a ridiculous question. He was just nearly choked to death by a man who is like a second father to him. Of course he's not okay. I know how he feels. I wish I didn't, but I do.

"I'm so sorry," I whisper, squeezing his shoulder. "I didn't know. He seemed better. I thought he was better."

"It's not your fault," he mumbles, his eyes drifting closed. "Or his…" It's not long before his breathing slows and he drifts off to sleep. Careful not to disturb him, I stretch my legs out in front of me onto the hearth rug and lean my back against a chair. I'm certain that it's been a day or perhaps two since he's slept at all, and so I stay as still as I can to let him rest until my back aches and my legs are numb. My father sleeps, too, and with the warm air of the crackling hearth washing over me, I doze in and out as well. As I do, I go over in my mind the things my father said during his fit of madness. *You and your never-ending secrets! You knew she'd have to stay there! You should have stopped her!*

I turn the words around and over again and again in my mind, trying to see them from every angle. Uncle Gaethon knew it was dangerous for Mum to travel to Kythshire. Da says he knew because it was in Uncle's blood, too. But what is in their blood? Gaethon is my mother's brother. They share the same parents and the same lineage. I think back on it and realize that my mother has never talked much about our family line on her side, though I can name my father's tree for several generations. *I trusted you Lisabella. You swore you'd never go back.* It can only mean that my mother has been to Kythshire before. If his accusations were right, she knew she'd have to stay if she went back. I remember how reserved she was at our last guild meeting, and the note in her saddle bag. Still, I can't bring myself to believe that she would choose to leave us behind.

I twist my torso from one side to the other to stretch my back, careful not to wake Rian. His scroll case and books are piled on the chair I'm resting against and I reach up over my head to feel for something to occupy myself while he sleeps. My fingers find the scroll case and I pull it to rest on the floor beside me. I hesitate for a moment. I know that Rian has been researching the curse, and that his notes and Uncle's are tucked inside the case. It isn't forbidden for me to see these. I would only have to be careful not to study anything that might teach me to use magic. At least, I think that's the way it works. I slide the thick roll of parchment from the tube and smooth it out beside me. The first page is headed with the title of a book of curses, followed by a list of names and dates. The last name and most recent on the list is Viala Nullen, who Uncle assigned to teach Rian in his absence.

I leaf through several similar pages and find her name on every one of them. There are books of curses, books about Kythshire, books about the fae, and a tome of records listing the lineage of the families of Cerion. At first I'm suspicious to see her name appearing so frequently, but then I realize it can't be that unusual. Someone in her position has probably read most of the tomes in the vast library. I scan the sheets again and realize that my uncle's name and even Rian's are scattered here and there on them. With a sigh I slide them aside and come to the first page of Rian's notes. Much of them are written in the scholar's language and despite my uncle's relentless pestering, I never showed a talent for learning it. I fleetingly wish I had tried a little harder as the strange words swim on the page before me. He has written here and there in the commoner's tongue, which I have much less trouble discerning, but his notes are brief:

Border curse. Defensive? Breakable? Lost treasure. Act of goodwill. Must be prepared to cross. Pure intent?

I shuffle through the pages and a small note falls out. The handwriting on it is unfamiliar and has a grace to it that is easy on my eyes after pages of Rian's rough scratches. It reads:

Rian Eldinae
Sixteenth Circle Exam
20 Autumnsdawn
Report to studio "Grace" at dawn to begin your testing.
Exam will be both practical and written.
Attended by the High Council
Failure will retest in one year.

I sigh and look down at Rian, who continues to slumber with his head comfortably in my lap. I know he's been training for his Sixteenth Circle for two years now. He didn't tell me he was called in for his test. And now he's spending all of this time researching my problems. I stroke my thumb over the Mage Mark on his jaw. No wonder it's grown so quickly. He's pushing himself too far, too fast. The door handle rattles and someone on the other side knocks, startling me.

"I'll be!" Luca's muffled voice is barely audible beyond the thick wood. He knocks again.

"Do you have a key?" I call out, trying not to disturb Rian. He turns his head in Luca's direction, but I shush him and pat his arm and he goes back to snoring softly in my lap. On the other side of the door, keys jingle. The latch clicks and Luca pushes it open.

"What do you mean, locking the door, eh?" His eyes glide from Rian's slumbering form to my father slumped unconscious against the wall beside the hearth. "Well that's a puzzler," he murmurs. "What happened? Looks like a blow of sleep dust or some." I press my finger to my lips.

"Da wasn't himself, so Rian made him sleep. And Rian hasn't slept for days, so I think the spell wore him out." I whisper. Luca looks from one man to the other and shakes his head.

"Strange goings-on lately. Don't like it." he walks over to Da and nudges him gently on the shoulder. I brace myself, but Da doesn't even stir.

"Well, now." Luca paces around him, one hand on his hip, the other stroking his own beard thoughtfully as he assesses the situation. He's a wiry old bow-legged man who's as weatherworn as the fisher boats lashed along the cliff side, and just as hearty. That's why I'm not at all surprised when he stoops, pulls Da up by his arms, hoists him over his shoulder, and carries him to the door. "He'll be up to bed," he whispers. "I'd come back for the lad, but it'd probably wake him." I nod.

"He's fine here," I whisper. "Stay with Da, won't you?" Luca grunts his agreement and lumbers off into the corridor with my father hanging limply over his shoulder. I turn my attention back to the roll of notes. The rest of them have to do with his studies, and I feel strangely like I'm invading his privacy even looking at the first page, though I can't understand anything they say. I arrange the pages into the order I found them, roll them up, and tuck them back into the tube.

"Can I come back yet?" Flit's voice dances in my mind again. I close my eyes and let out a long, slow sigh.

"Are you sure you want to?" I whisper to nothing. "The stinky Mage is here." I hear a giggle and Flit appears, hovering right above Rian's brow.

"I'm sure. Do you want to play?" she asks, her fluttering wings lifting her to perch on my shoulder. "He's not so bad when he's asleep," she says. I shush her and consider her offer. I definitely have questions I need answers to.

"I do, but we'll have to be quiet. I don't want to wake him."

"Oh!" She hovers out again and digs into one of the pouches at her belt to produce a glittering white powder. Before I can stop her, she sprinkles it directly into his ear, which begins to glow with white sparkles. Rian nuzzles my leg and dozes on.

"What was that?" I ask.

"Muffle powder. My turn!" She does an excited little flip in midair.

"I didn't mean to start yet—oh, alright." I roll my eyes.

"Are you going to the ball?" she asks, coming to perch on my shoulder again.

"How did you?—"

"Ah, ah, ah!"

"I think I am, yes." I say. I wonder if she heard about it somewhere in her travels today, or if she spied the invitation that I left in the kitchen. I decide not to waste a question on it; how she found out isn't really important to me. Instead, I take some time to think about my first question. I have so much to ask, and I know her game now. Tiny master of misdirection. She crunches in my ear as I try to concentrate, and I turn to see her munching on another sugar cube. That reminds me of Margy's pitcher, and the diamond hidden inside. I decide to start there.

"A few days ago, I had a dream about a beautiful place. I was there for a long time, so long that I became part of a tree. Then a fairy visited me and a star fell from the sky into my hand. When I woke up, I was still holding it. It's the diamond in your pitcher in my room. How did that happen?"

"Whoa, you've been practicing. Good question. This will be fun! The fairy that you met was a Greeter. She has powerful magic that can be used to cross objects over the edge of our world into yours. So, she gave it to you in your dream so you would have it with you." She pushes her bangs out of her face with sugar-coated fingers, causing them to stick up erratically. "I heard shouting before. What was your father going on about?"

"He was confused. He thought Rian was my Uncle Gaethon and he was angry about what happened to my mother." The words he shouted swim in my thoughts but I shake my head to clear them. I'll ask about that later. "I don't understand why she gave me the diamond. What is it for?"

"She gave it to you so I could get here." She does a twirl, sending her ribbons out in a spinning blur, and then flies to the wall where my father had been lying earlier. She looks at the empty space for a moment and then drifts upward to land lightly on the edge of the hearth mantel. She walks along it, weaving through the collection of awards, statues, and trophies on display. "Why was your father confused?" she asks, taking particular interest in a bronze figure of a man just a little taller than she. She links her hand through the crook of his arm and bats her eyes up at him. I chuckle at her flirting and then shake my head.

"I don't know. Since he came back from the quest, he's been different. Something happened to him in Kythshire. I was hoping you could tell me why, actually." Tears sting my eyes. I try to blink them away but it's too late. "I don't know if he'll ever be the same again." I've been holding my emotions back for too long and now that they've forced themselves out, I can't stop it. I shake with a torrent of sobs, but I try to keep them as quiet as I can so Rian can sleep. Flit comes to land on my shoulder.

"You aren't supposed to cry! It's a game, it's meant to be fun." She pats my cheek with her sticky hand, and I try to calm myself, but it's too difficult. So much has been weighing on me. I need this release. "It's your turn to ask a question. You wanted to know about the diamond, right?" I nod. "Well, I'll give you a good answer if you promise to stop crying. I don't like it. It makes me sad, too."

"Okay," I sniff and wipe my eyes, and make a good effort to settle down.

"There." She pats my damp face again and then wrinkles her nose and wipes her hand on her skirt. "In my world, we all have different jobs, just like you do here. Only ours don't involve killing people or animals, or brutally beating anyone, or stealing magic and using it for selfish reasons, or taking things that don't belong to us, or starting wars, or making fires, or chopping trees, or humiliating each other, or enslaving each other, or hoarding treasure, or making ourselves feel powerful while others around us suffer. You know, like you all do," she says matter-of-factly. I open my mouth to protest, but she goes on before I can. "My job is called Traveler. That means that I get to go places that other fairies don't. But I can't just go on my own, I need help. That's what the tether is for. Tethers are made by Creators. They can be made of anything.

"One time, my friend Sorwa had a tether made from a leaf! And then a caterpillar ate the leaf and you know what happens to a leaf after a caterpillar eats it, right? It comes out the other end and poor Sorwa tracked to her tether and she was covered in such a mess!" Flit doubles over with laughter. "Oh!" she gasps after a long bout of hysterics that is so infectious that I find myself laughing despite my lingering tears. She smears a tear of her own with her saccharine fingers and goes on. "Anyway, since then we try to make sure that our tethers aren't edible. And also it helps to make them valuable so that if someone finds them, they take good care of them."

"You call it a tether. What does that mean, exactly?" I shift a little. Rian's head is getting heavy in my lap and my leg is full of pins and needles. I wriggle my toes to get the blood flowing.

"Uh uh, my turn." She taps her lips and looks up at the ceiling thoughtfully. "Have you ever done magic before?" she asks.

"Once, when I was very young," I say. "I got a scolding for it, and I haven't done any since. I don't really want to, anyway. Now, my question."

"A tether is an object that helps me focus, so that I can flit to it. I just close my eyes and wish, and then, pop! There I am! I can only do it once while the sun is up and once while the moon is up, though." I look at her to see if she's joking with me. It seems impossible that she could travel that way, but she gazes up at me with earnest. She's completely serious.

"Amazing," I whisper.

"And before you ask, no, you can't have a tether, and no I won't take you with me. And no I won't wish things for you. So don't even try." She smirks and shakes her head, and then chews her bottom lip thoughtfully. "Will you wear my diamond to the ball?" She asks.

"If you want me to," I say. "Why are you answering so easily today when the last time we played you were so infuriatingly vague?" I ask. Flit giggles.

"Because this time, it's important for you to know. If anyone was to steal the diamond and I didn't know it, I could accidentally reveal myself to someone dangerous. So you have to guard it, okay? Don't leave it rolling around under the bed like before." I nod in agreement. She looks down at Rian, whose ear is no longer glowing and glittering. "He can hear us now," she whispers right up to my ear. "Is he really as nice as you say?" I nod and smile.

"He really is," I whisper. "Do you think you can try to be friends?"

"Maybe if he says sorry, and he really means it. But I'm still not telling him anything." She floats down close to him and then flits back to my face. "He's awake!" she squeaks. Then in a twinkle of light, she's gone.

Chapter Ten

RIAN'S RESEARCH

Rian blinks the sleep from his eyes and looks at me with a lazy smile.

"Hey," he says, his hazel eyes glinting with the glow of orange embers from the hearth. I feel my heartbeat quicken. What is wrong with me lately, I wonder? My emotions are all over the place. I clear my throat self-consciously.

"Hey," I reply, "feel better?"

"Mmm." He pushes himself up and scoots so his back is against the chair beside me. I follow his eyes to the spot where my father had been lying.

"Did Benen wake up?" he asks.

"No," I say. "Luca carried him to bed."

"Ah." He reaches up and scratches through his hair. "I'm sorry I had to do that."

"I know…it's okay. It's for his protection, too." I tip my head to the side and rest it on his shoulder. "Why didn't you tell me you were testing in two days?"

"I only just found out."

"But Rian, you're supposed to have months to prepare for your trial!" My head bobs up, then down with the movement of his shrugging shoulder.

"Mistress Viala feels that I'm ready, she talked the masters into it. She wants me tried and entered into the Sixteenth Circle before the ball," he says. "She wants me to do an exhibition there."

I pull away and look at him. I'm not sure that I've heard him right. The idea of exhibiting one's magical skill at a princess's birthday party is unheard of. He meets my eyes and reaches up to gently stroke my cheek.

"It's nothing," he says, but there is a hint of fear in his eye as he turns his gaze away.

"Why does she want you showing off?" I ask. "Don't you find it a little strange?"

"She's trying to convince His Majesty to drop some sanctions on magic."

"Which sanctions?" I ask. The thought of changing any of the laws that govern magic makes me very uneasy, and I can't help but find Viala's timing especially suspicious.

"Mostly the ones which prohibit magic from being taught to the royal family. Those laws have been in place for generations, ever since the last dynasty fell. They were sanctioned to keep any reigning sovereign from gaining too much power."

"You need to write to Uncle and tell him" I say. "He needs to know. This isn't right."

"He has more important things on his mind."

"What are you going to do? Are you actually going to go through with it?" I picture him standing in the center of a ballroom filled with royal subjects, showing off, and I push myself angrily to my feet. It goes against everything we've ever been taught. Magic requires a certain reverence. It isn't meant to be flaunted around like some jester's folly.

"I haven't gotten that far." He sighs. "I'm going to focus on passing my trial first. I was hoping we'd be on the road with your father before the ball, but it's obvious now that that isn't going to happen. And after what I found out last night, I need an excuse to get into the palace."

"What do you mean?" I ask as he scoops up his books and his scroll case and spreads them out on the table. We slide onto the bench together and he pulls out the book lists with the signatures and fans them out.

"These are all of the books that were missing the pages that possibly described your affliction." I'm not surprised when he points to Mistress Viala's signature on each of them. "She signed them out, and look where she took them." He points to the section under the heading of 'location'.

"The palace," I whisper.

"Someone there is very interested in researching curses. Especially ones that cause a serious aversion to weaponry of any kind." He taps the page. "So interested, in fact, that whoever it is wanted to keep those pages so that no one else could find out about it."

He slides the lists away and opens a children's book of fairy tales. He shows me the space where a page has been torn out.

"This story is about a group of travelers who were seeking the way into the land of fae. They had heard the tales of riches beyond measure and magic powerful enough to let them live forever and defeat any foe. See here?" He points at a grotesque illustration of a man writhing on the ground and a group of tiny fairies hovering above him, laughing. "He crossed into the land with ill intent, and when he came out, he was afflicted with madness. The next page is torn out." His eyes meet mine and immediately I think of my father.

"But Da was helping to return the lost treasure," I say. "He didn't have ill intent. Why would it affect him this way?"

Rian shakes his head.

"I don't know," he says. "That's why I want to get into the palace. To find the torn out pages, and maybe figure out who in the palace is so interested. Then we'll have answers and maybe even figure out a way to reverse this."

"But you can't compromise your integrity that way, Rian! You've worked too hard to turn it all into some cheap entertainment act!"

"Some things are more important," he says. "As an apprentice, I can't refuse my Mistress, even if she is a substitute. And I need to get into the palace."

"I'm going, too," I say, and he starts to protest, but I interrupt. "I got an invitation this morning."

"Really?" His eyebrows arch up and mischief plays in his eyes. "Are you going to wear a gown?"

"Much to Mouli's delight," I say. His grin is so adorably pleased that I can't help but laugh as my cheeks go red. "What?" I ask.

"Nothing." He starts to roll the pages up again. "Oh! I almost forgot what I really wanted to show you!" He grabs my hand and pulls me up, through the door to the training square. He takes me by the shoulders and guides me to the center of the square. Then he positions my hands so that I look as though I'm holding an invisible sword. "There, hold them just like that," he says. "Now, do you trust me?"

"Of course," I keep my hands still as he steps back from me, his concentration steadily fixed on my hands. He makes a sweeping gesture with his arms and then moves his fingers apart as though he's writing something in the air. He speaks the strange incantation and I feel something cool and solid materialize in my hands. I tighten my fingers and gasp in wonder at the graceful sword in my grip, formed of ice.

A rush of excitement courses through me as I slice through the air with it. I spin and step and slash in an intricate combination, laughing and crying at the same time. The sword is more perfectly balanced than any I have ever tried. It's weighted so precisely that it seems like an extension of my own arms. Most importantly, holding it doesn't make me pass out or lose my breakfast.

"Rian!" I laugh. "It's unreal!" I spin again and run across to a training dummy. When I slash at the thick canvas, it hisses and steams as a chunk is sliced clean away. I turn to him and grin, and he smiles back. That's when I see it. The Mage Mark has crept up further on the left side, its inky black line already thick and prominent against his pale skin. My grip loosens and the sword vanishes as it's released. I cross to him and trace the black line with my finger. His eyes meet mine and I scowl.

"It's Sixteenth Circle," he says. "After my test I can cast it without worrying about this." His hand covers my fingers, and he turns his head and kisses my fingertips softly.

"But you shouldn't…" I start, but a warm tingle spreads from the gesture all the way to my toes. He moves closer to me and slides my hand to the back of his neck, then moves his own hands down to circle my waist. My breath catches as he leans closer to me. My eyes close slowly. His lips are warm and soft when he presses them to mine. Everything around us falls away, and for one moment there is nothing else in the world except for Rian and me.

"So romantic, now you can kill people!" Flit's voice jars me and I jump back and spin around. Rian drops his hands to his side, looking dejected.

"Was it that bad?" he asks. I shake my head.

"No, it was amazing. Flit!" I can hear her giggling, but she doesn't show herself.

"What?" he looks around, too, but there is no one else in the square.

"The fairy. Her name is Flit. She just said something rude in my ear."

"Ah, Flit, that's right." Rian nods. "I remember." I reach for his hand and hold it. We've held hands countless times before, but this time, after that kiss, it feels very different. Wonderful.

"That reminds me," I say, looking down. I can't seem to meet his eyes. "I have a lot to fill you in on."

"Not really," he grins. "Last night after you said you were going to tell me everything, I figured it'd be okay to eavesdrop. So I listened through the wall. And just now in the hall, well, I wasn't really sleeping and…" He taps the ear that had been sprinkled with muffler and then taps his other one. "I have two ears, don't I?"

"So rude!" Flit pops into view between us and spins to face Rian. "Listening to a private conversation!"

"What about interrupting a first kiss?" Rian rolls his eyes and shakes his head. "I'd been working up to that for months, little fairy."

"Serves you right," says Flit. "Why not steal your kisses? Your kind steals everything else, don't they?"

"Stop it, you two," I groan. I try to set aside the fact that Rian has just admitted he's had feelings for me for months. Instead, I turn to him with my best attempt at a stern expression, though I'm fairly sure it fails since I can't stop smiling. "Rian, can you please apologize to Flit for the Revealer?"

"Sorry," Rian says as he draws me closer, his eyes fixed on mine. He's going to kiss me again, I know it.

"You call that an apology?" Flit humphs. "It doesn't count if someone else asks you to do it. And it doesn't count if you don't even look at the person you're apologizing to. No sincerity at all. So typical."

"How do you make her go away?" His cheek touches mine as he murmurs into my ear. I'm torn between hoping for that second kiss and wanting to defend poor Flit.

"I heard that! You just forget it!" Flit stomps her foot down in midair and she's gone in a blink, just as before. Rian looks around.

"That worked," he says.

"You're awful," I shake my head, and my wish is granted as I'm quieted with another kiss, this one even softer and longer than the first.

When we finally separate, I'm eye-level with the Mage Mark that curves along his jaw. "Why does it happen, exactly?" I run my finger along the black line. Despite its dark connotations, it is beautiful the way it curves and swirls gracefully.

"There's no distracting you, is there?" He smirks. "It's caused mainly by overreaching your skill. If you try to perform magic that's too powerful or too high above your Circle, the Mark grows. If you spend too long in certain levels of Rumination, also." His lips brush my forehead as I lean against him, listening to his heartbeat.

"I have it," I say quietly. "It's just a small circle, here." I tap my breastbone just over my heart. "But I didn't perform any magic."

"I know, it's in the notes Master Gaethon left me." He sighs. "Just another mystery that's eluding me. Mouli says you didn't have it when you were put to bed, but it was there when you woke up." I nod, and he continues. "I have been meaning to ask you about your dreams, but with everything that's been going on there hasn't been time. You didn't tell Master Gaethon about that dream you were asking Flit about, did you? That wasn't in his notes."

"No," I say, thinking back to that afternoon right before my father was brought home. "It felt wrong to tell him. I felt like he wasn't supposed to know." We go back to the guild hall, where Rian clears a space on the table and pulls out a fresh sheet of parchment and a quill as I sit beside him.

"Tell me about the dream," he says, his quill poised over the page. "Try to remember as much detail as you can." I remember the first dream, when I lay among the golden wheat, listening to the peaceful sound of the breeze and birdsongs. I try to think of how to describe it, but no words seem adequate. The more I think about it, the more unsettled I feel. It's too personal, too private even to share with Rian. It feels wrong, as though describing it would somehow desecrate the memory of it.

"I don't know," I say. "Maybe we should do this later. You need some sleep, and then you need to study. And eat. When was the last time you ate?"

"Azi, this is important." He shakes his head.

"So is your health, Rian. How can you even think straight when you're starving and exhausted?"

"Ugh, you sound just like Mouli." He leans over the page and rubs his forehead. "Listen, just give me this, and I promise I'll eat and sleep and all of that."

"Promise?" I ask. He nods and dips his quill.

"If I can get one solid answer in all of this mess," he gestures to the pile of books and scattered notes, "then maybe I can shut my mind up long enough to get some sleep. And I think I've almost figured this one out, so, please." He scrawls the words "Azi's Dream" across the top of the page. I take a deep breath and close my eyes and think. I can almost smell the wheat. The sky is impossibly blue...I don't want to ruin it. This place belongs to me. I try to speak several times, but words fail me. I glance at Rian. He's getting annoyed.

"How about this?" He sets the quill down and pushes the paper away. When he speaks, his voice is so quiet that I need to lean much closer in order to hear him. "When I enter Rumination, the first stage is black and terrifying. The screaming drowns everything else out. It sounds like a thousand souls being tortured. I can barely think. I feel like I'm becoming one of them."

"Rian, don't..." my voice trails off as he holds his hand up to stop me. What he's telling me about is the Mage's secret of trained meditation. Rumination is a special art that they practice to open their minds and increase the flow of magic. He could be severely disciplined if Uncle or Viala or anyone else caught wind of him describing it to me in such detail.

"When I'm able to push through it, everything goes white and quiet. It's the most beautiful, peaceful feeling after all that noise and pain. That's the second stage. It lasts for a long time, Azi. Some people spend days there and never reach the next stage. You start to go mad from the stillness of it if you stay too long." He watches me. I still don't understand why he's sharing this.

"In the third stage, if you're ever patient and quiet enough to reach it, the sky is vast and blue, so blue that it dazzles you. The ground is a field of golden wheat that stretches as far as the eye can see."

My heart starts to race. How did he find out? I didn't tell anyone about my dreams. Even when I was talking to Flit I didn't mention the field or the sky. He's joking with me, he's got to be. He must have used some Mage's trick to peek into my mind. I shake my head slightly, dismissing the thought. I'm starting to sound like Flit.

"Stop it," I say. "I don't know how you knew that, Rian, but just— don't. It's not funny." He tips his head toward me, his expression something between puzzled and intrigued.

"I'm not joking, Azi. It's written, and I've seen it myself. Do you remember last week when you asked about the Mark, and I told you I went too far and Master Gaethon tore me out?"

I think back to that morning. Was it just last week? It seems like ages ago. I nod slowly.

"Was it in your dream? Is that what you saw?"

I hesitate, but I nod again.

"Ha!" He claps his hands once and I jump. "I thought so! That explains your Mark!" He pulls the blank page close and starts writing frantically. "Somehow in your sleep you managed to enter the Third Stage. It's unheard of! In your sleep! Some mages spend their whole lives trying to reach it and you just doze off and there you are." He chuckles and shakes his head. "Amazing."

I have a hard time sharing his enthusiasm. The wheat field is mine, my private, beautiful, peaceful place. Knowing that others have been there or have tried so hard to reach it and it's not mine alone makes it feel sullied in my mind. I'm reminded of the dark cloud on the mountain and the smudge of rain in the distance. I fold my hands in my lap and sit silently, listening to the quill scratch on the page. When it finally slows and stops, I look up at Rian. He's so pleased with himself. One mystery solved. He doesn't realize that it's made me feel violated somehow.

"All done?" I ask, forcing a smile. He nods and stretches. "Now will you go to bed?"

"A quick nap," he says. "Wake me for dinner, okay?" He brushes my cheek with his fingertips and I feel it warm with his touch. I close my eyes and he kisses me again, shorter than I'd like. He smiles at me and then stands and stretches before he slips out of the room. After he's gone, I pick up the page of fresh notes. Reading them over makes me feel nauseated. They are so impersonal, so precise and analytical. I fold the paper and without thinking I cross to the hearth and drop it in. I watch the page brown and curl against the coals until the flames lick it into black char, and then die away. Somehow, I feel much better.

Chapter Eleven

PREPARATIONS

My father's spell-induced sleep disturbs me when I go to check on him. This sort of spell is one I'm vaguely familiar with, but it's usually reserved for criminals and madmen. No one needs to sit with him. He'll sleep until the spell is lifted. I try to settle myself in there with him, sitting near the open window.

As I sit, I think back on my last game with Flit and what she told me about my mother. When I go over the conversation in my mind, I realize how vague her answers were, and how she manipulated the game carefully and distracted me whenever I asked anything about my mother. I suddenly wonder whether anything she told me was actually true. The dreams I've had certainly tie into all of it to make it more believable, but legend has always said that fairies have strong magic. I imagine that if they wanted to, they could make me believe anything.

Should I have trusted her so easily? Should I write the guild and tell them what I know? What would I say? That a fairy told me Mum is safe, and they shouldn't bother looking for her anymore? They'd think I'd lost my mind. Fairies are mythical creatures who haven't been seen for over a century. Nobody believes they're real anymore. The notion makes me realize that we haven't had a note from Elliot yet today, and so I leave my father and go to look for one.

It doesn't take long. When I pass my room on the way to check the guild hall again, a rustling sound catches my attention, not surprisingly coming from the pitcher on the window ledge. I cross to it and bend to look inside, where I find a lovely blue and black songbird nestled in the scraps.

"Well, I was just going looking for you," I say to the bird. It blinks up at me, and then it hops out onto the ledge and lifts its skinny leg, where a tiny scroll is tied. I free the scroll as gently as I can with shaking fingers and unroll it to read:

On course. Will arrive at border three days.

"Thank you, thank you," I whisper. Now I can send my own reply.

"Wait here," I say quietly as I scoop the fluffy creature back into Flit's house.

"Hey! Get your feathers out of my—oh, it's you." Flit presses herself against the wall of her house to edge past the bird and then stands at the lip of the pitcher with her arms crossed, scowling at the opposite wall.

"A bit of a tight space for a house guest," I say suspiciously. Elliot's birds are highly trained and very intelligent. They know to go directly to one of us at the guild hall. If we want to send him a reply, they always find him. Elliot is a wood elf, and wood elves are highly tuned with nature. They claim to talk to trees and animals the same as they do to humans. Flit pointedly turns her head away from me.

"Oh Flit, are you giving me the silent treatment?" She pulls her arms tighter across her chest and raises her elbows up and down sternly. She's certainly angry with me, but I ignore it for now as I pen my reply to Elliot, carefully squeezing everything I can think of onto the tiny square of parchment.

Da still unwell, sleeping. Don't expect us. Have word that Mum is safe across the border. Unsure if true. I pause and try to think of anything else they need to know, *Rian's trial tomorrow.* I consider waking Rian to make sure the message is okay, but I decide it's important for them to know either way, and he really does need his sleep.

"Thank you, little bird," I whisper as I tuck the note in place, "please bring this to Elliot." She stands and shakes her feathers and darts off into the sky to the west.

"Wow, you even used your manners. I'm so impressed," Flit says dryly from inside of the pitcher.

"I'm sorry about before," I offer. "I didn't defend you very well against Rian, and I should have. I was caught up in the moment." Flit gradually comes into view. She ponders me while I try to look as sincere as possible.

"That's alright," she says finally. "Kissing is pretty amazing, even if it is with the stinky Mage. I almost felt bad interrupting. But he was doing High Magic. Above his skill. Did you know that it's forbidden? He should know that, being an Apprentice. It seems like every time I see him his coils are higher and higher. If he doesn't watch out, he'll be swallowed up in blue-black. He'll be just like a giant, walking bruise. Then he'll be just as ugly as he is stinky! Although I do think blue is pretty. And black has its moments. Just not together. And not on skin." She shivers and dives into the pitcher and rummages around, then comes back out sulking. "I'm all out of sugar cubes."

"If I get you some more, will you play the question game?" I ask.

"Oh! Can you show me where they are? Then I can get my own whenever I like!" She squeals and claps her hands when I nod. I show her the jar in the kitchen where the sugar is kept, and she takes several and stuffs them impossibly into a pouch at her belt. I gaze out the window as she does. The afternoon is bright and clear, and the air is so temperate I can barely feel it on my skin. A gentle breeze carries the perfume of the fresh flowers on the windowsill. I stand on tiptoes and breathe in the sweet scent.

"There you go, loving dead things again," Flit murmurs in my ear. "Creepy!"

"But it's not, they're not dead. They're lovely. Don't fairies like flowers? I thought you made dresses from them and wore them in your hair."

"Well, we do. But we collect the petals after they've fallen. Or we grow them right in our hair. We don't chop their stems off or ruthlessly tear them apart just so they can look pretty as they slowly die on our windowsill." She flies up to the beautiful pink and white bunches and strokes them gently, "Poor little dears. It'll be over soon." With her back to me, I roll my eyes. There are some things we'll never see eye to eye on. Many things, probably.

"Can we play now?" I'm eager for answers, but I'm not very hopeful. Flit's behavior is especially ornery today. She settles in a sunbeam on the windowsill and nods.

"Yes. My turn. How did you get that bird to take messages for you? I'll bet your tortured it, or brainwashed it, or did something just as horrible." She looks up at the flowers and sighs and looks away. I blink at her in disbelief, and I wonder if all fairies have such a horrible opinion of our people.

"My guild mate, Elliot, is a wood elf. I don't know how he does it. But I do know he'd never hurt an animal."

"Oh! A wood elf? They're okay. I like them. Your turn."

"Do you remember the dream I told you about, where the diamond was given to me?" I start.

"Yes. My turn!" Flit giggles, and I groan and remind myself to be more careful with my wording. "Why did the stinky Mage make you an ice sword?"

"Um," I think back to Rian's spell, and how the canvas of the training dummy frosted and steamed as I sliced at it. I suppose it was an ice sword. I want to tell her the real answer, but I'm afraid it'll disrupt my current line of questions. But then I weigh the two. I want to find out if I entered the third level of Rumination in my dream, like Rian suggested, but if Flit knows anything about the curse and how to break it, then I need to know right away. "I can't wield any weapons right now. So he created that one so I could fight again." I center my thoughts. If I play this correctly, I can get both of my questions answered in one game. "Rian believes that I entered the third stage of Rumination by having that dream, and that's how I got Marked. How is that possible when I've never been trained in meditation?"

"Oh! That's a good one, Azi! There are many ways to visit what you call the third level, or what I call home. It very rarely happens, but sometimes you can be pulled there by a group of special fairies named callers. The callers pull you in, usually while you're dreaming, so others can talk to you and show you things. They're kind of snobbish, those callers. You really have to convince them to get them to do anything for you. They're rather annoying. But anyway, the stinky Mage was right. Traveling there will make you get the coils. That's what we call the Mark, coils. He's clever, I'll give him that!" She wrinkles her nose a little, "Why's it so important for you to be able to kill people with a sword, anyway?"

"Not to kill people…" I sigh. How do I explain this to her in terms she'll understand? My world is so much different than hers seems to be. "I've been learning to swordfight since I was a girl. I took it up because my mother and father are both Knights. It's part of my birthright, it's in my blood. I'm not bloodthirsty, Flit. It's just… it's different here. There are people out there who are ruthless, exactly the way you seem imagine all of our people to be. I took up my sword to defend others against those people. There are those who are too weak to fight, or too innocent to want to. I fight for them. To protect them. Everyone here in our guild does. We don't fight for money or personal gain. We try hard not to be selfish or punishing."

For some reason, it's really important for me to make her understand. We're good people. She pushes off from the windowsill and comes up to my eye level. Slowly she moves toward me and presses her hand to my forehead. I feel a soft tingling there and then she laughs and moves away so we're eye to eye.

"I didn't think you were lying. I hoped you weren't. Sure, I've been around the kingdom these few days and I've heard whisperings about you, you know. Everyone talks about 'Azi the great new promising Squire,' or 'that Azaeli girl who's so sweet and inspiring,' or 'one day I want to grow up to be just like her' or "mummy, please buy me a sword so I can learn to fight like her' or 'can't you make my hair golden like hers,' or 'their family is such an inspiration,' or 'Cerion is a safer place with them in it,' it gets a little sickening, actually. Seems I can't flit from one street to another without hearing your name on someone's tongue. Hammerfel, this. Azi, that." She looks at me, and her expression is very different from the scowling fae that glowered up from the pitcher earlier. She seems enamored, now. "Your turn for a question!"

"I..." Her description of my fame throughout the kingdom jars me. She's exaggerating. If it's true, I've certainly never noticed it. I press my fingertips to my hot cheeks as she gazes at me, blinking expectantly. She's on the verge of giggling, I can tell. I wonder if it's a diversion, to push me off my line of questioning. If it is, it worked. I try hard to redirect my thoughts, to remember what I was going to ask. "You said that the callers bring people from their dreams into your world, and your world is the same as the third level. How does that work? Does my spirit go to your world?"

"Your consciousness does. So it would seem like you're sleeping to anyone watching. But inside," she taps her head, "you're not there. You're in Kythshire. Why can't you wield a sword?"

"I've been cursed," I say, "Whenever I try, I black out. You said I go to Kythshire? Where my mother is? Can I go there again? Can I talk to her?"

"Whoa, it doesn't take long for the game to fall apart with you, does it? Which question do you want me to answer? You have to pick one." She floats down to rest on the edge of the windowsill again. Her wings catch the sunlight and send it sparkling in rainbows across the kitchen.

"Can I go to Kythshire again and talk to my mother?" I ask, hoping it's okay to put two questions in one. Flit gives me a look. She shakes her head and smiles.

"Typical. If you were to go again, you could talk to her if you could find her. But visiting that way, you'd probably need a guide. It's not easy. It'd be much easier if you were really there. Kythshire is bigger than you think. And a lot more complicated." She twirls her purple ponytail around her finger, "What exactly happens when you pick up a sword?"

"I hear screaming, and the room starts spinning, and then I black out, or I get sick." My heart races just from the memory of it. "Could you guide me?"

"Not my job, you'd need a guide for that. They're haughty, too. Very full of themselves. Think they know everything about everything. Then what happens?"

"What happens?"

"After you black out? What happens?"

"I let go of the sword..."

"Well, did you ever keep holding onto it?" Her tone chides me and I suddenly feel embarrassed. Not once in all of those swords and clubs and maces that Rian handed me did I think to keep holding on.

"I never did. Why? What would happen if I held on?"

"Azi!" The front door bumps open and without a thought I turn to shield Flit from Mouli's view. When I glance behind me, she has already disappeared. "Oh, you're here, I'm so glad. Look, I've got your dress and it's just as I imagined it!" She closes the shutters and beckons me into the sitting room.

"I brought the tailor to measure you. It'll need hemming and letting out in the arms." The tailor files into the house followed by two assistants carrying a shimmering, deep blue gown with gold slashing at the sleeves and in the skirt pleating. It's more extravagant than anything

I've ever worn before, and as Mouli helps me out of my plain dress and into the rich, heavy gown, I find myself wishing that chain mail could be acceptable attire for a princess's birthday ball.

"We'll let it out there," the tailor murmurs as she and her assistants circle around me. "Not so many ladies have muscles like yours, my dear." They pinch the fabric here and there and take measurements and notes while I fight to keep from scratching the itchy lace at my neckline. I try to stay still as one of the assistants measures my bicep and the other kneels at my hem to pin it up.

"Plenty of extra fabric here," she chuckles. I find it odd to have my body so scrutinized, but I try to hide my discomfort for Mouli's sake. The door opens again, and I look over my shoulder to see Rian silhouetted against the waning sunlight.

"Whoa," he mouths when he sees me standing there in my gown.

"Out!" Mouli yelps, rushing past me to bat him out of the door, "out, out out!"

I'm a little annoyed with her for sending him away. There are more important things right now than this dress, or the ball. I wanted to tell him about Elliot's note, and my latest game with Flit. I wanted him to be there when I tried to keep holding the sword as long as I could. Suddenly I find myself angry with Mouli for interrupting my game with Flit. I shift and fidget in the dress as the three confer with her about all of the work that needs to be done, and the short time they have in which to do it. They quote her an extravagant price that I know we have the means to pay, but I could never imagine spending so much on an article of clothing I'll only wear once. Mouli glances at me with concern and I know she can tell what I'm thinking. Before I can protest, she agrees and signs the order.

"Yes, yes, that's fine. Just fine. I'll pick it up tomorrow afternoon." The assistants carefully disrobe me of the gown and help me back into my familiar soft, plain dress. I scratch at my collarbones and give them all a half-hearted thank-you as they file out of the door.

"I'd better be getting supper started!" Mouli pauses and hugs me and then rushes out before I can issue a word of protest about the assault of the dress. Hoping that Rian went back to his room, I take the stairs two at a time and tap as I slide open the hatch. He has left his side open, and his room is empty. I groan and run back downstairs and into the guild hall. His books and notes are cleared from the table. I'm sure he's gone to the Academy again. I'll have to wait until he comes back. Sighing, I cross to the training square and choose a small dagger, which I pick up carefully by the sheath. I take a deep breath and start to close my fingers around the handle.

"You're going to try it in here?" Flit's voice echoes in my mind.

"Why not here?" I murmur.

"Well, if it makes you black out, wouldn't it be better to do it someplace more comfortable?" She's right. I decide to go back upstairs to my bed where I brace myself, take another deep breath, and close my fingers around the hilt. The deafening screams thunder in my ears and I resist the urge to clap my hands over them. I keep my resolve and squeeze my eyes shut as the blackness floods my vision and the room starts to spin around me. My stomach churns, and I'm grateful that I skipped lunch as I swallow the bile that rises in my throat. I remember Rian's description of the stages of Rumination as the darkness and screaming slowly fade, and I find myself bathed in an endless white light.

Here, I'm floating inside of a gentle white cloud, and my awareness of my body slips away from me. I'm no longer in my room, lying on my bed. I'm here in this beautiful, peaceful place. My curiosity is piqued. I know the next stage will bring me to the field, to Kythshire. To my mother. Distantly, I feel my heart racing in my chest. I start slipping back into the black, spinning. I fight it, gripping the hilt more tightly and clearing my thoughts until the white claims me again.

I float in endless white and eventually I forget why I've come, what I'm looking for, who I was. All that matters is that I'm here in this wonderful place that I never want to leave. The sun is warm on my face and the wheat is fragrant around me as I emerge in the field, and soon the trees of the forest tower ahead. My feet find the soft carpet of moss at their base, and I grin. I have never left the field before, and yet here I am at the precipice. I turn to look behind me across the golden field, and in the distance the now familiar dark mountain stretches across the horizon, dwarfed beneath the black storm cloud. Gold and jewels of every color glint amid a strike of lightning.

I am not interested in stolen treasure, though, and the sounds of revelry within the cover of the trees is so enticing to me that I turn my back on the storm and the gold and instead step into the shelter of the trees. As I walk I find that I'm getting smaller, or the trees are getting taller, until I'm as small as a fairy.

In between the tree trunks ahead I glimpse flashes of color: red and yellow, blue and orange, purple and green streaks and glints and wavering lights. The spectacular show draws me closer and closer until I'm standing at the edge of a glittering meadow lined with pristine white mushrooms. Figures streak and dart past me, laughing and singing and dancing. Someone grabs my hand on the way past, and I am pulled into the whirling frolic.

My laughter blends with the beat of the drums, and my feet seem to know the steps without my bidding. I dance in circles as they play song after song. All around me are bright wings and colorful costumes and glittering light. The voices singing are the sweetest I've ever heard, even sweeter than Mya's. They meld with flutes and strings and birdsong so perfectly that it's impossible for me to discern one sound from another. My heart is light and free, and nothing matters to me except that I keep dancing and laughing and circling and spinning.

For hours, the forest streaks past me in splashes of green and gray and brown, until a glint of silver catches my eye. I try to focus on it as it blurs past, and catch a glimpse of yellow and blue. Golden hair tugs familiarly at my heart. I try to focus as we come around again, and see a boot as large as I am, tapping in time to the music. Around again, and I look up. Blue and yellow livery. Chain mailed sleeves. Things from a long time ago, important things. I try to remember, but my thoughts mingle with the music and are carried off into the tree tops, and then everything goes black.

"Azi." I know this voice. It belongs to someone I love. It comes again, deep and full of concern, and something important is torn from my grip. My ears throb and my head pounds. Suddenly I'm aware of the bed beneath me, and my hands which lay limp and empty at my sides. I squeeze my eyes shut, and my hand feels foreign as I slide it around, desperately seeking the dagger. I need to get back. I saw something, something important. Something I was searching for. I don't remember what. "Looking for this?" Rian's voice booms in my ears. I wince in pain and force my eyes open just enough to see him towering over me, the sheathed dagger in his hand.

"Give it," I croak as I reach out, but he holds it away.

"What's going on, Azi?" His accusing tone sends a burning anger welling in my chest. Who does he think he is, pulling me out? How could he, when he knows how painful it is?

"What are you doing in here?" I'm as surprised by the fury in my voice as Rian seems to be as his brow raises high. Still, I can't control it. He has no right to pull me away from my field, my forest, and my dancing fairies. Then I remember…my mother. She was there. I grab my pillow and hurl it at him, "I don't have to tell you anything! Leave me alone!" Rian ducks away from the pillow and blinks at me in disbelief. It hits the far wall next to the window and falls to the shelf beside Flit's house. Outside, the silvery light of the moon cascades onto the distant rooftops. I close my eyes and press my palms into them to keep my head from splitting open.

"You're back!" Flit's voice grates on my ears. "And you're throwing stuff at the stinky Mage! I'll help!" I hear something whiz toward Rian and I peek between my fingers just in time to see my hairbrush stop in mid-air in front of him at his gesture and fall to the floor with a clatter.

"Great, just what I need," Rian groans. The mattress dips down as he sits beside me and slips his arms around me. My instinct is to shove him away, but I stop myself. Rian hasn't done anything but wake me up. There's nothing wrong with that, I tell myself. My anger is raw and irrational and I know it.

"Aw, you're not going to let him kiss you again, are you?" Flit makes a noise that sounds like choking. I take a deep breath and continue to try to calm myself, staring at my hands in my lap. The bandages must have fallen off while I slept, and the slices across my palms have healed to soft pink scars now.

"How long was I…?" I let myself trail off. My throat is too dry and sore, my thoughts too confused.

"All night and all day. I knocked in the morning but you didn't answer, so I went to study. When I came back later in the afternoon, you were still asleep so I figured I wouldn't wake you. I had to study again anyway. I don't know why I bothered…" his voice trails off and he looks down at a note in his hand. I flex my own fingers, staring at the scars in my palms. A day and a half wouldn't have been long enough heal them up so well.

"So," Rian interrupts my thoughts, "I think I've figured out why you were in bed with a dagger, but how about proving me right?" He reaches for a cup of water on my side table and hands it to me.

"It's a secret. Our secret, right, Azi?" Flit comes to light on my knee, a safe enough distance from Rian. I sip, considering her words. I do feel just as protective about this dream as I had the others, but it seems as if Rian's already figured it out anyway.

"Rian's clever," I say to Flit. "And trustworthy. I've told you already he's my best friend. I think it's okay to tell him. But I think he has something he wants to say to you, first." I look pointedly at Rian who blows out a puff of air and looks up at the ceiling.

"Fine," he says and leans down so he's eye level with the little fairy. "Flit, I am very sorry that I cast the Revealer on you. If I had known it would upset you so much, I never would have done it."

"Really?" Flit eyes him. Rian nods. "Okay! We're no longer enemies!" She dives at him and throws her arms around his neck.

"Get it off," he mouths silently, and I laugh despite my aching head.

"Not friends, though?" I ask. Flit wrinkles her nose at me.

"No, not yet. Maybe soon." She darts to her house and comes back with a sugar cube, then sits beside me on a wrinkle in my blanket. When she's settled, I turn to Rian and explain to him about the dagger, the Rumination, and the dream.

"I think Mum was there," I sigh. "I was about to get a good look when you pulled me out."

"No wonder you were angry," he says. "I'm sorry. I was worried. I had no way of knowing."

"And yet you poked your nose in anyway," Flit mumbles around a mouthful. "Typical." An awkward silence fills the room. I feel as if I should scold Flit, or defend Rian, but I find myself agreeing with her. If he hadn't pulled me out, I might have actually been able to talk to my mother. The silence stretches to an uncomfortable length, until Rian finally clears his throat.

"Azi, did you send word of my test to my father?" I try to think back through the haze of dancing and colors and flashing armor, and vaguely remember the songbird flying off with my note. I press my hand to my throbbing forehead and nod.

"I told them your test was tomorrow."

"Today. It's past midnight now. I couldn't sleep, so I thought I'd try to eat something and practice a little before the trial. Not that it matters. This came for me while you were sleeping." He shakes his head and hands me the note he's been holding. Two words are scrawled on it in Uncle Gaethon's handwriting, written in the scholar's language. One of them is familiar enough. I've seen written across my own work in the same hand plenty of times. *Fail it.*

Chapter Twelve

THE TRIAL

"Fail it," I whisper. I look up at Rian, who suddenly seems to have found the ceiling very interesting. His jaw is clenched tight. He swallows, and I know he's fighting tears. I read the words again. "But, why would Uncle order you to fail?" My voice catches, and I clear my throat, "Rian, you're not really going to, are you? You've worked so hard for so long. You've never missed a mark in any of your trials."

"I don't know why he'd tell me to fail, but of course I'm going to. I have to. As his apprentice, I can't ignore a direct order from him. I need to trust him. He has to have a good reason." His shoulders rise and fall in a half-hearted shrug, "I can retest next year. It's not a big deal."

"Couldn't you bow out instead? Delay it? Say you need time to come up with the fee? I've heard of other students who declared they weren't ready and their trial was set back."

"That won't work. They know we have the money. Anyway, it's too late," he says, "Viala posted it public today. So I get to fail before an audience."

"There's got to be some way—" I start, but he holds up one hand to stop me.

"Azi, this is bigger than my turning a Circle. Something is going on that I'm just beginning to understand. If Master Gaethon wants me to fail, then I don't care who's watching. It isn't just about me anymore."

"What do you mean?" I ask. Rian's arms slide from my shoulders. He goes to my window and closes the shutters, and then he crosses to my door and closes that, too. He gestures his hand across both openings and murmurs a spell. All at once I feel secure, as if we've been wrapped in a cocoon of quiet, and I know that anyone who might be outside listening in on us would never be able to hear our voices. He comes back to sit beside me and his eyes rest on Flit.

"Ooo, stinky Mage's secret time." She licks her fingers and smacks her lips and grins up at him with a sticky smile.

"Flit, maybe you should..." I start, but Rian stops me again.

"It's okay. I think she knows more than she lets on." He watches her lean back and wipe her sugary hands onto my coverlet while she blinks up at him innocently. "I found another log in the library yesterday," he starts and turns to me. "Do you remember two years ago when Prince Eron chose to journey on his 16th birthday?"

I think back. It's common for the royal children to take an expedition on that milestone. It's meant to symbolize their maturity and desire to learn of distant cultures and strengthen alliances.

"He went to Ceras'lain," I say, nodding. At the time, I remember that Rian and I thought it was an odd choice. Ceras'lain is our next door neighbor in terms of countries. He could have chosen to travel across the green channel to Cresten to explore the deserts of Elespen, or visited the Stepstone Isles which are filled with colorful birds and hospitable people with dark skin and bright smiles. He could have gone north to Haigh and trekked the snowy mountains and glorious caverns where Bryse's culture of stony-skinned goliaths boasts of impossible strength and an immeasurable bounty of raw metals. He could even have chosen to go as far away as one of the Three Sunteri, the great island continents where the people have sleek black hair and exotic slit eyes, and are known for their skills in meditation and subterfuge and extravagant magic. Still, he chose Ceras'lain, land of the elves.

"Ceras'lain, where he spent several weeks exploring the countryside," Rian nods. "Then he came home, and that was when the books began to find their way to the palace, courtesy of Mistress Viala." Rian glances at Flit, "Based on the records, it seems he suddenly became very interested in curses and fairies after that trip."

"Oh!" Flit giggles and claps, "You *are* clever!" We watch her dart back to her house and rattle around inside for a moment. She comes out carrying the diamond, which she drops in my lap. "Hold on to this today, will you? I'll be back later!" I close my hand over it.

"Wait, Flit, I wanted to ask you—" Rian starts, but in the blink of an eye, she's gone. Rian groans, "She's really irritating, you know."

"I know," I say. "But her occasional usefulness makes up for it."

He quirks a brow at me and our stomachs grumble in unison. "What do you think happened? Why did Eron suddenly become so interested in fairies?" The creatures are considered the ravings of madmen. It's unseemly for a prince to be so interested. Sometimes, even with Flit right beside me crunching her sugar cube in my ear, I worry that I'm losing my mind. Rian glances at the window and the door before he ventures a reply.

"Think about it. Before his journey, Eron never missed an opportunity to show off with his sword. Remember at the games the year he turned fourteen? How he insisted on showing off in front of the crowd before the squires began their trials? Everyone was so awed by his skill." I remember that day well. His fighting had even impressed my parents, who have always been overly critical of anyone's technique, especially those still in training. He fought like a seasoned swordsman. It inspired me to work harder.

"I remember." I massage my temples and Rian hands me the cup of water again.

"Drink, you'll feel better." He goes on. "After his journey, do you remember ever seeing him fight again? And there are reports in the conclave of a dark mood that overcame him for several months after his return."

"Rian...are you saying you think Eron is cursed, too?" I think back over the past two years and realize that it all matches up.

"If he is, he's spending a good deal of time searching for a way to break it, and covering his tracks while he does." He frowns, "I think he's behind Viala's prodding to change the laws. If he can't fight by sword, he wants to learn magic." I nearly drop my cup.

"Rian, you can't say things like that. That's...it's treason to even think it. Everyone knows it's forbidden for royalty to study the arcane. Nobody would stand for it." King Tirnon is the fourth king in the Plethore Dynasty, which has come to be known as the Age of Peace. His ancestor, King Asio made the declaration over a century ago at the start of his rule, that no king or member of the Royal family would be permitted to practice or study magic. This came after a terrible time in our history, ending with the Reign of Diovicus, who was said to be a Mage of the Forty-Fifth Circle. His cruelty and oppression melded terribly with his thirst for power and immortality.

Since then, the palace keeps Mages at arm's length. Their skills are allowed and appreciated, but never depended upon or flaunted. In Cerion, we're only just now beginning to feel completely recovered from those dark times. There are some cultures who still find it hard to trust us in the wake of our dark history. "We all know the risks that come with our rulers having too much power. His Majesty would never allow it."

"His Majesty wouldn't. But we know who his heir is, don't we?" His stomach growls again, and I notice the soft lavender light of pre-dawn through the slits of the shutters.

"Eron." I shiver. Even if the king stands his ground and refuses to change the laws, it's only a matter of time before his son takes the throne and does it anyway. "You have to eat and go," I say reluctantly. It seems as though a full conversation is a luxury that won't be ours any time soon. "You can't be late. Or maybe you can…if you're going to fail it anyway." Rian pushes himself to his feet and stretches his arms up over his head.

"Will you come and watch?" he asks. "If I'm going to fail, I might as well do it with a flair."

"I wouldn't miss it," I come up on my tiptoes and kiss him. In this moment, everything falls away and it's as though nothing in the world exists but Rian and me. I wish we could stay this way forever, locked together, his lips soft and warm on mine. Eventually and reluctantly we pull away from each other and each of us sighs in unison, which gets us laughing. I wonder if it will always be so sweet between us. I hope it is.

***

Mouli insists on accompanying me to the Academy to watch the trials. We make a colorful show together as we make our way through the winding streets to the southernmost corner of the city, she in her yellow dress and I in my blue and gold surcoat. Mouli chatters hopefully about Rian as we walk. She's as proud as a mother hen of his accomplishments, and completely unaware of his plans to fail. From time to time, we're stopped by a passerby or an acquaintance, and they get to chatting for so long that I have to remind her we'll be late to watch the trial if we don't hurry.

My hand frequently slides into my pocket to find Flit's diamond.

I'm so paranoid I'll lose it that I've tucked it into a pouch and tied that pouch to a hidden loop sewn into the lining of my tunic. Occasionally, someone calls my name from their window or doorstep and I wave, and more than once a child runs up to give me a ribbon or a flower or some small trinket. When we finally arrive at the Academy, I'm blushing profusely. I'm also crestfallen.

A massive crowd has gathered near the entrance to the public audience hall. I can't recall ever seeing such a gathering to watch an exam. Poor Rian. As we near, I realize that people are being turned away. A harassed-looking yeoman is standing on a platform near the door and gesturing emphatically.

"No more room, no room. Clear out!" he shouts. My heart sinks at the thought of breaking my promise to Rian.

"I never saw the likes of it," Mouli says, and a dejected looking passerby stops.

"Should have expected it," he says. "Considering. The youngest to try for Sixteenth in more than forty years, he is. Of course everyone would want to see it."

"Protégé of Gaethon himself," says another, "You know that though." He nods at my livery, "Azi, right?" I offer the man a half-hearted smile and a nod. Of course everyone would turn up to see Rian's trials. It's just as they said. He's the youngest from Cerion to reach this Circle in decades, and rumors have been flying for years that Master Gaethon is molding him to take his seat one day. The thought of it makes his order to fail that much more of a puzzle to me. My eyes scan the crowd of disappointed would-be onlookers. Are they all here just to see him? My Rian? There's a tap on my shoulder and I turn to see a page in purple livery. He bobs his head.

"Squire Azaeli Hammerfel?" he asks. I nod. I recognize this page and I know he recognizes me, too, but of course we have to observe the formalities. "Your presence is requested by Her Highness Princess Sarabel and His Highness Prince Eron. Your chaperone is welcome as well." I nod again, stunned. Though the palace keeps the Academy at arm's length, it isn't unheard of for its members to attend an exam from time to time. Naturally, a trial of such high profile would pique their interest. *Especially Prince Eron*, I think to myself, knowing what I know now. I try hard to keep my expression neutral as Mouli and I follow the page through the parting crowd and up into the narrow corridor that leads to the viewing area. It's difficult, considering. All I can think of is my dear Rian having to throw away his chance to shine, and not just in front of an audience, but in front of royalty, too.

The royal viewing area is dimly lit and cozy. It resembles a theater box about one story up from the floor of the exam ring. It's set into a recess in the wall, and as Mouli and I enter, I can sense the same spell Rian used in my room earlier has been cast between us and the floor below. We'll be able to hear what goes on in the ring, but we won't be able to distract him with our comments.

The ring itself is small, about the same size as our training square at home. It's set in a circular stone room with a domed ceiling about seven stories up. A section of the dome has been opened so the early morning sun casts a single beam of light across the floor. Rian sits cross-legged in the center of the beam, his head bowed. I swallow nervously and tear my attention away from him to the princess who is waving me over. I offer the assembly of royal siblings a respectful bow before taking the offered seat beside Sarabel. Princess Amei and Prince Eron are seated on her other side. The prince leans away from his new bride, his rapt attention on a conversation with the stunning woman seated beside him.

Her sleek black hair falls like a curtain as she tilts her head to talk to him. Her dark almond eyes flick to me and away quickly. She's dressed in long, wine-red robes with the high styled collar commonly worn by a master. An intricate black design weaves across the fabric of the robes, meant to echo the lines of Mage Mark. I recognize her almost immediately as Mistress Viala, and my hands curl into fists in my lap. It's her fault Rian is being put through this.

"Thank you for the invitation, Your Highness," I tear my attention from the two and whisper to Sarabel, who giggles and bats my arm playfully.

"No need to be so formal, Azi. Can you believe the turnout?" She flicks her eyes to the ceiling where I can hear the thumping and creaking of dozens of feet. "The common seating is standing room only, Viala says." I try to keep my expression neutral as I look down at Rian. He seems so small and alone, kneeling there in his wedge of sunlight. "He's awfully handsome, isn't he?" Sarabel says, making me shift uncomfortably. "I never realized how good looking he is."

"Poor Sara," Amei says with a singsong accent from beside Sarabel, "Anyone looks good after Prince Beaky." She pinches her nose and pulls her fingers outward, miming a bird's beak.

"Or Prince Eyebrows," Sarabel furrows her brow dramatically, and the conversation dissolves into the two of them lightheartedly teasing about the line of suitors who've recently come calling for Sara. They go on as I watch Rian sit in perfect serenity, and I wonder if it's possible that I'm more nervous for him than he is for himself.

"Ah, it begins," says Viala as Rian rises to his feet. "He will demonstrate his spell range in order, from First Circle to Fifteenth," she explains to the rest of us. Our box goes silent as we watch.

The knees of his robes are coated in dust and badly rumpled. He sweeps his hands down and away from his shoulders in a smooth movement and all at once the dust is gone and the wrinkles fall away until his appearance is impeccable. He moves his hands again, and the air around him seems to shimmer slightly and then settle.

"First Circle. Novice spells. A little something to tidy himself, and a shield spell." I find myself annoyed by Viala's droll tone as she describes his efforts. I can tell she's eager to get through the review of simpler spells and into the more impressive ones. I try to block out her voice as I watch Rian use his magic to arrange a wall of glass vases behind him. One of them falls to the ground and shatters, and with a flick of his fingers it repairs itself and sets itself back into place. The ring goes pitch black and I'm momentarily alarmed until Viala explains that he's just performed a Sixth Circle darkness spell. Then, a burst of colors and blinding light flashes through the ring and I'm forced to squint and look away.

"Seventh Circle. Dazzle."

I blink rapidly and peer down to see Rian floating several feet above the ground. He rises higher and higher until he's eye level with me, and he points at me and gives me an exaggerated wink. I wave hesitantly and Sarabel grasps my arm and squeals with excitement. He bows to her and then to the Prince before he disappears from view and continues to rise to the next level. Above us we can hear the muffled sound of cheering as the common crowd goes wild, stomping their feet and clapping.

"That was a Thirteenth Circle levitate. He's skipped several. He'll be marked off for that, he's meant to go in order." There's an edge to Viala's voice as she raises her chin to indicate the box across the ring. For the first time, I notice the group of Masters seated there. They'll be grading Rian, and he hasn't missed them. He lowers himself to the ground and then trots over to face them and repeats the spell again until he's at their level. He offers a midair bow and a flourish before lowering again.

His feet touch the ground and there are suddenly two of him, then three, then four, then a dozen. All of the Rians walk away from each other in opposite directions, and I have trouble recognizing the real one until he bends to pick up a stone from a stack across the ring from his carefully arranged wall of vases. He tosses the stone up once and catches it, and then he turns to wink at his audience. I shake my head. He isn't supposed to make such a spectacle of it. He throws the stone with great force and I wince as it goes hurling toward a row of vases, waiting for the crash. It doesn't come. Instead, the stone hits what seems to be an invisible wall and falls with a thud.

"Fourteenth Circle Mirror Illusion," Viala says through clenched teeth. "Fourth Circle Ward."

"What is he doing?" Eron murmurs. Viala remains silent, and I imagine that she's shaking her head, but I don't risk looking away from Rian's exhibit to see for certain.

Rian's mirror images begin to fade as he walks over to retrieve the stone. He raps on the barricade shielding the wall of vases and shrugs. He waves his hand across a section of the wall and it shimmers and fades, much like my bedroom wall those nights ago. He steps through it, and there is an audible gasp from Viala. In the Masters' box, several of the Mages have risen to their feet. Two of them are arguing with each other, two others are frantically scrawling notes on their parchment.

"Sixteenth Circle, Cross Borders."

At Viala's narration, I understand the sudden uproar in the Masters' box. It's utterly brazen of him to perform a Sixteenth Circle spell when he's only Fifteenth, especially in this setting. Mouli reaches for my hand and grips it, and my own knuckles are white as I continue to watch. Rian steps back through the wall again and the vases solidify. Then he bends and picks up the stone and murmurs a spell over it. He takes a few steps away and tosses the stone casually over his shoulder. It hits the vases and bursts into a violent explosion, sending a spray of glass shards littering the floor. A collective scream echoes from the royal box and the gallery above, which then erupts into cheers. He is certainly failing spectacularly, just as promised.

"Fifteenth Circle, Explosive Stone," Viala huffs as Rian performs a series of intricate gestures. His lips are moving silently and his brow is knit in deep concentration. The shards of glass collect together in a swirling mass in front of him. "Oh, what is he doing now?" Viala ducks her head and covers her eyes. "I can't watch. He's ruining everything."

"Careful," I catch Eron's warning just as the tinkling of glass ceases. We all gasp as the glass glows deep orange as though molten, and shapes itself into the form of a man. It's a perfect replica of Rian except in glass, like a sculpture made of ice.

"Seventeenth Circle," Viala's voice quivers. "Golem-Self. Excuse me." She rises to leave, but Eron gestures for her to sit.

"Leave it. I want to see how far he'll go." I see him lean forward from the corner of my vision, obscuring Viala who has slunk back into her chair with her arms tightly crossed over her chest.

In the center of the ring, Rian commands the golem to follow him. He walks a lap around, and the golem obediently trails behind. Rian gestures at the floor at the golem's feet, and a group of vines break through the boards and climb upward, entangling it.

"Fifteenth Circle, Command Plant," Viala croaks. We watch as the vines carry the golem as high as the ceiling, and Rian thrusts his hands upward. Through the opening of the dome, a thunderous crack of lightning pulses. It crashes into the vines, instantly charring them, and the golem shatters again into thousands of shards of glass that rain down like ice.

"Nineteenth…Lightning Strike." I watch the glinting shards as they fall, and I'm worried that Rian will be cut, but they slide away from him as though he's protected by an invisible bubble. He sweeps his hands together and the shards of glass swirl and link together into their previous form, a wall of glass vases. The gallery above erupts into applause.

"What was that one that reformed the vases?" Eron asks. The rest of us turn to Viala. She shakes her head. She has no answer for him. I feel a nudge in my pocket and I clap my hand over it protectively.

"What did I miss?" Flit's voice echoes in my mind. I shake my head slightly. The crowd above us is still roaring and the sudden racket makes my ears ring as the masters in their box drop the sound barriers. One of the two who had been arguing steps forward and rests his hands on the ledge. He looks quite weary as he peers down at Rian.

"After much deliberation, it is decided that Apprentice Rian Eldinae is condemned to silence for a period of two weeks week as a punitive measure for his indiscretion in this ring." The common crowd jeers rudely. The master raises one hand and waits patiently for them to calm down. "After which," he pauses again, waiting. "After which, it will be recognized that he has risen to the Sixteenth Circle and therefore appointed the title of Mentor."

"He didn't fail it?" Flit's tone is disappointed. *"Why I am not surprised?"*

"No," I whisper. "But he won't be able to perform at the ball tomorrow, either." Suddenly, my uncle's command makes a little more sense to me. He must have known about the plan to exhibit magic at the palace. Part of me hopes that he also knew how Rian would show off in his effort to fail. Perhaps he foresaw that it would turn out this way.

"Oh, that's right," says Sarabel sadly. "I was so looking forward to seeing what he would do. Perhaps they'll make an exception, just for tomorrow."

"Don't be ridiculous, Sara," Eron sounds as though he could spit venom. "The Academy doesn't make exceptions for anyone. Especially not us." Viala rests a hand on his arm but he pulls away petulantly and signals to the royal guard. "Let's go." He files out first, and I rise as he passes. Sarabel offers me a hug in his wake.

"Tell Rian he's still welcome, even if he isn't able to perform, okay? And tell him we said congratulations, it was really very impressive." Over her shoulder, Amei gives me an awkward smile. Eron calls for them to hurry and they rush out together. Viala remains in her seat, glowering down into the ring that Rian has already vacated. Mouli tugs on my arm and we leave together after an awkwardly rushed farewell to the brooding mistress.

"Oh, if his parents could've seen that," Mouli frets in my ear. "Your uncle is going to have ten fits, I know it. It oughtn't have happened." She wrings my arm nervously. "What was that boy thinking, honestly! Always showing off." She clicks her tongue.

"I thought it was amazing," I say. "Despite the trouble he got himself into. I had no idea what he was capable of." I mean it. Even though he never should have attempted half of those spells, and certainly not in front of an audience, I'm so proud of him.

Chapter Thirteen

THE ROYAL BALL

"My turn!" Flit perches on the window seat beside me, where I sit watching the street below. The afternoon hours have crept by, and as the sun dips low to touch the castle spires, I grow increasingly worried about how long it's taking Rian to get home.

"Did you like the dancing?" she asks. Her question conjures a blur of colors and sweet music as fairies dance across my memory. I smile.

"It was wonderful," I reply. It's strange, I usually don't really care for dancing, but there in the forest it felt so natural and free. I'm reminded of the ball tomorrow, where I will probably have to dance in the formal way, and my stomach twists into knots. I push the anxiety away and recall the forest again. "Was my mother really there?"

"Uh huh!" Flit nods. "What spells did the stinky Mage perform at his test?"

"I wish you wouldn't call him that," I scowl. Someone rounds the corner in the street below, but it's just a passing neighbor. He waves up at me and I wave back. Flit wiggles her feet. "Shouldn't you hide?" I ask. "He could have seen you."

"My question first." She tips her head to the side. I sigh and think back to the trial. There were so many spells, I'm sure I miss one or two of them, but I list them off to the best of my memory. Her wings move slowly back and forth as she listens, casting a glittering spray of rainbows across the rough wood of the window molding and the walls beyond. The effect mixed with the peachy glow of sunset is breathtaking. When I'm finished with my answer, she gives me hers.

"People can't see me unless they believe in me. So, a stranger walking by who has no reason to think about fairies has no chance at all." She pulls a sugar cube out of her tiny belt pouch and starts to crunch on it. "Did the prince say anything interesting while he was watching Rian?" I chew my lip thoughtfully.

"Mistress Viala said something about Rian ruining everything, and Eron warned her to be careful. It seemed like he was reminding her not to say too much in front of me." I think for a while about my next question, careful not to allow her line of questions to distract me. "Why is it that my father and I were both affected by the curse?"

"Hmm." Flit's eyes fade from pink to lavender and then green as they slide to the side thoughtfully. Her lips purse together and scrunch to the opposite side, making her look rather silly. "Your Da crossed into Kythshire with ill intent. Anyone who does that gets touched, and all of their descendants do, too."

"Touched?" I ask, but she wiggles her pointer finger to chastise me. Her turn.

"Do you have something else sweet? I'm getting bored of sugar cubes." She stuffs the half-eaten cube back into her pouch, and I imagine it must be getting rather sticky in there.

"I'm sure we do. We have fruit. What does it mean, touched?" I ask.

"Well, most see it as a curse, because they're not so bright, are they? I mean, you pick something up and it hurts you and frightens you, so you put it down and worry about it. Some folks are really stubborn and they just keep picking it up and dropping it and trying until their minds get all befuddled and confused and even cruel. And it makes the worst of them come out, and they get even more greedy and even more hungry and they don't know that it just pushes them farther and farther from what they wanted in the first place. But others are clever, and they figure it out. And if they make the right choices, then we can be friends. But only if friendship is all they really want, and they don't want to get anything else out of it. But nobody ever really wants that. No one from here, anyway."

I stare at her in disbelief. It's a lot to take in. Before I can wrap my mind around it, she asks her question.

"When you get to the field, you never choose the riches. How come?"

"They're not important to me. Why did you say my father entered with ill intent?"

"He wasn't invited but he crossed anyway with your mum. When the guardian asked him to leave, he tried to fight." She looks down into the street, where Rian has just rounded the corner. "Why aren't riches important? Everyone wants riches."

"My family and my duties are most important to me. I don't need riches, I have everything I want." My thoughts are already on my next question. I think about my father, and the pieces of conversation we've had, sane and insane, since his return. I think back to my mother's sad goodbye, and his rant in the guild hall when he thought Rian was Gaethon. *It's in our blood*, he said. "Flit," I think long and hard before I ask. "My mother was able to cross over, and she knew when she left here that she may not come back. My father blamed my uncle for this, he said he knew it would happen, and he didn't try to stop it. Why are my mother and our family so important to Kythshire?"

She pushes off from the window seat to float up to my eye level, and her eyes fade all the way to white as they gaze into mine. They change from yellow to blue and lavender as she tilts her head from side to side considering me. "Oh," she sighs with disappointment after a long time pondering, "I can't tell you yet. You win this time! It was such a good round, too. I think I'll go try and find some of that fruit." Before I can protest, she's gone, leaving me to stare in confusion and disappointment at the empty space she leaves behind. I would have been much happier with an answer rather than a win.

A blur of blue in the street below catches my attention, and I look down to see Rian waving me down. I hop from the sill, and in the time it takes me to get to my front door, a small crowd has gathered around him. He grins and nods cordially as people flood around him to shake his hand, clap him on the back, and congratulate him. Some of them are girls our age, and I lean against the door frame, watching as they bat their eyes at him and flirt. Rian's sheepish grin clearly shows his embarrassment, but the girls, who aren't at all familiar with him, seem encouraged by it. They fall over each other giggling and fawning at him. "Help me," he mouths in my direction as more girls flock around him, bombarding him with questions that he has no hope of answering in his silence.

"Rian, you're needed in the hall," I call after I enjoy watching him squirm for a little while. Maybe next time he won't be so flashy with his magic. He nods to me and extricates himself from the enamored crowd. When he reaches the stoop, he takes me in his arms and kisses me deeply and unabashedly right there. The collective groan of disappointment from the crowd of girls sends me chuckling as he pulls me inside of house and shuts the door behind us. "I think they got the message." I say, watching through the window as the group of rejected girls disappears around the corner.

He leans heavily against the door and lets out a long sigh of relief, closing his eyes. When he opens them, they hold that familiar glint of mischief. He offers me a low bow with the same flourish he gave the masters in their booth at the end of his trial. I roll my eyes and shake my head.

"Only you could fail at failing so impressively," I say. "What took you so long getting home?"

Rian gestures at the door with one thumb, indicating the crowd that has now dispersed.

"Really?" I scoff. "You were so mobbed that it took you all afternoon to walk across the city?"

He shrugs and huffs impatiently. We both know that I'll scold him if he tries to talk after he's been ordered to silence, but it's still frustrating trying to have a conversation.

"I was worried that you were being punished, or at least getting an earful," I sigh.

He nods. That's when I notice that the Mark has crawled up past his jaw and around his ear, and disappeared into his hairline. I reach up and trace it with my fingertips.

"Oh Rian, you went too far."

He bobs his head from side to side and rolls his eyes as he nods. I imagine what he'd be saying if he could, his tone thick with annoyance. *I know, I know.*

Mouli is just finishing setting out the flatware as we reach the hall together, and she looks up with a grin from the feast she's spread out.

"Well done, well done!" She rushes to Rian, hugging him, "and congratulations!" She lets go of him and then smacks him hard on the arm. "And that's for overreaching! Oh, if Gaethon had seen you! He'd have had you stripped and you know it!" Rian winces away from her, looking injured. "Well, sit down and eat. I know it's a little extravagant,

126

but I couldn't help myself. Oh, and this came for you earlier." She sets a tiny roll of paper on the table between us as we sit side by side. Rian unrolls it and I read Elliot's note over his shoulder.

"Will reach border 2 days from now. Have reason to agree with Azi. Stay put. Behave." I snort indelicately. "Behave. If he only knew." I say. Rian's head bobs once as he offers me the platter of roast before serving himself. Mouli makes sure that we have piled our plates amply and then takes off her apron.

"Well now, that's done. I'll be off," she says.

"Aren't you having supper?" I ask her.

"Oh, I ate already, Dear. Too much to do. I'll be back to clean up after." I nod and take a bite of meat, which is so tender I barely have to chew it. As soon as Mouli leaves, Rian turns to me and takes my face gently in his hands. He gazes into my eyes and I fall into his, watching the soft glow of the fire reflect in flecks of green and gold. This time when he kisses me, it's just for the two of us. It's warm and deep and perfect, and time seems to slow while we melt into each other. When we part, he smiles softly at me and strokes my cheek. He doesn't need to say anything at all.

We dine hand in hand, and I tell him about everything from the comments in the booth to the questions and answers in Flit's game. It's an odd one-sided conversation, but he manages to take his own part without a word. He's mostly interested in Eron's interactions with Viala, and pushes me to remember more and more details as our plates are slowly emptied.

After we're both completely stuffed, we clear everything to the kitchen where we find Flit splayed in a half-empty bowl of berries. Her hands rest on her bulging belly which pokes out between her corset and the belt of her skirt, and her lips are stained purple with juice. She smiles lazily up at us as we come in bearing our trays.

"Found the berries!" she says, patting her stomach.

"Looks like you ate twice your weight in them, too," I say. She giggles and then looks over at Rian, who is stacking the dirty plates at the basin. He pauses and frowns and turns to Flit. She grins widely and tilts her head to the side. He takes a step toward her, looking alarmed, and then his eyes flick to me. "What's going on?" I say. He points at Flit, and then taps his own lips, and then his temple. She's talking to him in his mind, like she does with me sometimes. I can't help but feel a little jealous. "What did you say?" I ask Flit.

"I said his coils are reaching." She strokes a finger from her own chin up around her ear, leaving a trail of purple juice in the green section of her hair. "He's got to do something about it." Rian gestures one palm up and shrugs. "You know, something pure. Something kindhearted. Make them go away." I think about my own Mark on my chest, and realize that it has indeed faded some since it appeared. I can't really think of anything I've done that has been outstandingly kindhearted, though, since then. Flit scoots out of the bowl of berries and lands lightly on the counter. She walks across and puts her hands on her hips to survey the platter holding the remains of our roast. Her nose wrinkles up and she screws her eyes shut and shakes her head. "Disgusting." Before I can object, she's gone.

We go back into the hall, where Rian settles at a desk and starts writing. His quill moves frantically across the paper while I drowse in a chair near the fire. Eventually, Mouli comes and drags me away. I let her fuss over me for another dress fitting, listening to her go on and on about how much there is left to do before the ball tomorrow afternoon. When I finally fall into bed that night, I drift easily into a deep, dreamless sleep.

I'm woken midmorning by Mouli, who ushers me off to the bath. I relinquish myself to her scrubbing and trimming and buffing and fussing through the morning hours and into the early afternoon, when I'm finally allowed a bite to eat in between primping and dressing. I convince her to let me take it in the guild hall, hoping to catch Rian, but unfortunately I find it empty. He's left me with a long letter in his place, the cover of which explicitly declares it's for my eyes only. I unfold it and read while I chew a bite of apple.

"Azi, we have to be careful tonight. I think I know where to look, but it should probably be only one of us, and you're the least likely to look suspicious wandering around outside of the ballroom. Margary might be able to show you where he keeps his books. I think that would be the most likely place to find the missing pages and more information to help break the curse. I've found more that confirms our suspicions, but I won't say it here. It'd be a good idea for you to pack for a trip, just in case. I'm going to the Academy, I'll be back in time to get ready for the ball. XO, R"

I read it twice more, and then drop it into the fire just as Mouli comes to get me, and the whirlwind starts up again. She spends what feels like hours wrapping locks of my hair around a hot iron and I spend just as long blowing the bouncing golden curls off my tickled face while she works. It takes her and two tailor's apprentices another hour to get me into my dress and looking perfect. By the time I'm ready to leave, the sun has sunk low in the sky, and I'm completely exhausted.

"How do women do this every day?" I groan, trying hard not to scratch at the pins in my hair as I slip my feet into the satin shoes offered to me by one of the girls. The heels make my ankles wobble, and they click noisily on the worn wood floor as I take a few hesitant steps to the mirror. I don't recognize the young woman looking back at me through the glass with Mouli beaming over her shoulder. The neckline of blue satin trimmed with gold lace is just low enough to show my pale shoulders and collarbone, but high enough that it covers the remnants of the faded Mage Mark over my heart.

The full skirt cascades to the floor and shimmers beautifully in the low light of my bedroom. When I turn, the wide slits between the pleats show flashes of the glittering gold underskirt. The sleeves puff out at the shoulders in the latest style, and then hug my arms until the light silk drips down to the floor. When I move my arms, the fabric trails along behind them like a dancer's scarf. Looking at myself this way feels odd, like I'm a stranger in my own skin.

"Oh, if your mother could see you," Mouli bawls, and when I go to hug her, she brushes me away. "No, no, I'm a mess, I'll get you all smudged and rumpled."

"Mouli…" I hug her tightly anyway. "Thank you." There's a knock at the door and Mouli claps her hands excitedly.

"That'll be Rian!"

"Why's he knocking?" I frown. "He knows he can just come in."

"Oh, don't be ridiculous!" Mouli shakes her head in exasperation and rushes down the stairs to greet him. While she's down there, I steal into my father's room and sit on the edge of the bed.

"It feels wrong, Da," I whisper as I adjust the corset that digs into my ribs, "to go flitting off to the palace dressed like this, leaving you here, while everyone else is out there somewhere." I sigh. "But I really hope that I'll find some answers for us. If I find a way to break the curse, then we can go together and bring her home. I promise Rian and I will figure this out. In the meantime..." I let myself trail off. It's so difficult looking at him lying here so still and silent. I know he's not aware of me, but it makes me feel better to say the things out loud that have been weighing on me all day. My curls brush his face as I press my lips to his cheek. "I love you."

"Azi, dear!" Mouli calls from downstairs.

"I'll be right there!" I rush back to my room, suddenly remembering Flit's diamond. She never really said whether she wanted me to bring it, but I'm sure she'll want to be able to find me at the palace tonight. As I search the little trinket box where I had stowed it after the trial, I realize I haven't packed a thing like Rian instructed me to. There simply wasn't time. I start to panic as the stress of the upcoming evening and what might lie beyond blends with the fact that I can't find the diamond anywhere. Mouli calls me again from below.

"Coming!" Panicked now, I spill the contents of the little box onto my dresser and sift through the little baubles and mementos I've collected over the year.

"Looking for this?" Flit appears on my shoulder. The diamond dangles from her hand by a woven bracelet of frayed, stained, rainbow colored ribbon. "Like it? I did it today."

"It's lovely," I whisper as she darts down to tie it around my wrist. Its craftsmanship is childlike, but something about the contrast of the perfect diamond woven tightly into a messy nest of discarded ribbon makes me smile. When I lower my arm again, the long draping sleeve of my gown covers it. I shake my wrist, testing it.

"Is it safe to bring it to the palace? Will it fall out?"

"Nope!" She answers, and she pops out of view before I can discern which of the two questions she was answering. Mouli appears in my doorway, looking quite annoyed.

"Azi!" she yelps and takes my hand, "You'll be late!"

"*I'm coming, too.*" Flit whispers into my head as I descend the stairs, careful not to step on my delicate skirts or fall down in these wretched heeled shoes that crunch my toes together uncomfortably. I'm concentrating so hard on those efforts that I don't notice Rian until I reach the bottom of the stairs and look up to see his eyes on me. He stares with a mix of awe and something else it takes me a moment to recognize, because I seldom see it in him: nerves. I grin and reach a hand out to him and he leans away dramatically and gestures from my head to my toes and shakes his head. He starts to say something and I start to stop him, but I don't need to as he stands there, his mouth hanging open.

"Wow, is stinky actually speechless?" Flit giggles. I ignore her. I am, too, as I take him in. He's set aside his robes tonight in favor of a calf-length, midnight blue jacket cinched with gold buttons at his waist over a crisp white shirt. The Mage Mark that had curled up around his ear just yesterday has already faded so much that it barely peeks up over the edge of his collar. His black slippers are polished to a mirror-like shine, their gold buckles bright in the waning sunlight. Together, we're perfectly coordinated. He offers me his arm and we say our farewells to Mouli, leaving her to bawl into Luca's shoulder about how grown up we both look.

The road to the palace is decorated with curls of thousands of purple and gold streamers that sway gently in the breeze. A crowd lines the streets near the gates to watch as the attendees of the ball arrive. Most come in carriages drawn by horses or footmen, but we live close enough that we didn't see the need. I regret that decision now, in these awful shoes. Thank goodness for Rian, whose strong arm I cling to in a concerted effort not to catch my heel in the cobbles and fall.

As we turn the bend and the palace rises up before us, we both gasp. Elegant lanterns line the walkway, floating like miniature moons, casting a soft light over the arriving guests. They remind me of the dazzle spell that Rian used during his exam the way they flicker colorfully. As we pass beneath them and I get a closer look at one, I can tell for certain that they're held floating and aglow with magic. There are dozens of them, nearly a hundred, scattered across the vast lawns of the grounds as well. I glance up at Rian, whose jaw is tightly clenched as he takes in the scene. It's hardly a reverential use of magic. Despite the soft and lovely effect of it, it feels ostentatious, edging on disrespectful. The other guests don't seem to agree with me as they ooh and ah over its beauty and remark on how it's unlike anything they've ever seen.

Inside, the receiving hall has been lined with live trees bedecked with tiny glittering lights. As we near them I realize the lights are actually hundreds of miniature fairy figurines of blown glass, enchanted to glow with colors that change in such a way that they remind me of Flit's eyes. We file in behind the crowd of guests and make our way down the line, greeting the row of honored guests assembled to receive us, finally coming to the royal family just before the entrance to the ballroom. We meet Margary first and she tugs my sleeve excitedly as I curtsey down to her level.

"I have something to show you after," she whispers, "once the music starts." Her eyes twinkle as she grins at me.

"It must be something very important," I say, "if it means you want to miss the dancing."

"Oh, it is." The tiara pinned to her hair sparkles brilliantly as she bobs her head.

"We'll find each other, then?" I whisper as I rise from my curtsey and she nods again fervently before turning to the next guests in line.

"Squire Hammerfel!" Princess Amei takes my hand in her gloved one and squeezes it, obviously relieved to see a familiar face among the throngs. When Eron offers us a polite but cold acknowledgement, I'm glad he's so dismissive. We move quickly from him to Sarabel, the guest of honor. I dip into a formal curtsey and rise again and the princess beams at me, her eyes sparkling.

"Oh Azi, isn't it amazing?" She gestures to the decorations. "Eron and Margary dreamt it up and they had the Mages working all day on it." She turns to Rian. "I hope you're not still upset about it, Rian, now that you've seen it." She rests a hand on his arm. "After all, it's just a bit of display, and it isn't hurting anything, right?" I look at Rian, who offers a cordial nod to the princess and a genuine enough reassuring smile. "You're such a dear. I'll save you a dance, then. See you inside," she says to the two of us. Then she turns to the next in line, leaving us to curtsey and bow to King Tirnon and the queen.

"Good of you to come, my friends," he says to us sincerely. "How fairs your father, Squire Azaeli?"

"He still sleeps, your Majesty." I leave it there. This isn't the time or place to go into further detail. When he offers me his apologies and his hopes that my father is well soon, I know in my heart that he's being genuine. He then turns to Rian, who he offers a smile with a hint of apology. He must know that Rian's been silenced, and he is respectful enough not to speak to him. Had he done so, Rian would have been obligated to reply. I notice as we turn to leave how very tired the king looks. It isn't overly obvious, but I've seen it before in my own father: the hunch of his shoulders, the circles under his eyes from too much worrying.

Rian and I follow the crowd into the ballroom and I stare in awe. As if the grounds and the reception hall hadn't been extravagant enough, the ballroom has been washed and draped in white. Thousands of crystals dangle from the ceiling by silken ribbons. They turn and sway and cast brilliant reflections across the shining floor. It has the same effect as the sunlight through Flit's wings, and it's just as dizzying, so much so that I have to hold tight to Rian's arm to keep myself from tipping among the dancing beams.

"It's absolutely stunning," I whisper. Rian shakes his head and waves a hand dismissively at the décor, then points at me, leans down, and steals a quick kiss. I grin and feel my cheeks warm. A squeal of excitement shatters the moment. Over his shoulder, I see a team of giggling girls peeking around a pillar. "Brace yourself," I say. Just then, the royal family files in and the musicians begin to play. The king and queen and Prince Eron and Princess Amei pair up together to start off the ball, and a page taps Rian on the shoulder.

"Her Highness requests you join her on the dance floor," he says. Rian flashes me a helpless, wide-eyed look before he turns to meet the Princess's request. I try to hide my disappointment as he bows to Sarabel and takes her hand. If either of us had to dance, I truly hoped it would be together, especially for the first dance. I watch the three couples move gracefully across the floor and soon they are joined by more and more pairs until the crowd of dancers is too thick for me to see much. Occasionally I catch a whirling glimpse of him. It's then that Princess Margy tugs on my skirt and looks up at me, feverish with excitement.

"Let's go now. Nobody will notice. They'll just be dancing." She takes my hand and we weave together between the guests and the pillars of the ballroom until she waves me in through a hidden door off the side of the ballroom. When she pulls it closed behind us, the sounds of the ball beyond are blocked out completely.

"What is it you wanted to show me?" I crouch to her level. She looks perfectly in place here amongst the exquisite furniture, dressed in her lavender silk gown that shimmers with silver embroidery and drips with pearls. The walls are lined in dark, ornately carved paneling, and warm fire crackles merrily in the hearth. The room is otherwise empty.

"Not here," she whispers secretively, and leads the way out of the room and through a narrow corridor lined with the occasional pair of palace guards.

As she passes each guard, Margy calls out to them: "'lo Fen. "'lo Mari." "'lo Vince." In turn, the guards wiggle their fingers at her and offer her a smile, and their eyes scan over me appraisingly. After dozens of similar greetings through the winding corridors, the princess stops at an elaborately painted door, pulls it open and then waves me through again. "Wait 'til you see," she whispers.

I step through the door into another richly decorated room, but this one is a little less pristine than the last. Here there are stacks of books piled about, and a half-finished needlepoint is draped on one of the velvet arms of a chair near the fireplace, where the embers have died to a quiet black crackle. Two large desks adorn opposite walls, set in front of shelves that stretch up so high that they require a rolling ladder to reach the top. I lift my skirts to step over a tiny model of the kingdom carefully arranged with miniature subjects. Across the room, Margy disappears behind a drape that's stretched from the corner of the desk to the wall.

"I'm not sure I should be in here," I say to her uneasily as I cross by the desk, which is piled with official-looking documents. Still, I'm hopeful. My goal tonight was to find the missing pages of those books to help us break the curse, and also any clues that might lead me to what Eron could be plotting. This is a perfect place to begin my search.

"It's just our study," she says. "It's okay. Look here." She waves me into the little cubby behind the curtain and I have to gather my skirts up in order to keep from bumping anything. The drape closes behind us and suddenly I feel as if I'm someplace secret and wonderful. This small corner of the room is the princess's own, private space. Her colorful drawings are scattered over the walls, and the book shelves are piled with storybooks and dolls and stuffed toys. She kneels and peers at the little tarnished silver jewel box that had previously been in the garden.

"Twig," she whispers as she kneels there, her hands folded neatly her lap. She grins. "Twig, it's okay. Yes, she's here." she pauses. "Oh, you want me to show her that first? Okay." She slides a children's book from the shelf and hands it to me. "Will you read this to me?" she asks, and tucks her knees up under her chin beside me.

The cover of the book is plain and unadorned, but when I open it I'm enchanted by the fantastic illustrations that greet me. I turn the page and gasp at a drawing of a woman with a long, blonde braid dressed in shining armor. She wields a great glowing two-handed sword against a twisting, dark mass. The artist has drawn tiny glimpses of hands, feet, wings, and frightened faces spinning and whirling within the harsh black twisting lines of the mass. The warrior wears a grimace of determination as she arcs her sword to slice at the foe.

"She looks just like you, doesn't she, Azi?" Margy scoots closer to me and points to the blond braid.

"She does," I say, a little rattled. "Where did you get this?"

"Oh, here somewhere," Margy answers dismissively.

"*Go on, read it,*" Flit's whisper almost makes me jump. I had forgotten about her. I take a moment to compose myself before I begin to read aloud.

Chapter Fourteen

FAIRY TALES

"There once was a fair warrior whose aim was always true, because her heart belonged to her sword, and her sword was one with her heart. Together, the two left no foe undefeated. But this power did not intoxicate her as it would most men. Instead, she traveled the lands seeking to snuff out all manner of evil, and wickedness, and selfishness and cruelty. She journeyed over mountains and plains, through deserts and snow, until one day she crossed into an enchanted forest.

"The creatures who dwelt there were so pure of heart and so innocent that they did not know deception or danger. They lived in peace and prosperity, and kept themselves well hidden from outsiders. And so imagine their surprise when they one day came upon the warrior sleeping on a thick bed of moss at the edge of their forest. They did not know what to make of the warrior, for she was such a giant to them, and foreign. At first when she woke, the warrior was startled to find herself so surrounded, but the creatures were trusting of her, and she was delighted by their kind spirit and playful manner, and they soon became friends.

"As it was her quest, the warrior spent many months exploring the land of the fairies seeking out wickedness to defeat, but despite her efforts, she could find no evil in their land. One day, when she had been walking endlessly among the golden grasses and colorful flowers, she came upon a curious sight. A deep pool of glimmering light stretched out before her. It was perfectly round and still, and its contents glimmered like the stars in the sky even in the sunlight. The warrior was entranced by the sight, and knelt to dip her fingers into it, but the fairies cried out to warn her.

"'Do not touch the pool, for it is the source of all magic. It must not be tainted by those who do not understand it!' The warrior knelt quietly, enticed by the sparkling surface. From time to time, streaks of it would shoot off into the sky in a powerful, glittering jet like a shooting star. Eventually, her curiosity swayed her, and she removed her glove and dipped her fingers into the pool. When she held them up, she saw that they had blackened with coils that wound in thick lines. In the distance, for the first time in the many months she had spent in their land, she heard the ominous rumble of thunder.

"Lightning struck the mountain in the distance, and all of the fairies fled the pool in fear. The warrior rose to her feet and turned toward the storm. A strange sound chilled her to her very bones, and she readied her sword as she watched the coming foe. The twisting shadow shot her through with terror as it approached, but she did not falter. Even when she could see swallowed within it the faces of her small friends, she stood her ground. She swung her sword true and sliced through the shadow, which all at once disappeared, leaving her battered friends in a heap in the grass.

"The warrior tended to them until they were well again. She swore an oath that she would forever guard their Wellspring from harm, and defend the fairies from the twisting shadows which she believed to be birthed by the abuse of their magical source. And so she stayed with them until she grew weary from uselessness, and lonesome for her own kind. Because the fairies did not like to see their friend so downtrodden, they agreed that she should go and find her true love, which is the right of all those with hearts that are pure. But before she bade them farewell, she made them promise that they would call on her if they ever had need of her sword again.

"The warrior did eventually find her one true love, and when she was too old and weak to keep her promise, she passed her sword to her own daughter, and with it her vow. And they all continued to live in peace happily and forevermore."

I stare at the drawing on the page of the woman that could be me, or my mother, kissing a man who doesn't at all resemble my father, with fairies circling them joyfully, throwing sparkling bits of magic at them. In her arms is a baby with wispy golden hair, and the sword strapped to her back has a familiar blue glow to it. I shake my head. It's just a strange coincidence. It has to be. I flip to the front again and read the bookmaker's mark. It's over a hundred years old. But why have I never heard the tale before? It seems like just the sort of story my mother would have told me at bedtime.

"*Aren't you going to say anything?*" Flit prods.

"Now will you come out, Twig?" Margy whispers, "What? Who? Who's coming?" Her eyes go wide and she snaps the curtain closed and presses a finger to her lips. Not a moment later, the door opens and slams shut again.

"Someone will hear," a familiar voice whispers. Margy clings to me, her eyes still wide. I peer through the narrow crack between the curtain and the desk and see Eron gripping a woman by the arms. He pushes her against the wall beside the door and kisses her. Her long blue-black hair falls in a curtain over her bare arm, which is almost completely covered in the black coils of the Mark. Viala. She tips her head back against the wall as he bends to trail his affections along her black, swirling Marks.

"I told you we'd win him over," she whispers, "just a little at a time. Patience." The prince raises his head to meet her eyes and I look away as they grow more passionate. Margy blinks up at me, her face pale, and her lips pressed tightly together.

"It's hardly a win," Eron growls. I hear a thud and I duck my head and close my eyes, trying with all of my might to be completely silent. "Some fancy lights and twinkling stars? That's nothing. He's a fool not to see what a waste it is to deny ourselves the power we could harness."

"And that," Viala's voice is silky smooth, "Is why we're taking things into our own hands." There's another period of kissing and breathy whispers obscured by the rustling of fabric and I slide my hands to cover Margy's innocent ears. "Patience," Viala says again through a soft moan, drawing out the end of the word like the hiss of a snake.

"That's easy for you to say, while I sit useless. Those fools should have arrived at the border by now. Why hasn't the offering worked yet? What if we were wrong in sending her?"

"Don't worry," she purrs. I peek out to see her caressing his hair back. "I'm certain she was the best offering. Just give it time. Curses don't break as easily as they're doled. And if it doesn't work, then we move to the next on the list." I press my back up against the side of the desk as I hear the prince's footsteps approach. A spattering of glitter puffs in front of my eyes.

"Don't make a sound. He can't see you, but he might hear you." Flit says silently. I hold my breath and look to Margy, who I can feel pressing into my leg, but I can't see her at all. When I tip my head back, the prince is standing just an arm's reach away from me, rifling through the mess of pages on the desk.

One of them drifts to the ground beside my knee, old, yellow, and torn into the shape of a fairy's wing. I know it immediately as Uncle's research from so long ago, and now I see that it's a list. My mother's name is at the top, followed by my own. Beneath them are listed a variety of legendary magical items, and some lesser known objects I'm unfamiliar with. At the heading of the list is written: Lost Treasures. My mother's name is circled, and so is another object, an amulet.

The prince shoves the curtain aside to retrieve the list, and I have to quickly pull the fabric of my skirt away to keep him from catching it accidentally. He storms back to Viala, who is casually adjusting the incredibly low neckline of her deep red gown. "We should have sent the real amulet with them, not the replica. I told you that. Just in case they didn't accept that Paladin. We've based this entire plan on some old baby story!"

"That amulet is too important," she presses a hand to his chest and leans in to kiss his neck. "I've told you. You need to keep it safe." She takes him by the collar and grazes her painted lips across his jaw. I look away again, thinking of Princess Amei who seemed so alone in the reception line despite the fact that she was standing right beside her prince, who ought to have been trying harder to make her feel more at home. I think of how cold he was to her at Rian's trial, how he spent the entire time sitting with his back angled away from her, talking to Viala. It all makes sense now. Beside me, I feel Margy shudder, and I close my arms around her as Viala goes on.

"It's not just a story. It's history based on fact. I researched their line. We're rid of the Paladin already. When Gaethon arrives at the border, Redemption will take care of him and the others just for good measure. Then we just have to worry about the girl, who conveniently remains oblivious. You can easily lure her to you when the time is right, and then I'll finish her myself. With their line out of the way and your curse debt paid in full, nothing will stand between us and the Wellspring. Then, we build our kingdom. Be patient, my darling."

"*BAD MAGE!*" Flit's voice booms in my mind, and I clap my hands over my mouth to keep from yelping. Viala's eyes flick to our corner and I hold my breath, certain for a moment that she can see us.

"Come, they'll be missing you," she snaps her attention back to him and they kiss, forcing me to avert my eyes as he slides his hand over her chest. When the door eventually clicks shut, I finally allow myself to breathe.

"See, they're plotting bad things," Margy whispers. "Twig told me. I didn't believe him at first, but then I started to pay attention." A cascade of silvery dust shimmers down over us and I feel a strange crawling across my skin as I become visible again. Margy looks up at me gravely. I close my eyes, rest the back of my head against the desk, and press my shaking hands into my skirts to still them. Of course Rian and I had our suspicions about the prince, but I never would have dreamt that he'd be so brazen and so…I don't know. I can't even think of a word to describe what I just overheard, what I just saw.

"How long have those two been…" I try to think of how to put it delicately to Margy's innocent ears. "…friendly?"

"Oh, a long time," she whispers. "I saw them together after Brother returned from his touring, and he told me I'd better not tell anyone. And I didn't! I kept his secret. I'm good at secrets, Twig says."

"Does Viala know that you know?" I smooth a fold in my skirt, forcing myself not to seem overly concerned.

"Only if Brother told her," she says as she peers into the shelf again. I'm sure he must have, which makes me frightened for her safety, but I'd never say that to Margy. She reaches her hands into the shelf, palms up, and leans forward.

"They mean to kill us," I whisper, mostly to myself. "But why?" If Margy hears, she doesn't answer.

"Won't you say hello now," she asks her empty hands sweetly as she draws them close to her chest, "please?" She turns very slowly and carefully to face me, grinning. I look into her palms curiously, only to find them empty.

"Isn't he wonderful?" she asks. For a moment, I'm disappointed. I had really believed that she'd found an actual fairy of her own. "Oh," she looks down at her empty hands, "she doesn't see you. I really thought she would! Don't you believe, Azi? I thought it would be easy for you, by now."

"*Look harder,*" Flit whispers, and I do. I stare at Margy's delicate little fingers, gently curved around thin air, my eyes following along the lines of her palms. "*Not at her* hands*, genius. Look at* him." I purse my lips and shake my head and try to change my focus to the fairy that everyone's telling me to see, that isn't there. I stare until my eyes blur and lose focus and then something strange begins to happen.

A tiny face with a pointed chin and long nose and a dark, wide-eyed gaze emerges slowly from the bend of her fingers. It looks up, studying me. Slowly, shoulders tufted in yellow dandelion appear, and a tunic of leaf green, and from the sleeves stretch impossibly spindly, long arms. His legs are just as lean, covered in trousers that are spotted with dirt and threadbare with holes. Every bit of exposed skin is brown and smudged with dirt. His black hair is streaked with green, and long fringes of it fall over his eyes so that I wonder how he can manage to see anything at all. Last to appear are his wings, which are quite different from Flit's larger, iridescent ones. His are two jagged twigs that jut straight out from his back. Just as I start to wonder whether they work to lift him, he pushes off from Margy's hands and punches the air joyously.

"She did it!" he cries, his voice adorably uneven, much like an older boy who is becoming a man.

"I knew she could!" Flit laughs and pops into view. The two collide together in midair, grasping hands and linking their feet at the ankles. They spin gleefully until both are just a blurred ball of color floating before our eyes. Margy claps and giggles and throws her arms around me.

"Is that your Flit?" she asks. "Twig told me about her. Oh, I've wanted to see her! She sounds so very pretty." The spinning ceases abruptly and Flit dives to Margy, stopping short right at her nose.

"I'm not *her* Flit. I'm *my own.*" She jams her fists onto her hips and glares, challenging the princess.

"Of course you are," Margy says gravely, "I misspoke, will you please forgive me?"

"Okay!" Flit gives her a peck on the tip of nose, and then she and

Twig go back to spinning. I watch them for a moment, dazed, until Margy tugs on my sleeve.

"She is awfully pretty. Exactly as I'd picture a fairy to look." She picks up the book again and begins turning the pages. "Imagine what it must be like there..."

I look down at the pictures of the warrior and think of my mother. I wonder whether the whirling shadows have returned, whether she's fighting right now, as I sit here tucked away in the palace. I think of our guild, rushing to save her, riding straight into Redemption's ambush orchestrated by Viala and the prince.

I need to do something, and my first instinct is to jump up and run for Rian. Run to the horses, ride hard for Kythshire. Get away from Eron. Warn the guild, especially Uncle. But then I remember all of the reasons that I can't. They are several days' ride ahead of us now; we'd never catch up to them. I can't fight without Rian's ice sword, and Rian can't rise to the Sixteenth Circle for two more weeks. Neither of us would be good in a fight, so what help would either of us be, even if we did reach them in time? Not only that, but we'd be defying the direct order to stay where we are, and I can't leave Da behind, asleep in his room, cursed.

I decide that our first step is to get a message to them quickly. Then we need to break the curse, and somehow stop Eron and Viala's plotting. I have no idea where to even begin, and then the thought strikes me.

"The king," I whisper, and the fairies stop spinning, and Margy stops giggling at them. "I have to tell him what Eron's planning. He can help." Margy starts to say something and then stops and looks at Twig.

"What is it, Margy?" I ask her. Twig slumps his shoulders and nods as if to say it's okay.

"Paba knows already," she whispers. "Knows a little of it, anyway. But Eron doesn't know he knows. Paba's trying to keep it quiet. He doesn't want Brother to get in trouble. He's trying to figure out a way to stop him without him knowing. He has a lot of faith in his Elite, but it's all making him very tired. I think it's even making him sick." Her eyes go wide. "What if it's a spell? She could be making him sick with her magic!"

"Oh, Princess," I whisper. It's all such a mess, and she's so young to be so heavily burdened with secrets like this. She curls against me and I hug her close. "You know there are wards all over the palace, wards on you, and on His Majesty. Complicated shield spells that protect against anyone who might try any spells against him. The Mages keep you safe, remember? But wait, he knows?" I think of the threat against my family, my guild, and my blood goes cold.

"Not all of it, not all of it," Twig darts up to me. "He suspects that Viala has a grip on the prince, and he sees how they are trying to influence him to change the laws governing magic. He doesn't know about the ambush, though, or what Viala is truly after."

"But why?" I ask. "Why do they want to kill us?"

"Oh! Questions! Do you want to play?" Flit does a little flip in the air and then comes to sit in the fold of my dress at my knee.

"No, I don't want to play," I say sternly, "I want answers. This isn't a game."

"If you want answers, then we'll play. If you don't want to play, then..." Flit shrugs, "you're no fun." Margy looks back and forth between us, her eyes wide.

"Azi's right. It's time to be serious," Twig says.

"Well, I don't like serious," Flit says. "Not much, anyway."

"Sometimes we have to do things we don't like, so we can hold onto the things we do like." He winks at her and pushes off from Margy's shoulder to hover in front of me. Flit crosses her arms and makes a face at him as he watches me. "Now you know the stories. You know what the prince is plotting. What will you do?"

"I need to be able to defend myself. I need to know how to break the curse," I say, and Twig nods.

"I think so, too," he says. "Though it isn't really a curse, you know."

"I know, but can you tell me how to reverse it? Does it have to do with the treasures on that list?"

"In a way," he says. "The key is to make a selfless gesture toward Kythshire. Can you think of why it didn't work for the prince?" Flit giggles a little, and when I look down at her she turns her head away and covers her smile. I knit my brow curiously at her and turn my focus back to Twig.

"Well, his gesture wasn't selfless. He thought he was returning a treasure to break his curse, and that treasure was my mother. He thought based on the story that if she crossed into Kythshire, she'd most likely stay. He knew our guild would go searching for her, so he set Redemption up to take care of them. But why do they want to kill us?" I ask again.

"Think about the story," Twig says. "The protectors, your line, have sworn to watch over our lands for generations. That kind of vow, honored for so long, holds a great deal of power. They believe they won't be able to take the Wellspring while your family still lives." He winks again at Flit, who is chuckling at my knee as she watches our exchange, and then turns back to me with his question. "Why are you so intent on breaking the curse, as you call it?"

"It's not as much for me, as for my father," I say. "If he can't wield, then his life will be ruined. He's a good man, and he truly loves my mother. When he crossed the border, he was only trying to keep from losing her," I explain. "I'd do anything if I could bring her back and cure him. Is there a way?"

"There is always a way," Twig says. "Knowing what you know now, can you think of how the curse could be broken, and your parents reunited?" Flit's giggles erupt into full-out laughter which spills over to Margy, who's pressing her fingers to her lips to hide it.

"Oh, will someone please let me in on the joke?" I cry, exasperated. Flit sits up.

"No, no, no," she holds her stomach, trying to catch her breath. "By all means, don't let us interrupt you *not* playing the game!"

"He," Margy giggles. "He's tricked you, see? You've been playing all along!"

"Shush!" Twig waves at her. "She's almost got it!" They all go quiet and stare at me, and I feel my cheeks go hot. At first I'm angry at being tricked, but then I can't help but laugh. I'll give it to them, fairies are clever creatures. Infuriating sometimes, but definitely clever. I sigh and shake my head.

"She isn't going to get it," Flit whispers to Twig.

"Quiet!" He hisses at her. "Give her some credit!" Margy chews her lip, looking from the fairies to me, her fine eyebrows raised so high they nearly touch the sparkling circlet in her dark hair. I look down at the blonde warrior in the storybook, and I think of Eron's list with my name just below my mother's, and suddenly I know what I have to do.

"A selfless act. I could break the curse for Da. Be his returned treasure. I could take my mother's place and fight the shadow cyclones myself. They could be together." I look to them. "Would it work?"

"Huh. You were right." Flit says to him. "She got it."

"That'd work," Twig says. "But could you really do it?"

I think it over. It would be difficult and strange to leave my life here behind and start a new one, a life I never planned on. But when I consider all that I've worked toward, I realize this is the path I was meant to take. I've never been interested in treasure hunting, or exploring new lands to claim for Cerion, or gaining riches. My training has always been with the hope that one day I could protect those who needed it. If I chose this, I would be guarding an entire race of creatures who are too small and too gentle to defend themselves.

My gesture would keep peace between Cerion and Kythshire, and protect the magic of the Wellspring. Uncle Gaethon could deal with Viala, and Rian—this is where a lump rises in my throat. Rian. Could I leave him behind, knowing we might never be together again? The notion sends tears to my eyes almost immediately. Margy, who has been silently watching me, scoots closer and hugs me around the waist. I close my arms around her and sniffle.

"I would miss you so much," she says. "But we could see each other in the dreaming place." I realize that she must have been to the wheat field as well, and I think of Rian's practice in Rumination. He and I could still be together there, maybe. But would I be able to feel his hand on my cheek, or the tenderness of his kiss?

"Think on it," says Twig gently. He drifts to Margy and wipes a tear from the corner of her eye. "Buck up, little princess. Things are starting to shine again, see? And now you don't have to be alone with your secrets anymore."

Flit, who has suddenly become unusually somber, comes to rest on my shoulder.

"You'd better get back to the ball," she offers quietly, "before they start to talk. You know how they are. Typical."

The melody of a gentle waltz drifts through the corridor as I follow the princess on a different course back to the ballroom, one on which we'd be unlikely to bump into Eron. In a daze I let her lead me through the dimly lit and highly polished hallways while my thoughts race with the information I have now. The decision regarding my parents hangs on the precipice of being made. I know what I have to do, and I would do it for them in a heartbeat if it wasn't for Rian. I don't know how I'll bear being away from him. I need to see him, right now. He needs to know that his parents and his mentor are in danger. And Bryse, and Cort. And Brother Donal. They'll reach the border soon. We need to warn them, and I hope that Rian knows a way to do it that's faster than a bird.

"Shadow Crag," Flit whispers into my mind. It's a moment before I realize that we've stopped in the alcove where Eron held me. Margy is gazing up at the same tapestry on the wall, clinging to my hand.

"I know this place," I whisper, and start to reach up with my free hand to touch the rich woven fibers depicting shadowy crag and the white lightning. Margy squeezes my other hand as I look closer. The black foreground is littered with tiny bodies and the bodies of men, all half-obscured by whirling shadows.

"I don't like this picture," says the princess. "Paba says it was the end of a dark time for everyone, but the start of a bright future for our family. It started the Plethore Dynasty. The Age of Peace. The Great War that ended King Diovicus's reign. He was a powerful Sorcerer-king, you know. The last ever of those. Paba thinks like everyone else, that we were too late to save the fairies, and none of them survived. I wish I could show him that it's wrong. I think he'd love Twig. But everyone else thinks so too, and Twig says it's safer for the fairies to be a secret, and he says we don't want people to think Paba's crazy." She whispers that last bit.

"See there?" Flit emerges only slightly from hiding, so that I can see parts of the tapestry through her as she rises up to point at the figure of a man standing on the crest of the mountain. I look closer and shiver as I realize why I hadn't noticed him before. His skin is completely blackened by the Mark so that he looks like part of the jagged shadows of the stones. Even the whites of his eyes are filled in. He stands beside a great rock that looks almost like a giant face.

Flit blows a raspberry at him and Margy giggles as the fairy fades from view again. Margy pulls me away from the dark image, toward the rising sound of the musicians and the revelry of the ball. Even as the richly dressed guests and sparkling dancers come into view, the images of the dark, twisted bodies of fairies and men alike haunt me.

I find Rian where I left him, at the center of the dance floor with Princess Sarabel. He looks so perfect among the distinguished group of dancers with the princess on his arm that I find myself wondering whether he'd suit her. As he twirls the princess around and she laughs merrily, I think he could be happy here in the palace. Sara would be happy, too. Then he looks away from her, and in the moment that our eyes meet, his brighten so much that his love for me is obvious. I smile and give a little wave, and then a tap on my shoulder startles me.

"*Oof! Rude!*" Flit's plaintive cry echoes in my head as I turn to the Page.

"His Royal Highness Prince Eron requests a dance," he says.

"Of course," I answer, curtsying my compliance even as my heart drops into the pit of my stomach.

Chapter Fifteen

THE UNKNOWN

My pulse races as I follow the page through the throngs of guests to the Prince. The image of him pressing Viala into the wall, kissing the Mark on her arm burns into my memory. I think of the tapestry and feel his hot breath on my shoulder and his rough hands on me. I'm desperate to think of a way out of it, but nothing comes to mind as the crowd parts and we approach Eron standing beside his father. The prince eyes me with a cold sort of greed and I duck my head and grip my skirts tightly to hide my shaking hands as I bend my knee to them. When I rise, the hand that's offered to me is not his, but the king's.

"I'm sure you don't mind, Azaeli, if I take this dance. That is, if Eron would be so kind as to allow his old father a moment of levity?" With a glint in his eye, he turns to Eron, who offers a reluctant nod.

"If it pleases you, Father," he murmurs, obviously annoyed.

"Excellent." The king offers me his arm and I rest my hand gratefully on it. As we cross the floor together, I dig deep into my mind trying desperately to remember any scrap of Mouli's teachings on etiquette in dancing with royalty. I curse myself for not paying better attention to her, but my worries are completely unfounded as we take to the dance floor. His Majesty is a gracious partner as he moves me swiftly across the ballroom in time with the other guests, and my long skirts hide the mistakes in my steps. I catch glimpses of Rian as we twirl and spin, and when we get closer to the musicians, the king leans in close to my ear. I feel Flit push off from my shoulder and land on the opposite side as he begins to talk to me so quietly that I can barely hear him above the music.

"Your family and mine have served Cerion for many years, Azaeli. You know this." I nod. "Your grandfather and my father were great allies, and I count your family among my most trusted friends."

"Thank you, Your Majesty," I say, feeling humbled by his praise.

"That is why," he tips his head even closer and whispers, "I would advise you to keep your distance from my son and his dealings." His eyes meet mine, and the exhaustion in them is plain. "I was unaware, when I sent the quest decree, what he was plotting. I did not want to believe him capable of such plots, and so I saw it only at face value. Since then, I have begun to see evidence of more selfish intentions. I owe you and your family an apology, Azaeli. I never meant for any harm to come to them." He bows his head to me as the music closes, and I curtsy. The musicians start another waltz, and he offers me his hand again.

"I would ask you to right it," he says as we glide across the floor, "if you can, as quietly as possible. I fear for my son. He is consumed by greed and lust for something that can never be his, and I am quite aware there is a stronger influence at work. I shall lend you any aid you need that is within my power. But Eron must not know, nor must anyone else." His request startles me.

"Your Majesty thinks too highly of me, surely you have other resources…" I say quietly.

"None that could be so discreet. If there is to be any hope for my son, then you and yours are my best course." As we come to dance beside Rian and Sarabel, I realize that my hands are sweating. To have the king himself put all of his faith in me this way is something I never could have foreseen.

"I can think of no one else more invested than you, at this time, or more suited. You do not give yourself credit where it is due," he says, and I know with his words there's no room for argument. He slips his hands from mine and bows to Rian. "Apprentice Rian, I do hope you will relinquish my daughter for one dance."

He offers his elbow to Sarabel, who takes it with a wistful smile back at Rian. Rian bows to both of them as they twirl away, and as I rise from my curtsy, he sweeps me off across the floor and into the crowd that loiters along the edge of the dance floor.

His hand tightens around mine as we weave through the milling throngs and finally push onto a grand patio overlooking the sheer cliffs that drop down to the vast black sea below. He pulls me to a quiet corner where we lean against the railing, tucked away from onlookers. I turn my back to the frightening drop and try to collect my thoughts. There's so much to tell him that I have trouble deciding where to start. I settle on the most immediate threat, tipping my head to rest on his shoulder so that my whispers carry straight to his ear.

"I saw them together," I say. "The Prince and Mistress Viala. "They were…quite friendly." I look up at him and his mouth drops open slightly. He taps his temple. He had an idea. "Much more friendly than they ought to be. They're plotting together, Rian. Redemption isn't searching for my mother, they're setting up an ambush to get rid of the others when they arrive at the border. They want Uncle dead. Mum and me, too." Rian holds me away at arms' length. He searches my eyes and then shrugs his shoulders to his ears, shaking his head. Why, he asks silently. "Viala wants us out of the way," I whisper. "She said once our family was out of the picture, the Well—"

"*Shush!*" Flit cries in my head as Rian's eyes snap wide in shock and his hand flies up to cover my mouth. He shakes his head frantically. I understand. Even here under the cover of darkness, in secret whispers, it isn't safe to talk about the Wellspring.

He grabs my hand and leads me back into the ballroom, where he seems to be searching for someone. Eventually, he tracks down a rather old-looking master in plain gray robes, with a long pointed beard that trails down to his chest in white wisps. He's deep in conversation with another Mage, who is only slightly younger looking. I stand beside Rian, feeling awkward as the two halt their conversation mid-sentence. The younger mage excuses himself, seemingly relieved by the interruption.

"Evening, Apprentice," the older Mage says, nodding cordially. Rian pats his chest with his hand and leans forward slightly in the Mage's greeting. The man turns to me, "and you are, dear?"

"Azi. Um, Squire Azaeli Hammerfel, sir."

"Ah, yes. I ought to have known. Anod Bental, High Master and Advisor to His Majesty, the King." My breath catches in my throat at his intimidating title, and I nod my head politely. Rian squeezes my hand reassuringly, and then steps closer to Anod and makes another gesture, one I haven't seen before. He taps three fingers of his right hand to his left arm, just above the bend of his elbow. The man's eyes snap to Rian's fingers and back to his face again.

"Is this some joke?" He reaches to cover Rian's hand with his, and Rian shakes his head. He pulls his hand free to make the gesture again.

"Well, don't do it again, boy!" His voice is slightly panicked as he claps his hand over Rian's again and checks to make sure no one has seen. "Come with me." He leads us quickly into the corridor with the alcove bearing the dark tapestry. With a quick look over his shoulder he moves it aside and whispers, and a passage appears.

We slip inside, and the opening behind us solidifies again. The walls grow damp and stony as we walk, and the floor slants downward. Eventually I realize that we must have long left the palace for the network of Academy tunnels that are rumored to run below the city itself.

My breath comes in cool puffs of white in the chilled air, and I hold on tightly to Rian to keep from sliding in shoes that were not meant for such a hard, slick path. My dress grows heavy as it slides along the narrow passage, collecting droplets of moisture from the walls and floor. Its fine threads pull on the rough walls, fraying the delicate fabric, opening holes in the once pristine blue and gold, ruining it.

The further from the palace we get, the more nervous I become. How well does Rian trust Anod, I wonder, to follow him into the depths of the tunnels where we could disappear and nobody would know? The king trusts him enough to call him an advisor, but with all of this plotting, whose side is he truly on? I decide there isn't much I can do but trust Rian's judgment as Anod opens a rough wooden door and gestures us inside.

The room is starkly furnished with a plain wood table and several stools. There are no windows or openings other than the one we entered through. There isn't even a fireplace. It reminds me of a prison cell, and when he closes the door, I hug my arms across my chest. Rian guides me to a stool and sits with his arm around me.

"*It's awful,*" Flit's whisper comes to my mind, "*So heavy in here.*" I give a very slight nod of my head as Anod locks the door and tucks the key into his pocket. He gestures over it with a murmur to set the ward, and then he turns to Rian.

"I release you from your bonds of silence, Apprentice," he says.

"Thank you," Rian says with great relief, clearing his throat. Anod bobs his head.

"Now tell me, what is the meaning of this? And do you think it wise to use such a gesture before…" he nods to me, "An untrained?"

"Yes, Grand Master, I do. Considering who the untrained is." Anod studies me for a moment and I fight the urge to look away.

"Very well, very well," he concedes. "What is it, then? Is there truly a danger?"

"Viala," Rian says simply, and Anod's eyes narrow into slits of fury.

"As we expected."

"She means to annihilate the protectors. The whole line." Rian says.

"I see," Anod strokes his beard thoughtfully, "Yes, that would be very effective, it would. Clever of her. And how does she mean to do this?"

"Ambush," Rian says, "Redemption's allegiance is with Eron. They lie in wait for the approach of His Majesty's Elite. They mean to attack them. That will take care of Master Gaethon. Sir Lisabella has already crossed the border, the cyclones will take care of her once they multiply, which they will once Viala begins to test the Wellspring. That just leaves…" he turns his head to me slowly.

"Me," I whisper. "But does it really matter? Can't they see that anyone could watch over it? You could, Rian. Or Da could. Anyone who cared could keep the cyclones away."

"What a charming sense of humility you have, dear Azaeli." Anod says with a gentle smile. "Yes, someone else could make the promise and act as protector, but it would take many generations for their bloodline to hold the same power yours does now. It is imperative that your line continues to thrive, in order to maintain peace. Kythshire is a land full of mysteries, Azaeli. Most of which even us learned scholars will never come to fully understand. Though we thirst for the power and knowledge within its boundaries, we have learned over the years that there is a high price to pay for it. Some things are best left to the unknown." He groans and settles onto a stool before he goes on.

"Viala, on the other hand, is young. She has no respect for this notion. In Sunteri, where she was raised, knowledge and power are valued above all else. They are ruthless in the pursuit of it. Her people see only the potential to own it all, for to master a Wellspring is to master magic itself. And now, with the prince as her puppet, she might just." He shakes his head. "She might just, yes."

Something nags at me as he talks, a tiny fact. Rian knew about the Wellspring all this time. At the very least, he knew that. I wonder how much else he's been aware of. Did he know, growing up, that my mother was a part of this promise that spanned generations? Did he know I was? What about the rest of the guild?

How much of this secret have they kept from me? How many of the choices I've made have been my own, and how many have been carefully orchestrated by my parents, who knew the path I was meant to follow? Why didn't they trust me enough to tell me the truth? Rian's hand squeezes my shoulder and I fight the urge to push it away. It isn't the time, now, to ask these questions. The people I love are in danger, and we're running out of time.

"We need to get word to the others," I say. "They need to know to expect an attack."

"Word?" There's a twinkle in Anod's eye, "We can do better than word. Yes, this falls within the guidelines, I'm certain. Important enough to send you to them straight away." He winks at Rian. "Prepare yourselves, and return to the Academy in a half-hour. The ceremony will be readied by then. Tell no one." He stands a little stiffly, and leans to stretch his back.

"Oh yes, of course." He turns to Rian and with his thumb draws a symbol over each of his shoulders, then his forehead. A reddish glow hovers in each spot before fading into Rian's clothing. "I hereby raise you to the Sixteenth Circle. Congratulations, Mentor." With no further ceremony, he rushes out.

"Yeah!" Rian shouts, jumping up from his stool. He throws his hand flat, and sparks of light fly from his fingertips in celebratory bursts, and then he dives at me and pulls me up into a hug. We spin in circles until we're both dizzy and laughing.

"Congratulations!" I say as he takes my hand, his eyes glinting with excitement.

"Azi, I have something to ask you," he says, his tone suddenly serious, "and it's important that you accept. There isn't much time." My head is still spinning with confusion about the protectors and the Wellspring, and I feel as if I should be angry at him for keeping secrets

154

from me, but his sudden switch from elation to utter seriousness jars me.

"What is it?" I ask. My hand is shaking in his now and I can't seem to meet his eyes until he takes my chin and gently raises it up. His eyes are bright with the promise of adventure, and also, as always, there's that underlying tone of mischief. I wonder how I'll ever live a day away from those eyes. He takes my other hand and pulls me closer to him, and my pulse quickens as I begin to imagine what the question could possibly be.

"Will you be my student?" his question leaves me flat.

"I...what?" I search his face. He's serious.

"Will you be my student, Azi? Officially." He starts to talk so quickly that it's hard for me to keep up.

"I'm a Mentor now, and by the laws I can only take on one student. If you agree, then I can't be forced to take anyone else. It's what she was planning. Viala. Master Gaethon had her take me as a student when he left so she couldn't secretly take Eron. I realize now that he wanted me to fail so she couldn't force me to teach him in secret, either. So if I took you on, that would solve it. Also, it helps to be bonded in some way if we're going to be teleporting. I'm sure that's why Grand Master raised me to sixteenth. And I could tell you everything. All of the secrets."

He shifts and steps back a little to read me, and I wonder if I look as beaten as I feel. I'm not a Mage. I don't ever want to be one. Choosing that path now would feel too much like abandoning everything I've worked so hard for.

"Nothing would change. I don't even have to actually teach you anything," he offers as though reading my mind. "It's just a quick agreement, Azi. A safeguard. There isn't a lot of time." His hands tighten around mine.

"I will," I say a little hesitantly.

"Good," he nods and presses his thumb to my forehead, and a warm tingle comes with the ebb of golden light just above my brow. "That's done," he says, and gives me a quick kiss on the cheek. "Now, we have to run home and get ready. I'll explain on the way."

I abandon my torturous shoes as Rian pulls me through the door, and we sprint off down the narrow passageway in the opposite direction we came from before. I try to keep track of our route, but there are so many bends and openings and doors that I eventually lose count of how many lefts and how many rights we've taken. Rian explains the laws of teleportation to me as we run.

He tells me that it takes a great deal of diplomacy on the part of the Academy, requiring several signatures of approval including the king's due to the amount of magic required. The spell will send us directly to a Master Mage who has been marked to receive, and thankfully Master Gaethon had himself marked several years ago as a precaution.

The law that strikes me as most disappointing is the restriction on metal. Any metal we bring or wear is considered magical payment, which means I can't wear my armor or bring any weapons, unless they're made of wood or leather. When I ask him if there is any way around it, he asks me if there's any way around our feet striking the ground when we run. Magic has a cost, and the cost for this extravagantly expensive spell is payment in precious metals.

He pushes a door open to reveal a ladder that stretches up overhead at least two stories. I crane my neck and wonder how on earth I'll manage to climb it in this dress.

"You go first," he says. "If you slip, I'll be right behind you." It's tedious and frustrating getting up to the top, especially rushing as we are. I curse the gown several times as it wraps around my knees and tangles at my feet. Eventually, we make it up to the top and I crawl out of a narrow doorway that leads onto a cobbled street that glows in the lamplight. We've emerged right outside of the glass blower's stall, which is just a block away from home if we take the alley shortcut.

"No more gowns," I puff as we trot to the alley's opening, "Ever again." I can't wait to be rid of the cumbersome thing. We reach the end and Rian skids to a stop.

"Brace yourself," he says, looking at my front door, "Mouli's waiting up."

"Oh…" I look down at the dress, which hangs heavy and damp from my frame. The once crisp pleats have fallen and rumpled, the hem is crusted with street filth, and many of the threads that caught on the rough stone have torn to gaping holes. One trailing sleeve is nearly torn off at the elbow. I imagine I stepped on it climbing up the ladder. "She's going to kill me."

"We don't have time for that," he whispers, and waves a hand over me, and I watch in wonder as the dress is transformed. The grime falls away and the holes close up. The sleeve repairs itself, and the pleats reform to even crisper lines than they had been when I first got dressed. I turn slightly, and the golden fabric shimmers in the lamplight. He looks at me, inspecting his work.

"Not bad," he grins. "Remember, no metal. We have just a few minutes, so hurry and change and only pack what you need. Don't worry about food."

"Are we telling Mouli and Luca what we're up to? What about Da?" I ask. Rian nods.

"I think they should know. Your father…" he pauses, thinking, "It may be best to leave him sleeping. If something happens to me, the spell will break. If all goes well, I can remove it easily enough." It's too painful to think of something happening to Rian. I push the thought away.

"I wish he could come with us," I gaze up at my bedroom window and picture him sleeping in his own room, just beyond it. Rian strokes my cheek.

"I know," he says. "Come on."

In my room, I explain as much as I can while Mouli helps me out of my gown and all of the constricting undergarments that it requires. She takes them away to store them, and I scratch my stomach and sides with great relief as I rush into the dressing room.

I pull out a thick pair of work trousers and a long-sleeved tunic. Out of habit I grab the belt I usually wear, but it has a metal buckle, and so I opt for a sash instead. As I tie it, Flit's diamond glints at my wrist, catching my eye. I rush to the hatch and push it open. Rian's is open already. He's rushing around his room, back in his familiar blue robes again.

"Is this okay?" I ask, holding up the diamond. He comes over and looks at it carefully, then nods.

"It should be fine. Are you almost ready?"

"I think so. I'll meet you downstairs." I look around my room and my eyes rest on the stand that holds my chain mail. I trail my fingers along the smooth, cool rings and sigh. It's the last thing I'd expect to be leaving behind at a time like this, but as Rian said, if I try to bring it, it'll be lost forever. I don't have time to dwell on it. Even my sword will remain.

I feel too light, too exposed as I grab the cross-body bag that holds little more than an extra set of clothes. I can't think of anything else I'd need that fits within the laws. I look around the room and I wonder if this is the last time I'll stand here. Flit's pitcher lies empty on the windowsill, and I realize that I haven't felt or heard from her since she whispered to me in the underground room.

"Flit?" I call quietly, "Are you here?" I hear the front door close, and Rian and Luca making hurried arrangements downstairs. There's no answer from Flit, and I can't help but worry as I rush into the hallway. I turn toward my father's room and pause. I want to say goodbye, and I will my feet to push me forward through his door, but I can't. It's too difficult to think it might be the last time I ever see him.

"He'll be okay," Rian says softly behind me. "Promise." He slips his hand into mine. "Come on, we can't be late."

We offer our rushed farewells to Mouli and Luca, who both promise that everything will be safe in their care while we're away. I can't tell if I'm imagining the hint of finality in Mouli's voice, and there's no time to dwell on it as Rian and I rush back to the Academy. Master Anod is waiting for us outside of the entrance and when he ushers us through, he turns to Rian with a nod.

"Good thinking, Mentor," he says as I step across the threshold and my forehead tingles where Rian pressed his thumb to it earlier. "That makes things much less complicated."

"There are wards on the door which keep everyone but students from entering," Rian explains quietly as we are ushered into an atrium of highly polished white marble.

As I gaze around at the circular space, I can't help but feel a little disappointed. All of my life I have passed by the grand and imposing Academy buildings, imagining how wonderful it must be inside. The only thing remarkable about this stark white room is how bright it is despite the late hour, which is about to strike midnight. There are no paintings on the walls, no carvings of relief in the shining white marble. Even the marble itself bears no veins or markings at all. After a moment I realize how very quiet the space is, too. The sound of our footsteps and the movement of Rian and Anod's robes are completely silent. The effect is slightly dizzying, and I'm relieved when Anod opens one of twenty doors on the opposite wall and motions us through.

When the door closes behind us with an audible click, we are immediately surrounded by a corridor full of tiny, floating globes of multicolored light. They remind me of drifting, rainbow-colored snowflakes. Master Anod and Rian raise their arms out to their sides and I mimic the motion. I feel a sense of curiosity emanating from the orbs as they drift around us, changing color.

Several of them cling to the diamond tucked into the weave of my bracelet. Rian's travel bag seems to be covered in them, many are stuck to a button of his vest, and a few others are attracted to the places in his robes where I know there to be hidden pockets. When Master Anod turns to us, the entirety of his robes is covered in them. His eyes glint with amusement at Rian, and then me.

"Ah," he nods at my wrist. "It seems that we are not the only ones with secrets, eh, Mentor Rian?" The globes that cling to my diamond are pulsing a soft, friendly yellow, while Rian's are a mix of green, blue, and purple. The orbs on Master Anod continue to fade through the entire spectrum as Rian leans to me.

"They detect magical objects," he explains. "Different colors for different types of magic. Also, if we had any metal, they'd go red."

"Master Anod's robes are magical?" I whisper as Anod opens the next door and the orbs separate from us to continue drifting along their small space. "What do they do?"

"As lower Circles, it's considered rude to ask," says Rian. "But I imagine they're imbued with protective magic. That's why the orbs have trouble discerning the type."

"Right you are, Mentor, right you are." Anod beams, and we follow him through into another circular room. This one is spectacular. The walls are painted in intricately entwined runes of every color creating an effect that's dazzling.

The dark, low ceiling is dusted with sparkling white specks that remind me of the night sky. Ten alcoves are set into the wall, perfectly spaced, and the floor is a spiral of mosaics. A closer look at the tiles under our feet reveals them to be tiny squares of silver, gold, and pearl, and at the center is a disk of rough, unpolished sapphire. Within the sapphire is a glass cylinder that stands as tall as my waist. Gold coins and gold nuggets and chains fill the glass to the brim, and I estimate that such a great amount of wealth could set up a small family to live in comfort for a lifetime. Anod instructs us to stand face to face on either side of the cylinder, and Rian takes my hands.

"Don't let go," he says. "No matter what. I won't let you go, either." He squeezes my hands and I try not to panic as I realize what's about to happen. One moment we'll be standing here, and the next, we'll be thrust into the unknown. As a group of Mages in gray robes file into the room, each one settling into an alcove, I suddenly feel completely unprepared.

"I'm not ready," I whisper to him frantically. "Will Uncle be expecting us? Shouldn't we have some shields put on us in case we're attacked when we arrive? What if something goes wrong? What if there's fighting? Shouldn't we have a plan?"

Rian's hands tighten around mine as Master Anod steps into the last empty alcove and the Mages begin speaking the ancient words that will send us on our way.

"Can't do shields." Rian's eyes glint with the reflection of the gold between us. "Teleportation strips them." He raises my hand to his lips and kisses it. "And we have a plan. That plan is hold on to each other. Don't let go."

The floor seems to rise up around us in shafts of gold and silver and shimmering pearl. The sapphire at our feet begins to glow and rise and a strange sensation starts in the soles of my feet and slowly crawls upward. It tickles and itches, like an army of tiny ants crawling over me. I squeeze my eyes shut and grip Rian's hands as tightly as I can as the blue light envelops us.

We're jolted and we start to move, but I'm too disoriented to tell which direction we're going. The wind whistles painfully in my ears and slaps my face. Rian's fingers slip from mine but we catch each other and he pulls me against him and I realize that the glass cylinder has been taken. Then the wind is gone, and the light is gone, and we hit the ground hard, and there is nothing but darkness.

Chapter Sixteen

REUNION

The ants crawl over every inch of me, biting, skittering, and pinching. They're in my hair, in my nose, in my mouth. I fight to brush them off, but my arms are too heavy and won't move. I try to roll, to writhe, but my body is dead weight. Instead I lie whimpering, cloaked in darkness, paralyzed.

Slowly the sensation fades, and as I begin to feel the prick of pine needles beneath me, I remember that there were no ants. Just magic. When my arms can respond, I reach up to scratch my scalp, which still tingles from the odd sensation. In the back of my mind, as I push my fingers through my hair, I'm haunted by a feeling that something isn't right. And then I remember. Don't let go. I hold my empty hands out in front of me, but I only see darkness.

"Rian?" I whisper, pricking my ears to my surroundings. I roll with some difficulty onto my side, and the small movement makes my stomach churn. I lie still again and listen, waiting for the feeling to pass. In the distance I catch a ring of steel on steel, a booming voice. Fighting.

"Rian?" I call a little more loudly as I try to blink away the blackness.

He promised he wouldn't let go. I swore not to. That was our only plan, don't let go. Maybe he's nearby, paralyzed like I was. I fight through the queasiness and push myself to my knees and begin to frantically search around me with my hands, but all they find are more pine needles and the trunk of a tree.

In the distance the clashing fight intensifies, and I press myself against the safety of the massive trunk. My hand closes around a stick as thick as my wrist and I clutch it to my chest, waiting, listening to the distant screaming as the air grows thick with smoke. There's a battle cry that sounds comfortingly like Bryse, and then the deafening boom of some spell quiets him.

"Please, Rian," I whimper and rub my eyes, terrified that the blindness is permanent. Someone comes crashing toward me through the forest from the direction of the battle, and I hold my breath as they near, unsure whether it's friend or foe. The footsteps are light and swift, and they slide to a halt only an arm's reach from me.

"Blindness," Cort curses apparently to himself. "Can't see a damn thing. Mages. Give me a sword any day." He takes a few steps back and shouts into the woods, "Gaethon, Donal! Bryse is down! Need you due south!"

"Cort!" I call out as the footsteps retreat. They pause, and I push myself to my feet in relief, but he doesn't answer. Instead, he continues to run away from me, back to the fight, still cursing.

"He can't hear you," Rian says from beside me, causing me to jump.

"Oh, Rian! Thank you, thank you!" I fling my arms around him in the darkness.

"It's a blindness ward, really complex magic," he says as he takes my hand and guides me away from the noise. "Step through and you can't see a thing, and anyone outside can't hear you call for help."

"We're going away from the battle," I say as I pick my way through the darkness, "They need us back there! Bryse is down."

"They need a healer. He's over here." I follow him a short distance until he pulls me down. I kneel and grope the forest floor until I feel him sprawled there, unmoving.

"Brother Donal?" I ask as my fingertips graze the smooth skin on top of his head.

"He's been knocked out," Rian says as he shakes Brother Donal's shoulder. After a moment, he groans and sits up.

"Brother Donal, are you all right? It's Azi and Rian," I say, "we came to warn you, but we were too late. Bryse is down—"

"Who's there?" A familiar voice calls from a short distance away in the darkness. Brother Donal coughs beside me and Rian moves protectively closer. I feel the air shift around us several times as Rian murmurs, and I realize he's casting shield spells over us. It takes me a moment to place the new voice, but when he calls again, I'm certain I know who it is.

"Dacva," I whisper.

"Who is it? Declare yourself!" he calls, his voice shaking. Rian grips my arm, signaling for me to be quiet.

"It's Donal. Over here, boy." Rian and I hiss our disapproval, but Brother Donal pushes himself to his feet. "Where's Gaethon?" he asks as he moves away from us into the darkness.

"Over here," Dacva's footsteps crunch heavily in the underbrush as he leads Donal away. Another crash of magic booms in the distance. "Something came out of nowhere and slammed into him. Knocked him out."

"That would be me," Rian murmurs as he moves to follow them. I grip his arm as we move along in the darkness, and hear something that sounds like soft chimes, and then Uncle coughing. He speaks a quick spell and our sight is instantly restored. I blink at the shock of it, squinting into the group, all of whom are already running into the fray again. Dacva brushes past me in a blur of blue and gold, and Rian and I blink at each other in disbelief.

"Why is he in our colors?" I whisper, and Rian shakes his head with no reply to offer. The trees in the distance are silhouetted against flashes of red and orange as magical bursts thunder through the forest. Rian and I chase after the three, into the fray. "Stay close to me," he says as we crash through the underbrush and into a charred clearing. Bryse lies in a mountainous heap of burnt blue armor and Dacva and Donal stand beside him, their hands streaming a whitish glow as they administer healing. Again, Rian and I exchange glances of disbelief. Since when is Dacva a healer?

Opposite them, on the far side of the clearing, Cort's swords flash ferociously against three foes in Redemption's colors. As I charge to help them with a battle cry, I feel the cool familiarity of Rian's ice sword take shape in my hand. I raise the weapon high over my head and bring it down in a graceful arc that meets my opponent's armor with a sizzle. The pauldron at his shoulder slices clean away and he falls backward, stunned by my attack. A spell shoots over my shoulder and I watch the man's eyelids go heavy and droop closed.

"What in black stars?" Cort says under his breath. I don't have time to think as he drives the remaining two men back, both of whom are twice our size. One of them swings his axe wildly and I'm too slow to block it. It slices at my knee and I brace myself for the impact, certain of the peg-leg in my future. But it simply glances off, and the air around me shivers. The axe-wielder growls in fury and swings again, missing me by a long shot, almost as if he's attacking something he can't see.

I swing my sword, aiming for the weak spot in his armor where the arm meets the chest plate, but one of his wild swings strikes a hard blow at my sword which sends me crashing backwards into Rian. We tumble to the ground with our opponent looming over us, grimacing, his teeth blood-stained. He swings at the air above me and again he misses horribly.

It's puzzling to me that it really seems like he can't see us, even though we're sprawled on the ground right in front of him. He whirls to meet Cort, who looks a bit pale now, and the ground beneath us shudders. Just as Rian raises a hand to cast, Bryse crashes over us both, his right foot landing just a finger's breadth from crushing my hand. I look away as his sword finds its mark deep in our opponent's skull.

"Spirits in these woods," Cort spits blood as he slides his own sword from his own opponent. "I don't like it."

"Least they seemed to be on your side." Bryse claps him on the back and they turn toward the bursts of magical battle. "I'm up to six, you?"

"Bah, four. And a half. I think that one's asleep." He jabs his sword to point at our sleeping opponent.

"Rian got him," I say, pushing myself to my feet. I give a hand up to Rian, who is watching the other two curiously.

"Back into it?" asks Bryse, not bothering to acknowledge either of us.

"With pleasure," Cort grins, and the two jog off to the tree line.

"Not even a greeting?" I frown at Rian as we follow them.

"It's strange," he agrees.

Past the clearing's edge, the battle belongs to the Mages. Uncle is holding his own against Redemption's Mage, Rikstarn. They exchange endless bursts of spells: lightning, fire, ice, wind, until the trees around them are charred and iced and half blown-over.

"Leave it, Rik. We're done!" A towering man calls from the opposite side of the small clearing.

"Dar," I whisper, remembering the giant knight from my trial.

Mya's voice rises above the crash of magic with an eerie song, and Rik slowly lowers his hands, the mesmerizing effect of the music causing his eyes to glaze over.

Dar curses and crashes into the clearing, grabs the Mage under his arm, and drags him off. They disappear quickly, accompanied by their own cleric, into the darkness of the forest. A streak of red darts after them.

"Was that a fox?" I ask Rian, but he doesn't hear. He's fixated on the others. Donal, Dacva, Mya, Uncle Gaethon, Cort, and Bryse stand in a semi-circle on the edge of what is clearly their destroyed camp, looking beaten and exhausted.

Though we are just a few feet away, they don't notice us as they talk quietly together. Rian takes my hand in his and we move closer, until we're standing in front of them. Uncle looks up for a moment, but his eyes pass right through us and he turns back to Mya.

"It was an ambush," he says as Rian waves his hand in front of his eyes. "Caught Donal and I by surprise. He used blindness. I should have expected it."

"Rian, why can't they see us?" I ask, watching him circle around his mother.

"We came through it," Mya says, her eyes fixed on the point in the woods where the fox disappeared. "No worse for the wear."

"I don't know," he tells me. "MUM!" He shouts in Mya's ear. She turns her head vaguely in his direction but her full attention remains on the woods beyond.

"Speak for yourself," Bryse grunts. "I got a splitting headache. And they burned our rations. I'm starved."

"As always," Cort shoves him.

"Elliot will have something for us to eat," Mya says. "In the meantime, let's recover what we can and then try to rest. I don't think they'll come back. They've only got three left. It'd be uneven in our favor, and they won't have that."

"Cowards," Bryse grumbles, picking through a charred pack and pulling out a blackened hunk of bread.

"They'll be going to the Outlands now," Dacva says, drawing a map in the soot. "To pick up some friends. They won't be back through here. That was the plan all along. They just had to put on a good show of it, in case they had to answer to the prince later." Uncle raises a brow.

"And who do they expect to collect in the Outlands?" he asks, his tone thick with disdain.

"Anyone who's left." Dacva shrugs. I glance at Rian and we follow as the others move away from Dacva to whisper in secret.

"I don't believe anything that creature utters," Uncle hisses, "and I would advise you not to formulate any plans based on his information."

"Yes, we all know how you feel about the boy, Gaethon," Mya says gently, "but need I remind you that he's saved our lives? Yours twice?"

"I have yet to be convinced that his allegiance has changed."

"It's not enough that he's cast his weapon off and still aided us in battle?" Donal offers. "He is a fast learner. He shows real promise as a healer."

"I can't believe we're standing here listening to them discuss whether or not Dacva makes a good ally. I feel like we've stepped into some awful other realm." I gasp. "Have we, Rian? Is that why they can't see or hear us?"

"I don't know," Rian scowls. "It's all very strange." I feel a tug at my wrist and I raise my arm up to eye level to see Flit squeezing herself up out of the diamond. She stops midway, sighing with relief as her wings stream out of the stone and rise slowly up. She rests her palms on the facets and pushes down, and she's out from the waist up before she turns to me, her eyes wide.

"Azi! What are you—" she squeezes herself the rest of the way out, sliding one leg from the shimmering surface and then the other with a little grunt. "Ungh, you aren't supposed to see that. It's not very graceful. Actually it's a little embarrassing, having to squeeze out of there, but I couldn't find you otherwise. Anyway, what are you doing here?" She sneezes and rubs her nose.

"Well, we teleported," I start, "and then—"

"Wait, where's here?" Rian asks.

"Oh, stinky Mage is here, too!" She circles around him, sniffing, and sneezes again. "Not so stinky anymore though. Actually, you smell kinda nice. Like, ah..." she takes in a deep breath, "Pine. And berries. And pine berries. Or are they pine nuts? I don't like those so much.

Not very sweet. So, how did you get here? Oh! We're going to have such fun now!"

She darts around us and then flies over to Bryse, who's occupying himself by peeling the charred crust off of the loaf to get to the white inside. "Don't know how you can eat that stuff," she says to him.

"He can't hear us. None of them can," I say.

"Nope, but he can feel us! Watch!" She flies up and tickles his nose, and he reaches up and scratches it.

"Flit!" Rian says sternly. "Where's here?"

"Oh! You want to play!" She giggles. "Yes, me too. Let's go someplace that isn't so dead, though. It's not very fun here." She comes to settle on our clasped hands and starts to close her eyes.

"Wait, Flit! We don't want to go anywhere else," I say, "We came to help them. If we leave, we might not be able to find them again."

"Oh," she sighs, disappointed, and sneezes three more times. "Oh! What if we make it easy to get back to them?"

"Well, I guess they've come through the fight and don't need our warning anymore. We can go if we really need to. As long as we can get back to them again." Rian looks at me and I shrug. He's right. The whole point in coming here was to warn them. We can't do much in this state, and now we need answers. I nod to Flit, who flies to my wrist and pulls the diamond free of the bracelet, and then darts to the others.

"Who should get it?" she asks, pausing at Uncle. She wrinkles her nose and shakes her head fervently, then skirts to Mya who stands beside him, still talking. "This is your mum, right, Rian? Oh, she's so pretty. Look at how red her hair is, almost as red as mine!" She tips her head to the side and holds her red ponytail up against Mya's spikes.

"Yes, very red. Can you please get on with it?" Rian says with annoyance and I squeeze his hand. I must be getting used to her. I find myself trying not to laugh as she pulls open a small pouch at Mya's belt and slips the diamond inside.

"It'll be safe in there, okay? She probably won't even notice it. Then we can find her. Now can we please go? The smoke is filling up my brain." She sneezes again as I glance at Rian. He shrugs, and we nod our assent. Flit takes our hands, still sneezing, and in a blink we find ourselves slipping away once again.

The grotto where we appear is more beautiful than any place I have ever been. A soft green bank of moss sparkles beside a pool of crystal clear water, just large enough that I could sit in it with little room for anyone else. The water reflects the moon and the stars in ripples caused by a sparkling waterfall on the opposite bank. The stone face there is made up almost completely of mica, which shimmers and shifts in the moonlight.

Willow-like trees dip their colorful wispy fronds into the water, grazing its surface. Fraying ribbons dangle from the branches, some tied with trinkets so that when the breeze blows, it creates a soft tinkling sound. Flit settles onto the moss and Rian and I duck beneath the tree branches to join her.

"This is my place," she says. "Do you like it?" She dips her fingers into the water and a swirl of colorful fish with graceful trailing fins swims up to greet her.

"You can teleport, just like that?" Rian asks. "No payment? No ceremony? No rules?"

Flit sighs and rolls her eyes in my direction. "Azi, we'll have to teach him to play."

"I'm not playing any game. I want to know what's going on." He pulls at a frond of leaves, inspecting it. I rest a hand on his arm.

"Let me, Rian." I turn to Flit. "I like your place very much, Flit. It's beautiful. I've never seen anything like it." I nudge Rian. "Now you can ask." He lets go of the branch and presses his fingers to his forehead, thinking.

"So serious," Flit whispers to me. "Typical."

"When we arrived in the forest," Rian starts slowly, "our friends couldn't see or hear us. You said it was because we were 'here' with you. Where did you mean when you said that?"

"Ooh he's good, Azi." She pulls off her tiny boots and digs her bare feet into the carpet of moss with a satisfied smile. "We were in the Half-Realm. The In-between. Not really here or there. But also in both places at once. Here, and there. In between realms. Do you see?"

"Not really," Rian sighs. "What does it mean? How did we get there? How do we get back?" Flit scowls and looks at me, gesturing to Rian in annoyance.

"One question at a time," I say. Rian gives me a look of disbelief.

"I'm sorry! Those are the rules. You have to choose one. You ask a question, and then Flit asks. The game is over when one of you can't answer."

"Alright." Rian closes his eyes and takes a deep breath. "I'll start at the beginning. How did it happen?"

"Oh," Flit sighs. "I was hoping you wouldn't ask that so soon. I don't want the game to end yet, but I don't have the answer. Mage type teleporting is so different from what we fairies do. Too fussy, too many ingredients and words. Lots of things can go wrong. I expect that's why it's done so rarely.

"Maybe it was the diamond. Or some other spell interfered. I don't really understand why you all have to complicate things so much. Here, we just think about who we want to see or where we want to go and poof! There we are! I'm hungry. Are you hungry?"

She pushes off from the moss, leaving Rian and I alone at the edge of the pool. He stares at the rippling water, and I know his thoughts are racing, formulating his next question. Flit comes back bearing three hollowed out acorns filled with a pink liquid. She passes one to Rian and one to me, and then settles back onto the moss.

"No, thank you. I'm not hungry," Rian says, tipping the acorn to inspect its contents. "How do we restore ourselves and get back to our realm?"

"I don't know that, either. You aren't supposed to be here, really. No people have ever been, as far as the stories tell. I can't say it isn't allowed, though. If it wasn't allowed, you couldn't have done it." Flit's answer sends my thoughts spiraling.

I set my emptied acorn on the moss and draw my knees up to my chest to rest my forehead on them. It's all too much to take in. Ever since the King's Quest was declared, I feel as if my life has been spiraling out of control, and just when we arrive at a solution to one problem, we're presented with another. I'm not sure how much more of it I can take. Rian slides an arm around my shoulders, but it does little to comfort me.

"It's not all bad, Azi," Flit says. "Can't you imagine the possibilities?"

"Not supposed to be here," Rian murmurs. "Flit, are we in Kythshire?"

"Answer mine first!" She says, slurping at her acorn.

"Can't I imagine the possibilities?" Rian repeats her question. "I thought it was rhetorical. Alright. No. No, I can't imagine the possibilities because really I have no idea what you're talking about. Now, are we in Kythshire?"

"Yep! Do you like it?"

"It's very nice. But, does that mean we crossed the border?"

"Well, you did and you didn't..." As Flit rambles on, I don't hear her. My heart starts to race. We've crossed the border to Kythshire. My mother is here. I can break the curse, I can take her place. I can send her home to my father. They can be restored. They can be happy. I remember what Flit said about just thinking of who we want to see and where we want to go and I concentrate as hard as I can.

"Mum. Lisabella." I whisper, and I find myself suddenly elsewhere. Rian remains beside me with his arms around me, and we sit together in a field of moon-washed wheat that stretches off into the black, craggy mountains on one side and the inviting forest on the other.

I push myself to my feet and stand on my toes in order to see over the tall grasses. I see her standing there, her armor glinting silvery-blue in the moonlight, sword in hand, eyes scanning the horizon.

"Mum!" I cry, and take off toward her, leaving Rian behind.

Chapter Seventeen

FAITH

Rian shouts after me and I can hear Flit calling my name, too, but I don't stop. The tall fronds of wheat whip my face. I crash through it to my mother. She's so close now, so close. I see her armor flash as I reach the edge of the wheat. The blue glow of her sword is right there. Two more steps and I'll be in her arms. I burst forth from the wheat and she swings with a ferocious battle cry, barely missing me as I dive to the side to dodge the blow.

"No!" Flit shouts as she darts from behind me. My mother lowers her sword and shakes her head.

"That's a dangerous game, Flit," she warns. "What are you doing all the way out here? How is my Azi?" The wheat rustles behind me and my mother gestures to the fairy and readies her sword. "Get behind me. They're coming through one after another tonight." Flit glances to the wheat and darts in front of my mother, raising her hands.

"No, no, no! It isn't a cyclone! It's Rian!" she cries as the wheat parts beside me and Rian appears in the clearing. Mum blinks at the space where the wheat settles again and lowers her sword.

"What do you mean, Flit?" she asks, stepping forward. Her eyes narrow as she squints past Rian, who steps closer to me.

"Oh," he breathes. "She can't see us, either."

"Could you cast a Revealer?" I ask. "Like you did on Flit when she first showed up in my room?"

"Rian and Azi!" Flit answers my mother and giggles as she comes to perch on my shoulder. "They're here, in the Half-Realm." Mum edges closer. She reaches out and grazes her gloved hand to just below where Flit is perched, and touches my arm. Her eyes glint with excitement and she pulls her glove off and reaches again. "Go on, Azi.

171

Give her a hug." I step forward and throw my arms around my mother, and feel her embrace tighten around me. She reaches up and strokes my hair and presses her cheek to mine, mixing our tears together. When she looks down at me, she grins, and I know that she can see me now as clearly as I can see her.

"Oh, my sweeting," she whispers, and she hugs me again and kisses the top of my head. "I've missed you, I've been so worried."

"Mum," is all I can manage to say as I cling to her, crying. I didn't realize how much I truly needed to see her until this moment. Now that she's here, I feel the weight of everything that's been on my shoulders melt away. The relief of it is so sudden and so glorious that I can't stop myself from sobbing in her arms.

"You didn't have to worry," says Flit, who is now perched on top of my head. "I was doing a good job keeping you informed, wasn't I? I was looking out for her."

"Yes, you were, Flit," Mum sniffs. "Thank you." She keeps one arm around me and stretches the other one out. "Where's Rian?" she asks. He steps forward within her reach and the three of us embrace, and I don't even care that he's nearly suffocating me against the hard steel of her plate armor. When we finally pull away, she looks him over. Her eyes find the mark on his jaw and she frowns.

Behind us, the thunder rumbles and I turn in time to see a flash of lightning. My mother gives me one more squeeze before stepping around us both and drawing her sword. "Get to the tree line," she says, her eyes fixed on the horizon. Flit squeaks and races to the forest in a rainbow-colored blur. Rian and I exchange glances and follow after as fast as we can. We skid to a stop as we cross onto the mossy forest floor and turn to watch.

The cyclone parts the wheat, taller and more terrifying than it ever was in my dreams. It dwarfs my mother, who stands with her sword ready as her golden hair whips around her face. Flit whimpers behind me, clinging to my neck. Rian grips my hand.

"What is that?" he whispers as my mother swings her sword. It slices the cyclone midway through, but not completely. She swings again as black tendrils stretch out from the dark, swirling form, licking at her arms.

"We call them coil cyclones, or shadow twisters. If we get too close, they'll swallow us up," Flit says, cowering behind me. "They happen when the Wellspring is sapped too quickly. When you Mages do too much, too fast, and the coils appear." She points to the Mage Mark on his neck. Rian reaches up to cover it with his hand, looking guilty. "Then the lightning flashes over the Crag, and the cyclones come swirling. In the dark days, they swallowed nearly everything and everyone up, until there was almost nothing anywhere. It's been better for a few generations, but lately they're getting bigger and bigger, and harder to destroy. That's why we were so glad when Lisabella crossed over."

"Funny how they don't teach us about those at the Academy..." He frowns, dropping his hand. "I mean, we know they exist, but I had no idea they were directly caused by our carelessness..." Mum's sword meets the black twister again and this time it slices it in two, eradicating it. She kneels down and combs through the grass with her hands, but unlike in my dreams, there are no fairies to retrieve.

"It was empty." I say as my mother comes to my side. We settle on the edge of the forest, next to the trunk of a great pine tree. In the quiet I can hear the sound of merry-making coming from the depths of the woods and I remember the dancing. It tugs at my heart and makes me want to run to it. I look over at Rian, whose head is turned in that direction. He hears it, too.

"Most are," she says quietly. "The fae rarely come out this far anymore. They're aware of the danger, and now that I'm here, they don't need to risk themselves to defend the woods. And the ones on the Crag are clever enough to avoid them." Her brow knits together as she gazes off at the mountain. "It's been bad tonight, the worst night since I arrived. Something's going on out there. Do you see?" She points into the distance.

Just beyond the line of golden treasure I can make out a blemish in the black face of the mountain. Something strange, that I've never noticed before. I can't quite describe it.

"What is it?" I whisper, leaning into Rian. He shakes his head. Flit darts away from us to chase playfully after a passing firefly.

"Dark magic," Rian scowls. Another cyclone comes, and Mum charges into the wheat again. Lightning strikes the Crag and the thunder is so loud it shakes the ground beneath our feet.

"Is anything going on in Cerion?" Mum asks when she comes back. "Anything out of the ordinary?"

"Sarabel's birthday." I say, thinking of all of the frivolous magic used to decorate the party. I turn to Rian. "Could that have caused it?"

"You didn't perform, did you Rian?" Mum asks, eyeing his Mark again.

"No," he replies. "But there were others who did. I tried to argue against it, but it was difficult, being silenced and all. Viala was very convincing. She wanted it to be a big show."

"Viala," Mum sighs. "I ought to have known. Gaethon has been suspicious of her for some time. He shouldn't have joined them to search for me. He needs to be home, watching things there. Flit has been keeping me informed, but it's difficult to piece things together. I thought there might be a danger and I tried to send word, but it's difficult to judge things here. By the time I realized the threat, the guild was already on its way here. Even then, for me it was just a suspicion. I only knew for certain that she was plotting tonight, when Flit came to tell me what you saw in the palace, Azi." I turn to Flit.

"So that's where you disappeared to," I say. She nods and floats down to sit on the moss between Mum and me. "His Majesty wants me to quietly put a stop to it. He knows they're up to something dark, and he asked me to stop them. I don't understand why he'd ask me, of all people. I don't know how to even begin..." I trail off as Rian stares at me, wide-eyed.

"Is that what he was talking to you about while you were dancing?" he asks. I nod.

"You need to have more faith in yourself, Azi," Mum says. "If His Majesty asked for your help, then he must believe it's within your power."

"That's what he said, too," I sigh. "But how can I stop this?" I look at her. "Do you know about Da? What happened when he crossed the border?" She nods and her eyes fill with sadness as they look away toward the Shadow Crag.

"I tried to tell him to let me go," Mum says. "but he refused. He didn't believe I'd ever return to him. He fought it, even though we discussed it before we arrived. I tried to warn him." She reaches up and pinches the bridge of her nose. "I never meant for him to get hurt."

"What happened?" I think back to what Flit told me about my father crossing the border. "Flit told me that the guardian forced him to leave."

"The guardian of the East," Mum nods. "It did, and I tried to explain to it that he didn't mean any harm. But the guardians take their duties to protect the borders very seriously. They're strong, relentless. In some ways, single-minded." Mum shakes her head as Flit starts to protest. "I'm sorry Flit, but it's true. Their one obligation is to keep everyone out. They don't listen to explanations. If you cross with ill intent, if you're able to without an invitation, you're punished. Your life is forfeit," she says, her voice growing thick with anguish. "And your father was so distraught when he followed me through, it was an easy mistake for the guardian to think he meant to force his way. I should have stopped him before he crossed. I could have prevented him from being hurt." I watch her swallow and turn away. Flit hovers up to her shoulder and strokes her cheek.

"I told you he's all healed up now except for his mind." Flit says. "And that'll come after a while. You can't even see a bruise anymore." My mother shakes her head in her grief, and Flit turns to me, scowling. "Why'd you have to go and bring up your father? She's been so sad, and she was finally just starting to forget. Now she'll be crying all the time again." I slide over to my mother and hold her, and she tips her head to rest against my arm.

"I won't ever forget, Flit." She sniffs. "I should have made him stay away. I watched the guardian fling him back across the border. I tried to explain but it wouldn't listen to me." She's shaking with tears now, her eyes squeezed shut. "By then it was too late, the damage was done. I looked across and your father was being carted off by Elliot and Donal. I could see them, but they couldn't see me. I knew he was safe in their hands, and I knew that I had to go on and complete the quest, but when I presented the amulet, I was told it was a forgery. Then they told me how bad the cyclones were getting here, and how much they needed me here in the North, and I couldn't ignore it. I agreed to help. A part of me had known all along that I would end up having to stay as a Protector."

"Your name was on the prince's list. Mine was, too. He was counting you as a treasure to return."

"It wouldn't have worked anyway, whether it was me or the necklace. His intentions aren't pure of heart." Mum says.

"Why didn't you tell me?" I ask. "You knew we were both destined for this place but you kept the stories from me."

"I hoped to spare you," Mum says. "Hoped I could come and complete the quest and return home, and keep you from all of it. I didn't want you to feel pressured. I didn't want to ever lose you to this place." she sighs. I think about the afternoon of the quest announcement. How quiet she was at the guild's table. How apologetic her eyes were.

"You made sure my name wasn't on the list, didn't you? You knew it would be here in Kythshire and you had Uncle or someone get me stricken from it." Fresh tears prick my eyes and I push them away in irritation.

"I'm sorry," she whispers. "It was selfish of me. I wasn't ready for you to face this. If either of us was going to have to stay, I wanted it to be me. You're so young, with so much of your life still ahead of you. It wasn't fair to shove you into this fate. I didn't want it forced on you." I don't even know what to say. I simply shake my head. Rian's hand on my shoulder does little to comfort me and I snap my head toward him.

"And you," I turn to Rian, my temper rising, "you knew, too. You told Anod that Viala was plotting to get rid of the Protectors. How long have you known? How could you keep this from me?"

"Don't be angry with Rian," my mother says softly. "He hasn't known for long, have you Rian?"

"I only discovered it when I was researching about the curse, following Viala's trails," he says. "I've known about the Wellspring and the legend of the Protectors. That's apprentice-level privilege. But it's forbidden to talk about it, and I didn't suspect that it was your family until after my trial. And even then, I didn't want to believe it. I was silenced too, remember? But then when you told me at the ball that you knew about the Wellspring, I couldn't ignore it anymore. Your dreams, Flit appearing to you, I knew it more than just a coincidence."

"You knew, too, Flit. You knew from the beginning."

"You didn't ask..." Flit whispers, dipping behind my mother's shoulder at my fury.

"I didn't ask?" I shout. "How could I ask when I didn't know anything about it?" I don't fight the anger now. They need to be blamed. I want them to feel how I've been suffering. I would never keep so many secrets and lies from either of them, and they couldn't show me the same courtesy. I push myself to my feet as the lightning strikes the mountain.

"Well," Flit comes to stand on my mother's shoulder, hands on hips, her tiny voice squeaking over the rumble of thunder. "How can you be mad at me for not answering a question you didn't even ask?" I have no reply for her. My thoughts are a jumbled mess of hurt and rage. I watch the wheat part in the distance, watch the cyclone come, and think of how good it would feel to release my fury on it. I need to take these feelings out on something.

"I wish I had my sword," I whisper to myself, and it's suddenly there in my hand. I grip the hilt and I'm shocked when nothing happens. No screaming, no pain, no darkness. Somehow, the curse has lifted. The thought does little to calm my anger. Instead, the feel of the cool, smooth leather wrapped around the familiar handle bolsters me. I charge into the wheat with a deafening battle cry, ready to meet the terror-filled swirling shadow.

"Azi, no!" Mum cries out, and I hear her crashing in behind me, but I don't slow my pace. The cyclone is just ahead of me. The black tendrils reach out hungrily between the golden fronds. It licks at me with a searing heat, grabbing at the fabric of my sleeve, wrapping around my arm painfully. My rage builds as I try to pull it free and swing my sword, but another tendril stretches out and grasps my other wrist. Along with the pain I'm consumed by a sensation of terror. The feeling isn't just my own, it's deeper. The agony of every creature ever harmed by the cyclones consumes me, embedded in the dark tendrils that bind me. I scream as it pulls me into the black, swirling abyss. I begin to spin inside of it, seeing flashes of lightning, hearing thunder and screaming, feeling torture. The wheat streaks past me in swirls of gold, and I catch a flash of blue and silver, my mother. I feel her calm aura swirl into the darkness around me as her sword arcs sideways. It finds its mark and the darkness falls away, and I tumble into the soft golden grass.

At first I can't move. I stare up into the sky, which is slowly brightening in subtle washes of a lavender and pink sunrise. Mum moves impossibly slowly as she sheaths her sword to her back and bends to lift me. It takes what feels like a full day for her to carry me back to the edge of the forest. Everything is quiet around me. I can't feel myself. I imagine that a part of me was left inside the cyclone, and I struggle to get away from her and retrieve it. It stole my rage, it stole my power. I wriggle desperately, but her arms are strong. She doesn't care that I'm pleading. She lays me down and holds me there. I'm vaguely aware of Rian beside me. He's talking, but I don't know what he's saying. A pink glow settles over me and my eyes start to close. Though I try hard to fight it, sleep takes me.

When I wake, I find myself nestled in the sparkling roots of a great white birch. Far above me, golden sunlight dapples through the swaying green leaves of the canopy. Now and then, a group of colored orbs drifts by. Sometimes, they pause over us and I hear a sound like a chime or a giggle, and see a flutter of a wing, and then they go along on their way again.

Rian strokes my damp hair away from my face and Flit hovers over me looking slightly frightened. Just beyond them, my mother leans against another birch and keeps an ear cocked to the distance as her healing calm pulses around us.

"Back again," she whispers with relief, searching my eyes. I realize they're all watching me with trepidation, as if they're waiting for some onslaught, and I remember my rage with embarrassment.

"I'm sorry," I say softly. "I don't know what came over me..." part of me feels like I had every right to be angry with them, but I push it away. So they kept secrets. They were only doing what they felt was right at the time. I'm ashamed of myself for losing my temper so quickly and acting so irrationally. One of the orbs dips low enough to rest on a root beside me. I turn my head to focus on it but it darts away, leaving behind a delicious looking, juicy pink berry. I watch it float up again and join with another one, and they giggle and fly away together.

"Are they fairies?" I ask, reaching for the berry. I scoot up to sit against the tree trunk and inspect the plump fruit. My mouth waters.

"Yep!" Flit says.

"Is it safe to eat?" I ask, suddenly realizing how hungry I am.

"Sure it is! They know you're here to help us. They've been

bringing you presents all morning." She gestures to the carpet of grass surrounding the roots and I gaze in wonder. They're piled with a colorful assortment of everything from berries to fruits to garlands of flowers. My mother smiles.

"I had the same reception, once things settled down," she says. "They really are lovely little people." I pop the berry into my mouth. It's so sweet and delicious that I find myself looking around for another in the scatter of presents. I push myself to my feet and tiptoe around the grass, picking them up as I go. With each bite I feel a little more of my troubles disappear, and my spirits lift. Once my belly is full, I feel like I can accomplish anything. I drop down next to Rian with a grin and offer him a handful. He accepts and he and my mother feast on them, too. By the time we're finished, we're all laughing together, and all of the things that have been troubling me feel as distant as Cerion itself.

"Now everyone's happy, right?" Flit grins, her teeth stained disturbingly pink from the juices. "No more shouting, no more crying."

"For now," Rian says, laughing softly. "But it's obvious Kythshire has an effect on us. I was ready to blast you with a wind gust and throw you against a tree before you ran off, Azi." His smile fades a bit as he reaches out to a passing orb. "As amazing as it is, we don't belong here."

"It does take a great deal of self-control to keep it from affecting you," Mum says. "Even with my calming meditation I find my thoughts slipping irrationally more often than I'd like. It's as if the very air makes you drunk with emotion." I realize that she's right. Even with my untrained senses, I can feel the magic thick around me here. Just now, I was so easily amused by our beautiful surroundings, and at the edge of the forest I was so quick to anger. I remember wishing for my sword, feeling it in my hands. I sit back on my heels and look around the little clearing for it, but it isn't here.

"What are you searching for?" Rian asks, following my eyes to the grass.

"My sword," I say. "I had it in the field, before the cyclone swallowed me." He and my mother exchange a worried glance.

"Azi, you were unarmed." Mum says softly. "You just charged out there like..." she trails off, shaking her head.

"Like you were offering yourself to it." Rian watches me with concern. "You can't wield a sword, remember?" My heart sinks. I remember it so clearly, the feel of the sword in my hand, the weight of it as I swung it, the tendrils catching my arms. I try to look at it differently, to imagine that I was empty handed, but I can't.

"But I did," I whisper, gazing at the green grass. "I was so relieved," I say. "I thought the curse was broken." I'm suddenly overwhelmed with sadness but then I remember what my mother said about this place. I focus on her pulsing calm, and I push it away.

"Let's play!" says Flit suddenly, startling me.

"Oh great," Rian groans and rolls his eyes. Mum chuckles.

"Okay, you go first, Flit." I say as I lean back against the trunk of the tree comfortably. Rian settles in beside me. I'm beginning to learn that when Flit asks to play, it usually means she has something she wants to tell me.

"Well," she starts as she comes to perch on the toe of my boot. "You wished for a sword, and then you believed you got one, and then you believed you used it, and you believed you weren't cursed anymore. So how come you changed your mind when these two disagreed with you?" I look from her, to Rian, to my mother, thinking.

"I don't know, I just...I trust them. I believe them. Why shouldn't I?"

"Because you need to believe in yourself, first. Think about it. That will get you into trouble here." She shakes her head, sending her multicolored ponytails swaying. "You believe in them more than you believe your own eyes and your own hands?" she asks.

I look down at my hands and then over to my mother. My eyes trail to the sword at her back and I flex my fingers. It seemed so real.

"What are you saying, Flit?" Rian narrows his eyes. "That Azi wished for a sword and got it, and Lisabella and I are both lying about it?"

"Uh-uh," Flit shakes her head and wiggles her finger. "It's Azi's turn to answer." Rian rolls his eyes.

"I don't know what I believe now," I say. "It's all so confusing. Is the curse broken, or not?"

"It is," Flit shrugs, "or it isn't. Here in Kythshire, it's all about what's up here." She flies up and points a tiny finger to my forehead.

180

"And there." She points a little lower, to my heart. "You all say it's confusing here, that this world has some effect on you. But all Kythshire does is show you what's truly in your heart. You can have whatever you want and do whatever you desire here. Sure, you have to be careful. Your choices still affect everyone around you. If your heart is kind, you don't have to worry about it so much. But if you are a cruel person, you can cause a lot of destruction. If you're just trying to help, though, and you ask for a sword, then you should be able to use it, right?" I think over her words as I watch a glowing pink orb drift by.

"Right..." I say, beginning to understand. "You're saying that I lifted the curse myself, just by wishing for the sword so I could battle the cyclone. But then why didn't Rian and Mum see that I had it?"

"Because they still believed you couldn't do it. Maybe they didn't hear your wish, or maybe they were too distracted by your yelling."

"Wait a moment," Rian interrupts again. "You're saying that we can just wish for something, anything, and we'll just get it? But others can't see it unless they believe it, too?" he shakes his head. "That doesn't make any sense. You either have something or you don't have it."

"Just like faith." She sticks out her tongue at him. "You either have it or you don't. Whether or not it makes sense is entirely up to you, Mage. I'm just telling you how it works." She turns to me. "Rian ruined the game by interrupting. I win!" I shake my head, speechless, but I think I understand. I push myself to my feet and cross to Mum.

"Can I borrow your sword?" I ask her. She looks at me for a moment and pulls the weapon from its sheath, offering it to me. Its blue glow illuminates my hands as I close them around the hilt. I feel a rush of peace as I swing it slowly between us. My heart swells and laughter bubbles in my chest as I turn to Rian to show him. His smile seems forced, but I don't dwell on it. Instead I practice a long combination of thrusts and blocks and slashes, so relieved by how easily it comes back to me that I barely notice Rian get to his feet and walk away.

"Azi,' Mum says quietly after a while, resting a hand on my shoulder. She holds her other one out for the sword and I return it to her a little reluctantly. "I have to get back to the field," she smiles. "You have work to do, too." She nods off into the forest and I realize that Rian has wandered out of sight. I find myself torn between the two of them for a moment, and I vaguely remember that I came here to do something important. Bits of my conversation with Flit and Twig at the palace drift into my memory. They seem like a dream now, so far away.

"I was coming to take your place," I say, remembering. "Rian and I were going to warn the guild of the attack, and then I was going to find a way to get through the border to relieve you. So you could go home to Da." She steps closer to me and takes my face gently in her hands. Her blue eyes mirror my own, sparkling with tears, and her smile is filled with such love that I feel it like a cloak around my shoulders, soft and warm. She doesn't say a word, but when she embraces me, I'm reminded of her carrying me out of the wheat.

In my mind I see her standing vigil at the edge of the forest, her sword glowing blue. The cyclones come one after another carrying terror within them, and each is sliced in two by her blade. I remember the dream I had the first time I saw them, when I was the size of a fae and she turned to look at me and she was me. The image is clear in my mind, but I realize it was never me. It was always her. Her peace pulses around her steadily, calming her, keeping her head level. She's more suited to that duty than I am.

"Could you really stay here, simply battling the dark cyclones, knowing what's causing them, and knowing that there is a larger threat out there? Could you keep your head, knowing who might be risking their lives to the forces at play? We all have our places. Your part in this is much bigger than mine," she whispers. "Believe in yourself. Trust Flit. The fairies are difficult to understand at times, but they are kindhearted, and they need you."

She leans back and searches my eyes again, and I force a smile through my own tears. My heart knows that what she's saying is true, but still, I don't want to leave her here. As though she can read my thoughts, she tips her forehead to mine. "It's easy enough to find me," she says. "Just think of me, like you did before. As long as we're both in Kythshire, you'll find me. For now, Rian needs you, and the fairies, they need you."

"Okay," I manage, brushing my tears away. I try to do as she says, to believe in myself, but right now all I want is to stay here with her, washed in her peace, and let everything else fade away. I tighten my embrace, and I'm so reluctant to let go that my mother has to finally pull herself away from me.

"I love you, Azi," she says. "I'm proud of you." She kisses my cheek and smiles again, and then she closes her eyes, and she's gone. With the sudden absence of her calming pulse comes a rush of sorrow so powerful that my knees go weak.

"She didn't even let me say goodbye," I croak. I start to drop down into the grass but a tiny finger under my chin stops me. Flit's touch sends a tingle through me all the way to my toes. The strength in my knees returns and my eyes are dazzled by the prisms of her wings as the fairy flutters up to my eye-level.

"Because it isn't goodbye, not really." Her smile is contagious, and despite my tears, I smile back. "That's better," she says. "Let's go find Rian. Then, I have someone you need to meet."

Chapter Eighteen

THE BARGAIN

As Flit and I move deeper into the forest in search of Rian, I can't help but be amazed by its strange beauty. Giant mushrooms of every shape and color sprinkle the forest floor. The trees are adorned with fluffy blossoms of every color. The morning dew sparkles in the golden sunlight that streams through the canopy. Flit glides along beside me, unusually quiet. My boots and trousers grow soaked with dew as I scan the grass for Rian's path, but there's no sign of anyone passing this way. Just when I begin to feel slightly panicked that I might not be able to find him in this vast forest, I realize I've been going about it the wrong way.

"Why didn't you say anything?" I ask Flit, laughing.

"I wanted to see how long it'd take you to figure it out! Go on, then." She perches on my shoulder as I close my eyes and think of Rian.

The ground shifts beneath us and falls away, and then I feel Rian's arms catch me. His laughter is drowned out by the rushing wind as we soar high above Kythshire. I cling to him and squeeze my eyes shut as we rise. The height invokes memories of Dacva and his gang dangling me over the cliff wall, and as we climb even higher I try hard not to imagine the sickening thud my body would make or the crack of my bones if I was to plummet to the ground so far below us.

"Isn't it beautiful?" he asks, oblivious to the chatter of my teeth. I'm not sure whether I'm shaking from the chill wind or my own terror, but either way squeezing him tighter and burying my head into his chest seems to help.

"Where is it, Flit? I want to see..." Rian swoops even higher.

"You can't," Flit cries from somewhere beside us, "you shouldn't!"

"Is that the ocean to the west?" Oblivious to her protests, Rian speeds our pace.

"It's the ocean, watch out for the Guardian!" I turn my head and peek for just long enough to see the torso of an enormous man forming from the sands of the beach. It rises up, watching us, and Rian laughs as we swoop past.

"Amazing!" he cries.

"Please, Rian," I'm ashamed by the pathetic whimper in my plea as I close my eyes again. My heart is racing so fast that I fear I might suffer an attack. I need to get down.

"Look, Azi, your favorite." The grass brushes my feet as we speed along, and behind us we leave a trail of bright yellow roses in our wake. "Or would you rather pink?" As he says the words, the roses we leave change to pink. "It has to be close, I can feel it." He soars back into the sky and I can't hold back my sob as I press my face against him again.

"Rian, please listen!" Flit cries as our speed increases so that my skin feels as though it might be torn from my bones.

"There," he whispers with awe, and we skid to a stop so quickly that my stomach lurches. I drop to my knees in the moss, immensely grateful to be back on the ground. As my fingers push into the spongy green I look out over the vast, quiet, perfectly round pool of glittering gold. The dazzling sparkle of the surface lures me. I have to touch it. Distantly I'm aware of Flit's protests, but I don't care. This is power. True power. With it I could have anything. Do anything. Rule anyone. I come to the very edge, reach my hand out, and then I feel Flit's soft touch on my cheek and suddenly I'm sprawling away.

I land hard on the dewy grass of the forest. Above me the multi-colored tree puffs sway wistfully in the breeze as Flit's stern scolding brings me back to my senses.

"Reckless Mage! You need to listen! It's forbidden to go there, it's too much for you! And poor Azi, you scared her nearly to death and you didn't even care!" I push myself up and blink at Rian beside me, who seems to be going through the same awakening.

Immediately, he summons a journal and writing stick and begins to write feverishly, recording everything he's seen, oblivious to Flit's scolding. Slowly, I push my hand between his and the book.

"Rian, you can't," I whisper. "No one can know." He pauses and looks down at the notes and his face goes pale.

"You're right," he says, crestfallen, "What was I thinking?" He grasps my hand and pulls me into his arms.

"I'm so sorry," he whispers into my hair, "I didn't mean to scare you. I was drunk with it, all of it. I never should have..." His voice trails off weakly and he shakes his head. "We can't stay here," he says as he pushes himself to his feet. "I can feel myself slipping all the time, Azi. I can do anything here. Anything at all. No incantations, no restrictions. It's such a rush, it makes me feel amazing, like... like I could rule it all." He pauses. "We have to leave."

"Wait a moment," Flit says, surprised, "You mean to tell me that you want to leave even after you've seen the Wellspring because there's too much magic?"

"Right," Rian pulls me to my feet and kisses the crown of my head, "I know it sounds mad, but I know I'm not supposed to be here. When I let myself think about the power, really think about it, I start to spiral out of control. Think about it, Azi. Once you realize that you can have everything you want, forever, then what?"

"Isn't that everyone's dream?" I ask, still somewhat dazed, "To have what they want? To be happy?"

"If you could stay here," he asks, "stay forever, and always have everything your heart desires, what would you do then?" I think of the way the Wellspring compelled me, how it made me feel.

"I don't know. I'm afraid it would change me. And even if it didn't, I'd at least want to share it. With you, with my family, with the guild." I say, "I wouldn't want to be alone."

"And then," he says, "They'd have their hearts' desires, too, and they'd want to share. And then the people they bring would want the same. Eventually, one of them would let it get to them. One of them would spiral. At the very least, it wouldn't be able to sustain us all. Everything has a balance. Our being here upsets it too much." He pulls me close and gazes into my eyes, and the Wellspring's draw becomes a distant memory. I know in my heart that all I really need is him.

"He's right!" Flit claps, startling us both. "You're both right! Oh, I'm so proud of you both, I really didn't think you'd get it! And now, now, you're finally ready to meet them."

"Oh?" I say, reluctantly tearing my eyes from Rian's, "Who are we meeting?"

"The Ring," Flit says, her eyes wide, "but first, we have to do something about this." She points to the two of us and taps her lips thoughtfully.

"The Ring?" Rian asks as Flit circles around us, turning her head this way and that as though measuring us up.

"Really, you need to practice the game if you're going to meet them. I never win when I play against them. You two have no hope at all. You can't even get the order right. You ask a question, I answer. I ask a question, and then you answer. Then you, then me. Then you, then me."

"I swear..." Rian murmurs, rubbing his forehead as I rest a reassuring hand on his shoulder.

"You go first, Flit," I offer, but she shakes her head.

"Nope, I don't want to right now. Come with me." She grabs a handful of each of our shirts, and we pop into her grotto again.

"A little warning next time?" Rian says, ankle-deep in the grotto's pool.

"I said come with me. That was your warning." she turns away from him to give me a secret, mischievous grin and I shake my head, trying hard not to laugh. As Rian trudges up out of the water, I wonder whether Flit will ever tire of tormenting him. I suppose after what he just put us through, he deserves it a little bit.

"As I was saying, before we go," she tips her head at us as Rian sweeps his hand across his robes to dry them, "we need to do something about you both. First, smaller." She nods at us and we begin to shrink.

"No way," Rian says midway to her size. "Taller." he stretches back up to his own height again. "You, too, Azi," and the words have barely left his mouth before I'm back to my own height, too. "Tell us why, first." Rian crosses his arms as I blink my eyes rapidly, trying to clear the odd lightheaded feeling that came along with the transformation.

"I'm taking you to meet the Ring. They're a little bossy, but it's okay, because they're supposed to be. But you're too big to get in, and they'd send you away if you tried to because you might step on someone. So you have to be small like, me. It's all right though, I'd probably get into trouble bringing someone like you in, anyway, especially if they found out what you just tried to do. On second thought, you stay here. I'll just take Azi." She points at me and down I go again, shrinking toward the moss. I look up at Rian and feel a little dizzy at his enormity.

"I'm not going without Rian," I say.

"I'm really sorry, Flit," Rian says sincerely, "Honestly, I am."

"Oh, fine, he can come," says Flit. "Shrink yourself, then, Mage." If it was odd to see Rian so much larger, it's even stranger being eye to eye with Flit. The light that scatters from her wings is much more blinding at this scale, making me squint. Her many-colored ponytails are impossibly brilliant, and from this close up I can see that each strand of her hair shimmers with a light of its own. She stops in front of me and I blink rapidly.

"Could you be a little less...bright?" Rian says, shielding his eyes.

"What?" she scowls. "Oh, right. Sorry, I was thinking." Her glow dims a little as she chews her lip. "Azi, you can't go in that, it's not very fine." She points at the plain blue tunic and brown trousers which I chose for comfort and utility.

"Oh," I say, thinking about the similar outfit in my bag. "Does it really make a difference what I wear?"

"Well, would you go to the palace dressed in that?" She wrinkles her nose.

"If she had something urgent to tend to she would," Rian says defensively, "And they wouldn't really care, either."

"Rian..." I whisper.

"It's okay, I've learned to mostly tune him out," Flit says matter-of-factly as she looks me up and down again. "Just think of who you are and how you want to look, and then make an outfit." She looks up at the sky, "And hurry. It's almost noon. They'll be starting soon." I think of Flit's bright ribbon skirt that reminds me of a bright prism, and Twig and his brown and green leafy outfit that looks like he walked out of the bark of a tree. It's harder than it seems, trying to imagine how I might dress to show who I am. I close my eyes and think about my mother and father, and the guild hall, and the castle, and the city and the ocean. It takes quite a while for it to come together in my mind, but after a short time I feel my clothing start to change. When I finally open my eyes, Rian is grinning at me.

"Perfect," he says.

"I'm impressed!" Flit nods her agreement as I take stock of myself. My arms and legs are swathed in a clinging, shimmery silver fabric that resembles chain mail, but is soft to the touch. Over it is draped a surcoat of soft yellow gauze which is short in the front and trails to my ankles in the back. It's cinched at the waist with a light blue sash, and of course at my back, my sword is strapped securely in its sheath. Flit's frayed ribbon bracelet, which I've grown fond of, still hangs at my wrist despite its missing diamond.

"Can I bring my sword?" I ask.

"Well sure, as long as you're not thick enough to try and use it. Everyone at the Ring is important, and very powerful. If you tried to attack them, you probably couldn't even draw it. But I think it's good to have it. It'll remind them of who you are." She turns to Rian, "Now for you, Mage." Rian's nostrils flare out slightly as Flit paces around him, inspecting him.

"I don't see why I can't just go like this," he says. "I'm a Mage. You can see that plainly by what I'm wearing. If they're anything like you, they'll hate me right away, anyway."

"Oh, Rian," I say, "Flit doesn't hate you..." I look at Flit, whose ever-changing eyes dance from orange to bright red. "Do you?"

"Hate is a strong word," she says. "They'll need to see your coils, Mage."

"Why? Are you sure?" Rian tugs uncomfortably at his collar.

"Well, that's kind of the whole point of the coils, you know. So our kind can see quickly how responsible someone is with the magic they've been entrusted. So, yes. You'll have to wear an open shirt. Or no shirt. Probably no shirt is best." She steals a secret glance at me and winks. "It shouldn't be a problem. Your kind is always flashing around their coils, showing off anyway."

"Rian isn't like that," I say. Flit gives me a look of disbelief. "Sure, he gets carried away sometimes, but it's not to show off... he's just...interested. He tries to be respectful, he just likes to learn."

"It's fine, Azi," Rian says, clenching his jaw, "We're losing our focus on why we're here to begin with. What I'm wearing isn't really important." He glares at Flit, "Or not wearing." He's right, I think. As always, Flit is a master of distraction.

It takes Rian much less time to make his transformation. He waves his hand and his clothing shimmers into a long, sleeveless vest that's creamy yellow at his shoulders and deepens slowly to midnight blue as it drapes to his ankles. It buttons at his waist over an off-white shirt that is just sheer enough to show the Mark that swirls from his heart up to his collarbone and down to his buttons. His trousers are deep blue dotted with pinpoints of light that twinkle like stars.

"Amazing," I breathe.

"Yes, that's fine," Flit says. "Now, when we get there, you should probably let me do the talking. They'll want to play, and you're both still pretty terrible at it. Oh, and if they're dancing, then join. Sometimes that goes on for a while and it's important, so best not to interrupt. Remember it's all in good fun, so don't be uptight. And try not to be rude." She looks pointedly at Rian.

"I swear," he mutters again as I link my arm through his and squeeze it.

"I think that's everything," she says, rising up from the moss with a flutter of her wings. "When in doubt, just do what everyone else is doing. Ready? Follow me!" She speeds across the grotto's small pool, which is like a vast lake to us at our tiny size, and splashes right into the waterfall on the opposite side. I start to follow, picking my way around the edge of the pool.

"You just go along with it, don't you?" he says quietly, taking my hand to hold me back. "You're very trusting, Azi. More than I am. Sometimes, I wish I could be that way."

"What choice do we have?" I ask, "You said it yourself. We don't belong here. Mum said the same thing. There's too much going on out there for us to stay here, and I can't think of how to leave without crossing the border on foot. If we tried that, we might end up just like Da..." My voice trails off and he takes my chin in his hands.

"I'm not saying it's a fault," he says, "It's one of the things I love about you. Just don't let your guard down, okay?" he leans in and kisses me, and we stay locked together until we're interrupted by a splash and an angry squeal from Flit.

"Really? I leave you for less than a cricket's chirp and you can't keep your hands off of each other? I thought this was important, Mage! Stop slobbering all over Azi and get through the waterfall!" She darts to us and takes each of our hands, and then we're flying fast over the water and splashing through the trickling falls on the other side.

We come through dry, and my first impression of the Ring is that I've been here before. Blurs of colorful dancers streak past us as we stand outside the edge of the small meadow clearing, which is dotted with bright blossoms among the thick, green grass. The Ring itself is made up of pristine white mushrooms which create a perfect circle. Surrounding the circle of mushrooms, between them and the thick line of forest trees is a narrow strip of moss where a great crowd of fairies has gathered.

Some of them look like us, tiny people without wings, while others have stunning iridescent wings like Flit. Some are covered in fur so they might be mistaken for a mouse, and others resemble insects until they turn to look at us with human faces. There are creatures covered in tiny mushrooms, and fairies with sprigs of grass sprouting from their backs. Some of them are twisted and dark and spindly like the roots of a tree, with deep black eyes that sparkle, while others are bright and ethereal, with impossibly beautiful faces. I cling to Rian as the group closest to us turns to point. Their whispers rush through the crowd until almost all of the creatures around the Ring are craning to watch us pass.

"Hello!" Flit cheerfully greets those nearby. "Excuse us," she squeaks as she pulls us through the path they create. As we approach the blur of dancing, it slows. At first I think it's because of us, but then as they come to a stop I see Twig sitting in the grassy center of the ring. A few of those who were dancing fly up to perch on the mushrooms, and others settle beneath the caps to watch. "Hi, Twig!" Flit calls out, and he looks in our direction and gives her cheerful wave. Something pokes from the soil in front of him, and at first I think it must be a worm or a mole the way it's burrowing upward, pushing the earth from below.

"There's Crocus," Flit points at the delicate spring-green bud that emerges and continues to grow just to Twig's chest height. The petals transform to a beautiful deep purple as they fall open, revealing an elegant child-like fairy. The crowd around us gasps in approval and bursts into applause, and I find myself doing the same as she opens her arms in greeting. She has a delicate build that is not unlike a flower's stem, and wears a crown of dewdrops on her puff of yellow-green hair.

"Twig," she says, and her sweet voice carries the same warmth as her smile. "Please present your name to the gallery," she nods to the crowd with amusement in her bright green eyes, "which I see is quite occupied this noon." Twig sticks his thumbs into his belt and rocks far back on his heels. His stick-like wings blur as they work to keep him from tipping backwards.

"Tufar Woodlish Icsanthius Gent," he announces with a tone of importance, "currently reporting from the palace of Cerion City."

"And what news have you, Twig?" she smiles gently, tilting her head to one side.

"The eldest princess's ball was held last eve, with a great deal of magical decoration."

"That would explain the flood of cyclones," a large green fairy perched on one of the mushrooms offers in whispers. He has long, lean green legs and wings that fall sleekly over his back like tear-shaped leaves. At first I think he must be some sort of mantis or grasshopper, but when he turns and I can see his face, it's quite human. His hair is swept back in long streaks and his high cheekbones come to sharp points, making him look as though he's flying into a strong wind. His large eyes are covered with a protective mask resembling the eyes of an insect. He pushes it up to his forehead as Crocus nods to him.

"We recognize Soren Hasten Udi Swiftish Haven," she says, "Shush, what word from the North field?"

"Thank you," he whispers quickly, so that I have to lean forward to hear him, "an unrelenting stream of cyclones throughout the night, and the trespass of a half-elf Mage and a human warrior." A murmur rushes through the fairies, and those closest eye us cautiously. "Investigation tells us it is Lisabella's daughter and her friend."

"Is that so?" Crocus' brow lifts gracefully as she scans the crowd and her gaze rests on Flit. She nods and beckons to us. "We recognize Felicity Lumine Instacia Tenacity and her charges." Flit leads us to the center of the Ring to stand beside Twig, and Crocus waits for the buzzing crowd to settle before she speaks. "Please present your name, Lisabella's daughter."

"Azaeli Hammerfel." I dip into a curtsy.

"A. H." Crocus announces my initials thoughtfully. "Is that all?" I nod. "Well, Ah," she says as the crowd giggles, "we are pleased to meet you." She turns to Rian, "And the Mage?" she asks, folding her hands elegantly on top of her skirt petals.

"Rian Eldinae," his formal bow spurs another giggle from the crowd.

"Re." she nods again, "such short, strange little names. Ah, and Re. We now recognize you." I glance at Flit, who is pressing her lips together, trying not to laugh.

"No, no," she giggles. "Azi and Rian."

"Well, it doesn't match up, does it? And why is it she has a sword, but her name is Hammerfel? Did she drop her hammer? It fell and now she needs a sword?" Crocus covers her mouth and her laugh is sweet and melodic as a chime. I can't tell whether she's serious or teasing me. She turns to Rian, "Eldinae, though. That's an old name. An elven name." She tilts her head at Rian.

"My father is a wood elf," he says.

"A half-wood-elf-high-Mage," she claps her hands, "how oddly delightful! Oh, but you have the coils." She swirls her finger in the air in the direction of his chest and leans forward, then gestures him closer as the scandalized crowd whispers around us. I try to follow, but Flit shakes her head at me and pulls me back, and my hand slips from his. He doesn't hesitate. Instead he crouches down before the little flower, allowing her to reach her slender fingers out to him. All around us, the crowd of fae lean in, trying hard to get a closer look.

"How did you come by these?" She asks and lowers her hand, reluctant to touch him. Rian clears his throat awkwardly and glances back at Flit.

"I've been studying to rise to a new Circle," he says, his voice a little feeble. "I came across some spells that were beyond my level and I was curious. I wanted to try them. Also, I was trying to help my friends, who were touched by your border wards." The two study each other for a long time, and I feel awkward for him as I shift uncomfortably.

"Rian," Flit leans forward to whisper. "It's your turn to ask." I groan inwardly. I don't think either of us realized a game had started. Poor Rian.

"Oh, uh..." he glances back at Flit and then looks around the Ring, up at the vast array of fairies perched on mushrooms, hovering in the forest, and milling around the grass. I can guess how he feels. There are too many questions, where does he even start? "Is it true that the Mage Mark, that is, the coils, causes the cyclones?"

"Indeed, they are directly related." She bows her head in grief, and the sadness drifts over me like a perfume. "Both mean that the balance has been disrupted, and that our Wellspring is abused. Were you unaware?"

"I didn't realize," he shakes his head apologetically, "that it was causing harm. I only meant to learn and grow so that I could be helpful to others." Crocus nods, waiting for his question. "Why do you believe me so easily? I could be lying to you. I could be a danger right now." All around us, the fae erupt into a fit of giggles, and even Crocus presses her delicate fingertips to her lips and looks down coyly.

"It is impossible," she says, "to deceive us here within the Ring. Please, try. Tell me a lie." I watch Rian as he opens his mouth and closes it several times, pausing in between to think, or scowl, or scratch his head. "So, do you see now?" she asks among a scatter of laughter from the others.

"I see. That's very interesting," he says. "Does it mean that you trust us, then?"

"To a degree, Mage. You may step away now." She gestures back to the center, and then meets my gaze.

"Ah," she beckons to me, and I exchange places with Rian. "You have the student's print." She gestures to my forehead. "Are you also a Mage? We understood that you followed your mother on the warrior's path."

"Rian chose me as his student," I say. This close, I catch the floral scent of her petals. It's so lovely that I have trouble forming my thoughts. "Just before we left to come here. It was easier that way to..." I glance back at him, trying to remember the events that happened just last night, but my mind is already foggy. "To get into the Academy. As a student. It's very private. They keep things secure." There was another reason, which I try hard to remember. "Oh, also I was affected by your border when my father crossed it. I wasn't able to wield my sword. But that's changed now. I'm still a warrior."

I shake my head and rub my eyes. "Why do I feel so strange?" I ask her. Up close I feel enchanted by her. My eyes fix on the petal skirt, which is so full that I can't see beneath it to tell whether she has a stem or legs and feet. I ponder that while she starts to reply, and I have to focus hard on her lips in order to understand.

"Oh, I'm terribly sorry," she smiles. "My perfume has such an effect sometimes. You may step back, if you'd like. That will help." I step back, and as the distance grows between us, I begin to feel my wits returning to me. "We are well aware of the Academy and its workings. You need not explain. Now," she smoothes her petals, "how is it that you and Re came to be in the Half-Realm? The in-between?"

"We were trying to get to our guild, to warn them," I say. "They were about to be betrayed. They would have been ambushed and killed. Do you know of Mistress Viala, and her plotting?"

"Yes, Twig has kept us well informed of the Mage and her hold on the young prince." Some of the fairies perched on the mushrooms start to protest, but she raises a hand and they go silent. "It is an issue much debated within the Ring these days. Some feel that the prince is acting of his own accord, but we are of the belief that Viala has enchanted him. Either way, it is a dangerous pairing for the Wellspring."

"He came here seeking treasure and power," a fairy perched on one of the mushrooms raves, "his greed has blinded him! Without the Oculus which their people stole," she jabs a finger at us, "our northern borders lie open and unprotected! There is peril on the Crag, and the prince is well aware. He's the one who sent them here. Do not underestimate his motives!" The fairy is charcoal-skinned and wrinkled, with long orange hair and a dress of bright red embers. She floats up above her mushroom as though readying to dive into the circle. She sends a spray of orange and red sparkles behind her as she moves, which remind me of the sparks that fly from my father's hammer as he strikes the red-hot steel at his forge. There is a long pause before Crocus replies.

"We do not recognize Ember at this time. The game will continue." she turns back to me. I watch from the corner of my eye as Ember sits back down on her mushroom and crosses her arms with a huff. "We would like to be certain of the origins of this Mage. Are you aware of her past?" she asks. I try to remember what I know of Viala, which isn't much.

"She's from Sunteri, I think. She came to study a few years ago..." I turn to Rian for help. He looks from me to Flit and then Crocus.

"May I?" he asks. Crocus nods, and he continues. "She arrived six years ago from Sunteri to study at the Academy. Do you know of Sunteri?"

"We do. It is the triple continent, beyond the sea and the desert and the sea again. Far to the south. A land of mysteries not unlike our own. And so why do you suppose she would travel to Cerion to study?"

"Our methods are different here," he says. "I imagine that she wanted to learn ways other than those taught by her countrymen. She rose quickly through the Circles until she became a Master herself. Everyone was quite impressed at the time." There's another stretch of silence and I nudge him with my elbow.

"Your turn," I murmur.

"Oh," he thinks. "You refer to yourself as 'we'. Are you royalty? Should we call you Your Highness?" This causes a spattering of giggles from the onlookers again, and Crocus looks down at the ground with an adorable smile.

"No, we aren't. I'm afraid we never properly introduced ourselves. My name is Chantelle Rejune Cordelia Unphasei Seren. And his name is Subter Crag Rever Enstil Evrest." She gestures to the ground beneath her petals, which begins to rumble. Rian stumbles into me and we hold each other steady as Crocus is lifted up by a jagged-looking rock that emerges from the soil and grass beneath her.

"Scree!" The crowd shouts in unison, cheering. Flit joins the excitement, squealing and clapping.

"It's a rock." Rian utters under his breath, and I'm just as perplexed as he seems to be by the very ordinary-looking dirt-crusted rock. The only thing remarkable about it is the way Crocus's delicate white roots weave over it.

"All of their kind wants something. What is it they want?" A deep voice booms through the circle, sending the very ground vibrating. Crocus blinks at us expectantly.

"What do they want? What do they want?" The fairies cry in unison. The sudden chaos makes me uneasy, and Rian squeezes my hand reassuringly as we wait for the fairies to calm. When they don't, Crocus claps her hands and the dancing starts again, blurring around us. Shush grabs my free hand and pulls me into it.

We dance for what feels like hours, and I feel the tension of the game fall away. Laughter wells in my heart and bubbles from me. I turn to look at Rian, whose own grin is wide and carefree. It reminds me of the rare afternoons we shared chasing each other through the forest park beside the guild hall, when he was allowed a break from his studies. The dancing slows when the sun is low in the sky, casting bright coral beams through the trees.

"Your reply." Crocus says as we fall into the grass before her, laughing, and now I understand why the dancing is important. The long session of wildness has lulled everyone into a state of serenity.

"We want to get out of the Half-Realm," Rian says after a thoughtful pause. "So we can tell our guild that Lisabella is safe, and they can stop searching for her. We want Azi's father's sanity restored. We want to do something about Viala and the Wellspring. Can we help?"

"Yes." Scree's voice thunders. I stare at the rock, trying to figure out where the sound is coming from. "Viala has shared secrets that were put in place to ensure the safety of this land. She encourages and aids in the abuse of the Wellspring. She has invited darkness upon the Crag and her actions have opened the North. In our eyes, she is no longer a Mage, but a Sorcerer. Our laws and agreements with Cerion clearly state that Sorcery is forbidden. Our bargain is this. We will free the father from his afflictions and restore you. In exchange, you shall strip the Mage Viala." I glance at Rian, who has gone pale.

"That's Archmage-level magic. Fortieth Circle at least." His voice is barely above a whisper and I can tell by his expression that he's completely repulsed by the idea of it. Once Mages have been stripped, not only do they lose all of their ability to perform magic, but their minds also unravel slowly. They eventually become so simple that they can barely manage the most basic tasks of dressing, walking, and even talking. Once Mages have been stripped, they can never be restored. They're better off dead.

Chapter Nineteen

THE BORDER

"We will provide the means to do so, if you will agree to our bargain." Scree's thunderous voice booms through the Ring. Rian turns to me, searching my eyes for answers.

"He's right," I say quietly, thinking of the draw of the Wellspring. "She needs to be stopped."

Rian nods and turns back to Scree and Crocus. "We'll return to Cerion and find out exactly what she's planning. If she is as much of a danger as we all believe her to be, then," he steels himself, "yes, I agree it needs to be done." There's a stretch of silence while Crocus gazes around the Ring and up into the sky, not unlike a daydreaming child, with her eyes distant and her smile serene. As she tilts her head this way and that, there's barely a whisper among the crowd.

"Well enough," Scree finally rumbles. The ground shifts again, and he burrows down into it amid the cries of farewell from the assembly. Crocus makes a sweeping gesture at the churned up dirt surrounding her petals, and thick green grass springs up from it as though Scree was never there.

"Flit," Crocus smiles and gestures, and Flit floats forward to take her hand. "You have done well in your duties, and now you may be dismissed. Unless of course, you wish to continue." Flit turns to look at us. Her eyes trail over me first and she smiles, and then she turns her attention to Rian she wrinkles her nose at him dramatically.

"Yep." she says as she beams back at Crocus. "Wouldn't miss it!" The crowd bursts into applause.

"Very well. Take your place," she says with a nod, and Flit comes to stand beside me.

"Shush," she nods to the mantis-like fae who spoke earlier. He shoots down from his mushroom and lands lightly beside us. "Twig," she says, and Twig steps forth. She pauses for a moment and her eyes fall on the coal-skinned fairy who ranted at us from atop her mushroom.

"Oh, Please. No, no, no." Flit murmurs through her teeth beside me, barely loud enough for me to hear. Crocus doesn't seem to notice as she gestures to the fiery fairy.

"Now we recognize Elia Magest Brimstone Envis Rife," she says with a respectful bow. Ember's red dress trails behind her and her long orange hair shifts from red to yellow and back to orange, giving the effect of a coal on fire. When she lands at my side, I can feel the heat emanating from her like a campfire. Crocus nods again. "The four of you have been chosen for this quest," she begins, but Ember interrupts.

"I'll send someone in my stead. I can't leave the Crag. I shouldn't even be away now." The wrinkles of her brow deepen as she scowls, and her eyes flash bright red.

"Here we go," Flit says under her breath.

"Impossible," Crocus waves a hand dismissively. "You and Shush must work together on this. We are all depending on you." I watch as Shush leans forward slightly and attempts to catch Ember's eye, but she looks away from him pointedly.

"A jaded fairy entourage. Not what I was expecting," Rian whispers to me.

"We shall leave it to you to devise a plan," Crocus says. "And Ah, we have restored your father as a gesture of good faith. He continues to sleep, though." She tips her head to Rian. "That is a spell not within our power to undo."

"Oh, thank you!" I rush forward in my excitement and hug her. Her skin is cool to touch, and she feels so frail I fear I might break her if I squeeze too hard. "Thank you," I say again, tears flooding my vision.

"Of course," she whispers, patting my shoulders. Her perfume drifts to my nose again and I retreat to Rian's arms as it starts to affect me. I sniffle softly, undisturbed by the dozens of eyes that I know to be watching me from outside of the Ring. My father is cured. My mother is found and as safe as can be in her situation. My curse is lifted. My family is well.

"As for your second request," Crocus goes on, "we feel it is a boon for you to be in the Half-Realm, considering the task at hand. It will aid you on your quest, if you remain unseen in your world. If you succeed, then we shall restore you to your realm."

"How will we get word to our guild?" Rian asks. "They're still searching for Lisabella."

"There are ways," she says, gesturing to the group of fairies beside us. "Your new companions shall help you in that. Now, the dusk comes, and I'm sleepy." She rubs her eyes, and the petals of her skirt begin to rise around her, enclosing her. She looks so child-like and small as she stretches up and yawns, that it's hard to believe the authority she seems to hold here.

Her yawn carries through to Rian and me, reminding me that it's been a full day since we've slept. As Crocus continues to close up, a deep serenity washes over the Ring. All around us, the fairies either settle sleepily into the grass or fly away into the depths of the forest. Crocus is now merely a pale green bud held up by a single stem.

"Well!" Flit's wings flutter, raising her up to her tiptoes. "That's that I guess! Let's go to my place and figure out what to do next."

"If you think for a moment that I will be taking orders from you—" Ember starts, but Shush quietly interrupts her.

"They're her charges," he whispers. "She knows them best." Ember doesn't argue with him. She simply glares, her eyes glowing a hot yellow-white.

"Perhaps it would be best if we let the humans rest. They are both tired," Twig offers. "And I'll need to check on Margy. I'm sure you two have arrangements to make before we get started, too."

"Of course," says Ember haughtily. "I can't just up and leave without any notice. I shouldn't have even come to the Ring. There's too much strife on the Crag right now."

"Yes, yes." Flit rolls her eyes. "We all know how important you are, Ember. You remind us every chance you get."

"We'll meet up at Flit's in the morning." Twig nods, and then vanishes. With a final glare at us, Ember goes, too.

"She's charming," Rian says.

"Very." Flit giggles.

"I have arrangements to make as well. I'll see you at sunrise,"

Shush's whisper is like a quick breeze, and he crouches down and then springs up with a powerful jump that sends him into the treetops in a streak of green.

"Back to my grotto then?" she asks us.

"We need to see our guild first," I say to Flit. "Can we get to Mya through the diamond?"

"Even if we can, how will we be able to communicate?" Rian asks. "They can't see us, remember? We're still in the Half-Realm."

"Oh, they can." Flit says. "We just have to make them believe we're there."

"What about the Revealer spell?" I ask. "Would that work?"

"It might, Rian says a little reluctantly. "I honestly don't know." He looks down at the ground and digs the toe of his boot into the earth, frowning.

"Are you okay?" I ask him softly. He's quiet for a moment.

"We think we're so brilliant," he says finally. "We study and we practice and we work so hard to figure out all of the mysteries and knowledge and to gain our Circles. We compete against each other..." He trails off, shaking his head. "If I had known about any of this, really known, I mean." He gestures to the Ring of sleeping fairies and shakes his head. "Viala and I, we pushed each other. She passed me quickly, but it made me work harder. She was awful to me, but I still looked up to her. I never suspected. Sorcery. I should have seen this coming. I should have tried to stop it a long time ago. Master Gaethon, too. How did we not realize?"

"It's not your fault, Rian. You can't blame yourself." I hug him, and he returns the gesture silently.

"Typical," Flit says. "There always has to be someone to blame, with you people. What good is blame, anyway? Sometimes things just happen because they happen. It's when you don't do anything to stop it that makes you part of the problem." When we don't say anything in reply, Flit wraps her arms around both of us. "Let's go play with your mum, Mage," she says. "Ready?"

Squeezing through the diamond is an experience I don't think I'll soon forget, or ever want to repeat. Flit's warnings weren't enough to prepare me for the discomfort of it. At first, everything is dark and blurred, and a loud thumping and ringing jab at my senses. The sound of Mya's soft song is muffled thickly by the leather pouch where I appear. I do as instructed and stretch my arms up over my head as far as they will go, and I feel a little resistance before Flit's hands clasp mine and start to pull. Every inch of me is squeezed from head to toe as I'm pulled out of the diamond and spill into the contents of Mya's belt bag.

"You do this every time?" I ask her. "Flit, that's awful."

"Not every time. It's just a precaution," she says. We help Rian through after me, and the space in the bag is so cramped that I can barely breathe. "Hang on," Flit says. She grabs our hands and in a blink we're standing on the ground at Mya's boot, still fairy-sized. Rian whispers a spell and we begin to grow again, and I wriggle my toes and shake the tingle out of my arms gratefully as I reach my proper height.

Mya is leaning against a tree, gazing to the northwest. I can feel the hint of some unseen force just in front of her, and somehow I know it's the border of Kythshire. In the distance to the east, heavy footsteps rustle the brush as they move away from us. Along the border in the opposite direction, Uncle's blue robes flash between a thick of trees as he moves toward us. Together we watch him creep, raising his hands up and down meticulously along the invisible wall.

"He's looking for a weakness in the border ward," Rian says as Mya's song ends.

"Take a break, Gaethon," she says. "You've been at it for hours now."

"I still don't see why one of us can't just step through quickly. So there are guardians. We could ask them where she is. They're sure to know, aren't they?" Cort calls from above, where he's perched on one of the branches of Mya's tree. Beside him, curled in a nook where the trunk splits, Elliot snores.

"Believe me, I've considered it," Uncle mutters as he continues to test the wall. "But the risks are too great. You saw what happened to Benen. I won't have it repeated."

"No one has even charted the borders," another voice calls out, and I see Dacva peer around a nearby tree. "It'll take days for you to make the full circuit of Kythshire. Weeks, even." One icy glance from Uncle is enough to make his face go pale. He slides back behind the tree and out of sight without another word.

"Gaethon," Mya offers hesitantly, "they know you. Are you sure you couldn't just cross—"

"Absolutely not," he interrupts her. "I will not say it again, Mya. I cannot cross into Kythshire. I shouldn't even be this close." He drops his voice so only she can hear. "As I have explained to you before, the draw for a Mage of my Circle is intoxicating. If I were to cross, it would be devastating. I don't expect you to understand, but I do ask you to respect my stance." He stands back, dropping his hands in defeat, his voice still just above a whisper. "As much as I hate to admit it, though, the boy is right. This approach is taking too long. Even if I was to find a weakness, I couldn't guarantee the safety of anyone crossing through."

"You aren't suggesting that we give up on Lisabella?" she crosses her arms defiantly.

"I wouldn't." He sighs and raises his hands again to continue his work. "She's my sister. My suspicion is that she is safely carrying out her work. Still, I find it troubling that she hasn't sent word to ensure us of her safety."

"He's right," I say to Rian and Flit quietly. "I wonder why Mum didn't try to reach them, to tell them she's okay. She knew they were looking for her, didn't she?"

"Nope," says Flit. "She was so worried about you and your da that I think it slipped her mind. You know how Kythshire affects you. She spent a lot of the time when she wasn't fighting crying about you both. I think that swallowed up her thoughts on anyone else. Plus I told her that they brought him home, but I don't think I told her that they left again to look for her. She mainly asked a lot of questions about you, Azi, when we played."

I think about my own irrational anger after my reunion with Mum, and I guess I can understand how Mum could lose sight of one thing in favor of another. Still, it seems odd to me. I look up at Rian, who shakes his head slightly.

"Either way," he says, "I think it's time to try and get their attention." He raises his arms up over his own head and murmurs an incantation. The words are slow and rhythmic and slightly familiar. One look at a very dubious Flit confirms my suspicions. He's casting the Revealer spell. I watch as the air around him shimmers softly and then settles again.

"Hi Mum," he says from right beside Mya. When she gives him no reaction, he groans. "I was really hoping that'd work!" he sighs and rustles his hair thoughtfully. "Here. I'll try it on you, Azi. Maybe a Revealer isn't meant to be cast on oneself." He motions me closer and repeats the spell along with the intricate hand movements. The air shimmers around me this time, and Mya jumps back and lets out a yelp. Instantly, Cort drops out of the tree and lands lightly beside her, swords flashing, and Uncle whips around, his hands raised and ready to cast. The heavy footsteps I heard earlier crash toward us and I throw my hands up in surrender.

"It's me, it's me!" I cry.

"Azi!" Mya claps her hands over her mouth in shock and then throws her arms around me. "What are you doing here? Where did you come from?"

"Bah, was hoping it'd be some action for a change," Bryse says with disappointment as he emerges from the woods, shoving his sword back into its sheath. "Ay, Azi." I grin at him and look at Uncle, whose jaw is dropped in disbelief. Cort sheathes his own swords, seemingly just as disappointed as Bryse by the revoked promise of a fight.

"It's a long story," I say, "but we came to tell you that Mum is okay. She's helping in Kythshire. You don't need to search for her anymore." Uncle circles around me slowly, watching me as I talk.

"Is it some trick? Some spell of deception to send us away?" Cort reaches out to poke my arm.

"If it is, it's quite convincing," Uncle says.

"Rian's here, too," I say, pointing to Rian. Uncle turns, and though Rian's standing right beside me, he looks right through him. "Here," I say to Mya, taking her hand. I place it on Rian's shoulder. "See?"

She steps a little closer, sliding her hand up to his face and into his bristly hair. Her eyes light up and she pulls him to her and hugs him. I think of how strange it must look to those who can't see him yet, as though she's hugging thin air. Then Uncle steps forward and juts his hands out and casts the Revealer, and Flit darts away just in time to keep from being caught in it. The others gasp, and there is a great deal of hugging and laughing and congratulating before Uncle finally takes Rian by the elbow and leads him away.

"Mage secrets," Mya says as she watches them go. "Necessity doesn't make them any less irritating." We settle together against the same tree while the others go back to their watch points. Still safely hidden, Flit comes to perch on my shoulder. "You were inside, then?" Mya asks quietly. I nod. "What is it like?"

"*Careful.*" Flit whispers into my head.

"It's beautiful and strange," I say. "Easy to lose yourself."

"Did you meet any of them? The fae?" she looks at me with hope in her eyes. The very little I know about Kythshire came from Mya. She sung to us as children about the dark times, and the Sorcerer king, and the legend of the fairy folk. Songs are safe, passed down from generation to generation, unwritten. Not as secret or forbidden as the writing locked up in Mages' libraries. How I wish I could tell her what I've seen and how perfectly her songs described the fae. Instead, I look away. The words just won't come.

"Sorry," I say quietly. It's the safest answer I can give her.

"I understand," she sighs and takes out her lute to strum a lazy melody. The music soothes me, and it isn't long before my eyelids grow heavy. I'm comforted by Flit's steady breathing as she lies nestled into the crook of my neck. The exhaustion that I've been fighting for so long finally wins its battle, and it isn't long before I drift off to sleep.

My father is the first one to greet me in my dreams, which are mottled and confused. He sits on the edge of his bed, looking out the window. Beside him, tucked inside the rumpled blankets, a red fox dozes. I'm vaguely aware of the smell of bread baking. Downstairs, Mouli chatters away. Da offers me his hand and we go downstairs together to breakfast, but when we arrive in our cozy kitchen, we find Viala and Eron sitting at our table. They've just finished eating our breakfast, and Mouli is fussing over the prince, wiping his cheek with a napkin the way a mother would dote on her own child. I hear movement under the table and bend to see Luca kneeling there, brushing the dirt from Viala's fine slippers. He's quite happy in his work, and it leaves me feeling disgusted. When I turn to my father to ask him to put a stop to it, I find him sitting beside the prince, picking the crumbs off of his plate to eat them. I'm so repulsed by the sight that I turn away, and that's when I see a streak of red slip through the door to the street.

I trot after the fox as it weaves through the deserted city and out of the city gates. It picks up its pace to a run and I chase it into the thick of the woods. The space between us widens; it's too fast for me. I stumble over roots and underbrush while the fox leaps lightly, far ahead of me. I wonder why I'm so slow and then I realize that I'm weighed down by my armor and my sword. I try to keep chasing it as I struggle to free myself from the weight of the chain mail, piece by piece. Now it's just a tiny red dot against the green, far in the distance.

I will my feet to go faster as my last piece of armor falls to the ground, and I start to close the space between us. I'm so compelled by the creature that I follow it through the day and into the night. We never slow, but eventually I catch up to it and we run together. We come to the charred clearing of the guild's first camp, and we run through it and dive into the trees again. Far behind us, I hear the pounding of horses' hooves. I look over my shoulder and see in the distance the banners of orange and red. We find a place to hide and watch the riders pass, and then we start again, only this time we're following them.

Our journey lasts for several days and nights, never stopping. We travel through beautiful plains and along coastline and into the snow-capped mountains. We're careful never to let the riders see us, but we always keep them in our sights. Eventually the mountains fade from green pines and snow into charred black stone. A false step would send the horses careening over the unforgiving cliffs, so the riders dismount and leave them behind.

The fox and I creep along behind them, undetected as we descend into a deep ravine. I wonder where we are going as the chill in the air bites at the bare skin of my face. We follow them until they reach a fortress of black stone cut into the mountain. The doors swing open and they disappear into its depths, and the fox whimpers and trots back and forth to skirt the boundary of the strange place. Outside the door, several sentries stand guard. The fox does not seem to be afraid, and so I approach them to investigate. It's then that I realize that I must still be in the Half-Realm, because the sentries' helmed heads don't turn in my direction as I near.

As I peer up at the nearest sentry, I realize that something about it isn't right. The eyes behind the barrel helm are dark and vacant. I look down to its arm and see bare bone. The sentries aren't men. They're skeletons. My screams echo through the canyon and they don't stop even after I jolt awake and feel Mya's arms around me, quieting me. Her gentle voice washes away the horror of the dream until I feel safe again.

There are no skeletons, no black rock mountains. The image of them shifts in my mind and I see them from another angle, with a great golden field of wheat stretching out before them. I blink myself back to my senses. Rian sits beside me, opposite Mya, rubbing my arm to comfort me. The rest of our party have rushed to investigate. Bryse is the last to crash through the woods. When he sees me lying in Mya's arms, shaken, he tosses down his shield in disappointment.

"Bah, still no fighting? Sounded like someone was gutting you, Azi."

"Sorry to disappoint you," I attempt a smile. "It was just a nightmare." Mya and Gaethon exchange glances.

"There didn't happen to be a fox in it, did there?" she asks me. My eyes widen.

"Yes, actually." I go into detail, including everything from the creepy breakfast scene to the disturbing skeleton sentries.

"I told you," Dacva pipes up from behind the tree where the horses are tethered for grooming. He drops the brush and meets Gaethon's eyes a little fearfully, but steels himself. "They're going there. They plan to collect anyone that's left. To gain their allegiance."

"But that's impossible," Mya says. "Nobody has lived there for generations aside from the banished, and the last of them were sent off nearly twenty years ago. It'd be a wonder if they survived this long."

"The banished?" I breathe. Dacva's expression darkens.

"All of Redemption is obsessed with them," he says. "You know the history of my former guild." He spits the words with distaste. "Everyone knows it. It's why they feel like they have so much to prove. I'm sure you've heard some version of the story." He dares to edge closer, still eyeing Uncle as though waiting for a scolding, but Gaethon simply nods his assent for Dacva to continue.

"Years ago, my old guild was called Knights of Conquer. They prided themselves on claiming more and more land for Cerion. But their greed for power and control grew so fast and so strong that many started to question whether they were really doing it in the name of the King, or just for their own gain. Their Mages were powerful and covered with Mark, and their warriors were ruthless to any who stood in their way.

"Soon, the crown started to suspect that the Knights had selfish motives. Claiming distant lands in the name of the king and looting treasure for the kingdom wasn't enough for them. They wanted more of a share for themselves. Everything, even the throne. When word got out about their treachery, King Victens, Tirnon's father, ordered the guild dissolved and sent its high members to be banished to the Outlands. The Academy had their Mages stripped." Rian shifts uncomfortably and I reach for his hand.

"The weaker members were allowed to stay in Cerion, and they reformed under the name Redemption. They've fought hard since then to gain the king's favor, but he's never been able to trust them fully. The prince, however, admires their perseverance. He sees their potential."

"But those banished members, if they're even still alive, must be very old by now," I say. "In their seventies or eighties, aren't they? What good would it do to have them back?"

"For Redemption, I think," Mya says, "it's a matter of pride. That was their family, just as everyone here is ours. Imagine if we were all sent away when you were just a girl, what kind of effect that would have had on you."

"But that's different," I say, avoiding Dacva. "You would never plot against the king. And if you did, then you'd deserve any sentence he handed down."

"Some people," Brother Donal sighs from beside Dacva, "create their own sense of right and wrong, Azi. It's easy enough to justify one's misdeeds if you have the mind to."

"It's not just that," Dacva says. "They have other motives, too secret to ever talk about around me. They haven't trusted me for a while. I think they knew I was looking for a way out. Anyway it's not just the elders in the Outlands. Lots of men have gone to settle there. Rebels." He looks from me and Rian to Uncle. "And I can tell you who else is involved. That Sunteri Mage who's seen around the prince. The pretty one with the dark hair."

"Do you mean Viala?" Mya asks. I try to catch Rian's eye, but he and Uncle are already exchanging their own secret glances.

"Yeah," Dacva says. "Dar has it bad for her. I walked in on them once. He'd walk off a cliff for her if she told him to."

"Here's what I know," Bryse interrupts. "Azi never woulda missed that cake of mud on Celi's knee." He nods to his grey charger pointedly.

"And mine still has burrs on the hind near the saddle." Cort offers lazily. "Azi never let my horse stand for a moment with a burr." Cort and Bryse grin at each other as Dacva slinks away to his place again and picks up the grooming brush. I look at Bryse and he gives me a wink.

"I think the boy is well aware by now how much more you favor Azi, what with your constant reminders." Donal says quietly. I feel my cheeks grow warm. So, Bryse and Cort have been giving Dacva a hard time. Thinking back over the years of torment he put me through in training, I'm glad he's getting back a little of his own.

"Nah, I don't think he's got it yet." Bryse chuckles and bends for his shield. He raises it in a quick salute to me and then clomps back off into the woods again to take up his watch. Donal sighs and shakes his head, and then tucks his hands into his sleeves and bows himself into a prayerful pose.

"It seems we have a new mission," Mya says, steering the conversation back. "Stop Redemption, and if what Dacva says is true, then we should send a note of warning to Cerion regarding Viala."

"Viala will be taken care of," Uncle says, giving Rian a meaningful look. "I shall draft a letter to the king to update him on this turn of events."

"I'll have Elliot send a bird for you when he wakes," Mya says, looking up into the nook of the tree where he's still snoring soundly. "Or Rian and Azi can ride back on his horse to deliver it."

"Rian and Azi have their own path to take in this," Uncle says. "They'll be leaving us soon."

"I might have known," Mya sighs, her tone rich with sadness. She pushes herself to her feet and offers Rian her hand, and they walk together into the forest.

"A word, Niece," Uncle says quietly. He gestures to the woods in the opposite direction. Flit follows along behind us a little hesitantly until Uncle stops among a tall grouping of pines. I wonder what this will be about, and I can't help but feel like I did as a child preparing for a scolding. I cross my arms over chest and stand in silence, waiting for him to start.

"Rian," he says in his usual stern tone, "tells me that you kept him in check within Kythshire." I nod and hug my arms tighter. "You stopped him from making records." I nod again, shifting uncomfortably. "It is highly unusual for a student to stand against her teacher in such a way. The binding between mentor and pupil prevents it. And yet you managed it anyway."

"Yes, Uncle," I say, looking down at his feet.

"The two of you have a strong bond. You depend upon each other. I would ask you to continue to keep your eye on him." My eyes snap to his and his expression softens. "Are you prepared for what lies before you?" he asks me. I'm not sure of his meaning, and so I shrug. "Is there anything you need from me? Anything at all?"

"I'm sure there is," I say. "But right now I don't know exactly what lies ahead, so I don't know what we might need." It's mostly true. I'm not sure how much Rian has told him or how much he already knows, and I wouldn't dream of mentioning the fairies. He nods and we stand in awkward silence for a long stretch before he slips a ring from his finger and offers it to me.

"Take this," he says. I turn it in my fingers, looking at the fine scrollwork of the Headmaster's ring inlaid with a G and a furling quill.

"Your crest?" I whisper. He nods.

"It will show any who question your actions that you have my full support."

The gesture shows me that he sees me not as the silly child I always feel I am in his presence, but as a young woman worthy of his trust. I swallow the lump in my throat and tuck the ring safely into a pouch at my belt. I can't manage to say anything and so I hope a simple nod of appreciation will do.

He pats me on the shoulder and offers me another rare smile before leading me back to the makeshift camp. We're greeted by Cort, who wriggles his brow at me and goes back to watching Dacva closely inspect the hind quarters of his horse. Mya and Rian emerge from the opposite side of camp, and Flit whispers into my mind.

"Time to go if you're going to get any rest before morning," she says. I notice that Rian's eyes are wet with tears as he offers me a smile as we take each other's hands. Echoing Flit's whisper, he announces that it's time for us to leave. We say our farewells and then duck into the forest together, far enough away that they won't see us vanish back to Kythshire. As Flit rests her hands on us both, I close my eyes and hope with all of my heart that all of them remain safe.

Chapter Twenty

THE ENTOURAGE

The carpet of moss in Flit's grotto makes the most comfortable bed imaginable, and despite all of my worries, I sleep through the night with pleasant dreams of fairies dancing through my head. When Flit wakes us it's not yet dawn, but I feel completely rejuvenated. We nibble on the pink berries that she brings as we sit shoulder to shoulder in the moss, and Rian tells me about his conversation with Uncle the previous night.

"He's always been unsure about Viala," he says, "but no one else seems to see anything suspicious about her. That's why he had her mentor me when he left to look for Lisabella. He wanted me to be close to her, to watch for anything off. When he heard that she moved up my trial, he realized that she was trying to use me to forward her plots. That's why he told me to fail, just as we thought."

"Did you tell him what we've been sent to do to her?" I ask. He nods.

"He thinks it's the best course." Rian looks into the sparkling pool where the elegant fins of Flit's fish swirl and dance beneath the surface. "I agree, even though part of me feels like it's unimaginable to reduce someone so brilliant to almost nothing."

"It's her own fault," Flit pipes up, coming to land before us. She picks up a berry and nibbles it. "She's a danger. A real danger. A bad Mage. A Sorceress, even"

"I know, Flit," Rian says, "and I agree. So it's time to make a plan."

"Not without Twig and Shush and that Ember," Flit says, "Which is why I woke you up early. I think I've figured out why Screecus chose who they chose."

"Screecus?" I ask.

"Oh!" Flit giggles and covers her mouth, and her prisms of light dance over the waving fronds and the surface of the water playfully. "That's what we call them. Scree and Crocus. It's not an official name, more like a nickname. So you should never, ever call them that. It might make Crocus close up and refuse to talk to anyone. The two of them are inseparable. Really inseparable. They need each other. Crocus can't be without Scree, and flip that, too. Do you remember when she went all funny and started daydreaming? She was talking secretly with Scree. So, anyway, I know Scree chose Twig because he can get us to the palace, and from there we can find Viala, since Mya has your diamond now, Azi. I think he chose Ember and Shush because they can make the container for the stripping together. But it's going to be tricky." I think back to a question game we had long ago, when Flit told me about some of the roles fairies play.

"Are they Creators, like the ones who made my diamond into a tether?" I ask.

"Yep! I told you they can be tricky, right? Well, they are. And those two are always bickering. So, it'll be fun to see if they can work together." She raises her shoulders up to her ears and offers a grin, her eyes flashing pink with excitement.

"Great," Rian says.

"Don't be sour, Mage. Have some more berries." She tosses some at him and they hit his chest and roll down, leaving streaks of pink along the white. Rian shakes his head and gestures over the stains, clearing them. Then he collects the berries and pops them into his mouth.

"I'm not being sour," he says after he swallows. "I just expect that this isn't going to be as straightforward as we imagined."

"Most quests aren't, are they?" I stand up and stretch, and pick up my sword to practice my footwork. The familiar feel of the leather-wrapped handle in my grip makes me smile. In my mind I wish for someone to spar with, and a glistening figure emerges from thin air and stands before me. It is nearly invisible, and holds a sword in one hand and a shield in the other. I stumble backward, shocked. Behind the figure, Flit giggles.

"He's alright," she says, "Just a helper. I think Mages call them elementals, or golems. He's made of light. Careful what you wish for,

Azi."

"I didn't even say anything," I say, raising my sword to signal that I'm ready to begin.

"You don't need to say anything, silly! Go on, let's see the famous Azi fight."

"As I was saying," Rian goes on as I circle around the golem, swinging to hit it or block its attacks. It feels so good to be back in practice that I can barely concentrate on Rian's train of thought. "Maybe we'll have to gather some things. Ingredients, so they can make an object or a potion or something to do the stripping." The elemental quickens its attack and I answer with a flurry of spins and slashes. I aim for the space beneath its arm, which is a weak spot in most opponents' armor, and my blade slides in easily. Red light spills from the wound and the elemental stumbles backward. I pause and lower my sword, but the red vanishes and the figure comes at me again. Rian goes on, "Unless Shush and Ember will be doing the stripping themselves, somehow."

"Not likely," Flit says, "I can't imagine them leaving Kythshire. They aren't Travelers like me and Twig. But it isn't unheard of. What they're going to do is pull away really powerful magic. Too powerful to just leave it lying around in some object that could get stolen or misused. Or trust it with another Mage. They might just come with us after all, so they can collect the magic in whatever they make and bring it back here to the Wellspring. Anyway, before they came, I wanted to give you a warning." I'm about to deliver another devastating blow when the figure vanishes and I stumble forward.

"Sorry, Azi, this is important. I'll call him back after." She gestures me closer and I come to kneel in the moss in front of her. "You can't expect them to get along," she says, "Ember and Shush are longtime rivals. They used to…" she looks up at the colorful swaying fronds of the willows thoughtfully. "…spend a lot of time kissing. You know. Anyway, it was a long time ago. And then something happened and Ember got angry and Shush got all strange and apologetic and it's been that way for years. Everyone keeps trying to get Ember to forgive Shush for whatever he did, but Ember is too proud and Shush is too quiet and neither of them will talk about it. So I just wanted to tell you that. Just so you know." Rian blinks.

"With everything else going on, her biggest concern is a lovers' squabble." He shakes his head. "Fairies." The elemental appears again and charges me, and I jump to my feet to meet it.

"Well, it's important. You'll see," Flit says. A single beam of sunlight splashes over the grotto's pool, and with a swish of wind, Shush appears. He's joined almost immediately by Twig, who does his little gleeful spinning dance of greeting with Flit. Ember is the last to arrive. She stands with her chin up, her arms crossed, and her shoulders angled slightly away from all of us. As if spurred on by their arrival, the elemental speeds its attack, sending me into a frenzy of blocks, parries, and dives until I manage to deliver a final blow to end the spar, slicing it from shoulder to waist. Red light spills out of it, and Flit, Twig, and Shush applaud enthusiastically.

"Great job, Azi!" Flit says proudly, and then turns to Twig as the elemental fades away, "Any news from the palace?"

"Everyone's sleeping," Twig says, "It's a good time to show up." I stow my sword back into its harness and cross to the others, where Rian pushes himself to his feet and takes my hand.

"So, what's our plan?" he asks. Ember scoffs.

"How quaint, the Mage is trying to take charge." She flies up to circle around him, leaving a trail of glittering orange and yellow behind her. "Why am I not surprised?"

"I'm not..." his eyes follow her path cautiously, "I'd just as soon get it over with."

"Listen here," Ember says, jabbing a finger and sending a burst of sparks at him which he ducks away from. "It's your kind that caused all this mess to begin with. You rise and you rise like a flame, leaving nothing but destruction behind you. If you saw half of what I've seen even in the past day--"

"Ember..." Shush whispers, but is promptly ignored.

"He's not like the others," Flit pipes up, and Rian and I exchange glances of surprise as she comes to his defense. "What?" She looks at us. "Well, he isn't! Not entirely. Well, mostly not. Okay, maybe he is a little. Actually Rian, you should probably let one of them do the leading." She bobs near his shoulder and whispers dramatically loud in his ear, "Just let Ember be in charge. She's going to do it anyway." She floats down again to rest in the moss and I watch in silence, thinking that this is not a very strong start to our quest.

"True," Twig's stick-like wings are a blur of brown as they carry him up. "But it would make more sense if our leader was someone familiar with the workings of Cerion, considering."

"Oh, like you?" Ember huffs, "I suppose you're an expert on the subject, having spent a few weeks as the princess's playmate."

"I don't claim to be, no," Twig settles cross-legged on my shoulder. "I didn't mean myself, anyway."

"Surely you don't mean this one?" she descends to face Flit, and the way she circles around her bothers me. It's as though she looks down on her, like Flit is some lesser being. Flit presses her lips together and looks away, refusing to meet Ember's gaze. I can tell she's upset; the dancing light that I've grown accustomed to around her dims so much that even the color seems to drain from her hair. A short distance from the two of them, Shush murmurs a warning to Ember to let Flit be.

"Stop that," I reach them in one stride and dip to my knee to offer Flit the safety of my cupped hands. She dives into the shelter gratefully and I scoop her up to my unoccupied shoulder, where she hops off to perch. "We're all here to work together," I say. "If you can't do it without bullying, then we'll figure out a way to do it without you." Ember's red dress seems to burst into flames as her eyes narrow into bright yellow slits that burn against her charcoal skin. When she flies up to confront me her heat burns my nose and cheeks, but I don't flinch away.

"Careful," she says, flaring angrily. "You don't know who you're dealing with, and you'd be in a real fix if you were to lose me." The air shimmers around me and I feel a cocoon of cool air settle between us.

"Back up a little, please, Ember," Rian says, lowering his hands as his shield spell takes hold. "I agree with Azi, and I'll follow her."

"As do I," Shush whispers clearly as he darts to me in a blur of green iridescence. "I shall follow Azaeli." He hovers in front of me and taps his chest with his fist, bowing.

"Oh! Me too!" Flit says. "You should lead!"

"Just what I was trying to suggest," Twig says from my other shoulder. "I'll follow you, Azi." Ember floats back a little, her arms crossed, assessing me.

"Fine." she says with a scowl. "I'll follow you. But if it goes to your head, I'm taking over." The other fairies join together and cheer. They link arms and ankles and spin in place in a joyful celebration. I can't say I share their enthusiasm. I've always considered myself a follower, not a leader. I think of Mya's strong and steady leadership. I could never measure up to that, but if they're putting their faith in me, I'll try my best. Rian meets my gaze and offers an apologetic shrug and a grin, and I'm pretty sure he knows me well enough to realize how reluctant I am to take up the role.

"Now," I say a little hesitantly as the celebration settles down. "We were talking before you arrived, and we think we've figured out everyone's role, except for Shush and Ember. Flit says that you're Creators? Would you be able to make us something to…" I trail off as I notice Ember floating there, shaking her head, already protesting. "Ember?"

"That's not how I would have started. You should have begun by asking everyone what they have to contribute. For example," she reaches into a hidden pocket in her dress and pulls out a nugget of gold the size of my thumbnail, "I've brought the main component. And he," she jabs her thumb at Shush, "is the only other one who knows what's required to imbue it. With my help, of course."

"Alright…" I think about what Rian mentioned earlier regarding ingredients as I eye the gold nugget Ember has produced. "Are there more pieces that we need to collect in order to work the spell?" I ask.

"As if we'd tell you," Ember huffs. Shush darts over in a blur to hover at my eye level.

"Several," he says, his voice barely a whisper as he speaks so quickly that I can barely pick out the individual words, "but it's highly secret magic. We wouldn't be able to share with you what it is we need—"

"Even if we wanted to," Ember interrupts with a haughty roll of her eyes.

"You already shared one!" Flit darts to my shoulder and makes a face at Ember. "So, ha!" Ember slides her gaze slowly to Flit, who ducks behind my head. "Well, she did," she mumbles.

"Or did I?" Ember smirks. "It might be a decoy. Did you think of that, little spark?" This time, it's Flit's turn to huff.

"There's no need for insults..." Twig trails off from my other side.

"Okay, okay," I say. "I understand. It's a secret." I turn to Shush, "How long will it take you to gather what you need?" I ask.

"Not long," he whispers. "We could have everything by midday, at my pace." He rocks back in mid-air proudly.

"Doubtful," Ember murmurs. "Rushing around, missing half of what's right under his nose." I ignore her.

"What if we split up, then?" I turn to Rian. "Twig could bring you, me and Flit back to Cerion, and we'll see what we can find out about Viala while Shush and Ember gather what they need. Then, Twig can come back for them at midday and bring them to us." Rian nods.

"That would work," he says.

"Ha!" Ember shakes her head, sending a spray of golden orange sparks from her hair. "It won't. See? You humans don't know everything."

"Sorry," Twig says, "Ember's right. I can only travel to your realm once while the sun is up and once while the moon is up. So if I bring you now, I can return to Kythshire at any time, but we'd have to wait for the moon before I could bring Ember and Shush across."

"Oh," I say. That would give us a whole day to find Viala and figure out whether she's deserving of the fate we've been assigned for her. My pulse quickens when I realize that we wouldn't have to rush. "We could go wake Da," I look to Rian hopefully, and he nods.

"Of course. It'll be our first stop," he says.

"Huh." Ember shakes her head. "That didn't take long. Already straying from the task at hand to tend to selfish wants."

"Nuh uh!" Flit pipes up, flying forward, "He promised. He's keeping a promise! I keep telling you they aren't like the others! Well, the Mage is, a little. But only a little! So you just—"

"I'm sure you aren't presuming," Ember drifts closer to Flit, her eyes burning, "to boss an Elder."

"Flit, it's alright," I say, turning a little to shield her from Ember's wrath. I wait for Ember to calm down before trying to turn the focus back on planning. "Then we'll go this morning, while Shush and Ember—"

"Really?" Ember interrupts again, her nostrils flaring as she shakes her head. Her eyes are narrowed with such fury that I can barely make out the line of yellow against the charcoal of her lids. I glance at Rian, puzzled. He shrugs. One look at the other fairies, who are all wearing embarrassed expressions, tells me I've committed some terrible insult.

"What?" I ask. "Did I say something wrong?"

"You should have said Ember and Shush," Flit settles on my shoulder.

"I did…" I think back.

"No," says Twig, "You said Shush and Ember." I watch as Ember flares up again. I glance again at Rian, whose brows are raised, and I'm relieved that he seems as clueless as I am.

"I don't understand," I shake my head, "Isn't it the same thing?"

"No," Flit breathes. "Ember is an elder. You should always list her first."

"See, Ember?" Twig offers, "Azi didn't know. I'm sure she apologizes." I take a deep breath and let it out very slowly as I find myself wondering whether this is a task we can manage without Ember after all. Her attitude is draining. I close my eyes and try to calm myself.

"Yes, I apologize. Ember and Shush will collect what they need, and Twig will bring them to Cerion when the moon comes up. In the meantime, the rest of us will see if we can find out exactly what Viala is planning. Does that work?" I look from one to the next, waiting for someone to protest. Shush is watching Ember with the forlorn expression of a shunned puppy, while Flit and Twig are nodding enthusiastically.

"This'll be fun! We'll get to explore some more," Flit says. "Twig, you can see Azi's house!"

"I might stay with the Princess." Twig says. "She's been needing me more and more lately."

"We'll go, then," Ember avoids looking at any of us. "We've got a lot of work ahead of us while the rest of you are off gallivanting around with the humans." She vanishes before any of us have a chance to reply. Shush offers me an apologetic smile.

"Guess I'll be going with her," he says, and streaks up to the treetops in a blur of green.

"Poor guy," Rian murmurs. "He's definitely pulled the short straw of the bunch."

"I think he's used to it by now," Twig says. "They're often paired up. Scree keeps trying to get them back together."

"Don't know what he sees in her," Flit says, her light dancing much brighter now that Ember has gone. She flashes a smile at me. "I'm ready! Can we go now?"

"First things first," Twig says. "You're both in the Half-Realm, that's true, so you'll be unseen until someone believes you're there. So you need to be careful not to knock into things or make any sudden noises."

"And you should come down to our size again," Flit says. "It's easier on us to move you when you're smaller. Plus there's less of a chance of bumping into anything or anyone that way." Rian and I exchange glances. I don't relish the thought of being fairy-sized among my own kind, but they're right. It's less risky. Reluctantly, I nod my agreement.

"Tiny it is, then," Rian says. He waves his hand and I feel the ground rising up and the trees stretching high above once more, until I'm up to my shins in spongy moss.

"Right then," Twig says as he drifts down to join us. He holds his hands out to us, and Flit, Rian, and I grasp them together.

"Wait," I say, looking at Flit. "Is this going to be like your diamond?" I distinctly remember the discomfort of squeezing myself out of the cramped space into Mya's belt pouch, and being crammed in with Flit and Rian once he came through, too. Flit turns to Twig.

"What's your tether?" she asks him.

"A little poppet of a fairy," he says. I try to imagine arriving inside the cottony stuffing and having to tear my way out.

"How does that work? How do you get out of it?" I ask.

"Out of it?" Twig asks. "We'll just arrive beside it." he gives Flit an odd look, and she ducks her head and her eyes flash mischievously as she grins back at him.

"I had a little fun with them their first go," she whispers to him.

"Flit!" I shake my head in disbelief.

"What?" She shrugs. "Not many people can say they've seen a diamond from the inside. Think about it. I gave you an experience not many will ever repeat!" Rian lets out a sigh of exasperation.

"That's one way of putting it," he says.

"Ready?" Twig asks. We nod, and the air around us begins to

shimmer. The grotto fades away, and the ground beneath our feet transforms from soft moss to something plush and fluffy. I squeeze my eyes shut until I'm aware of something warm and soft settling over my head. I reach to push it up, but it's too heavy, and I'm forced first to crouch to my knees in the darkness. Thankfully, Flit is not far behind. Her colorful light brightens the dark space, which reminds me of some sort of pillow-like cavern. Nearby I can see the poppet that Twig mentioned lying on the plush pink ground. It's a ragged little doll just our size, with button eyes and locks of brown yarn for hair. Something massive slides toward us as Rian and Twig appear, and we fight the soft ceiling to move away from it. A giant hand pats the spot around the doll, finds it, and closes around it. It's then that I put it all together.

"Where are we?" whispers Rian.

"I think," I breathe, "we're in Princess Margy's bed."

Chapter Twenty-One

BENEN

"Come now, your Highness, we can't sleep the day away," a muffled voice wafts from beyond the thick ceiling of blankets pressing on us.

"That'll be the nursemaid," Twig whispers to us as we lie on our bellies, face to face, "Tirie. She's alright." There's a great rustling and sliding that bounces us around as the princess sits up in bed.

"Time to get dressed. His Royal Highness is waiting to breakfast with you." The coverlet goes up and Margy peers wide-eyed at the space we occupy. Twig gives her a little wave and she beams back at him and beckons for him to come to her. He nods and holds up a finger. One moment. She nods and lowers the cover carefully.

"Purple or blue today? Or pink?" The nurse comes to the bedside and I feel something light drop onto us.

"Blue, blue, blue, please, but don't put it there!" Margy cries a little urgently, and the newly added weight is lifted quickly away. "Who else will be at breakfast? Just Brother?" Between the heat that Margy is giving off and being sandwiched in between her bedclothes, I'm starting to sweat. I wipe my brow on my wrist and turn to the others.

"If she's going to breakfast with Eron," Twig whispers, "I'd better go with her. I'll meet up with you later," he says. We nod, and Margy throws the covers off of us and glances at Twig, who flies up to rest on her shoulder. The rest of us remain unseen. We watch as the two follow the nursemaid out of the bedroom into what I can only assume is the dressing room.

"That was an experience," Rian says as he ruffles his hair and Flit drifts up and darts to the door to peek out.

"Thought so," she squeaks. "They're coming to make up the bed!

You have to move!" I peer over the edge of the bed and shove myself back to the center. It's as high as the sea cliffs. Flit flies back and takes my hand with both of hers to help me down. My heart jumps into my throat and pounds so loudly I'm sure everyone else can hear it.

"Don't let go!" I screw my eyes closed as we lower to the floor. I hold my breath for what feels like hours until my feet meet the solid ground.

"Whew! You're heavier than you look!" she giggles and scoots under the bed skirt. Rian floats down gracefully to land beside us.

"Levitation," he wriggles his brows at me.

"That would have been less traumatic," I say as we join Flit under the bed just in time to avoid the attendants who've come to make it up.

"Why are you so pale, Azi?" Flit whispers. Rian slips his arm around my shoulders and squeezes me reassuringly. "Even your lips are white."

"She doesn't like heights," he says, rubbing my arm.

"Or flying," I say. "Add flying to the list."

"The very, very short list of things you're afraid of?" he grins as he ticks them off on his fingers. "Heights, Master Gaethon, and now, flying." I elbow him and shake my head, and we laugh.

"Shhh!" Flit waves her hands at us to be quiet as a maid's foot pokes beneath the bed skirt.

"They can't hear us though, can they?" I whisper.

"Well, you know how sometimes your thoughts get dreamy when you're doing some mindless task?" Flit whispers. "And then you think you heard something, but nothing was there?" I nod. "It was probably something in the Half-Realm. So you have to hush. Just in case."

"I think it would be best," Rian whispers. "If we return to our size if we're going to walk home." Flit nods.

"I thought we could fly, but I forgot that it makes Azi go all white like that." She sighs. "It's too bad. Flying would have been so fun!"

"We couldn't anyway, here in Cerion," I whisper. "Could we? We don't have wings. Here, Rian only knows how to levitate, not fly."

"You don't need wings to fly, not even here if you're in the Half-Realm." She shrugs. "You just think about it and go up!"

"Flit, we're not in Kythshire anymore," Rian whispers. "It doesn't work like that for us here. Besides, if you don't use your wings to fly, what purpose do they serve?" Flit stares at him in wide-eyed disbelief. She waves her wings elegantly, sending bright, dappled prisms of light across the polished wood floor under the bed.

"Oh! Let's play!" she whispers and claps her hands very quietly. "Our wings are our identity," she says. "They catch the magic and hold it for us. They show everyone who we are and what we can do. Think about it. Twig has his stick wings that tell you he's an Earth fairy. You know? Earth? Ground? Roots? Trees? Ember's wings throw out sparks to tell you that she's a Fire fairy. And Shush! Based on his wings, what do you think he is?" I don't have to think long before the answer comes to me.

"Wind," I say. "Shush is a wind fairy." Flit nods excitedly.

"Good!" She whispers.

"I can see it," Rian murmurs. "It makes sense now. Spells are broken down the same way: Earth, Wind, Fire, Water, Light, and Dark."

"Course they are, I bet it's starting to come together in your Magey head now, isn't it? We share the Wellspring with you, so of course you'd have to follow the same laws we do."

"What about Crocus, though?" I say. "She didn't have any wings."

"She does. Her roots are her wings. They come from her back and hold her close to Scree. They need each other, you see. Can't have one without the other. I'll tell you a secret, though. I like my wings much better. They're awfully pretty. Don't you think?" She turns her back to us and looks over her shoulder, showing them off. I shield my eyes from their brightness and Rian squints and nods.

"Very," he says. Above us, the bed making has finished and the door closes softly after the servants as they file out. "I think you win this round, fairy. We need to get going." We crawl out from under the bed and Rian starts casting.

"Remember," Flit whispers to us as me and Rian grow to our normal height. "Be careful not to bump anyone or say anything too loud or sudden. The guards especially are always looking out. If they believe something is there, they'll see you."

It's surprisingly easy to move through the palace undetected. So much so that it makes me a little uncomfortable. Our intentions are good, but if someone with darker motives were to figure out how to get to the Half-Realm, they could cause real damage to the royal family. I make a note to myself as we secretly skirt around a gathering of guards to make the king and his advisors aware of it as soon as I'm able. We meet with a crowd gathered at the palace gates, waiting for entry, which proves a little more difficult to navigate through. Rian holds my hand tightly and pulls me along as he weaves us through the narrow openings between the subjects and we finally reach the safety of the forest park.

"I like it here," Flit whispers from her perch on my shoulder. "So pretty. Look at how the leaves are going golden and red."

"Well, it is Autumnsdawn," I whisper, looking up into the treetops where the clear blue sky shows in patches beyond the gold and red. Beside me, Rian pauses. I follow his gaze through the trees to the guild hall. At first, I can't tell what's made him stop, but then I realize something is off. "No smoke." My breath catches in my throat.

"Hmm?" Flit asks.

"Mouli's fire is out. She's always baking or cooking a stew," he says. "And the hearth fire, that's out, too." Chills prickle at my arms. He's right. Those two fires are always burning, even when the others aren't lit. Even in the heat of midsummer, Luca keeps them well-stoked. I can't remember a time when there hasn't been smoke rising from the hall chimneys. Not only is it a warning to us, it's also a signal to anyone passing by that the place has been left unoccupied. Immediately I think of my father, helplessly asleep in his bed.

Rian and I look at each other, and without a word we break into a run for the hall. I can feel Flit clinging to my braid as we crash through the forest and out into the street to make for the main door of the guild hall. Rian reaches it first and finds it unlocked. He throws it open and we thunder inside, through the hallway to the main hall. He pushes that door open and we're met with a scream as he nearly collides with Mouli. She reacts quickly, swinging her broom at us, sending a puff of soot as it meets Rian's chest.

"Rian! Azi!" she cries. "What do you mean, crashing through here like that? You'll wake your father, let alone give this old woman a heart attack!"

"Could be a boon," Luca's voice is muffled by the hearth. "High time he woke up." A soot-stained oilcloth is spread on the floor before the great fireplace, piled with ashes and burned out coals. All we can see of Luca are his legs. The rest of him is up in the flue. There's a scraping sound and a rush of soot falls down to the fireplace in a black puff. Flit lights on my shoulder again and she presses her face into my braid to cover the sound of her sneeze.

"We saw the fires were out and we thought…" Rian's voice trails off. It takes Mouli a moment to realize what he means, and when she does, she rushes to him and hugs him.

"Oh of course you did, poor dears!" She pats my cheek. "No, no, all is well, all is well. It was just high time for a chimney sweep, that's all. Have you had breakfast?" she wipes her hands on her blackened apron. "It'll be cold, I'm afraid. We're doing mine next."

"Wait, you can see us?" I ask before thinking. Flit tugs on my hair and shushes me and my eyes go wide as I realize I shouldn't have said anything.

"Well, of course I can, you're standing right there, aren't you?" She chuckles. "Come on, we'll go to the kitchen."

"Thanks, Mouli," Rian says, "but we're not staying long. We just came to check on Benen."

"I'm afraid there's not much change there," she says sadly. "Like Luca said, he's just been sleeping. I can't even get him to sip some broth." Her eyes light up. "I'll make you a basket to take along with you when you go." She nods to herself and rushes off, dusting off her apron as she goes. Luca ducks down and blinks at us, and his bright white eyes against the black soot smudged across his face remind me of Ember.

"That came from the palace for you round about midday yesterday," he lifts his chin toward the table and bends for a brush before disappearing into the flue again. I cross the hall, careful not to track any of the black dust with me, and pick up the note sealed with the prince's crest. I crack it open and unfold it to read:

Apprentice Rian Eldinae and Squire Azaeli Hammerfel
of His Majesty's Elite
Your presence is requested at the palace at your earliest convenience
regarding the King's Quest, the progress of which
your guild has neglected to make its report.

Ordered on 22 Autumnsdawn
by
His Highness Prince Eron Plethore
Heir to the Throne of Cerion

Rian and I exchange a glance as he finishes reading over my shoulder. I tuck the parchment into my tunic. We've never neglected our duties in reporting the guild's progress before. If the order had come from the king himself, I'd rush to the palace straight away. But this note tells me that Eron is probably still cursed, and growing impatient.

"We'll deal with it later," he says.

"I'm not worried about the prince," I reply as I carefully step around the soot again. "His Majesty knows why we're not reporting." I'm reminded for a moment that Margy and Eron are having their breakfast together right now, and I'm concerned that he might take out his impatience on her, but I'm comforted by the knowledge that Twig is there for support.

As Luca sets another rush of soot cascading from the chimney, we make our way out of the hall and I take the steps two at a time to my father's bedroom. He's exactly as we left him the night of the ball; his blankets folded over neatly at his chest, his arms limp at his sides over them. I settle beside him on the bed and brush a lock of silvery-blond hair from his forehead. Flit drifts up and begins a fit of sneezes, each one sending a burst of light splashing across the room.

"I'll be back," she says, and she darts out the window with her sneezes trailing behind her.

"Ready?" Rian comes to stand beside me and raises his hands over the bed. "If you hold his hand, it might help him believe you're here enough for you to appear for him. I think the waking spell alone will do that for me."

"Will he wake peacefully?" I ask, taking my father's hand.

Rian nods.

"It won't be like before," he says. "He's of sound mind now. They promised." I nod and watch my father as Rian begins the incantation that will wake him. There's a pause, and his eyelids flutter before his gray eyes find mine.

"Lisabella," he says hoarsely as his eyes search mine, and I see the hope in them fade as he realizes it's me and not my mother. "Azi."

I smile, and relief washes over me.

"Rian's here, too," I say, and he blinks up over my shoulder and nods, his expression slightly apologetic. Rian hands me a glass of water, which I press to Da's lips. By the time he's had three cups, I'm surprised to find that he's strong enough to push himself up in bed to sit against the pillows.

"She's still there, then." It's a statement rather than a question. He sighs. "I was a fool to follow her across. Gaethon warned us, but I couldn't bear to see her walk away from me, knowing it might be the last time..."

"She'll come home again, Da, when her work is done. I'm sure of it." I think of the cyclones and try not to dwell on it. "Rian and I are going to see to it. We have a quest of our own now." I watch Rian close the shutters and door, and place his wards against them.

"Do you, now?" he watches Rian a little dubiously.

"It's complicated, but it's all traced back to Viala," Rian says, "so we're going to go take care of it." My father's eyes narrow.

"Her again?" he grunts. "It seems like all of your problems trace back to Viala, Rian. Just like Azi and that Dacva boy. What would Gaethon say?"

"It isn't just my problem. It affects everyone. Master Gaethon knows," Rian says, "and he agrees that she needs to be taken care of. It's on the verge of Sorcery now." Da's eyes grow wide at Rian's explanation. Such a threat isn't to be taken lightly. After a moment, though, they narrow slightly.

"How could he know?" Da says. "He's off with the others, isn't he?" He shakes his head as if trying to clear his confusion. "How many days have I been sleeping?"

"A lot has happened," I say. "You've been asleep for six days. Almost a week," I say after taking a moment to count back.

He throws the blankets off of himself and jumps out of bed, crossing the room in two strides. I rush after him, expecting him to be weak from starvation, but physically he's as strong as he was the morning Rian put the sleep spell on him. He disappears into the dressing closet that connects our rooms and starts to rummage for a change of clothes. "Da, what are you doing?" I ask, watching as he pulls out some leggings and a gambeson.

"Too much time wasted," he says. "I have to ride. I can meet the others at the crossroad to the Bane if I ride hard." He pulls on the leggings and discards his night shirt. At first I'm confused, but then I remember my dream when I followed the fox day and night and finally into the dark mountain pass that led to the citadel guarded by sentries.

"Bane's Pass," I breathe. "The only road to the Outlands. But, how did you know that's where they're going?" He grunts as he hefts his chain mail vest from its stand, and I cross to help him into it. He meets Rian's eye over my shoulder as his head emerges from the neck hole.

"A little fox showed me," he winks. I turn to look at Rian, who's grinning.

"I thought you said he wouldn't dream?" I say.

"Under normal circumstances, he wouldn't. But that situation is one of the exceptions," he explains.

"What situation?" I work the buckles of Da's hauberk with ease, tightening the leather straps at his side.

"Dream messaging," Rian says. "It's kind of a Half-Realm thing." His explanation does little to clear up my confusion, but I nod anyway, diverted by another thought.

"Da, it's not safe for you to ride out alone," I say. "Redemption turned on us. They're out there. They'd kill you." He tucks his gauntlets under his arm and pats my cheek softly.

"I know. Don't you worry about me," he says. "I won't be going alone. The king will lend us some good men, I'm sure."

"You can't," I say, remembering the king's request of me. "Eron can't know. Nobody can know. His Majesty made me promise to take care of it quietly."

"Then I'll make my request quietly," Da says, stepping into his boots. "Don't worry about me," he repeats. "You and Rian, you focus on your own quest." He kisses my forehead and looks into my eyes with his ever-smiling ones.

Since he jumped out of bed, I've had a nagging worry that this was all another episode of madness, but the truth is right there in his eyes. I believe in my heart that the fae healed him, and his mind is whole now. I trust that somehow the fox delivered the message that his help is needed. His bright red fur flashes in my memory and suddenly my thoughts trail to Elliot and Mya, and Cort and Bryse, and Brother Donal and Gaethon, and even Dacva. I understand that the guild will never be able to face Redemption and the skeletal sentries alone, not with our small numbers. In my heart, I know this is my father's path, and my own path must divert from his.

"All right," I whisper. "But...please be careful." He hugs me close and reaches for Rian over my shoulder. I feel him press against the two of us and his arms encircle us.

"Take care of each other," he whispers. "I'll see you when we return."

Rian removes the wards from the window and door and my father leaves us after another round of hugs and promises of a safe return. I lean against the frame of his door and watch him go, brushing the tears from my eyes. It was such a whirlwind reunion that I can't help but feel a little cheated.

"Rian," I say as I tuck a stray lock of hair behind my ear. "What's going on with the fox? Is it some sort of spirit guide or someone's pet? I don't understand. Why does everyone seem to know about it but me?" Rian comes to stand before me and his lips stretch into a crooked smile. He opens his mouth a couple of times to speak, but shakes his head and laughs quietly instead.

"Apparently, I can't say," he says. "It's interesting that you've gone all this time without ever having that revealed to you. But...does it remind you of anyone, the fox? Think about it. In the meantime, we have work to do." As we make our way together down the hallway, Flit bobs in front of us. Her arms are loaded with a stack of sugar cubes, and she grins up at me.

"Mouli must have gone to market and got more," she beams. "She's all right!"

Chapter Twenty-Two

VIALA

We decide that our best first course of action is to search Viala's quarters in the dormitory, since she's likely to be out this time of day. It takes some convincing on Rian's part. Despite the importance of our quest, I'm very uneasy with the idea of sneaking around someone else's private rooms.

The dormitory building is a smaller echo of the Academy building beside it. With the backdrop of the sea's horizon beyond, the Academy complex rivals the palace in beauty and majesty. The dorms are made up of a block of twenty rooms, which house visitors, students, and instructors who don't otherwise have homes in the city. They have their own entrance at the rear of the campus, where a waist-high wall borders the cliff face. A young boy sits just outside the door, hunched over a book he has propped on his robed knees. We duck into a corner a short distance from the entrance, where Rian begins a spell.

"What's he doing?" Flit whispers. I watch Rian's movements and listen carefully to his incantation.

"I think he's determining the wards," I whisper back. "He's trying to find out if we can go in undetected."

"We can," she says, pointing up at a circular drain hole cut into the stone far above our heads, which is meant to drain water out to the sea far below. I shiver and watch Rian, hoping he's figured out another way, but he shakes his head apologetically.

"She's right," he says. "That's the only way if we want to remain hidden. The door is protected."

"Yay, you can be small again like me," Flit whispers, patting my jaw excitedly.

"Hooray," I groan under my breath and wipe away her sticky

smudge as Rian's spell falls over us. I try to stay calm as I fix my eyes on our entrance, now even higher up. It's right over the cliffs, directly above the whitecap waves crashing on the rocks below. Panic starts to take hold, but then Rian comes to me and circles his arms around me. He presses his lips to mine and my fear ebbs a little. When he smiles at me, his eyes sparkling golden and green and brown all at once.

"Close your eyes and trust me," he says. When I do, he kisses me again I feel us levitating. The smooth stone of the dormitory wall slides against my arm as we rise, and then it gives way. We hover there for a moment, locked in our kiss, until Flit clears her throat.

"Go in," he whispers and I grope around with my eyes still screwed shut to pull myself through the drain hole. "That wasn't so bad, right?" he asks as he crawls in behind me. "Now, where are we?" He looks down the corridor from left to right and turns a couple of times to get his bearings. "This way," he says, leading us eastward.

We walk for what feels like miles, though if we were our true size it would have only been a few paces, before we reach the door that Rian identifies as Viala's. I wonder for a moment how or why he knows the location of her private quarters, and I feel a pang of jealousy. I dismiss it straight away though, and decide it's not worth the risk of a whisper to find out. I trust him. Rian points up at a rectangular slot in the wall, about two hands widths wide, carved into the stone beside the door.

"For messages and meals if one chooses to stay in and study," he whispers, and takes me around the waist so we can float up together into the slot. We walk across a sealed envelope to the sliding hatch door on the other side, and the three of us are able to push it open just a crack in order to peek through into Viala's room.

It is small, but lavishly decorated. Rich red velvets are piled on the plush, ornate bed which stands on a platform flanked by two narrow doors against the far wall. Golden silks billow lazily at the doors on either side, which lead to a private terrace overlooking the ocean. A long desk stacked with scrolls, books, and various piles of parchment stretches along the wall beneath us. A collection of various strange objects from stuffed birds to odd wooden carvings and glass orbs clutters the space. She even has her own hearth, where the fire has burned to coals. More oddities line the mantle shelf, and as Flit crosses the room to walk along it, her light dances over shriveled mice, ragged feathers, oddly shaped skulls, and jars filled with objects that looks suspiciously pink and fleshy. She hugs herself tightly and darts back to us again, her face twisted in disgust.

"That's enough for me," she whispers. "I vote for stripping!"

"We need to be sure," Rian says. He hops down to the desk-top and I follow, finding it very strange to walk among the enormous books and stacks of parchment piled high overhead.

"It'd be easier if we were our own size again, wouldn't it?" I ask him as I cross over a polished slab of blood-red stone.

"I don't want to risk using magic—" he cuts himself off as his eyes widen at the slab beneath my feet. "Step away slowly," he whispers. I look down at the toes of my boots and as I move carefully away, a thin golden line rises up to the surface of the slab, forming elegant script.

"*You're late,*" it reads.

Flit comes to land beside me and peer down at it.

"Oh!" she exclaims. "I've heard of these. It's a Scrier. Someone's trying to talk to us."

The words fade slowly from the polished surface and I look up at Rian for an explanation.

"I've never heard of a Scrier," he says. "Do you mean someone is writing messages to Viala on this?" He bends and places a hand on the cool stone, and the gold line emerges again, swirling into script. "Remarkable."

"*We are not amused,*" it reads.

"Write something," Flit whispers, nudging me.

"We'd better not," Rian says as the words fade again.

With a sudden crash, the door to the room flies open. I yelp and Rian claps a hand over my mouth and pulls me to the safety of the wall between two stacks of books. Flit crowds in beside us and dims her light as Viala strides in. She gestures behind her and the door slams shut again. Breathless, she rushes to the desk, snatches up a quill, and presses it to the slab.

"*I'm here,*" she writes. The words swirl into a thin golden line as she leans over the desk waiting for a response.

"*We know. You are late.*"

"*I'm sorry,*" she writes.

"*We are losing our patience.*"

Viala fumbles at the clasp of her hooded robe. When she releases it, the cloak flies off on its own to rest on a hook near the door. She gazes in our direction, and for a moment my heart leaps into my throat as I think she has detected us, but her focus is on the mirror hanging just above us on the wall. She turns her face to the side and I'm grateful that Rian's hand still covers my mouth to stifle my reaction.

The Mark has crept to cover most of the porcelain skin of her face, swirling across the bridge of her nose, circling her slanted eyes, reaching up beneath the curtain of blue-black bangs. Rather than seem concerned, she smiles at herself with admiration. As the golden glow from the letters fades, she tears her eyes away from her reflection and scrawls across the stone again.

"*I need more time.*" Her hand is shaking. It causes the lines to jut out of control in places. She takes a slow, deep breath, trying to calm herself. Her eyes are wild as she forces her focus on the tablet.

"*Need we remind you who your masters are?*"

"Stars forbid you ever fail to remind me of that," she mutters with contempt.

She writes and speaks in a mockingly sweet tone at the same time. "*You are, of course.*"

"*Yours is a simple task, and yet it remains incomplete. You slow our preparations, after all we have given you,*" it reads.

"Ha!" She bursts out. She bends over the slab and whispers maniacally to it. "All you've given me? You? Everything I have, I've taken for myself. And I'm not finished. I'm not a fool. You aren't stopping me yet." With her jaw clenched and her nostrils flared, she writes, allowing each word to fade before she writes the next.

"*I.*"

"*Need.*"

"*More—*" the last word is interrupted, crowded with script from the other side.

"*Your insolence shall not go unpunished.*" The words fade. "*Who shall it be first? Your brother, perhaps?*"

Viala's laughter starts as a guttural roll and rises slowly, until she's holding her stomach in shrill hysterics. I push Rian's hand from my mouth and stand on tiptoe to whisper in his ear, confident that her manic laughing will cover the sound.

"What's the matter with her?" I ask. Rian bends and presses his cheek to mine.

"Overreach rapture," he whispers. "The rush of too much magic. She's intoxicated."

"My brother!" Viala shouts out incredulously. She glances at the door and quiets her voice. "Oh, no, please, not my brother." Her tone is thick with sarcasm. "Do you really think I care about them, after all this time?" she hisses at the slab. "They're already dead to me." She gazes thoughtfully at the falling golden script.

"*Please*," she echoes in that same mocking tone as she writes. *"I'm sorry. It'll be done by tomorrow, she'll be dead. Out of your way. I swear it."* The words fade, and she writes again. *"Please, don't hurt my family."*

"That should do it," she murmurs, waiting over a long pause as the slab goes blank.

"*You have until sunset tomorrow. Kill the Protector,*" it says. "*If not, then first your sister. Then at sunrise, the grandmother. Noon, the boy.*" The final elegant gold lines emblazon slightly and linger longer than the others before they fade.

She writes, "*It will be done,*" and then scowls and says aloud, "Bastards."

"One more day," she grumbles. She takes a moment at the mirror again, tracing the black lines on her skin with her fingers. Her eyes are strange. Hungry. I look down at Flit, who is staring with horror at the Mark. She scoots back against me as Viala reaches in our direction for an old tome.

When she opens the book, I shrink into Rian's arms at the shock of what I see. There, pressed between the pages like a bookmark, is Margy's ring from my trials. She takes it in her slender fingers and presses the blood-crusted ribbon to her lips as she scans the page. I turn to look at Rian, whose expression echoes my own disbelief. The last I knew, that ring was tucked safely in the keepsake box in my bedroom.

"Now, how to find you, you annoying girl," she whispers as she flips through the book. My heart thumps in my chest and I'm sure Rian can feel it as he tightens his arms around me protectively. "Oh, Azaeli," she murmurs as she reads, "I depended too much on Eron to lure you in. I ought to have done it myself ages ago… Still, it's been amusing to see how long I could delay them." She laughs again and then stops abruptly, her eyes cold and calculating as she stares directly at us. Rian's face drains of color.

"Can she see us?" I mouth to him. He very slowly shakes his head, his eyes wide.

Viala flings one hand in our direction and the three of us duck together, bracing for an attack. Instead, the candle beside us bursts alight accompanied by a puff of smoke that drifts right into Flit's face.

"Location spell, location spell," Viala scans the book. Beside me, Flit's nose scrunches up and I know the sneeze is coming. I shake my head frantically as she pinches her nose and her shoulders rise to her ears. Each of us holds our breath until she finally relaxes with a long sigh of relief. But it's too soon. The sneeze betrays us anyway, erupting loud and squeaky and clear as a bell. Even worse, it's followed by three more in quick succession. Viala's finger stops on the page. She looks up.

The words of her Revealer are aimed directly at me. As the spell streaks across the short distance between us, Flit throws herself in its path to block it. The air shimmers around her and Rian presses his hand over my mouth yet again to block my scream. I struggle to free myself as Viala stares in shock at the revealed fairy.

"Well, well," her red lips curve into a satisfied smile. "What do we have here?" She reaches for Flit, who darts away quickly. "Pretty little thing." Her eyes are full of the same hunger they showed earlier, when she was admiring her Mark in the mirror. Without warning, Viala flicks her wrist and Flit drops to the desk. She glares up at the Mage, the light from her wings so blindingly bright that it stings my eyes. I can't look away, though. I watch in terror, squinting. Flit crouches to spring up again, but instead of taking flight, she only manages a little hop.

Viala grins. "No more flying for you, little one." She reaches down and grasps Flit by the wings, then holds her up as though examining a specimen. She turns her this way and that and brings her close to breathe in her scent. "Do you know what Sorcerers do to fairies, little one? Oh, I'll bet you do. How long will you last me, hm?" Flit swings her fists furiously and kicks and glows brighter until Viala gasps and turns her face away.

"Stop that." She shakes Flit ruthlessly by the wings.

"Put me down!" Flit cries painfully.

"No point in fighting, little one. I've tasted the Wellspring, you know. Drunk it in. I think it's safe to tell you it'll be mine soon. You won't be able to reveal my secrets once I've drained you, will you? How does it feel to know that you'll be contributing to my power? Me, your soon-to-be Queen, hm?"

She hovers her other hand over Flit and my stomach flips as a sparkling purple streak of energy swirls up from the fairy into her palm, draining the color from Flit's ponytail. Flit struggles and reaches into a pouch at her belt. She pulls out a fist full of glittering red powder and flings it into the air. Viala screams and drops her to the desk, clawing at her eyes in pain, and Flit scrambles back toward us.

She isn't quick enough. Viala slams a hand over her and opens a drawer with the other one to rummage until she pulls out a slender dagger. With a cruel stab, she drives the gleaming blade through Flit's wings, pinning her to the desk. Flit whimpers as red light spills out of the wound, draining from her hair. Viala twirls her finger around the escaping energy, soaking it up as Flit lies helpless.

Enraged, I finally break free from Rian and dive at the two, but he's quicker than I am. In the time it takes me to reach Flit, Rian grows in size as he leaps across the desk at Viala, crashing into her. They stumble backward together onto the floor and Viala utters a spell that throws him across the room. He catches himself and jumps nimbly to his feet as she looks around, frantic.

"Show yourself," she growls as she raises her hands to weave a spell, but Rian is too quick for her. He charges again with his fingers outspread and Viala stumbles back, grasping at her throat. I tear my attention from them to Flit, who's deathly still before me. The light spilling from her wings has changed from red to orange now, and when she looks at me, her eyes are colorless.

"My wings," she whimpers. "My light." Viala overcomes the choking spell and sends Rian flying again. This time he soars through the door and lands hard on the floor of the balcony. I try not to imagine him being thrown over the wall to the cliffs below as I drop to my knees beside Flit.

"You took the Revealer for me," I whisper through my tears, grasping her hand. "Why? Why would you do that?"

"She was going to kill you if she saw you," Flit says. Her eyes close slowly as she shivers, her hair and skin draining to gray.

"Flit," I whisper frantically through my tears as I shake her shoulder and squeeze her hand. Her dim eyes flutter open weakly.

"I have to go to the grotto. Heal." She closes her eyes and I expect her to vanish as she always does when she announces that she's leaving, but instead she just lies there.

"Go, it's okay. You can get better and then come back to us with Twig later, right?"

"Don't let her see you," she whispers, avoiding my question. "Promise."

"Flit, I…" I swallow the lump in my throat and steal a glance at Viala and Rian who are now locked in a furious battle of lightning and flame on the balcony.

"Promise," she says again.

"I promise…" I agree reluctantly.

She wriggles her hand in mine weakly. "I can't take you, too. You have to let me go." I realize that it's her hand in mine that's keeping her from going. I let it fall away, and she slowly fades until the only thing that remains of her is the still-sparkling shred of her wing pinned by the dagger.

I keep my promise as Rian and Viala's battle moves inside again, and I dive behind a stack of books as she's thrown into the desk. Rian is thrust away once more and he's down for long enough to give her time to cast the Revealer. He tries to cast a shield to block it, but he isn't fast enough. The air shimmers around him and Viala stumbles back, shocked.

"Rian," she breathes. "What are doing here?" Rian cradles his right arm to his chest as he pushes himself to his feet.

"Stay right there," Viala growls, "or I swear I'll break your other arm, too. Answer me! How did you get past the wards? Why are you lurking in my room? What did you see?" I watch helplessly from behind my stack of books, wishing fervently that Rian had restored my size. Right now, all I have to fight with is a sword that would feel like no more than a pin prick to her. I curse myself for making that promise to Flit.

"I saw enough, Viala," he says bitterly. "Who are they?" He points to the desk where the slab lies blank. She steals a quick glance behind her, long enough to see that Flit has escaped the dagger. Her face falls and she clutches the chair for support as she turns back to Rian.

"Please," her tone changes instantly from venomous to desperate. "Please, you have to help me, Rian." Rian's eyes widen as she crosses to him. She reaches out for him but he leans away. "Please, you saw what they said. Help me or they'll…" her voice trails off.

"Who are they?" he asks again with a glare as he steps back. "How did you get tangled up in this?"

"Sorcerers. They recognized my skill. They sent me here to learn. They said I could repay them later. Just learn, they said. Learn everything you can, as fast as you can. Find out about the Wellspring, and Kythshire. Report it all. It was my only dream, Rian, to be a Mage, to gain power and fame. I never would have had the means to go to school otherwise. I would have worked in the dye fields all my life if they hadn't offered to sponsor me. It was too good to be true, but I didn't care. And now," she blinks piteously at him, "now they have my family."

"That won't work with me, Viala. I heard what you said. You don't care about your family. You're in it for yourself and you don't care what happens to anyone else." Viala eyes him like a predator watching a meal. Calculating. Thinking of an angle.

"You've always been brilliant," she coos. "I've shown you the rush. You've felt it with me, remember?" She steps closer to him, traces her fingers over the Mark on his chest. "And that was only Rumination. Imagine the feel of it in the flesh. The liquid gold slipping through your fingers. Tell me where Azi is, and I'll share it with you. We'll unlock its secrets," she slides her fingers through his hair, "together."

"Get away from me." He grabs her wrist and throws it down. "You're out of your mind. You've betrayed everything we stand for, Viala. You've stolen sacred knowledge, secrets, and shared it all. And with whom? For what? Look at yourself. Your greed is consuming you. And now you expect me to help you?" His eyes flash with a rage I've never seen before in him. "You know how I feel about Azi. Some of us value love over power."

"Enough. Where is she?" she snarls.

"I'm not telling you anything." At Rian refusal to answer, she thrusts her hands out, and her spell strikes him violently. He crashes against the far wall, grabbing the draperies to steady himself. His reply is a murmured word, an attempt to cast sleep. She interrupts with a black tendril that lashes from her palm and wraps around his throat.

"You *will* tell me," she growls. While Rian writhes and chokes, Viala looms over him and presses a fingertip to his forehead. "One way or another." A spark of energy flares at Rian's brow, and the vein at his temple bulges.

"Where," she demands over his moaning and gasping, "is she?"

I forget my promise to Flit. I can't bear to hide myself away and watch this.

"Here!" I scream. "I'm here!" I shove a glass jar off of the edge of the desk. It shatters on the floor and Viala whirls around. I push a second and a third. It works. In her moment of distraction, Rian dispels the choking tendril. He croaks out the sleep spell and thrusts his good hand out, and Viala collapses to the floor as the pink glow settles over her. Rian coughs and rubs his throat as he approaches her prone form with caution. He nudges her with his toe. When she doesn't move, he rushes to me, nursing his broken arm.

"Good thinking," he says, towering above me. "Are you all right?" Speechless, I simply nod.

"Flit?" he asks.

"Gone." I manage around the lump in my throat. "To the grotto."

He turns back to survey the wreck of a room. With a grunt of pain he begins to chant and I watch with amazement as the mess rights itself. The smashed bottles become whole and swirl up and settle on the desk. Books and papers stack themselves neatly beside them. Viala's twisted form floats to settle on the bed, and the velvet coverlet sweeps over her and folds itself neatly. The golden curtains, no longer shredded and torn, flap softly beside her in the sea breeze.

As he conducts the objects into place, I take an inventory of his injuries. His right eyebrow and half of his side lock have been singed completely away, and his ear is charred and blackened. He has an open cut over his left brow, leaving a streak of blood that drips to his jawline. His throat is badly bruised. His left arm is bent where it shouldn't be between the elbow and the wrist, and his hand is purple and swollen.

Once he's satisfied with his work, he turns to me.

"Come on," he says. I climb into his offered hand and he tucks me safely into his chest pocket. Close to his heart, I can hear it racing as he looks over the desk. He scoops up the shredded remains of Flit's wings and slides them into the pocket beside me with reverence. In his bag, he packs the slab, the tome Viala had been leafing through, Margy's bloodied ring, and several of Viala's scrolls and notes.

"What now?" I ask.

"We can't do anything until they arrive tonight. Hopefully the sleep will hold until then." He creeps to the bed and whispers something, and a soft shimmer falls over her. "A little extra, just in case," he explains.

"You need to get to the conclave," I say. I want to ask him to restore my size, but I know that would require both hands and I don't want him moving his broken arm anymore. "You need healing, Rian!" I call up to him as I poke his chest through the fine fabric of his vest.

"Shh," he warns as we cross the room. He brushes his good arm over himself with a quick spell to clean the blood away and repair the tears in his clothing. "Stay down," he whispers as he steps out and closes the door behind him with a soft click.

"Conclave," I say sternly once we're outside again, enroute to the guild hall. "Rian!"

"What happened to her?" he asks me under his breath. "Flit? She's not—"

"No," I reply firmly. "No. She went home to heal. She'll be fine."

"I had no idea Viala was so far gone," his voice is thick with emotion. "Nobody did."

"It's not your fault, Rian."

Salty water drops into the pocket and splashes me, and I look up to see tears sliding down his cheek. We walk in silence the rest of the way, past the loading docks with their colorful banners and the pristine palace with its white towers stretching up into the blue sky, and the forest park rich with red and orange leaves. Everywhere, the bright splashes of color remind me of Flit. The memory of her lying before me, draining to white is more than I can bear in the wake of our encounter with Viala. I curl into the privacy of Rian's pocket and allow myself to weep.

Chapter Twenty-Three

THE FOX

Emme, the nurse who sat with my father after his injuries, is a pious older woman who has dedicated her life to the healing arts. She has a kind, worn face which is always framed with the soft brown hood often worn by healers of the Conclave. She doesn't scold Rian or fuss at him as Mouli did when she first saw his injuries, she simply gets to work settling him into a comfortable position on a chair in the hall, and lays her hands gently on the break. Rian tips his head against the back of the chair and closes his eyes as she works, and soon he's sleeping.

Healing a bone through meditation takes time, and unfortunately, time is something we don't have much of. We both agree that Viala is deserving of the stripping, but doing so would doom her family, and neither of us wants their deaths on our consciences. Emme interrupted our discussion on how we intend to save them, though, and I'm left with little to do in my fairy-sized state but wait and try to be patient. At my current size, our cozy guild hall is as vast as the coliseum, and every piece of furniture is an insurmountable obstacle. I try not to feel intimidated as I settle onto a cushion tucked in beside the hearth. It's a safe spot with a good view of the door and the healing session, and out of the way enough that I don't need to worry about being stepped on accidentally.

With Rian in good hands and nothing to do but wait, my thoughts turn to Flit. I wonder whether fairies have healers of their own, and whether such a delicate and magical thing as a wing can be restored in the same way as a broken bone. My thoughts wander back to Viala's room and begin to darken. Images from the encounter flash before me, and I relive every moment as if it's happening again: Flit diving to take the spell, her light blinding Viala, Rian holding me back, the dagger driving through her fragile wing, the light bleeding out of her.

I should have done more to stop it. I could have shoved her aside and taken the spell myself. Saved her. It wasn't her battle to fight. It should have remained between us selfish, violent humans. Typical, her little voice echoes in my memory. She was right about us all along. We aren't to be trusted. We couldn't stop her from being hurt. I barely even tried. I glance up at Rian, remembering how he held me back and kept me from trying to help her. At first I want to lay the blame on him, but in my heart I know that I could have fought harder. I could have done more. I was useless and cowardly. I was selfish. I sacrificed Flit for my own safety, and now she could be dying.

My train of thought is a tangled mess, but the idea comes clearly to me that somehow it isn't too late. I could trade my life for hers. It would be valiant. It would show them that not all of us are selfish. Not all of us are wicked and greedy. Some of us are willing to make the ultimate sacrifice to save those who are weaker than us.

I don't realize I've left the cushion until I cross the threshold of the guild hall into the street, and then I begin to run. I know where I'm going now, and I want to get there as quickly as I can. The route to the cliff wall is an impossible distance at this size, but my determination to right things quickens my pace so much I feel as though my feet are gliding across the cobblestone as I sprint. The thought of the white foam crashing against the jagged rocks lures me as I dodge and weave around carts and horses. The closer I get, the more convinced I am that my course is the right one. Flit will live. The wrongs will be righted. As the air begins to grow thick with the odor of the fish market and sea air, my heart begins to race. I hope that my death will be fast and painless, but then again, maybe I deserve a little pain.

I reach the wall with surprising speed, but I'm met with another obstacle. The structure, usually waist-high, is now a mountain to be climbed. I find a fisherman's net draped over it and pull myself up. My mind is surprisingly clear as I place one hand over the other, one foot at a time, grasping the wet, slimy knots, not caring if I slip. With each inch I travel upward, my confidence is bolstered. I'm doing the right thing. It'll be over soon. My thoughts stray to Rian for a moment and I pause in my climbing. I didn't get to say goodbye. Won't he miss me?

Selfish, I think, you're being selfish. Keep climbing.

I'm almost to the top of the wall, and then I reach the ledge and pull myself onto it and the sea and the blue sky stretch infinitely out before me. I don't look down. I walk forward, right toward the crisp line of the horizon. It'll be over soon. All will be righted.

Then I'm struck. Flying back, falling to the net again, caught up in a blur of fox fur as I tumble back. It catches me with sharp white teeth by the fabric at my shoulder and I dangle just above the cobbles. When I look up I'm met with a black muzzle and red-orange fur that shimmers in the afternoon sunlight. Its golden eye winks at me, and the surety I felt about diving off the sea wall is replaced with a sense of danger and foreboding. It turns its head to its shoulder, inviting me to ride, and I grasp onto the sleek red fur and pull myself up onto its back. Then we're running fast, streaking though the city streets in a flash. Away from the sea.

Viala. The single name pulses over and over as we go, matching the rhythm of the fox's stride, until my thoughts slowly become my own again. My grip tightens so my fingers ache as I realize how close I came to throwing myself over the cliff, and how convinced I was that it was the right thing to do. The voice repeating her name in my mind is familiar to me, but I can't place it. Slowly, though, I begin to realize what it's trying to tell me. This was her doing. Sleep hasn't stopped her from her work, she's found a way around it. Somehow, she manipulated my thoughts. Convinced me to kill myself.

The palace guards don't see us as we race into the depths of the palace to Margy's cubby in the sitting room. Here the fox slows to a trot, cautiously investigating Margary's soft sniffling. In her lap are the shredded remains of Twig's poppet, which she's doing her best to piece together with a needle and thread. Twig's tether, destroyed. *Eron.* I reach out, wanting to comfort her, but the fox turns away and I have to catch his fur fast to keep myself seated at his sudden burst of speed. As we run, I hope that the shredded poppet doesn't mean that Twig is stuck in Kythshire for good.

We reach the terrace and I duck my head and squeeze my eyes shut as we clear the wall. My heart is in my throat as I brace for the fall, but the sensation doesn't come. Instead we're soaring, carried by the wind, high above the sea. I open my eyes and venture a glance and immediately wish I hadn't.

"Flying again, why does it always have to be flying?" I whisper. Some might see beauty in the crisp blue water rippling below, so clear I can see a world of sea life all the way to the sandy depths. Some might marvel at the endless stretch of sea fading into the horizon, and how very small the masted ships look from this height. All I can think of are the drop, the fall, the impact if I were to lose my grip. I hold on for my life and bury my face into the thick scruff of fur, desperate to distract myself. Rian's question before we left for Viala's hours ago comes to mind. Does it remind you of anyone? The fox?

I think of its red-orange fur and golden eyes, its quick feet and gentle strength. I remember it leaping into the woods after Redemption's retreat from the fight at the border, and I think of Mya's expression as she saw him go. When it comes to me, I can't believe it's taken me this long to realize who it is. I wonder if some sort of concealing magic has been in play to keep me from thinking about it too much.

"Elliot?" I call over the wind that roars in my ears as our pace quickens. I open my eyes to slits long enough to see the brown-tipped ears bob with his nod, and then I duck back into the safety of his fur. "Where are we going?" I shout, but he doesn't answer as we make our slow descent toward the water. A great continent stretches out before us, growing larger and larger as we near it. When the ocean changes to land beneath us his pace quickens impossibly, over the jungle and the desert and the jungle again and then we climb once more, far above another sea.

I close my eyes again and try to think of where we are, conjuring Uncle Gaethon's torturous geography lessons. You'll need to know this one day, he'd said. I hate that he's always right. I mentally plot our course. We've already traveled Southeast over the vast trading channel between Cerion and Cresten City, and across the continent of Elespen into the wide Sones Ocean. Here, I know, is the great triple island continent of Sunteri. Viala's homeland. We travel along the coast of the great island to an intimidating city which I know at once must be the capital, Zhaghen.

I barely have time to take in the opulence of the forbidding towers that stretch into the sky, each draped with silks of rich scarlet and indigo, and the stone facades that sparkle with jewels and gold before we dive down. Elliot slows his pace here, in the depths of the city, on the grimy cobbles of an alleyway strewn with filth. Nearby in the shadows, a huddled woman rifles through a pile of refuse with a sickly-looking baby strapped to her back.

Elliot trots past her and weaves through dark alleys and crumbling shanties in an endless maze of poverty and hopelessness until my heart feels as though it will break into pieces. Just when I'm about to ask him why he's brought me here, when I feel like I can't take another moment of it without taking some sort of action, he pushes off again and we're streaking away out of the city. We cross endless fields of scarlet flowers, where dozens of sunbaked laborers bend, picking and piling blossoms. Their clothes and skin are stained with red, their shoulders permanently hunched. These must be the dye fields that Viala spoke of with such distress.

Soon the ground beneath us fades from red and green to golden, and the desert here feels different from that of Elespen. I'm reminded of the wheat fields of Kythshire and with the thought comes the distinct sense that this place used to be the same. Littered along the grayish sand lie the blackened and petrified remains of a great forest. As Elliot takes us further into the desolation, my heart grows more and more heavy with grief for this place that I somehow know was once as rich and beautiful as Kythshire itself.

He picks up speed until we reach a great bowl-shaped canyon, and he pauses carefully on its rim. The perfectly circular canyon is empty, save for a small amount of sparkling gold liquid at the very bottom. As we watch, a glittering spray of it shoots up into the sky in the direction of Zhaghen, and it empties even further.

"Another Wellspring?" I whisper. "But it's nearly empty…" We trot along the vast lip to a small outcrop of three massive trees, the only ones in sight. As we approach, I realize something is odd about them. Their roots grow in tangles above the ground, twisted together as if clinging to each other for life. We stop a safe distance away and at first I wonder why, but then I see them. A dozen or so creatures huddle among the roots, their nearly white skin stretched tight across their spindly bones, their wings mere stubs at their backs. Their hair is wispy and colorless, and their eyes are black and cruel. One of them darts close to the roots and a whimper escapes from within them. Elliot and I creep closer and I spy a sprig of black hair wound tightly within the twisting prison. A close look reveals the figure of boy who wriggles and fights hopelessly against his bonds. Beside him the other two trees hold their own captives. I can't see them, but I can hear the occasional whimper and cry as the fairies peer in at them.

"Shut up, you three," one of the creatures hisses, jabbing at the roots. We move closer, so close I can touch one of them if I want to. It crouches possessively over something small, blood-red, and polished. An elegant glowing golden line rises up to its surface.

"*Not long now,*" it reads. The wasted fairy snaps its head over its shoulder and spies us. It screeches out a deafening warning and instantly Elliot leaps into the air and dashes away, northward, off again to Cerion.

"We have to go back!" I cry. "We can't leave them there!" Elliot's only response is to go faster until the torrent of wind against my face stings my eyes and I'm forced to bury my head again. I steal glances now and then as we run for leagues and leagues, back over the ocean and the jungle and the desert until the long cliffs of Cerion finally stretch out before us again. The palace walls gleam gold in the sunlight, and as Elliot's paws find the cobbles, I'm struck by the stark contrast between Cerion and Zhaghen.

Here, everyone has a place. It's a pretty kingdom, but modest. Here, we don't flaunt our riches. Here, we are charitable. I think of the wretched woman in the alley with the sickly baby on her back and my grip tightens. That would never happen in Cerion. Cerion isn't perfect. There are those who are lawless and those who are poor, but charity is an important part of who we are. When someone is in need, we help them. I wonder what has happened in Zhaghen to make it so cruel and uncaring.

Elliot carries me up over the wall again and straight to the guild hall, where Rian continues to doze with Emme working over him. At first I think that he means to leave me there, but we only slow to a trot as we pass Rian, and then we're off again. We leave the city walls for the trade road that heads West across Ceras'lain, toward Kythshire. Far ahead of us I can just make out a score of riders in gleaming armor and the livery of Cerion's Guard. As Elliot quickens his run and we near them, I see Da at the forefront in his blue and gold. As we match their pace and begin to gain on them, I watch proudly as he thunders authoritatively over the packed dirt road.

I wave to him as we pass, forgetting that he most likely can't see us as we remain in the Half-Realm. We speed up to a blur again, and it feels as though we're skipping forward in time along the road. We pass the fork that branches to Kythshire and instead of heading that way, we veer north along a different route. The air grows cold around us as we climb into the mountains, and this road is the same that Elliot took me on in my last dream.

It winds along cliffs and narrows dangerously, and I remember the point where the riders in my dream dismounted and left their horses behind. I think ahead to the black keep and the skeleton sentries and I steel myself. This time as we approach, he brings me along the side of the wall and leaps up impossibly high, to a parapet that is tucked against the black stone. We land lightly and silently on the wall, and Elliot slips with caution through the archway of a guard's tower.

Inside, the keep is as grand as Cerion's palace, but so dark it's nearly impossible to see. I can make out only the walls on either side of us, which are lined with countless sentries standing an arm's length apart from each other. There's an unnatural stillness as we creep past them and I realize it's because these aren't men. They're completely lifeless, not even breathing. I hold my own breath as Elliot pads softly along the corridor. He has shown me so much already, all of which I know are important parts of a larger picture, and despite the eeriness of the twisting corridors here, I feel safe with him. Here in this dark place, I'm filled with a sense of battle-readiness that makes me eager to see where this dark path leads and what he will show me next.

We ascend a long spiral staircase and the orange glow of firelight dances on the walls as we reach the top. Here, Elliot pauses just before the threshold of a grand circular room. He peers inside, through a ward that seems to be made of shadows and black coils. The effect reminds me of the cyclones in the field, and I lean away. Echoing my thoughts, Elliot takes a cautious step back. Beyond the magical barrier, I count six figures. Half of them are reclined in ornate cushioned chaises, sound asleep. The other half stand at a great arched balcony, shoulder to shoulder.

This room seems out of place in the otherwise sparse keep. The curved walls are draped with rich damask curtains in bold reds and purples, just like the towers in Zhaghen. A massive mirror over the hearth is set in a gilt frame, and even through the shadow barrier I can see Elliot's golden eyes reflected back at us. Opposite the fireplace, there is a circular table lined with ornately carved chairs. The table is set for six with a feast that has already been well picked-over. Another mirror stands in the center of the room, atop a disc of shining sapphire not unlike the one Rian and I stood on at the ceremony that teleported us.

Movement by the three figures at the window catches my attention. One by one, each of them raises an arm and a clap of thunder echoes over us, shaking the walls. Then, from each upraised hand, a stream of black energy begins to form and swirl until three enormous cyclones swirl before them. Each Mage flings a hand forward and the cyclones drop out of sight beyond the window. The view outside causes me to clap my hand over my mouth. A golden field of wheat stretches out beneath the crisp cool blue sky, and far in the distance I can just make out a lush green forest. My heart starts to race as I realize what it means. Elliot has brought me inside of the Shadow Crag.

In the time it takes me to come to this realization, the three at the window have summoned and released three more cyclones. I tear my gaze from them and scan the room again, looking for any information that we could use. It's difficult to see through the shadow barrier, but my eyes fall on the lap of one of the sleeping figures, where a blood-red polished slab rests gleaming in the firelight. One of the Mages turns away from the window and I see that his skin is completely blue-black from the Mark as he crosses the room to crouch nearby.

He yanks a crimson drape aside to reveal a cage stuffed with a score of tiny sleeping fairies. The Mage reaches in and pulls out a lovely one who instantly reminds me of Shush, with windswept blue hair and a green dress of feathers and dried leaves that shimmers with iridescence in the firelight. He hovers his free hand over her and I watch in disgust as he draws forth a stream of green and blue light from her which he absorbs into his palm. When he's finally through and the energy fades to a wisp, the fae's bright green skin and blue hair have drained to bone-white. I'm reminded of Flit lying on Viala's desk

252

and the twisted white fairies at the trees. My stomach twists as he tosses the helpless creature into a second cage, this one filled with similarly drained, unconscious fairies.

Elliot wriggles his shoulders slightly and I realize I'm gripping his fur so tightly in my fury that I've pulled some of it out by the roots. I loosen my grip and stroke it down apologetically. When he looks over his shoulder at me, his eyes echo my own rage. These Mages are using the fairies' own magic against them. I wonder how my mother is managing the torrent of cyclones on her own. The Mage returns to the window, and one of his companions leaves to cross to the cage and pluck out another windblown fairy. I can't watch it again. Instead, I lean to Elliot's ear and whisper so quietly I'm barely mouthing the words.

"Why would they do this?" I ask. His only answer is to turn his head and stare at one of the hanging curtains, where an elaborately embroidered crest has been hung. The symbol in golden thread is a hand with a glowing globe hovering over it. The crest of Zhaghen.

We're off again, this time he runs straight across the deep circular stairwell, toward the narrow slit of an archer's window. I brace myself thinking it will be too narrow, but we slip through with no trouble at all. I feel a sudden change in my mood as Elliot prances to the south. Suddenly I feel both calmed and bolstered. The air is thick with magic as Elliot turns to the balcony where the three Mages stand. We dive to the craggy slope that the keep is perched upon and my breath catches in my throat at the scene that unfolds before me.

We're running alongside the vast piles of gold and jewels at the base of the massive Shadow Crag. As the cyclones charge down the slope from the keep window, the black craggy stones of the mountainside grow to form human-sized figures. Golems, similar to Rian's glass one at the trials and Flit's figure of light that I trained against in the grotto. Some swing stone swords, while others have enormous clubs or just fists that they use against the cyclones, bursting them into wisps of shadow. With each defeat, tiny voices rise together throughout the battlefield in a victory cheer.

Elliot weaves carefully through the jagged battlefield of stone clashing with wind and I'm amazed to see that each of the rock golems has a fairy hovering nearby. Beside us, a glowing red golem of molten stone is torn apart by a cyclone, and the bright red-skinned fairy accompanying it is sucked into the swirling black mass. A larger gray golem rumbles up, trailing flakes of white ash behind it. It swings its stone club and the cyclone dissipates, dropping the captured fae to the ground and inciting yet another victory cheer.

"Thanks Ash!" the rumpled red fairy chirps and ruffles her short-cropped yellow hair before she waves her hand at a nearby pile of rock. It begins to glow red and liquid as it rises up into the form of a woman this time, with an elegant sword. She gives a squeaky battle cry and then charges together with her golem to an oncoming cyclone.

"Woo! Any time, Glow!" her rescuer calls after her as he sends his own gray golem against another attacker. "Get 'em!"

"Who let that one past?" Ember's familiar gruff voice shouts as she nears us. She points at Ash. "You! There's a hole on the east side, get over there!" Her red-orange hair ripples and glows with wrath, and the sparks that trail behind her flash brightly as she dives past us in a commanding fury.

"You got it, Boss!" Ash gives a salute and guides his golem off to the east.

"Ember!" I call out, and she whips around, her eyes narrowed.

"What are you doing here?" she snaps. "You're early! I'm not leaving until moonrise!" A cyclone surges toward her and she throws her arms to the side. Nearby, an enormous shining black golem with glowing orange veins crashes into it and throttles it into oblivion.

"I'm not here to collect you," I say.

"What, then, just to have a chat?" she growls. "If you're not going to help, then stay out of the way!" she screams over her shoulder as she speeds to the west side of the mountain, calling commands as she goes. "You, there, stop that one!" I whip around and watch as another cyclone finds a gap in the golems and charges away off across the piles of gold and jewels to disappear into the wheat. Ember's golem, which had been chasing it, skids to a stop at the edge of the treasure, sending a spray of gold coins into the air. Ember turns back to me again. "You see that? Every one that gets past us goes straight to your mother! We don't need you here distracting us! Fight or leave!" She darts away after her golem, calling it back to her.

"Fight," I say to Elliot as I start to slide from his back. Here, I can wish myself back to my own size again, or even bigger. I have my sword. I can help. But Elliot nudges me back with his nose and turns to look pointedly up at the window where the Mages continue their summoning. He shakes his head firmly, and I get his message. For now, my part in this lies elsewhere, away from the Mages who want me dead.

Elliot leaps up to the sky, and we're off again, faster and higher than before. My stomach sinks as we bolt eastward, away from the setting sun. To Cerion. I bury my face into his fur again and go over everything I've seen in my mind, from Viala talking me over the cliff to Margy mending Twig's tether, and all the way to Zhaghen and back. The scene in the tower and the mountainside battle have my blood boiling. When he lands softly and I open my eyes to find us in the guild hall again, I'm relieved he has nothing more to show me. Now that we have all of the information we need, we can start our planning.

Emme has gone, and Rian doesn't notice us at first. He's at the table now, bent over the books and scrolls he grabbed from Viala's desk. Her polished red slab lies on the table beside him, blank and gleaming. He's taking fervent notes from one of the books, poring over a map, and he doesn't notice me until Elliot deposits me on the table beside him and I step onto the page and lean on his quill hand.

"Hey," he grins down at me. "Back already?"

"Wait until you hear where I was," I say, tilting my head back to look way up at him.

"Oh, I know," he says, and gestures to the map beside him, which has been marked with the course Elliot and I just finished. When I raise a questioning brow at him, he glances over his shoulder at the empty space where Elliot was just moments before. "A little fox told me while I was healing. Either that or I need to get my head looked at."

Chapter Twenty-Four

MIND GAMES

"You saw everything?" I ask, thinking back over the journey that started with me trying to throw myself off the cliff. I try not to think of how far I might have gone if Elliot hadn't intervened. I'm too ashamed to talk about that now, especially to Rian. "Did you see Zhaghen?" I ask. His expression darkens slightly and he nods.

"Awful," he says. "The Academy is always using Zhaghen as an example of what could happen if magic is abused. There's a general idea among the students that the masters exaggerate. I had no idea it's really like that."

"It got that way because of the Mages?" I ask.

"Mm." He follows a passage in a book with his fingertip and takes a note. "You saw the city. Gold and jewels glittering in the bricks of the towers, ten stories of silk draping from the windows, all while others starve in the streets. It happened over decades, so they say at school. Slowly, so that at first they didn't realize the damage they were doing. It might have started with a few decorations at a party." He glances up at me meaningfully. "Magic has that effect. Slow intoxication. You do a little bit, and you want a little more until you're blinded by the beauty and the power of it and you no longer see the damage you're doing. And if you don't know something exists, you can't care about it. You just want more. And when there's no more energy to draw from, you steal it from others. That's when it stops being magic and starts becoming Sorcery. Those people you saw in the keep, they were wicked. Twisted by evil and selfishness. Sorcerers. Necromancers, too, from the looks of all of those skeletons." He shakes his head.

"It's why the Academy has so many restrictions and secrets. True students learn early on how important it is to have self-control. It's one of the reasons Viala's rising so quickly has always bothered me. It's not like them to allow that. But she has always found a way to get around the rules, and for some reason, they let her. Not only that, it's expensive. I always wondered how she was able to pay for her exams. Now I know. She had powerful backers."

I sit quietly, watching him work and thinking about what he's said. After a while, Rian pauses from his note taking and tilts his head to one side, offering me a half-grin.

"Are you going to stay fairy sized? I thought the first thing you'd do when you got back would be to ask me to grow you up again." I blink up at him. With my thoughts so full, it completely slipped my mind.

"Actually, yes, please!" I say, hopping down from my perch on a book spine.

"Oh, I don't know," his grin widens. "I kind of like you pocket-sized." He offers me his hand, palm-up, and I climb into it.

"Don't tease, Rian!" I chuckle at his mockingly serious expression as he ponders changing me back.

"Are you sure? I could make a little pouch for around my neck and carry you with me wherever I go. You'd be up high all of the time. You'd love it, I promise." He wriggles his brow at me teasingly.

"Rian…" I wrinkle my nose at him in a very Flit-like manner.

"Oh, you're no fun." He cups his hand over me gently and lowers me to the floor. "I could teach you to do it yourself, now that you're a Novice. Then you could grow and shrink whenever you'd like."

"No," I say straight away. I don't even need to think about it. After what I've just seen, I want no part of magic. "No thank you. Please just do it." I close my eyes and hear him murmur his spell, and I feel myself stretching up again. When I open them, I'm back to my own height. Almost. "Wasn't I a little taller?" I ask him, coming to his side. I put my hand on top of my head and move it in a line to his shoulder. "I used to come at least to your chin, Rian!"

"Maybe I've grown," he winks.

"Come on…"

"Oh, all right." He wiggles his fingers and I shoot up another hand span.

"That's better." I smooth my braid and peer over his shoulder at his work. A glimmer of gold draws my gaze to the polished red tablet, where the swirling lines are beginning to form script. "Rian," I whisper, and nod to it as a single word forms.

"*Sunset.*" It reads. Rian and I look at each other and then back to the tablet again.

"Should we reply?" I lean over it and watch as the words fade away. Rian does the same.

"Probably not," he says. "It's most likely the Sorcerers in the keep who are doing the writing, not the ruined fairies in Sunteri. Remember what the slab said to them? The ones crouched under the trees? It said 'not long now.' I expect that the Sorcerers are using that stolen magic to break their way into Kythshire. They need its magic now that their own is nearly depleted. They mean to steal it for themselves, and possibly for all of Zhaghen.

"Viala has been researching our Wellspring and the borders of Kythshire for quite a while now." He gestures to the array of torn pages and books strewn across the table. "I'm sure she's told them everything there is to know about it. That's why they paid her way to study at our Academy. They were using her to infiltrate our libraries and gather as much information as she could about our source." He picks up one of the books, a small, leather-bound journal filled with scarlet ink, and thumbs through it. "She writes that she eventually realized their dark intentions. She figured out exactly what they were using her for and tried to refuse to help them after that, and that was when they took her family."

"How horrible..." I trail off, shaking my head.

"Don't feel sorry for her, Azi," Rian says sternly as he tosses the journal back onto the table. "Have you forgotten she wants to kill you? She already tried once." He clenches his jaw as his eyes flash cold, but then he closes them and takes a deep settling breath, and I can see the discipline he mentioned earlier as his features settle back to calm again.

"I should have been able to tell that she was in my head," I shake my head. "I was so determined that jumping off the wall would make everything right." He places his fingertips under my chin gently and tilts it up to look at him.

"Sorcery," he says. "Mind control is a branch of magic Cerion's Mages never dare cross into. Viala has shown us exactly how far she's willing to go." He looks down at the tablet, now blank. The lines swirl again and then return to form the same word.

"So it's sunset. What do they want?" I wonder as I slip my arms around him. When he does the same, his touch sends a rush of warmth through me. I sigh and lean into him.

"They're just checking in on her, I imagine. To make sure she's doing as she's told."

"Sunset. They gave her until tomorrow at sunset to get rid of the protectors." I sigh and think of the pathetic bundles wrapped in the roots of the trees. Rian slides his page of notes to cover the slab just as Mouli bustles in with a tray of something that's still sizzling. My mouth instantly waters as the aroma of roasted fish and root vegetables drifts over us.

"Oh, Azi, wonderful! You're back in time for dinner." She sets the tray on the table and beams at me, opening her arms for a hug. I slip from Rian's arms a little reluctantly to accept hers. "Oh, dear," she tsks as she squeezes my shoulders, "Don't you two eat while you're out doing whatever it is you've been doing? Sit down, sit down. I'll fix you up with this and bring out seconds. Honestly!" She shakes her head as she sets out the plates, murmuring to herself. "Make me look bad, walking through the city looking like two starved strays!" She scoops a generous helping onto my plate, "Clothes hanging off of you..." she plucks at my tunic and pauses, rubbing the fabric between her fingers. "This isn't one I bought you, is it?" Rian and I exchange a glance.

"No," I shove a heaping portion of fish into my mouth to distract her, "Mmm... sho good." I say.

"Don't talk with your mouth full." She scolds me with a swat before she turns to Rian and prods him. "You, too! Eat!" She stands over him until he takes a bite to placate her and nods appreciatively, and then she rushes off to the kitchen again.

When she's gone, Rian pushes his plate aside and smoothes the map of the Known Lands surrounding Cerion. It's covered with a thin sheet of tissue which he has marked with the path that Elliot and I took on our journey. He circles Zhaghen and then draws a line back to Cerion, along the Trade Road, through the mountains of Cerion Proper, and then circles Bane's Pass. He draws a square and labels it "Keep/Crag?" I look at the map while he draws and realize something isn't quite right.

"How can that be?" I ask as I lean over to look. Bane's Pass, where we entered the keep with the Sorcerers, is in a deep ravine. According the map, one side of the ravine is bordered by a great lake and the other side is bordered by a channel of sea that separates it from Kythshire. It doesn't meet up with Kythshire on the map the way it did when Elliot and I were there. "It's wrong. It just shows water between Bane's Pass and Kythshire."

"Not wrong," Rian glances to the doorway and pulls his plate back. He takes several large mouthfuls in quick succession, just as Mouli reappears with another tray. She examines our plates and nods her approval as she serves a bowl of warm honey breads and soft cheese. I snatch one up quickly and spread it with cheese and take a bite that melts on my tongue like a cloud. When I look up at Mouli to offer my appreciation, I find her staring at Rian's marks on the map with a worried expression. She forces a smile when our eyes meet, and then she rushes out of the hall again. Rian is too focused on the map to notice. "Sorcery. That's the only way to explain it. There are six of them. It's certainly possible."

"What is?" I ask. He draws a line connecting Bane's Pass to Kythshire.

"The map is off, like you said. Only it wasn't drawn wrong. They changed the landscape." He shakes his head in awe. "I've only read about it in theory. No one has ever dared try it, as far as I know." He presses his fingertips to his brow and shakes his head. "Azi, if they succeed, if they succeed in entering Kythshire, if they claim the Wellspring, everything we know will be destroyed. They won't stop there. They'll take Ceras'lain, and Cerion, and Haltil…and everything else within their reach. And everything will *be* within their reach, believe me."

"How can we stop them?"

"With help," he says. "And stealth. It's already been set up for us, thanks to my da. Your father is moving here." He taps the map. My eyes follow the line of the trade road that leads to Bane's Pass, down which my father was leading a battalion of the king's guard. I imagine him and his twenty men clashing against the countless skeletal sentries at the keep.

"Rian, they can't!" I shake my head, "they'll be outnumbered ten-to-one!" He draws another line, this one a route from Kythshire's border to Bane's Pass.

"Not with the guild beside them. Your uncle alone could take out half of those sentries with his siege magic."

"They were trailing Redemption, though," I say.

"I know," he rests his chin in his hand and studies the map thoughtfully. "Da didn't show us about our guild or Redemption, which means whatever they're doing now isn't something we need to concern ourselves with. He only showed us what we need to know to make a plan."

"Which is what, exactly, then?"

"Well," Rian holds up his hand and starts ticking off the list on his fingers, "You swore to the king that you'd stop Eron's plotting with Viala as quietly as possible. We swore to the f—uh, anyway, we swore that we'd strip Viala if we saw good reason to, which we have, definitely." He taps another finger, "and obviously, being the only ones who can move unseen within the Keep, we're going to have to be the ones to stop the Sorcerers."

"Oh, obviously. So, nothing too harrowing, then." I groan and rake my fingers through my hair as he pats my shoulder reassuringly.

"We'll have help, remember. The others will be here at moonrise. But I think our first step should be to figure out a way to rescue Viala's family. Sunset tomorrow is the most pressing deadline we have right now."

"You don't want to strip her first?" I ask. Rian slides the map away and nibbles on a bite of his roll silently. "You think," I offer quietly, "if we save her family, we might be able to save her, too, don't you?" I shake my head, smelling the sea air and seeing the crisp blue line of the horizon stretched out before me as I step forward on the cliff wall. I see her kissing Eron's jaw in the royal sitting room, the black tendrils of the Mark displayed proudly on her bare arms. I watch her pinch Flit by the wings and eye her greedily, see the dagger driven through her wings at the desk, watch as she's drained of her vibrant color. All of it swirls before me as clearly in my memory as if it's happening again, right now. My eyes narrow and flood with tears. How could he possibly want to help her? I'm so angry I can't even look at him.

"Maybe," he answers gently. "Who are we to decide who's worth saving and who's worth punishing? What would you have done in such a desperate situation? Can you honestly say that you wouldn't do everything in your power to help the ones you love?" I realize I'm gripping the edge of the bench so hard my knuckles have gone white.

"She was plotting well before they had their hands on her family, Rian. Margy said she had her claws in the Prince back when he took his tour of Ceras'lain and crossed into Kythshire. Do you honestly think that sparing her will be enough to change her heart? Did you forget what she did to poor Flit? Some people are beyond help. She controlled me despite your sleep spell, Rian! Even unconscious, she's dangerous. How is that even possible?"

"My sleep is a weak spell, compared to her Circle," Rian sighs, "In theory, it really shouldn't have even stuck. I was surprised when it did, but it's not as strong as when I put it on your father. There are gaps. I suppose that's the easiest way to explain it." He frowns, "If she tries hard enough, she can push out of it. She already did, really. That's how she was able to feed you suggestions. It's amazing, really."

"Well, that should make you want to strip her even more!" I shove away from the table and get up. His sudden admiration of her skills turns my stomach. I'm so angry I don't even want to sit beside him anymore.

"Azi, you've seen firsthand what she can do. She's got incredible talent. If we could convince her to see our side of things--"

"You want to ally with her? After everything we've seen? Are you serious?"

"I am, if you'd just listen to me!" He slams a fist onto the table. "She could be an asset to us! If we could rescue her loved ones and bring them back here, then she might be out for revenge. Actually, we could take her with us to Sunteri. I bet she knows a way. If we could succeed in that, then she might help us against the Sorcerers. She's powerful, so powerful." His eyes grow distant and unfocused as he gazes past me into the fire. "She knows things." He picks up the worn journal and tosses it to me, "Maybe if you picked up a book once in a while you'd have a clue!" His words hit me like a punch to the stomach, and I have to stop myself from doubling over from their cruelty when the journal thumps my chest. I catch it, wide-eyed.

262

"Listen to yourself, Rian. This isn't you. You're not making any sense."

"I'm making perfect sense to anyone with half a brain," his tone is filled with disdain as he shoves his plate away. His hand flashes with blue-white energy that crackles in the air, leaving the scent of a lightning strike thick in the air around us. He pauses for a moment as he looks down and flexes his fingers, and then he turns away from me and speaks with a warning tone, "Azi. Get out." The lightning charges up his arm and he clenches his fist. I back toward the door as he hugs his arms around himself, locked in an inward battle.

"It's her, isn't it? She's doing this."

"I'll kill you," he says. "Go! Lock the door behind you!" He doubles over and grits his teeth as the energy crackles around him again. I take another step away and my gaze rests on the red slab on the table beside him. A fleeting thought enters my mind. I should take it with me. Take it, and bring it to the Academy. Bring it back, it doesn't belong to us. It belongs to Viala. I blink. Her name sends a flood of realization through me that breaks her hold. I cross the room and take Rian by the shoulders.

"Look at me," I say, ignoring the burn of the charge that surges into my hands as we touch. I don't pull away. Instead I grip harder, shaking him gently. "Look, Rian." His hazel eyes meet mine distantly at first and then slowly come into focus. The connection between us grounds him, and eventually the crackling energy fades until it's gone completely.

"I'm so sorry," he whispers as he draws me to the bench and we cling to each other. "We've got to end this. She's so subtle we don't even see it coming. So dangerous. As soon as the moon rises and they get here, we'll go straight to the dormitories and get started. In the meantime, we need a stronger ward." He tightens his embrace and begins to whisper an intricate spell over us both, and I bury my head into the hollow of his shoulder as the air shimmers and settles around us.

"Huhem." Luca clears his throat from the doorway. Something rattles in the heavy sack that's slung over his shoulder as he crosses to us. He slides one hand between us, pushing Rian's shoulder gently a hand's length from mine, then wiggles a finger at our legs, which are pressed together on the bench. We scoot away from each other and he eyes us, assessing our new proximity. "That's better. I'm watching you two. You especially," he points a crooked finger at Rian.

"Yes, sir," Rian nods gravely, but when Luca turns away he presses his lips together to keep from laughing, and I shake my head and cover my smile. We wait until he's gone through the training square and then he slides close to me again. "Everything we're going through and his biggest concern is with you and me…" he trails off. I try to ignore the bloom of red that has spread across his cheeks all the way to the tips of his ears.

"Anyway." He clears his throat and I press my fingertips to my own hot cheeks.

"I wonder if the moon is up yet." I offer quickly, jumping up to rush to the training square where the ceiling opens up into the overcast sky. "I think it's going to rain," I call in to him.

"Azi!" Flit's tiny voice squeals as she crashes into my neck. Her arms stretch as far as they can around my jawline and squeeze, and colorful prisms of light flash and dance before my eyes.

"Flit!" I laugh and reach up to pat her, but she's gone from my shoulder in a blink and then she's standing person-sized before me, just a bit shorter than I am. Her eyes dance from yellow to blue to green and I have to close mine against her gleam.

"That's better." She laughs as she throws her arms around me in a tight embrace. "Oh, and I got another T, so it's Flitt now." She giggles. "T for Teeming. I got it just now, and Crocus gave me these, too!" She steps back from me and I try to look, but she's glowing so brightly that I'm mostly blinded as she turns her shoulders away from me. I raise a hand to shield myself from the light but it does little good.

"Oh! Sorry!" She giggles again and the light fades enough for me to see the beautiful wings at her shoulders, twice the size they used to be and gleaming with a dazzling iridescent sparkle that splashes over us both.

"Oh, they're stunning!" I say.

"I know!" She jumps up and suddenly she's back to fairy size again. A trail of glowing colors streaks out behind her as she dives and loops around the square.

"Yes, yes, it's very impressive, Flitt." Ember says dryly from behind me, "Can we get on with this as quickly as possible? As all of you know, I have more important places to be." I turn to find the others, Twig and Shush, hovering beside her.

"Oh, is this where you live?" Shush whispers quickly. He flies forward and makes a circle around, stopping here and there to look at the weapons lining the walls. He comes back looking puzzled. "It's an awfully strange place. No beds. Nothing pretty to see. Lots of dead wood, though." He flies up to the wall and raps on it with his tiny hand.

"They do like dead things…" Flitt nods, "but once you get used to that, it isn't so bad here."

"Do you think we could get some of those sweet white morsels?" Shush rushes to Flitt. "The ones you told me about from the…what is it called? Kudgen?"

"Kitchen. Sure. Come on, I'll show you!" She grabs his hand but skids to a stop in midair as Ember circles to confront them.

"Nobody is going to the kudgen, or whatever it is," Ember bursts. "We have work to do."

"Right," Rian says as he comes to my side. "The sooner the better."

"You've made a decision, then?" Twig asks gravely.

"Yes. There's no way around it," Rian says. "She's too dangerous."

"We've got to be careful," Twig lowers his voice. "The prince is on a rampage. He tore up my tether. Luckily it still worked to get us here. But he's after you two now."

"After us?" I think of the royal summons, still resting unanswered on the hall table.

"Oh, yes!" Flitt darts to us, coming to a stop between Rian and I. "I almost forgot to tell you. He's sending men here. He said you're under attested."

"Arrested." Twig corrects her.

"Arrested, that's right." She nods.

Rian and I exchange looks of alarm and he runs back to the hall, where he starts shoving Viala's books and pages back into his bag. He tucks the slab in last, and the rest of us follow him down the corridor to his house.

"Ohh, is this the kudgen, er, kitchen?" Shush peers around at the cabinets while Rian kneels and rolls up the rug beneath the table to reveal a trapdoor. He shoves the bag inside and closes it up again. Once he's sure it's safely stored away, he whispers a spell and the air shimmers around us.

"Oh!" Flitt pauses with her arm halfway into the sugar jar. "You learned the hider. Good job!"

"The hider?" I ask Rian.

"Removes the Revealer," he says. "So we stay hidden in the Half-Realm."

"But when—?"

"Twig showed me, while you and Flitt were in the training square." He takes my hand. "Let's go." We jog together back through the corridor to the main door, where Mouli wrings her hands as she greets two palace guards through the half-door.

"I see," she says hesitantly. "Come in. They're just in here, in the hall." She turns to lead them down the hall, and Rian and I have to press ourselves against the wall as they pass by. "I'm not one to argue with the Prince, of course, but I'm sure it must be some mistake, or an oversight. They couldn't really be arrested, imagine!" she laughs nervously.

We don't wait to hear their reply. With my hand in Rian's and the fairies fluttering behind us, we slip out the door and run full-out to the Academy dorms.

"I don't understand. An order for arrest would have to be approved by the king," I whisper to Rian. "Eron doesn't have the authority." I try to keep calm, but the very thought that we're now running from the law has my heart racing with a mix of terror and shame.

"The king is ill," Twig whispers, hanging onto my collar. "He took to his bed around midday."

"Perfect," Rian utters as we skid to a stop along the cliff wall.

"Do you think it was her doing?" I ask him as I lean against the wall. I look up at the balconies overlooking the sea until I locate Viala's golden drapes blowing softly in the breeze.

"I'm sure it was. The timing is too much of a coincidence for it not to be." He shakes his head and turns to Ember and Shush. "It's time. What do you need from us?"

Chapter Twenty-Five

WINDSWEPT

As the first plump drops of rain begin to fall, we find a quiet alcove to huddle in just across from the dormitory. There, Ember explains the process of stripping to us. It is a long process, she says, and painful. Viala will need to be restrained or she will fight. Her magic will be drawn out a sliver at a time, and magic doesn't just go away, so each sliver will be placed into a grain of sand in a stone flask Ember carved from her own golem. Then, she and Shush will return the tapped magic to the Wellspring. I watch Rian, whose jaw is clenched as he stares across at the dormitories, listening to Ember's instructions. My part will be to hold her down and guard against attack. The whole thing makes me uneasy. As much distress as she has caused us, as dangerous as she is, I don't relish the idea of having to restrain her while others cause her pain.

My thoughts are interrupted by the approaching rhythm of boots marching in unison. All of us turn at once to see a dozen of the city guard rounding the corner. It's an odd sight. The city guard is usually a quiet presence, with one or two members milling here and there, keeping an eye out for trouble. These men, though, are stern and serious as they march in a grouping of three columns of four. Battle ready. As they approach the Academy, half of them split off and station themselves in front of the main door. The rest approach the dormitory beside it and round the corner to the side door.

"Those men are all armed up and ready to fight, aren't they?" Flitt bobs beside me.

"See?" Shush whispers quickly, "That's what I picture when you say human. Cold. Big. Shiny metal. Sharp things. A bit frightening."

"What are they doing?" Rian mutters, "The guards never bother with the Academy." As if answering his thoughts, the main door to the complex opens and an elderly Mage pops his head out. His shaggy white eyebrows rise into the cloudy nest of hair atop his head. When he speaks, his voice echoes across the square.

"Good evening, good evening, good sirs," he says, reaching up to scratch his nose. "May I help you?"

"Master Rendin," one of the guards nods. "We received orders to stand guard tonight, for your protection." The others with him stomp the ground in unison and stand at attention. "There's word of a threat against the Academy, and we're to keep watch and apprehend any attackers."

"Ho, ho!" Rendin's eyes twinkle with amusement as he looks from one guard to another, as if waiting for the punchline of a joke. When they remain still and serious, his smile fades. "I see, well." He watches them for a moment and then shakes his head. "I don't see any harm in it, I suppose. Carry on then." He ducks back inside and closes the door, and Rian lets out a long breath.

"He's letting them stay?" I peer out at the six men, who fan out under the awnings as the rain pelts harder.

"He obviously finds it amusing. The Academy is so well protected with magic that it's really pointless to station guards outside. Any non-student wanting to enter could never get through. Rather than argue with them, he's just going to allow it." His eyes narrow, "but they're not there to protect the Academy. You heard what they said. They're keeping watch, for us. This is her doing."

"Always so clever, and seemingly one step ahead." Viala's velvety voice sends a shiver through me. "But did you plan for this?" We turn quickly to see her lithe form sauntering to us through the rain, but something is off. She isn't solid like us, she's more of an apparition. The raindrops fall right through her. Still, I find myself reaching for my sword as she approaches Rian and slides her fingertip along his cheek. He ducks away from her.

"Viala. How?"

"How?" She tilts her head to the side and her lips form a seductive pout, "Can't you think of how? After all," she gestures to her nearly transparent form, "this is your doing." She circles around him, watching him beneath heavy eyelids as he goes rigid with discomfort. "It was difficult at first, finding a weakness in that wretched sleep spell of yours." She tilts her head to the other side as she grazes his shoulders with her fingertips. "But then I started thinking about how you eluded me in my room, and I thought of the fairy," she turns to Flitt and flashes her a cruel smile, "and I realized there are other states of being. Once I figured that out, the possibilities were endless." She gestures across the street at the guards, "As you can see."

"If that's the case," Rian says, "then you know that the guards are pointless. We could just walk in. They'd never see us."

"Not completely pointless," she purrs. "They gave you pause. They bought me time. They showed you my reach, my power now." Her eyes glint past him to me and the fairies. "You've brought friends." Her lips curl into a wicked grin as she saunters toward me. To my surprise, Flitt dives bravely between us as she approaches.

"You don't scare me!" she cries, her fists firmly on her hips.

"Oh, I ought to, pretty little wings," Viala coos. She reaches up to swat Flitt away, but her hand goes right through her.

"See!" Flitt jeers, "You can't do anything, can you? Nothing but talking. You're not really here."

"Flitt..." I warn, stepping closer.

"She isn't! She can talk but she can't do spells, and she can't even touch us. Look!" Flitt dives straight through Viala's chest and out the other side. "She's in the dreaming. You can't do anything from the dreaming. Only watch, and listen, and talk." Viala's eyes narrow and she spins back around to face Rian.

"And yet I've found a way," her voice is silky-smooth again, "to control. A suggestion is a powerful thing, isn't it, Azi?" She grins at me over her shoulder and I shrink away as I'm reminded again of my moments on the cliff wall. "There is always a way, Rian." She stands before him again and gazes up into his face.

"Set me free and I'll show you. It can all be ours. The kingdom, the Wellspring, it's all within our grasp. We'll rid that Keep of the Sorcerers together and claim it for ourselves. All of it. We can do as we please with no one to stop us. No more rules, no limitations. I'll even let you keep her, for your pleasure." She nods to me as though I'm some sort of object to be used as a bargaining chip. Anger floods me, and I have half a mind to march through the dormitory to her room and drive my sword through her where she lies in her bed. "Just wake me," she purrs to Rian, her lips against his ear just as they had been with the prince.

There's a long stretch while Rian and Viala regard each other, during which the fairies huddle together, whispering fiercely to one another. They seem to think he's considering her proposal, but I know Rian better. That's why when he gives her a slight nod and starts to cross with her through the rain to the dormitory, I'm completely shocked.

"Is he going to do it?" Flitt whispers to me.

"Are you really that surprised?" Ember drawls, "He's a Mage, after all. None of them can be trusted." She cocks her head toward Shush but pointedly avoids actually looking at him. "Time for the backup plan."

"But he saved me," Flitt says as I stand frozen to the spot. "I was almost going to let him be my friend…" My legs are too stiff, my feet too heavy to move as I watch Rian disappear into the sheets of rain. Flitt's voice is a distant echo as she goes on, "He wouldn't make friends with her. Azi, go after him!" She grabs my braid and tugs it, snapping me out of my daze. I dart across the street and the others follow. We reach the side door just in time to see Rian levitating over the oblivious guards. I imagine that he'll shrink himself down and climb in through the drain again, but instead he flies around to the back, where the balconies overlook the cliff side.

"Rian!" I cry as I run to the wall and watch him settle on Viala's balcony. "He can't be," I whisper, panicked, "He can't be waking her. I have to get up there!" The words have barely left my lips when I feel eight tiny hands grasp the fabric at my shoulders and the fairies hoist me up over the wall. I clap my hands over my eyes until I feel my feet settle firmly on the balcony, and then I take off inside. "Rian!" I skid to a stop at the bedside and I'm greeted with an apologetic shrug and a grin from him.

"Sorry," he says. "I had to make her believe I was agreeing to it. It was the easiest way to get in here, and get her back in there." He points to the bed, where Viala lies bound in a tight cocoon of red velvet bedcovers.

"Told you!" Flitt does a little twirl and sticks her tongue out at Ember, who rolls her glowing eyes.

"Of course it has to be raining." Ember grumbles and points at the floor just beside the balcony archway. "Put her there. We'll have to do it inside." Her hair glows red and steam rises from her wet black skin as she heats up to dry herself. Rian levitates Viala's sleeping form to the floor, and while the fairies prepare her for the stripping, he crosses to me and folds his arms around me.

"You didn't believe it, did you? That I'd join with her?" He murmurs into my hair. I'm too mortified to reply. How could I think he'd be so easily swayed? After all we've been through together, why didn't I have more faith in him? He seems to sense my shame and holds me closer.

"Sorcery," he whispers. "It's not always flashy and impressive. Sometimes it's subtle, so much so that you don't even notice it. So much so that it doesn't require an incantation or a gesture. But still powerful enough to break anything, even trust. Even love." He kisses my cheek tenderly. "It's almost over now. Ready your sword, just in case."

Shush and Ember take charge of the preparations, instructing Rian to remove her blanket bonds and stand ready at her shoulder in case she attempts an attack. I kneel at her feet as instructed, laying my sword by my right hand where I can easily take it up if needed.

"When I tell you to, you hold her down," Ember orders. She takes the flask of sand from her belt pouch and sprinkles it across Viala's forehead. Flitt's light brightens at my shoulder, dancing over the swirling black design on Viala's robes. A strong wind blows in from the balcony but it is quickly tamed by Shush, who waves a hand as if to send it away before it can disturb the sand. "Now, Mage," Ember says as she comes to rest at Viala's ear. "Wake her slowly."

"What?" Rian asks, shocked. "Are you sure? Wouldn't it be easier—"

"Perhaps I should just go and leave you to do it yourself, Mage," Ember spits, "if you feel the need to question my every move!"

"I'm sorry, I didn't mean…"

"What's that human phrase? Sorry doesn't mend the broken pitcher. Do as I tell you. She needs to be awake."

"But shouldn't we at least—"

"Oh, Rian," Flitt whispers beside me as Ember glows red.

"Fine. Here!" Ember throws the vial at Rian, hitting him square in the forehead, and then she whips around and points at Twig, who flies back a little to shy away from her rage. "Take me home! I won't be second-guessed!"

"Ember," Shush whispers.

"I-I-I can't. Not 'til Sunrise. R-remember?" Twig backs further away, wary of the sparks that crackle from her in her anger.

"I think Rian was just saying maybe we should take precautions first——" I interject, and it has the effect I had hoped for. Ember's attention is on me now, leaving Twig to slump with relief as she dives at me.

"Oh, now the non-magic human wants to boss me again? You don't know anything about anything, little one."

"I know that bickering with each other isn't going to help us get the job done." I square my shoulders and raise my chin. "And it's not going to make the cyclones stop, either." Ember smolders away, staring at me through the slits of her eyes. "I know you want to get back to the battle," I say quietly. "But you were ordered to do this first. The sooner this is done, the sooner you can carry on fighting." The silence in the room weighs heavily on us all as Ember seethes before me. Finally, she whips around to Twig.

"You, Twig. You hold her." She turns to Rian and jabs a finger at him. "Be ready to stop her casting. And give me my vial." She whips back to face me as she settles at Viala's ear. "Ready your steel." My fingers find the worn leather of my sword's hilt as Twig ventures close to Viala.

At first, I wonder how he'll manage to hold her as commanded, but then he raises his hands and the polished floor boards beneath her begin to pop and crack as the lines of the wood grain beneath her twist and grow like the roots of a tree. I snatch my sword and jump to my feet as they curl up over her legs and arms and neck elegantly, wrapping themselves like the coils of a grape vine around her. Twig doesn't stop there, though. The vines grow and tangle and twine across the walls and ceiling and grow fragrant white blossoms which drip down over us and reflect all of Flitt's glowing colors in a stunning display.

"Heh. Got a little carried away," he shrugs sheepishly. "Carry on."

Ember huffs impatiently as everyone else gazes around in awe of Twig's display. She claps her hands loudly and snaps at Rian.

"Good enough, Mage? Wake her up." She peers across Viala's face to Shush, who stands ready at her other ear, his hands pressed to the hollow of her cheek. Ember takes the same position on her own side and nods up to Rian. He hesitates and glances at me before he whispers the incantation to lift the sleeping spell.

Before anyone can react, Viala's voice screeches over us. Rian's shield spell is too slow. The force of her attack strikes me directly in the chest. I feel my feet leave the floor as I'm thrown back across the room. Pain explodes in the back of my skull and stars dance across my vision as I crash into the wall. Distantly I'm aware of flashes of light and someone screaming. I grip my sword tightly and try to shake away the darkness that creeps over me. It's no use. Despite my fighting it with every ounce of my strength, the pain in my heart burns and throbs and encloses me in darkness, and everything fades to black. The last thing I'm aware of is my legs giving way beneath me and the sound of my sword clattering to the floor.

I don't know how long I'm out, but I wake up to Flitt's face hovering over mine. Beyond that, there's only silence.

"I did it! She's awake!" she squeals with delight, and when she whips around to look over her shoulder and my eyes finally come into focus, I notice that her red ponytail and her orange one have lost their color completely, and her green one is dull and gray.

"Your hair," the two short words are agony to speak as my chest throbs in time with my head. I close my eyes again.

"It's all right," Flitt hovers beside my ear and keeps her voice low. "I used a little light to help you out. It'll come back in a while. Twig got hit, too, but he's back already. He was easy to help out, being so small and all."

"You're a healer?" I push myself up to sit and press my pounding head with my palms to keep it from feeling as though it'll split open.

"Sure!" She giggles. "I can use my light for a lot of things. Oh, shh." I feel her tiny fingers wrap around the curve of my ear as she leans against me. "They're right in the middle of it, we have to be quiet." At first I'm not sure what she means, but then I squint across the room to where Viala lies twined in the floorboard vines. Ember and Shush are just where they had been right before I was struck, but Rian has moved to kneel at the center, with his hands placed on the crown of her head.

"What's he doing?" I whisper.

"Getting all her magic," Flitt replies. "The sand was lost when she attacked. She burned it up and the vial was shattered. So they decided that Rian could hold onto what they strip out for now and then bring it to the W--um—bring it back to where it belongs."

"They're trusting him with that?"

"Well, they didn't have much choice. He's the only one who volunteered... Nobody else wanted it, and they don't want her to keep it of course. It's tainted magic. Too dark and creepy." I watch as Viala writhes and whimpers in the grasp of the roots, and Rian's brow furrows in time with her protests.

"It's hurting him..." I push myself to my feet and Flitt darts in front of me to stop me from approaching them.

"Course it is. It's bad magic. But you can't stop it or it'll make it worse. Besides, he's strong. He can handle it." She presses a hand to my forehead. "You need to sit back down until you feel better. Rest, like Twig." She points to the vines above us where Twig is curled up in a twisting nest of vines, sound asleep. "Stop crying, too, because that won't help anything." I shake my head and reach up to wipe away the tears I didn't even realize were falling.

"I don't want him to change," I whisper. "I don't want him to hurt."

"I know." Flitt sighs at my shoulder, stroking my earlobe in an effort to comfort me. We sit in silence, watching them wince and writhe, listening to them cry out. There is little evidence of the transfer aside from the occasional flash of blue or black at Rian's fingertips. Then, something strange begins to happen. The Mage Mark that stretches across Viala's cheek begins to move, its coils breaking free of her skin and reaching up into the air above her like black tendrils that lick at the space around them. They lash out like a whip, twirling and spinning violently as they expand and rise up to become a full-sized cyclone. In the enclosed space, the force of it is overwhelming. It rips the vines from the ceiling and sends fragile petals swirling through the air around us. Flitt cries out for Twig, who is sucked toward it. She darts to him and catches him fast, pulling him away as a tendril licks out for him.

Rian's brow furrows, but otherwise the four locked in the stripping seem to be unaware of the threat as the cyclone changes course to charge them. I don't think twice. I leap forward with my sword raised high and bring it down with a furious battle cry, slashing it from top to bottom. To my relief, it disappears in a puff of gray. Flitt and Twig cheer exactly the way the fairies on the mountain did at Ember's battle against the Sorcerers, and I can't help but chuckle at their enthusiasm.

My amusement is short-lived, though, as Flitt calls out a warning. I spin around to find myself face to face with two skeletal sentries. Each is armed with a spiked club and a tower shield. Their eyes glow eerily as two ominous voices ring out in unison.

"You will cease or die. She is ours."

"We won't cease, you creepy things!" Flitt squeaks. "She's getting what she deserves! We're taking back what you stole!"

"Flitt, I've got this..." I motion to her to move back as the sentries snap their heads toward us.

"You choose death," the voices shriek their wicked threat and Flitt ducks behind me as they charge us with their weapons raised. I ready my own sword and take a wide stance, bracing myself for the fight. The odds are against me at two against one, but it's only a small challenge. My personal best in training was seven-to-one, and all of them had minds of their own. These foes are empty-headed and predictable. I'm not afraid.

Rather than charge me in a fury, they stomp forward with a purposeful rhythm and raise their weapons and shields in unison. The first one swings at me with its spiked club. I parry the attack easily and bring my sword across in a powerful arc that catches the seam beneath the sentry's helm and sends its skull flying across the room. It makes a loud thump as it hits the velvet drapes on the wall and slides down to rest on the soft pool of red. The rest of the bones crumple at my feet with a clatter. Flitt cheers, but there's no time for me to celebrate.

The second skeleton bears down on me, charging behind its enormous shield. I dodge it easily and swing again. This time, my

sword glances off its chest plate with a loud clang. It spins to face me, its teeth pressed together in a deathly grimace. I aim again for the space beneath the helm but it's ready for me. It throws up its shield and the force of the block jars my arm as my sword strikes it.

"Surrender her to us!" The sentry hisses as it lashes out. I parry again, but not before a spike catches the back of my hand, tearing at my flesh. I grit my teeth and ignore the pain as I return with a barrage of attacks, trying to find an opening. I'm vaguely aware of Flitt at my shoulder as I press my attack. Her glow is nearly blinding, and I'm about to ask her to stop when I realize the wound on my hand has closed. A rush of confidence charges through me and I sidestep the sentry deftly. With a swift movement I swing my sword up and the shield falls away with a clatter, taking the bony arm still strapped inside with it. I duck behind the sentry and swing again, and the club clatters to the floor along with its remaining arm.

The sudden silence makes my ears ring as I watch the armless sentry, waiting to see if my move has ended the battle. It stumbles to one side and then the other and then turns to face me. Its glowing eyes surge and ebb and the wide grin seems to widen even further as it sneers.

"They will all be ours," it screeches and falls backward onto Viala, and her robes ripple and swirl over it in a blur of purple and black. The swirls of her robes lash out like a cyclone. Its tendrils grasp at Ember and Shush, who are too deep in their meditative work to even notice. A streak of purple curls around Rian's wrist, but he is oblivious. Then, they all begin to fade.

"No!" I scream and dive at Rian. He fights me as I work to free his wrist, but I'm stronger. I'm able to tear the fabric away and drag him a safe distance from the others. His eyes are half-open and vacant as I lay him down, but I don't have time to worry. I turn back to free Ember and Shush but I'm too late. Just as I reach out for Shush, he, Ember, and Viala fade to nothing along with the defeated bones of the sentries. All that is left are the empty floorboard vines and the sound of the driving rain that blows in through the now unprotected archway.

"No," I cry.

"They're gone..." Flitt whispers as she comes to rest on my shoulder. My outstretched hands fall empty to my lap as I kneel there, stunned.

"You tried your best, Azi," Twig offers quietly from my other shoulder. I shake my head in disbelief and my attention snaps to Rian. I close the space between us faster than I can think, and I scoop his head into my lap to cradle it.

"Rian," I sob, and I'm met with silence and a blank stare. I shake his shoulders and slap his cheek gently. "Talk to me. Can you see me? Are you here? Rian!" Flitt floats down to land on his chest and gaze up into his eyes. Twig does the same, landing lightly beside her.

"Shock," he says. "He's in shock. Get the blanket, Azi. That will help. Get him warm. Flitt, give him some light." I wrap him in the red velvet cover yet he still shivers as Flitt presses her hands to his heart.

The Mark has grown and swirled thickly across his face and arms. His chest is almost completely black beneath his sheer shirt. Flitt has changed, too. Her hair is almost all white now, with just the roots of it showing its usual rainbow of colors. Her own skin is paler than ever, but her light is unaffected. She glows and sparkles and casts her prism of colors out over Rian as I hold him tight to me, rocking him, staring into his unseeing eyes.

"Try kissing him, Azi," Twig commands, and I don't need to be told twice. I press my lips to his and it's strange at first not to be met with his usual welcoming warmth. His own lips are still and cool, but then they slowly soften and warm and press into mine. His arms wrap around me and his fingers slip into my hair and I can taste my own tears as our kiss deepens until there is nothing and no one but us, together.

Chapter Twenty-Six

SORCERY

"I swear, I'm fine, Azi. For the hundredth time. Really." Rian says as we move quietly through the dormitory. Still, he holds my hand with a much stronger grip than usual, and from time to time I catch a strange gleam in his eye that he hides by glancing away from me. We're alone. Flitt has gone back to Kythshire to rest, and Twig has left us for the palace. Their absence along with the disappearance of the other two leaves me feeling uneasy. We pause at the main dormitory door. He pushes it open, letting in the driving rain.

"Good," Rian murmurs, and shows me that the guards have gone.

"What does it mean?" I ask him as he pulls the door shut again and leads me on through the corridor.

"She lost her hold. Or rather, I took it from her. She made the suggestion for them to guard here, and when I received her magic, I was able to see that and remove it." We cross into the white room with many doors. This time, Rian chooses a door that opens into a passageway carved in deep purple stone.

"You took control of her spells, the ones she already cast?" I ask, pressing closer to him in the narrow space.

"Yes," he says. "That's what I was doing after you tore me out. Trying to take stock of her dealings here, determining everything she's got a hand in. It's intricate work, beautifully done. I see now how she's been able to rise through the ranks and go so unnoticed. It's like a long, slow dance of enchantment with many unsuspecting partners." He seems almost enraptured as he tries to explain it to me, and it frightens me a little.

"Where are we going now?" I ask as the corridor slopes downward and the walls begin drip with cool condensation.

"To the prince," his answer sets my heart racing, and with it comes the dull pain that has been creeping up on me since we left Viala's room. It throbs just beneath my breastbone, where her spell struck me. Now that the battle is done and the rush of the fight has faded, the pain is growing. I push it away, dismissing it as an injury that will eventually fade. There's no need to worry Rian with it. Not now, when he's been through so much himself and we still have so far to go.

Twig is already there to greet us when we emerge into the palace. As he guides us unseen among the guards to Eron's chambers, he chatters about how the king is well again and has called off the arrest order for Rian and I. "He's awfully angry at the prince, though," he nods his head. "As he should be, of course. For now he's locked him away in his room. And the king is meeting with his advisers. He wants to keep everything hush-hush, but they know he's been covering up for the prince now, and they want Eron held accountable."

"We should go to them, then, and explain. Why are we going to see the prince first, Rian?"

"He has something they need," he says matter-of-factly as he pauses in an empty corridor and rests his hand on the wall with his eyes closed. "Azi, is there a chamber door around the corner, guarded?" I look and nod.

"Four of them," I whisper.

"Stand back," Rian says, raising his arms as if readying to cast something.

"You're not going to attack them, are you?" I shift my stance slightly, putting myself between Rian and the guards. Skeletal sentries are one thing, but I refuse to fight a palace guard.

"Guess I shouldn't," he sighs and turns to Twig. "This is Eron's room, correct?" He pats the polished wood of the corridor wall with a slender hand. Twig nods.

"We'll do it this way, then." He runs his hand across the wall and starts an incantation, but Twig interrupts him.

"You don't need all that," he says. "You're in the Half-Realm. You can just go through. Like this." He dives at the wall and disappears through it. A moment later, he's back again. "See? Just like everything else, it's a matter of belief. The wall is there and it isn't, too. Believe it isn't, and you go right through. You try it." He gestures to me and I blink.

"It's a wall, Twig." I reach up and tap on the solid wood with my fingertips.

"Only if you want it to be, hm?" He sticks his arm through the wall. "The rules are different for us. For you now, too, since you're not here or there. You two, your heads are stuck in your world. You don't see the possibilities. Just like before, when I showed Rian how to slip in and out of view and he still needed a spell to do it, when he really doesn't. Go on, try it."

"We're wasting time," Rian rolls his eyes in frustration.

"And you'd have wasted magic, and you need to be careful now, don't you? More than ever before." He watches Rian knowingly.

"What does he mean?" I look from one to the other. "Why do you have to be careful, Rian?"

"Don't worry about it," he mumbles and sidesteps to disappear into the wall.

"Twig—"

"Come on," he interrupts me and darts into the wall after Rian. A moment later his head pops out again. "It's fun, try it." He glides back and forth along the wall, but all that's visible is his head, and I can't help but laugh. "Having trouble believing?"

"It isn't that, it's just..." I shrug. "Just because you can do something, doesn't mean that you should. Those are Eron's private chambers. He's still the prince. It's trespassing. There are guards posted for a reason. It isn't right to just go in simply because I have a way to do it without getting caught."

"You snuck into Viala's room, though. Even took things from her." He tips his head to the side curiously.

"That was different. She had to be stopped." I shiver and hug my arms to my chest. Even though it was several weeks ago now, I can still feel Eron's breath hot on my neck in the room with the paintings. I wonder for a moment whether I'm making the decision to stay outside out of fear rather than righteousness.

"You're too good for your own good," Twig chuckles. "That's probably why people find you so trustworthy." Rian's face pops through the wall and I jump back, startled.

"Coming in?" He wriggles his brow at me, causing the blue-black swirls on his face to dance. "I need a word with the prince, and it would help if you were here, too." His outstretched hand comes through to my side. "Come on. It's okay, I promise." I take a deep breath to steel myself, slip my hand into his, and step through the wall to the other side as if it isn't even there.

Prince Eron's outer chamber is a warm, lavishly decorated room with a grouping of chairs set around a fireplace that crackles brightly despite the hour being well past midnight. Its light casts deep shadows across walls hung with various trophies of stuffed beasts: Birds, wild boar, deer, and in the place of honor above the hearth, a plains-lion's head. When I turn to look at Rian, I'm met with the lifeless head of a fox. I yelp and jump back and nearly go through the wall again but he catches me. Perched atop the fox's head, Twig holds his belly as he laughs silently at me.

"Impossible," the prince's voice is low and cold as it drifts across the room. Rian moves closer to me, his hand squeezing mine so tightly that my fingers go numb.

"It isn't, my husband," Amei's tone is gentle, but I can sense the underlying hurt in it as we creep closer to the chairs where they sit. "It has been long enough since our wedding night."

"And you choose to tell me this now?" he snaps. "While I'm locked in my room, sitting vigil, possibly awaiting an accusation of treason?"

"I thought it would give you hope, or at least some small happiness." Even in her dressing gown, Amei looks regal. She holds her chin up and her back straight as she sits with a natural poise that enhances her beauty.

"Happiness?" Eron scoffs. "To learn that I might have a child who will grow up fatherless? Or to learn that my wife is just as much an enchantress as every other woman out there, weaving lies to manipulate me?" Amei doesn't lose her poise at his accusation. Instead she leans slightly closer to him, her gaze steady on the prince's as he slumps lower in his chair.

"I have never lied to you, nor will I ever. I have stood beside you while other," her eyes narrow slightly, "women have woven their spells. Against my own judgment I have not interfered. Do not ever compare me to her again." She shakes her head and closes her eyes. "What happened to the sweet prince who courted me? You've changed, Eron.

Still I love you as I ever have, as you used to love me, before she entered into it. I stand beside you, even through this, my husband." Her hand slides to rest on her belly as she leans back into the chair wearily.

I glance at Rian, who's watching the conversation with the same awkwardness that I'm feeling. This was a private moment, not meant to be overheard. As Eron stares into the fire, he absently rolls the gold chain of his necklace between his fingers. I'm stricken by the sadness in Amei's eyes as the prince broods for a long stretch of silence, and I wonder whether he regrets or even realizes what he's put her through.

"Now's as good a time as any," Rian whispers to me.

"To do what?" I ask.

"The necklace," he nods at the prince. "We need it."

"How are you going to--?" Before I can finish my question, Rian closes his eyes and takes a small step forward and Amei jumps in her chair and calls out to Eron. The prince is on his feet with a hunter's instinct, his hands closed around Rian's throat before I can blink. Rian clutches at him, fighting for breath.

"How did you get in here," Eron growls, "past the guards?" He lifts Rian up until his toes are grazing the floor and his eyes are bulging. I snap out of my own shock and charge them both, gripping the prince's fingers to pry them off of Rian. At the feel of my touch, he lets go immediately and steps back, staring in disbelief at his hand. Rian falls to his knees and gasps for air as he rubs his throat. The prince grabs a handful of his hair and tips his head back roughly. "Answer me, Mage! How dare you trespass here?"

"I came to help you," Rian says hoarsely, raising his hands. "Azi and I. We came to help you." Eron eyes the Mark on Rian's face suspiciously.

"I don't believe you. Guards!" Instantly the doors swing open and two guards enter. "Take him!" Eron gestures to Rian, who whispers a word as the guards stride forward and look around, bewildered.

"Seize who, your highness?" one of them asks as he searches the room. Eron blinks in disbelief and Rian grins at me with mischief as he gets to his feet.

"He was just here!" Eron swings his arm at Rian, who ducks back just in time to avoid it. "Rian, right?" He spins to Amei, who is watching wide-eyed. "You saw him, didn't you?" She nods slowly. "Search the room!" Rian follows the prince closely as he searches the room, his eyes dancing with amusement as Twig drifts down beside him.

"Told you it was fun once you get used to it," Twig chuckles.

"Still," Rian nods, "we're short on time." He closes his eyes and whispers something and the prince pauses in mid-stride.

"I was mistaken," Eron says. "Go out. Forget it." The guards stop their searching and turn to him.

"Your Highness?" one says hesitantly.

"I said go!" He shouts, and the two guards exchange concerned looks before filing out and closing the door behind them.

"Eron..." Amei whispers.

"Not now." He drops into his chair and rakes his fingers through his hair.

"Watch this," Rian comes to my side, grinning. "That chain is getting awfully hot, isn't it?" He points at the prince, who jumps up again and starts clawing at his neck.

Eron grasps the chain and yanks it with a snap from his skin, and then tosses it away with a cry of pain. It lands at my feet, a beautiful amulet with a rich blue stone laced with deep indigo veins and gold flecks. "Grab that, would you Azi?" I crouch and test it with my finger. It's cool to the touch when I take it. Eron's eyes go wide.

"It's gone! No!" He drops to his knees and searches the floor with his hands, nearly grabbing the toe of my boot. "No, no, no!"

"Don't panic," Rian says quietly as he steps out of the Half-Realm again. "It's not gone. Azi has it." He gestures to me and I watch the prince pause as his eyes focus on my boot and follow up the line of my leg until his eyes meet mine. He falls back and clambers to his feet as Amei rises from her own chair and backs away from the two of us.

"I can explain," Rian offers cautiously, "if you'll allow me to."

Eron's wild eyes find the amulet in my hand and he dives at me. Rian flings a silence ward at the door just in time to block Eron's cry.

"Give it back!" he shouts, and lunges again. I dodge him easily and Rian waves a hand to send me back to the Half-Realm again.

"Let me explain, please, Your Royal Highness," he offers patiently. "We aren't here to hurt you. We simply need the amulet, which doesn't belong to you. We want to help, but there isn't much time, and I need you to listen." He gestures to Amei, who is watching him with suspicion, her eyes tracing the lines of the Mark that nearly covers him. "Please."

"If he was going to harm us, he could have done so easily by now," Amei rests a hand on Eron's arm. "Perhaps we should hear him out." Eron's looks down at her hand, bronze and glowing against the deep purple of his dressing gown. His expression softens when his eyes meet hers, searching them. She watches him hesitantly at first, and then offers him a smile.

"Go on, then, Rian." The prince says, his voice still thick with suspicion. Rian paces the floor before them, collecting his thoughts.

"No doubt you feel lighter?" He asks the prince, who nods after a moment. "That necklace, the amulet, what did she tell you about it?"

"She said it would protect me as long as I wore it, since I--." he glances at Amei and trails off.

"Since you're held by a curse that prevents you from wielding a weapon." Rian finishes for him, and Eron's lips tighten with anger at his secret being revealed.

"You dare—!"

"She lied," Rian says plainly. "The curse is lifted. It was when Lisabella crossed into Kythshire, just as you thought it would be."

"It isn't." Eron protests. "I've tried every day since then to—."

"The amulet," Rian interrupts again. I've seen him this way before. When his thoughts go faster than his words, it's nearly impossible to hold a two-sided conversation with him. "It has many powers. She used it to convince you that you were still cursed. Used it like an enchantress's trinket. Mixed with her own cunning, it was foolproof." He shakes his head, laughing. "Brilliant, really, if you had any idea of its real power. But she knew you'd protect it if you thought it would protect you, and in the meantime, what a way to keep her hold on you, all the while keeping it safe."

"You're saying what? That the curse is broken?" Eron's eyes widen and he races to the wall where a weapon rack sits empty. His shoulders slump, but Rian pulls me from the Half-Realm again.

"Will you lend the prince your sword, Azi?" he asks me, offering me a reassuring nod. Eron turns to me, eyeing the hilt at my shoulder with a mix of hope and disbelief. I lean away from him as he approaches me, his hand outstretched. The last thing I want to do is surrender my sword, especially to Eron. "Trust me," Rian says again, and my hand finds the clip that holds the sheath to the harness at my back without a second thought. I feel the smooth leather slip into my free hand and I start to offer it to Eron before I realize what I'm doing. Beside me, Twig lets out a low, warning hiss and Rian's eyes go wide.

"Oh! Azi! I didn't mean—!" He claps his hands over his mouth and steps between Eron and me. "Azi, only give him the sword if you want to, okay? I'm sorry." I look down at the amulet in one hand and my sheathed sword in the other and I blink as the power of Rian's suggestion fades. "I'm sorry," he says again, searching my eyes. "I forgot. I didn't mean to."

"It's fine," I say, a little shaken by how easy it was for him to control me. My gaze catches on the growing Mark that curls just below his eye. I shake my head and look away as I tip my sword to Eron, holding tight to the sheath. "You can test it," I offer quietly. I watch his hands close around the worn leather at the hilt and my stomach flips a little. I feel my jaw clench as his eyes widen and he pulls the weapon free. The blade gleams and flashes, reflecting the orange glow of the fire as he swings it this way and that, laughing.

"Thank you," he says. "You've given everything back to me. Not just the sword, but..." he shakes his head. "I feel changed, lighter. I'm my own man again. I haven't felt this way in years, not since she..." he shakes his head. "I see it now so clearly, everything she's done. I'm in your debt," Eron presses his fist to his chest and bows.

"No," Rian says. "You aren't. We did what needed to be done. You don't owe us anything."

"Viala. She's defeated, then?"

"Stripped." Rian says simply.

"That isn't enough," Eron says. "She means to take over Kythshire, to own it. We were to rule it together." Amei looks away, shaking her head. "Forgive me, Amei, please," he pulls her closer. "She had me convinced that it was a wasted resource, now that the Fae have died off from those lands. She'll find a way to regain her power. She's unstoppable." I keep my expression neutral. Eron doesn't need to know that the fae are thriving. I still don't trust him. The less he knows about Kythshire, the better.

"It isn't just her," Rian comes to my side and helps me fasten my sword back into my harness. "Sorcerers from Zhaghen mean to claim the land for themselves."

"If that happens," Eron shakes his head. "It's only a matter of time before Cerion falls."

"Which is why our next course is an audience with your father. If you'll excuse us, Your Highness?" Rian says, taking my hand. Eron looks from me to Rian and then to his wife. He shakes his head, obviously trying to make sense of everything that has just happened.

"Go," he says. "And thank you."

"Ready?" Rian asks, turning to me. When I nod, he pulls us back into the Half-Realm, leaving Eron and Amei to sort things out together. We step through the wall into the corridor beyond and he takes my face in his hands. "Are you okay?" he asks as he searches my eyes.

"I don't want this," I say, holding up the amulet with distaste.

"I understand," he says, turning to Twig, who has just come through to join us.

"Kissing," he grins. "They're kissing. Amei is so happy. I'm glad. She's very sweet. Always kind to Margy. Oh." He looks down at the amulet in my hand as I raise it to offer it to him. "Ah, I can't," he says, waving his hands. "Sorry."

"It won't happen again, Azi. You're the best person to hold it though." Rian ducks his head apologetically. "I can't either, it's too powerful and I'm doing my best to keep it under control as it is."

"Can't we give it to someone else, then? Anod? Or one of the other masters?"

"Oh, no no," Twig says, eyeing Rian. "No, it isn't for Mages. It has to go back to Kythshire where it belongs."

"What is it, exactly?" I ask, dangling the bauble from its chain as though it's distasteful as a rotting fish.

"It's," Twig raises a finger and his mouth hangs open. He looks at Rian and then up at the ceiling thoughtfully, and back at the necklace. "It's a...I know, let's play!"

"There isn't time," Rian says sternly. "We've got to see the king straight away." He turns abruptly and starts down the hallway away from the prince's rooms into the main part of the palace. Twig darts off after him, leaving me alone in the dark, staring at the amulet that spins and sways lazily from its broken chain. Watching it puts me in a state of restfulness. I feel as though anything that happens doesn't really matter, as long as it is with me. Holding it, I realize, brings me peace. I gaze at it, smiling lazily, until I'm vaguely aware of a flutter of midnight blue and creamy yellow stopping abruptly in front of me. The amulet is plucked from my hand and I blink rapidly to clear the sense of serenity that had held me so fast.

"Rian?" My voice comes out far more dreamily than I intend it to. As I look up at him, I can't help but smile. Even covered in the Mark he's so handsome, so clever and brave. His hands are so graceful and strong as he pulls a strip of bandage from his bag and wraps the necklace in it. The spell he murmurs over it is like a gentle melody that's so pleasing to my ears that I feel as if I'll swoon right there in the hallway. Then when he's through, I feel foolish. The feelings are still there, of course, as they've always been, but not so strong. I shake my head. "What just happened?"

"I told you it's powerful. The stone is one thing, but the setting is something else. It's the setting, the gold part, that controls," he answers, handing the swaddled trinket back to me. "It saps power from the stone, keeps it in check. Put it away, okay? I worked something over it to dampen its effects a little, but keep it wrapped. Don't look at it. Now, let's go." He rushes off again as I tuck the awful thing into the pouch at my waist and jog after him.

"You want me to trust you," I say as I catch up to his stride, "and yet you expect me to just follow you blindly. I need a plan, Rian. I need to know what we're going to say to the king, and why it's so urgent." He spins to face me, his eyes half-wild.

"Are you joking? You're joking, right?" His long fingers rake through his cropped hair and tug in frustration at his side locks. "Azi." He takes me by the shoulders and I stare at the Mark that is now curled up over his left eyebrow. "Let me put it into perspective for you. This isn't simply about protecting fairies and saving your mother anymore. Not that both aren't incredibly important. Listen. The relationship between Cerion and Sunteri is shaky at best, and now six of their strongest Sorcerers have made camp in the only stronghold that separates us from the Outlands, where generations of men banished from our kingdom have waited for their chance for an uprising. So, not only are we talking about facing Sorcerers who are able to move mountains and raise a few hundred undead skeletons, but also possibly an army of thieves, outlaws, murderers, and generally immoral scum rallied by Redemption.

"But let's go back to the Sorcerers, because if you think I'm frightening right now, imagine six of me, but not as lovable. Cruel, demented, and with the monarchy of Sunteri held tightly in their fists. Because you've seen Zhaghen, right? That's what happens when the royals lose control of their Mages. But if you think it isn't urgent, then by all means take your time." He shakes his head and rushes off again with Twig trailing close behind, leaving me to turn over his words in my mind as we go.

The pain in my chest is a steady throb now, and I find myself rubbing it absently as the weight of Rian's explanation settles over me. It's too much for us to be expected to handle on our own. I wonder how much of it His Majesty is aware of, and how much we'll have to explain to him. I know that Cerion has reserves of soldiers for such a situation, but I have no idea how many, or how prepared they are. As we approach the planning room where Twig has told us they're meeting, Rian slows his pace. He takes stock of the six guards at the door and closes his eyes for a moment.

"This way," he says, and leads us away from the room, through to the main foyer, and out of the palace. We walk through the gardens and past the wall and pause in the forest. The moon is low in the sky now, nearly setting. It'll be morning soon. "We can't just go in unannounced," he explains. "We'll have to present ourselves at the gate and be escorted. His Majesty is meeting with Master Anod, several of his advisors, and four of his generals. They have some knowledge already of what's happening in Bane's Pass, beyond what your father told him. Anod doesn't know yet what's happened to Viala." Rian draws a hand up and over the back of his head, creating a deep blue hood that falls to cover most of his face. "You'll have to do most of the talking, Azi. I don't think they'll trust me, looking like this." I stare at him in disbelief.

"How do you know who's in there? How do you know what they

know, Rian?" His eyes are concealed by the shadow of his hood, but his lips press together tightly and he gives his head a very slight shake.

"I just know." he says, and his Revealer causes the air to shimmer around us. He guides me gently by the arm toward the palace gates, instructing me all the way on what they need to be told. "The king will be glad to hear that Viala's grip on Eron has been severed. You'll need to explain that he was held by her enchantments. Hopefully, that will be enough to clear him of the charges of treason that have been set in motion against him. You'll need to tell him about the Sorcerers, and the keep, and what you saw in Zhaghen. Tell him that Redemption is rallying the banished, wait no, he knows that already. The sentries, he'll need to know numbers. And that Viala has been stripped but they have her now. He'll need to know that."

"What?" I stop just at the edge of the park forest. "Who has her? You know where she is? Is she alive? Are Ember and Shush with her?" He turns to me, scowling.

"What do you mean? I told you that already. The Sorcerers claimed her, that's why she faded away. They were able to pull her through to the keep. I suspect they used that mirror in the center of the room. It's some sort of portal. We went over this." I shake my head in disbelief and look at Twig, who shrugs.

"You never said anything about what happened to her," I think back, trying to remember, but I'm sure I'm right.

"I told you..."

"When did you tell me?" I ask, watching as he presses his fingertips to his forehead.

"I could have sworn I told you, I'm sorry." He sighs and drops his hands. "They have her, and the fae, too. They're trying to restore her. Even now." He takes a breath and squares his shoulders. "Let's go."

"Wait." Twig drifts up to Rian's eye level. "They're trying to steal back the magic you're holding, right now?"

"Yes, I told you that. I told you both. I'm trying my best to hold onto it but it's a constant struggle. We have to explain things to the king before I lose my grip. Can we please go now?" He tugs at my sleeve, his tone that of desperation.

"You didn't, Rian. You didn't say a word of any of this." I cling to his arm now, afraid that if I let go I might lose him for good.

"Can't do it," Twig says, shaking his head.

"We have to. Have to see the king."

"No." Twig says firmly, darting closer to Rian. "If they're trying to steal it back, then that means that there's still a connection between you and Viala. Which means that if you walk into the midst of the king and all of his advisers, well—"

"That would be their way in," I whisper, horrified. He was so certain of this course and I was so willing to follow him...I shudder to think of what might have happened if we did reach the king. Could they have used Rian as a weapon against him? Is the connection that strong? If it did happen, if he attacked the king, Rian would be killed for certain. Either way, it's a smart move for the Sorcerers to send him straight to the throne.

"I'm too strong to allow that to happen," Rian growls, pulling me forward. "Why is it you have no faith in me? Either of you? You, Azi. You're supposed to love me. And Twig, I took that magic when no one else would. I'm guarding it with my life. Do you think I'd just let them steal it back, just like that? We're going to the king. Now."

His final word falls on me like a command, and I feel the power of it seep into every pore of my skin. This time, I'm prepared. I tighten my hold on his arm and close my eyes, and I try to think of the safest place for us right now. I know I need to do it quickly, before he can figure out what's happening. I don't worry about how, I just wish as hard as I can. As the ground falls away beneath my feet, I feel Twig land softly on my shoulder and cling to my neck.

"Good girl," he whispers as I tighten my hold on Rian and drive us through the Half-Realm to the safety of Flitt's grotto.

Chapter Twenty-Seven

IREN

"Oh, hello!" Flitt chirps cheerfully as my feet find the soft mossy carpet of her grotto. I let out a long sigh of relief as I cling to Rian's arm and open my eyes.

"You did it! She did it!" Twig darts to Flitt and they do their little dance together.

"No." Rian tears his arm from my grasp and covers his face, but not before I catch a glimpse of the panic in his eyes. "No! What were you thinking, bringing me here?"

"It's safe here, Rian, it'll be all right." I feel the peace of the grotto settling over me already. "We can make a plan--"

"No," he shakes his head beneath his rigid fingers, which crackle with energy that threatens to burst forth. "They'll see. They'll know. I'm not strong enough to hide this."

"Then we'll go to the Wellspring first and you can give the magic back. Will that sever the connection, then?" I look from him to Flitt and Twig, both of whom look away.

"Ohh, no, he can't do that without Ember and Shush," Flitt says gravely. "Those three started it, they need to finish it."

"She's right," Twig nods beside her. "They need to do it together or it could be bad."

"I need to get out of here," Rian whispers. "It's the worst place for me to be. They'll see everything. They'll use me..." His fingers crackle again and he thrusts them away from him, casting a ball of golden energy that bursts beside the waterfall, sending a cascade of glittering mica fragments into the clear water. "I'm sorry! Sorry!"

"He's losing it." Flitt nods matter-of-factly. "Here, take a nap." She reaches into her belt pouch and flings a handful of sparkling powder into Rian's eyes. Instantly his body goes slack.

"Flitt!" I jump to catch him, and lay him down in the moss, sound asleep.

"Well, he broke my sparklestone. I like that sparklestone. He scared Morley too." She hovers over the edge of the clear water and wriggles her fingers at the bright orange fish just below the surface. "And he was going a little too Mage for me. I'll wake him up after we figure out what to do." I slump back against the trunk of a twisting willow, one hand resting on Rian's shoulder. Tears sting my eyes and rather than fight them, I allow it. Maybe a good cry will help clear my head.

"We really can't help him without Ember and Shush?" I ask her.

"No," she replies sadly. "If it was the sand it would be easier, but now someone's got to sort through what belongs to Rian and what belongs to Viala and what belongs to those bad Sorcerers. What happened after I left?" I tell her all about Eron and the amulet and Rian's wanting to go to the king, and my decision to bring him here.

"It was the first place I thought of. We needed someplace safe, somewhere to think and plan away from everything. I'm so sorry, I didn't know that he'd react that way." I rake my fingers through my hair. "What are we going to do now?"

"Well, I think we ought to go to the Ring and ask them." She nods her head decisively, sending her bright ponytails bobbing. "Can I see the amulet?" I look to Twig, who nods at me.

"Rian told me not to unwrap it. He put a spell over it." I pull the wadded bandage from my belt and hold it up. "They wouldn't tell me what it is--"

"Couldn't," Twig corrects me, holding up a finger.

"Couldn't? Oh. Do you know, Flitt? I mean, can you tell me?" She comes to perch on my fingertips and carefully pushes the wrapping away just enough to reveal the deep black stone. Her eyes fade in and out of every color of the rainbow as they widen, and her lips form a tiny little "o".

"Is that..?" she looks up.

"I think it is," Twig nods, grinning.

"Ring, Ring, Ring!" Flitt cries gleefully. "Oh, Twig! I can't believe it! Azi, shrink down!" She points at me and my skin tingles as I begin to grow shorter. As I do, the amulet stays the same size, so that I have to hug it with both arms to keep hold of it when I finally reach fairy-size.

"I'll stay with Rian," Twig says. "Someone's got to."

"Oh." Flitt's shoulders hunch. "Well, I will then. You ought to get the credit for this. You might get another name! What will it be?"

"No, no, Azi is your charge and she's got it. The credit is yours." He grins. "Really, go on."

"Why don't you both go, and I'll stay with him?" I lean against Rian's giant shoulder. I don't want to leave him. We're supposed to be in this together.

"You're so funny, Azi. We can't carry it!" She rolls her eyes at Twig and he laughs.

"Everyone knows that! Can you imagine?" They both hug their bellies, laughing even harder.

"Really, go on. I'm getting used to this Mage. I might even call him a friend someday." He perches on Rian's chest. "You know, if everything turns out."

"What are you two talking about?" I burst out, exasperated.

"Maybe Scree can tell you," Flitt giggles. "Come on!" She takes me by the elbow and we fly off and dart into the waterfall together.

On the other side, the Ring is quiet. The pristine white mushrooms lining the edge of the clearing sparkle with dew in the pre-dawn light, and a number of fae sleep peacefully beneath them. We drift over them silently and land in the center of the Ring, where the fragile tip of a tiny green-white bud has just begun to pierce the soil.

"Crocus," Flitt whispers, kneeling before the tiny bud. She gestures for me to do the same and I kneel next to her, clutching the amulet to my chest. When the bud doesn't respond, Flitt laughs softly. "Sleepyhead." She opens and closes her wings slowly, and they glow bright yellow and warm as the sun. The light splashes onto the soil, drying the dew into tiny wisps of steam, and the bud grows taller and larger. Its bright fuchsia petals fall open elegantly, and Crocus stretches her dainty arms up over her head, yawning.

"Oh, sun, you're early today." Her eyes flutter open and she tilts her head at Flitt questioningly. "Why, Felicity Lumine Instacia Tenacity Teeming?" She turns sleepily to me. "And Azaeli Hammerfel. We recognize you. But why have you woken us?" Flitt nudges me with her elbow.

"Show her, Azi," she says excitedly. I kneel and unwrap the amulet while Crocus watches, her lips curved up in a smile of amusement and interest. When the stone is finally revealed, her eyes widen and the ground beneath her starts to rumble and shake.

"The Oculus!" her whisper is echoed throughout the Ring as the word travels through the gathering of waking fae. Their whisperings mix with cheers as Scree rumbles into view from beneath the soil.

"Scree!" they shout and dance and sing, and I wait until they settle down, which takes much longer than I'd like. Finally, Crocus raises a slender hand and they settle into quiet.

"Rest it here," Scree thunders, shaking the ground beneath us with his booming voice. I glance at Flitt and she nods to me and points to a flat empty area of the stone beside Crocus's white roots. A hush falls over the Ring as I approach the two of them. Crocus's sweet perfume is heavy in the air this close to them, and remembering its previous effect on me, I hold my breath as I set the amulet down on top of Scree.

"Step away, Ah," Crocus says gently to me, and I step back just far enough that I'm out of range of her pretty scent.

"Azaeli Hammerfel, are you the rightful owner of this amulet?" Scree asks me. I glance at Flitt, who nods encouragingly.

"I...I was told it belongs here in Kythshire, and Flitt said I should bring it to you."

"Do you surrender it freely to us, and all of the magic contained within, which is within your rights to give?"

"I don't, I mean," I look at Flitt again, who is nodding her head fervently, her eyes wide. "It's yours, isn't it? It isn't mine to give."

"The stone," Crocus says sweetly, "is ours. But the setting imprisons it, enchants it. Steals its power and twists it with Mage magic. No, Sorcery. We cannot undo such magic without assent from the amulet's owner. Have you the right to call yourself such?"

"It was surrendered to me, so, yes," I say, thinking of Prince Eron. "You have my permission." At my words, the ground rumbles violently and I fall backwards into Flitt, who steadies me. The vibrations created by Scree are so strong that the gold setting surrounding the stone breaks away and slips into the grass. Once freed from its bindings, the stone emits a soft glow of energy. Crocus smiles.

"You have done us a great service, Azaeli Hammerfel, in returning this." She pauses and looks down at Scree. After a moment, she nods and looks up sadly. "And yet we must ask more of you."

"Return this stone to its rightful place on the mountain," Scree booms, "and we shall grant you one True Wish." All around us the fairies whisper to each other with shock and surprise at his declaration.

"What is it? What does it do?" I ask them.

"It is the Oculus. It ceases the shadow twists. The cyclones." Scree begins to rumble down into the soil. "Return it to its rightful place. Do you agree?"

"Wait!" I call after him. "Ember and Shush, they've been taken by the Sorcerers. They stripped Viala, but Rian is holding her magic. He's suffering. He wants to give it back to you but he can't do it without them. We need to get them back. Your border is threatened at the Crag, Kythshire is in danger! The Sorcerers from Sunteri mean to take everything from you."

"We are aware." Scree responds as he disappears further into the soil. "Restore the Oculus. Do you agree?"

"I..." I look across at the stone that glows with an inky energy, considering. If it stops the cyclones, then Mum could come home. It might even stop the Sorcerers, or at least help to, if they're unable to summon them anymore. Even if it doesn't, I could use the wish to stop them. "I agree."

"Go, then, Ah. We wish you great success in this quest." As he sinks out of view, the stone from the amulet rises into the air and lands gently in my lap. It seems alive as I look down at it, and I take up the bandage and quickly wrap it up again to avoid becoming too entranced. Crocus claps her hands and the music rises up around us, starting the dance.

"We send you off with these thoughts," Crocus offers quietly as the colorful crowd whirls around her. "Magic is a gift we share willingly with your people. Its power alone is not wicked or evil. Only the way it is wielded makes it so. Choose your wish carefully, Ah. You will find the face at the highest peak of the Shadow Crag."

When we return to the grotto, Rian is still asleep with Twig tucked into the crook of his elbow, also dozing. I kneel beside the two of them and wish to return to my own size. "Okay, the highest peak of the

Shadow Crag," I murmur to myself as I think of an outfit suitable for climbing. "I'll need rope, and hooks, and boots that can grip. I'll need to figure out what to do with my sword, I don't want to leave it but I can't climb with it. I'll need food." My stomach growls loudly at the thought of it and I rub it absently. Its emptiness seems to exaggerate the now constant pain in my chest.

"I wish I had some of Mouli's sweet rolls," I sigh, and a warm tray of them appears in the moss beside me. Delighted, I pick one up and bite into it while I go over a plan. Suddenly, I realize what a fool I've been. "Wait a minute," I drop my hand into my lap. "I just agreed to do this task in exchange for a wish. But I can wish for anything already, can't I? He tricked me!" Flitt's eyes widen.

"No, no, no," she gasps. "Oh, you didn't realize! Sure, here you can think of food, and clothes, and going to see someone, and it happens just like that! But you can't make anyone else do anything, or wish too boldly. A True Wish, like Scree promised, is different. That means anything, anything at all, anywhere, not just here in Kythshire. It's a great gift. I've never heard of it being offered to a human before. It's far too powerful." She perches beside the tray of rolls and scoops up a handful of icing to lick from her fingertips. "Mmm, mmm, mmm. Mouli is the best!" She pauses as she cleans her sticky palm on the moss. "Do you see now?"

"I think so." I look down at the wrapped stone in my hand, which seems a bit larger now than it had been before we visited the Ring. "It's very important, I understand that. It's difficult to go blindly into such a difficult quest, though, and mostly on my own." I turn the bundle thoughtfully. It's definitely heavier. "I'd just like to know why."

"I guess I could bring you to the muses. They have all sorts of stories. I bet they could tell you about it. But it would take a while, and my sleeping powder doesn't last forever." She points at Rian. "If we go to the Crag now, we might be back before he wakes up."

"Right." I imagine an outfit suitable for climbing and it comes easily to me this time. My sword remains in its harness at my back. I know it'll be problematic to climb in, but I can't bring myself to leave it behind. The stone tucks neatly into the pouch at my belt, though it already seems even larger than it had been moments ago. I brush it off as my imagination as I look up to the sky to get my bearings. The mountains are in the Northeast, and the rising sun shows me the way. I kiss Rian goodbye, and trying hard not to dwell on leaving him behind, I turn away quickly to make my way through the forest.

"What are you doing?" Flitt asks as she drifts along to follow me.

"Going to the mountain. It's this way, right?"

"Sure, but why are you walking? It'll take forever going this way."

"Do you know a better...?" my voice trails off and I shake my head. "I can just think about the highest crest of the mountain, can't I? Is it really that easy?" She giggles as she rests on my shoulder.

"Believe it and do it!" She says.

"But I've never been there before, Flitt. I don't know what it's like. I can't imagine it, I've only seen it from a distance." I think of the ominous storm cloud over the massive mountain and the jagged lightning striking the black stone, and I shiver. Suddenly I realize what I've really gotten myself into. "So high," I whisper, feeling the color drain from my face. "I don't know if I can do this..." I sink against the trunk of a nearby tree. My heart races, my chest aches.

"Hey." Flitt hovers in front of my face. Her eyes are bright yellow as they look into mine, and her prisms glitter and flash across my vision cheerfully. "I believe you can. Come find me." Her light brightens and I turn away from it, closing my eyes. When I open them again, she's gone.

"Flitt?" I cry, spinning around. The forest is quiet, still sleeping as the sun rises. Deep down I know where she's gone: to the Crag. I steel myself and take a deep breath and close my eyes. I think of her dancing light and her bright colors. "Flitt," I whisper, and the ground falls away beneath my feet.

Immediately I'm struck by a chill wind that rustles my bangs and whips my braid into my face. I turn my back to the gusts and crouch down, grasping the frigid stone with my already numb fingertips. "Gloves," I murmur, and my hands are covered at once. I stay there, eyes squeezed shut, heart racing. I don't need to look. I know exactly where I am.

"You did it!" Flitt's voice is barely audible as the wind whisks it away. I feel a tug on my braid and I know she's holding on for dear life. My belt is heavy now, weighing me down. I reach to the pouch that holds the stone to find it bursting open, the bandages spilling out.

"Is it growing?" I shout over the roar of the wind.

"Well, it has to be able to fit, doesn't it?" She shouts into my ear. "The face is somewhere around here, come on. Azi, you can't do this with your eyes closed." She's right, I know, but I can't open them, either. The thought of the height turns my knees to jelly, and my hands tremble so violently I fear I'll lose my tight grip on the jagged rocks of the Crag.

"I can't." I cry. "You do it. You can have the wish!"

"You can," she clings to my neck. "What are you afraid of? In Kythshire you can float, you can fly. You won't fall. Just look, it's so beautiful. You can see the ocean and the prairies. You can see Haigh. You can see the Keep and the treasure field, and the wheat, and the edge of the forest where your mum is and—oh!" She clings tighter, and her sudden silence distracts me enough that I allow my eyes to open for a very narrow peek.

At first I can't tell what's startled her, but when I follow her gaze I see it just above us: the profile of an enormous face carved into the black rock. It juts out over the edge of the crag like a great, round head. The early morning sun casts a cool yellow glow over its burnished surface and I can easily make out the nose that is as long as I am tall, the mouth open as though it's crying out, and the single eye in the center of the forehead. I push myself to my feet and back away, following the line of the neck to where it meets the mountain. It isn't just a face. It's a shoulder, an arm, a torso. Legs. Feet.

"What is this, Flitt?" I whisper.

"Iren," she says with reverence. "The Guardian of the North. Spirit of the Crag." As she speaks, my belt pouch tears open and I catch the stone quickly as it slips out. It's as large as my hand now, and the inky energy seeps from it into the face. "It wants to go back where it belongs," she says, tugging my collar.

"It seems like it could get there on its own," I hold it out, feeling its strong pull.

"You need to put it in yourself," she calls over a gust of wind. "With your own hands. So it knows you're giving it back." My eyes trace the contour of the great head, fixed to the mountain only by a narrow strip of stony neck. It could crack and break while I'm out there. I could fall down the mountain. I imagine my bones snapping and cracking as I tumble down the rocky slope. Then I remember Flitt's words. Even if I fall, I can float, I can fly.

I stare at the nose where I know I need to be. I steel myself and think hard about it and I'm there, sprawled across the mouth, my feet firmly planted on the neck. I try hard not to think about how high we are but I can't help but look as the great glint of gold catches my eye at the base of the Keep. It's so far down that I can cover the entire keep with the tip of my little finger. In the crook of my arm, the stone wriggles insistently, pulling me toward the precipice of Iren's forehead. Beyond that, I know, is a drop that could surely kill me.

As I creep up across the stone face, I'm vaguely aware of the sky darkening above us. Flitt hovers over the eye, bright against the dark backdrop of a storm cloud that has just begun to form over the keep. A clap of thunder echoes across the mountaintop and as I cling to the bridge of the nose, a streak of lightning bursts forth from the cloud, striking the keep. Even from this distance I can see the cyclone that forms at the mouth of the balcony. I watch it twist and coil and drop away to the rocky bank, which immediately erupts with fairies and golems and flashes of light as the battle rages. The stone tugs at me again, now as large as my forearm. The eye is a great hole carved into the stone, its iris hollow and empty. Its edges have been chipped and broken where the jewel must have been dug out at some point. I slide the stone up until it slips neatly into the iris with a satisfying click.

Inky energy swirls out around it, clinging to the eyelid, spreading across the forehead, inching toward me. The stone beneath my knees rumbles violently, and a deafening cracking sound forces me to let go of my hold and clap my hands over my ears. The face tilts upward and I start to panic as I feel myself slipping. I tighten my grip on the nose with my knees and flatten myself against the rock, but I'm still sliding down. Then something catches me, grips me, pulls me away, tightens around me, and I'm encased in stone with only a small crevice to look through. I watch the ground below streak past in a dizzying blur.

"Flitt!" I scream, clawing at my stone prison, and she appears before me, beaming brightly.

"Don't be scared," she giggles. "You did it! You woke up Iren!"

My stomach jumps into my throat as I feel myself lifted up. When I'm face to face with the great eye, I realize it isn't a prison at all, but a giant stone hand holding me its grip. I step up onto one of the fingers as I catch a glimpse of the Oculus peering in at me. The stone is as large as my torso in its socket now, and the black energy swirling around it creates a depth that mesmerizes me. Looking into the eye is like looking into everything that ever was and ever will be. It's terrifying and fascinating all at once, and as I watch the golden flecks swirl within it, Iren pulls memories from me.

I see myself, a young woman caught by the wrist, being dragged by a horse in the center of the playing pitch while crowds of people toss brightly colored rings at me. I'm strolling in the palace gardens with Margy and Sarabel. I'm watching Rian's trials, clutching Mouli's arm, stealing glances at Eron and Viala. I'm sitting in the sunshine at my father's forge, watching my mother scrub my chain mail. I'm laughing with Rian through the circle hatch. I'm defending Flitt from Ember, I'm standing before Crocus and Scree, and I'm dancing with the fairies, hugging my mother at the edge of the forest, waking in Rian's arms, surrounded by glowing orbs and gifts among the trees.

The images come faster now, quick as flashes: soaring over the ocean on Elliot's back, drained white fairies, filthy streets of Zhaghen, six Sorcerers at the keep, Rian, Shush and Ember stripping Viala, my father leading the king's guard, myself kneeling before Eron and picking up the amulet, swinging my sword at the skeletons, choosing to walk away from the treasure in the wheat field, being dangled over the sea wall by Dacva and his group, holding Flitt's diamond to the light, kissing Rian in my ball gown, reaching up to slide the Oculus into place, steadying my cup as Bryse slams his fist on the dining table. There is no rhyme or reason to any of it. No order, just memories one after another as the gold flecks spin and swirl and dance within the enormous eye.

As fascinated as I am to see myself from the outside this way, it's also unsettling. The Oculus is using this information to judge me, and without my permission it feels like an invasion. I tear my gaze away from the powerful hold of the eye, and as soon as I do, the memories fade. With my attention averted, I take in the creature's face, which is like a beautifully chiseled stone sculpture.

Its features are neither male nor female but handsome and beautiful all at once. Its lips stretch into a slight smile as it watches me take it in. Its shoulders are strong but slender, its stone torso draped with folds of carved fabric that cascades to its knees. A rumble of thunder at the keep catches its attention, and when it turns to look in that direction, stony locks of curls slide over its shoulder with a fluid movement.

"Azaeli," it turns back to me again. "Despite your great fear, you have restored me from blindness. After nearly two hundred years of sleep, you have returned that which was most precious and woken me. You are noble, true of heart, generous and brave. You give these gifts of yourself freely."

A blinding flash of lightning cracks at the keep, followed by a clap of thunder that shakes the mountain. I try to peer past Iren, but my view is blocked by the mass of its shoulder as it continues to speak. "I am the Shadow Crag embodied. The Mountain Keeper. Esteemed Guardian of the Northern Border. I will crush all those who threaten the peace of Kythshire. Fight beside me, or remain safe upon the mountain. What do you choose?"

"Fight," I say without hesitation.

"As I knew you would. Then, be prepared." Iren's words fall over me like a spell. My body tingles from head to toe as a rush of power sweeps over me. I step back into the safety of Iren's palm and look down at myself.

"Oh, Azi!" Flitt cries with wonder as she watches the transformation. My climbing clothes have been replaced with a perfectly fitted set of deep blue armor. Describing it as plate mail wouldn't be accurate. It's smooth and shimmers like stone or glazed clay, though it carries little weight as it hugs my body. When I move, it gives me more freedom than chain or leather. Even the helm on my head is light and free, allowing me a full range of vision while safely covering most of my face. To finish the look, a cloak of pure white drapes my back. I sense something else about it as well, another sort of protection.

"Is it warded against magic?" I call up to Iren as we make our way down the mountain to the keep.

"To a degree, if you are not foolhardy," Iren's voice booms, rustling the leaves of the trees far below as we pass. Iren holds me close into its chest as we near the keep, and I climb up to watch the approach. The guardian's sheer size is breathtaking. Even from this distance I can tell that the keep will be as small as a doll's house to the Guardian of the North.

As we reach the base of the mountain, Iren stoops low and scoops up a heaping handful of the gold piled there. It tips its head back and opens its mouth to pour the treasure in, and I duck for shelter as coins and goblets and chains tumble and bounce and roll back to the ground. Iren lets out a long sigh of contentment at the snack and then we're off again into the fray.

Chapter Twenty-Eight

THE KEEP

The claps of thunder and torrent of cyclones are not as frequent this morning as they had been when Elliot first brought me through the battlefield, but Ember's stone fairies and golems are out in full force to face them anyway. Iren pounds up the slope causing the ground to quake, and we are met with cheers and dancing and cries of disbelief as we pass by those gathered to fight. Inside the safety of Iren's hand I turn to Flitt, whose excited glow is sending bright prisms across the stony enclosure.

"It's not safe for you here," I say to her. "You should go back to the grotto."

"Are you for real?" she asks, wide-eyed. "I want to see what happens! You and I, we're friends now. Azi and Flitt, together!" She grins at me. "Let's go get Shush."

"And Ember?" I grin.

"I guess so." She shrugs and wrinkles her nose and I laugh. A burst of lightning flashes just outside, crackling right above us with a deafening strike. Iren roars in fury and closes us securely in its fist as a shower of black stone rains down from its head.

"Sorcerers of Zhaghen, I address you. Cease this assault!" I clap my hands over my ears at the thunderous voice. "I am Iren. I am the Shadow Crag embodied. The Mountain Keeper. Esteemed Guardian of the Northern Border. Watcher of the North. Blinded by Sorcerer King Diovicus and restored by Cerion's Champion Azaeli Hammerfel. I will crush all those who threaten to encroach upon Kythshire. Cease now or face your utter destruction!" The lightning strikes again and I peek out between the cracks of its fingers to watch. Far below on the balcony, two Sorcerers stand with their arms raised as they summon the cyclone.

"You are nothing but stone," one of them cries. "Stone and words.

Begone, Iren of Nothing!" She thrusts her hands at us, releasing the cyclone. It twists and swirls with tentacles of darkness as it whips closer. Then Iren reaches out with its free hand, scoops it into its fist, and squeezes it. An earsplitting scream pierces the air, causing the Sorcerers to fall to their knees in agony. Iren laughs and puts its hand to its mouth, swallowing the cyclone like a plump black berry. Then it crouches down and, grinning, blows a great gust of golden light at them. Most of the light shoots up into the sky, but some of it dashes to the Sorcerers on the balcony, throwing them back against the stone wall where they both slide limply to the floor.

"Six of you there are. Soon to be none if you do not heed my warning. Cease this!" Iren's voice courses through me like fire. I feel as though it might split my bones. Then we're lifted again to its mouth, and as it whispers, glints of gold and white sparkle at its lips. "Free the others, Flitt and Azaeli. Keep your distance from the balcony." It swings its free hand down, crushing one side of the balcony to rubble and with the other deftly deposits me onto the ledge of a tiny window slit. I recognize it as the same one Elliot took me through, and I slip down onto the landing and quietly release my sword from its sheath as Flitt hovers beside me. As I creep toward the Sorcerers' room, I can hear their panicked voices over the rumble and crash of stone outside.

"I'm telling you, there's nothing in here about any of it. No Iren, no Mountain Keeper. Nothing about a creature that eats shadow twists and spits out pure magic." The panicked voice is smooth and familiar, and I swallow back bile as I creep forward to the doorway to see Viala's curtain of black hair shimmering over a pile of great tomes.

"Give it to me, you empty-headed whelp," an older man covered completely in the blue-black swirls of the Mark strikes her hard across the head, sending her crumpling to the floor. He pulls the book close and rifles through its pages frantically. "Mountain spirits, defeating rocks, natural enemies... there's got to be something."

"Dinaea!" another voice sobs from the direction of the balcony. "She's fading! Ornis, get the fae, do something!" A round man, also completely covered in the Mark and draped in rich burgundy velvet, lounges on a chaise across the room. He gestures to the balcony lazily, his attention deeply fixed on the polished red slab in his lap. The curtains against the far wall ripple softly as they part to reveal an empty cage, which slides across the floor to the balcony. One of the two Sorcerers that Iren had sent flying against the wall crawls inside and grasps at it, his eyes wide with fury.

"Ornis, you wretched slug! What do you mean, sending me an empty cage? Get the other! She's dying, she's dying!"

"And the stars wept," Ornis mutters dully, sneering as he flicks his fingers across the room once more, never taking his eyes from the slab. Another empty cage slides across the room, and when the curtains settle back again I catch a glimpse of Shush and Ember huddling together behind them. Both are bedraggled, but to my relief I see beside them all of the previously caged fairies. They huddle behind the curtain, looking drained but thankfully alive. Outside, another deafening crash sends the walls shaking.

"The creature is a common mountain spirit," he announces in a bored tone, reading from the slab. "Any fool can defeat it. Just rid it of its source. That would be the eye, witless," he calls to the balcony. "Gorgen, go and help the fools." The older man who struck Viala glares at Ornis.

"I'm sure you're not presuming to issue orders to me, Ornis," he growls, but he storms out to the balcony.

"Emris," Ornis barks. A wiry man with a hunched back and a Mark that curls up through his white beard continues to peer through the mirror at the center of the room. He makes a grunting sound, but doesn't turn away. I keep an eye on him as I step closer to the threshold. It's only a matter of time before they discover Ember and Shush and the missing fairies. I need to figure out a way to get them out of there before they do. "The High Master demands a report," he says distantly, his eyes reflecting the golden script of the slab. The man before the mirror leans closer to it.

"Six score and twelve sentries down. Serkin and Maj are trying to raise them as quickly as they're falling. Cerion's guard is relentless. The others have joined them. Gaethon is as impressive as tales would tell. He just took out seventeen in one strike."

"What of the Banished?" Ornis asks as he scrawls his report onto the slab.

"Rally failed," Emris leans closer, the spectacles on his nose reflecting bursts of light that shine out from the mirror. "Redemption was cut off before they could reach the Outlands." My heart races, amplifying the pain in my chest. My family is here, at the keep. They're fighting the sentries. They've defeated Redemption. Their victory bolsters me. I creep closer to the room, raise my foot to cross through the door, and a strong hand grasps my arm and holds me.

"Wards," Rian's voice is soft in my ear. "They'll see you if you cross."

"Oh, Rian!" I whisper, throwing my arms around him. "How did you know I was here?" I look up at him. His eyes are clear now, his jaw set and determined.

"The Crag's voice carries pretty far," he whispers. "It said your name and I knew right away I had to get to you." He steps back and takes me in. "You look amazing..." As if on cue, Iren roars outside.

"Puny, worthless, powerless little Sorcerers," it rumbles, and the walls around us creak as the keep shakes with the noise. Rian peers into the room and takes count of those inside. His eyes rest the longest on Viala, who is still out cold on the floor. He tears his gaze away from the scene and steps to the side of the landing. His feet hover just above the stone steps as he drifts along to the other side of the wall from where Ember and Shush are hiding.

The thunder rumbles again and the fiercest lightning I've ever seen flashes and cracks outside causing Flitt to yelp in surprise. I duck as a spray of golden light shoots in through the balcony doors, shattering the stone frames to a gaping hole. Debris pelts at Emris, who throws himself against the mirror to protect it. Ornis groans in annoyance, tossing the slab onto the cushion beside him. An uproar of cheers erupts from the fairy defenders outside on the slope.

"The eye, idiots! Just aim for the eye!" Ornis shoves himself up from the chaise with a grunt of effort and shuffles to the gaping hole that once was the doorway to the balcony. I turn my attention back to Rian, who is tracing his fingers over the stone, murmuring a spell. The wall beneath his hand shifts and fades into a tiny shimmering opening. He gestures to Shush and Ember, who immediately begin ushering the others through.

The first few are hesitant as they look up at Rian, whose Mage Marks continue to widen and creep to cover most of his face. He smiles at them kindly and nods, offering the safety of his arms to the weaker ones. With Ember and Shush to reassure them, most make it through to our side safely while the Sorcerers inside are distracted by Iren's fury. Many of them are battered and half-drained, and Flitt rushes to the weakest looking ones straight away. She bobs from one to the next in turn, offering hugs and shining light on them. Each is rejuvenated by her touch, and I'm relieved to see she doesn't seem at all drained by the effort herself. Shush continues ushering the remaining refugees through the hole, with Ember beside him keeping watch on the Sorcerers.

"Emris! Stop watching that and get over here. Corbin and Dinaea are fallen! The eye, I said, the eye!" Ornis screams at Gorgen, who I assume is perched on the remainder of the balcony outside the ruin of the doorway.

"We have to destroy the mirror." Rian says as he helps the remaining fairies through. "It's a portal, among other things. They can escape through it if we don't. And I have a feeling they'll be looking to get out of here soon enough, if Iren keeps it up."

"Tell us what to do," Shush whispers quickly as he gestures for Ember to go before him through the hole.

"Not so fast," a soft voice hisses, and an elegant hand closes around Shush. From my place at the threshold, I can see Viala kneeling before the curtain which has closed to conceal Rian's hole in the wall. She squeezes Shush tightly in her fist, watching him with wild eyes.

"Who are you talking to, pretty little windy?" She jeers at him, taking one wing in each hand to pull them slowly apart. "Where are your lovely friends?" Shush squeezes his eyes shut, his face twisting in pain. "I won't hurt them, I only wish to learn from them," she purrs. "Have they left? Do you know how to leave? I wish to leave," she whispers, ducking as another spray of rubble crashes through the room. "I promise I'll be good. Show me how to get out?"

"You're...hurting...me..." Shush whimpers, and Viala loosens her hold.

"That wicked man, he struck me. He hurt me," she says, reaching up to the bruise on her cheek. "Take me with you on the wind, back to Sunteri. I don't want to know anything anymore. I just want to go home." She leans against the wall, pressing her face into the curtain.

Outside, the battle rages on, the floor of the keep shaking and rumbling as Iren pounds at the walls, crumbling them. I watch Viala's back straighten slowly, her chin raise, her eyes slide to the side, to the wall where Rian hovers just beyond the curtain.

"He's here," she whispers, squeezing Shush mercilessly. "Isn't he?" Her eyes go wide and she tosses Shush aside. "I feel him. He's here!

"You thief!" Viala screams as the floor quakes and bits of the ceiling shower down over her. "You took everything from me, everything!" She thrusts the curtain to the side and reaches through the opening to claw blindly at Rian's face, but he steps out of her reach.

"Where are you?" she screams again, and though she's looking right at him, she can't see him. Shush dives through to our side just as Rian sweeps his hand across the hole in the wall, solidifying it. Viala is smart enough to pull her hand back before she's caught. In a rage, she pushes herself up from the floor and charges straight at me. I step aside just as she stumbles over the threshold. The shadow ward fizzles away with a loud crackle, and the collective cry from the Sorcerers the moment she crosses through is deafening.

"The ward!" they all scream in unison as the doorway shimmers and the magic fades. Oblivious to her folly, Viala spins on the landing, searching for Rian. We are still safely hidden in the Half-Realm. Over her shoulder I watch as Gorgen comes to hover in the gaping ruin of the wall. In a fury, he grasps Viala roughly by the throat.

"Worthless cur," he growls as he drags her back through the rubble. "Ornis was wrong. You're not worth keeping around, even if you are nice to look at." Viala's eyes go wide as she pleads and grasps at the old man's hands.

He lifts her up at the edge of the broken balcony floor and I watch in horror as he unceremoniously tosses her over the edge. Her terrified screams echo over the rumble of the battle outside until they finally end in a sickening thud. I take a step back, shocked by his callousness, and bump into Rian. When I turn to look at him, his face is drained of color. He's just as appalled as I am.

"The mirror," he croaks, more within his wits than I am as he nods through the door. "The wards are down." Outside, Iren's attacks have slowed. I steal a glance out of the gaping hole as we charge through to the mirror and see the Crag's great stone form hunched over, just outside. At first I'm afraid they've managed to damage it, but it straightens after it scoops something from the rubble.

"Your wickedness shall not go unpunished." Debris rains down again as Iren's voice sends vibrations through the weakened stone above us.

"The mirror, Azi!" Rian's cry tears my attention away from the scene. I charge into the room and raise my sword, and drive it through the wooden backing of the looking glass. What happens next catches me completely off guard. The room begins to spin around me as the mirror shatters. Shards of glass burst from the other side and time seems to slow as they drift around me like snowflakes. My sword is caught fast in the frame, which radiates powerful streams of magic.

I hear only silence as I watch the sparkling energy encase my blade and creep across the hilt. Magic erupts around me in slow motion as the shattered mirror holds my weapon in its grip. I'm vaguely aware of the fight, but my concern is with my sword. Flitt hovers before me. She's shouting something into my face, but I can't hear her. Lightning streaks past my shoulder from the balcony side, and it's blocked by a spray of red embers. I see Rian in the corner of my eye shouting, throwing spells.

It's as if I'm in another place and time, watching the battle rage around me but hearing none of it. Then they are on me. The wind fairies dive at my hands, wrenching my fingers, loosening my grip on my sword as the mirror's unleashed magic crawls up to the hilt. I fight them. I don't want to let it go. This sword was made by my father, a gift of love, a reward for hard work. I can't lose it.

One of the fairies is caught by the magic and pulled into the now whirling vortex where the mirror once stood. Still, the others work to free my grip as the energy creeps closer. I realize the fight is lost as I watch the single, brave little fairy swirling away into the unknown. As much as I love my sword, I can't allow the fae to be taken. I let the weapon slip from my fingers and lunge for the terrified creature to scoop it out of the vortex's hold. As my sword spins away, I throw myself away from it and the raging thunder of the battle around me pounds my senses. As soon as we're clear, the fairy squirms from my hand and darts to safety. Rian screams an incantation above me and the power of his spell clashes with one flung from across the room by Gorgen, who charges us both.

I find my feet and put myself between him and Rian as they exchange another round of spells, but Gorgen bests him, sending him sprawling into a heap of stone at the far end of the room. Relentless, he surges toward Rian again. I charge the old man in a fury, my arms raised as though my sword is still with me. When I bring them down something solidifies against my palms and as I close my hands around it, the ice sword streaks between us leaving a sizzle of steam thick in the air. Gorgen stumbles backward over a fallen beam and I take the opening. I expect to be met with some ward of protection or spell of shielding, but whatever he might have had on him has long been broken.

The sword slices cleanly through the front of his robes, sizzling as the chill of the blade meets his warm flesh. It's a killing blow, one that I've practiced a hundred times on the dummies in the yard. Clean and quick and merciful. Kinder than he deserves. His eyes go wide and distant, and by the time I pull the sword free, his life has left him. I turn away and lower my weapon, and Flitt stares at me in wide-eyed silence. As our eyes meet, I wonder fleetingly if she sees me differently now. Can we still be friends, now that I've killed someone? She's the first to look away, flying off to help the fairy who had been caught in the vortex.

"Go quickly, now's your chance! All of you, back home! Go, go!" she cries, shooing them. Shaken, I turn to Rian who has recovered from his fall. He doesn't seem harmed, but our reprieve is a short one. Ornis and Emris' attention is drawn from the battle outside to the fading whirlpool of magic that is slowing where the mirror once stood. One by one the wind fairies shimmer and dart past them through the gaping hole in the wall, off to Kythshire. Now, as the two Sorcerers approach, only Shush, Flitt, and Ember remain with us in the keep. I'm unsure whether the Sorcerers can see us at first, but if they can they don't seem to be interested in us at all. Instead they watch in horror as the vortex shrinks further and further until it is no more, and the broken frame of the mirror crashes to the cracked floor. Enraged, Emris turns to Ornis.

"See what your laziness has cost us!" he screams, thrusting his arms outward in a blast of orange flame that sends Ornis careening across the room. Above us, the ceiling rumbles and cracks. My instinct tells me to run, but instead Rian and I cling to each other, rooted to the spot, unable to look away as the enraged Sorcerers lock in a furious battle.

Ornis raises his arms and the pile of rubble around him collects into the form of a giant fist, which thrusts at Emris with impossible speed and force. Emris cries out and a powerful whirlwind swirls from his hand, breaking the fist to bits and sending chunks of stone in a spray across the room as swift as arrows. I step in front of Rian as we're pelted with them, shielding him with my armor. Rian whispers a spell and I feel us fade into the Half-Realm again.

Ornis is not so fortunate. One of the stones pierces his cheek. Another drives through his chest, leaving a blood-soaked stain that pools quickly, darkening the red velvet. Enraged, Ornis summons again, this time collecting broken shards of glass from the mirror in a shimmering ball before him. Emris is too quick for him, though. He sends a burst of dark matter careening toward the ball and it explodes in Ornis's direction, shredding his skin as easily as his fine robes. I turn away and bury my face into Rian's chest at the gruesome sight as Ornis screams in agony, and again the ceiling cracks.

"It's going to cave," Rian grips my wrists and pulls me to the door, but not quickly enough. A final deafening rumble sends the ceiling collapsing down on us. Rian calls out a quick incantation and throws his arms wide, and a circle of glowing white energy encases us. Massive chunks of the ceiling and thick supporting beams bounce and roll off the field with crash, creating a billowing cloud of dust beyond his magical wall. The ceiling is gone now, and sunlight streams in above us.

"Flitt!" I cry as I press my hands against the glass-like surface. "Shush! Ember!" I squint out into the dust, desperate to catch a glimpse of any one them, but it's no use. I can't see a thing, and the battle has gone eerily still and silent. Then, the tiniest sound echoes in our bubble: a sneeze, right at my shoulder.

"We're okay!" Flitt chirps happily, sneezing again. Beside her, Shush nods enthusiastically.

"Thank you for saving my little ones," he says to Rian in his usual rushed whisper. Rian has just enough time to nod before Iren's voice sets the floor rumbling again.

"Six there were, now three remain," it echoes across the one remaining wall. "Emris of Devniban. Sekrin, Defiler of Life. Majniver of the Desert Stone. You will not cross into our lands. Return to your own lands, depleted and wasted. Begone or forfeit your lives." Rian and I press ourselves against the invisible wall and peer out into the ruins. Our little bubble is framed by the arched doorway as we stand just outside on the landing above the spiral stairwell.

"Emris survived this?" Rian breathes as the dust slowly begins to settle. There is only one wall left standing after the ceiling's collapse, and the floor has also crumbled so that it slopes down into the mountainside. Outside, the stone fairies line the edge of the rubble, shoulder-to-shoulder with their golems. Ember bobs at the center of them all as they peer warily up, her own golem nearly double the size of the rest.

"How," the Sorcerer's voice comes in a wail from somewhere nearby, carried on the mountain wind that now whips through the battered keep, "how did it go so wrong, so quickly?" I search the piles of stone to see his frail form clambering over a wide beam. He reaches to the other side of it and pulls a limp hand to his chest. "Ornis, my friend," he says thickly, "how did this happen?" He presses the bloodied hand to his cheek, and I blink in disbelief as Ornis's wide apparition rises up from the rubble beside him. He bends to Emris's ear and raises a hand that's merely a wisp of energy as he speaks. We can't hear his words, but beside me I feel Rian go rigid as the spirit points in our direction.

"Oh, no. Spiritspeak. Get ready," he murmurs to me as Emris' expression changes slowly from despair to fury.

"Rian Eldinae!" The elder Sorcerer roars as Ornis fades away. "Show yourself!" He levitates to drift over the rubble. "What have you done? Ornis was my friend!" he howls with lament. "What have you made me do? Unforgivable and yet," his fury wanes slightly as he slows, his tone growing almost reverent, "yet brilliant. Rian Eldinae," he continues to search, at one point breezing right past us. "Your talents are wasted in Cerion. Brilliant, brilliant. I never even suspected...never saw it." He laughs a little manically.

"Rian, what's he talking about?" I whisper. "What did you do?" He glances at me and looks away, but not before I note the fear in his eyes. "Rian?"

"I didn't think it would really work. I didn't know it would go that far. They were so worked up..." He trails off as Emris picks up his pace, throwing spells left and right in his frantic effort to reveal us. He's growing tired, I can tell. Even in his anger his shoulders are hunched, his eyes drooping. "Ornis didn't attack him," Rian whispers. "I did. Or rather, I compelled Ornis to."

"What?" I stare at him in disbelief.

"He was furious. His mind was weak and clouded with anger. I controlled him. I attacked Emris through him. I didn't think it would work. A Sorcerer, fiftieth circle at least! I didn't think I had the power." His eyes flash with a frightening wildness, and I'm so shocked that I don't even know how to respond. It doesn't matter, though, because in that moment one of Emris' aimless Revealers strikes the force field, causing a crackle of energy to cascade to the floor as it's broken. Emris's eyes light with triumph and he casts the spell again. Before we can react, the air shimmers around us, and I know that the Revealer has taken. He can see us now.

Chapter Twenty-Nine

DARK DECISIONS

With Emris hovering this close to us, the intricate design of the Mark on his completely blackened skin is striking. It covers his wrinkled face like a shroud, and coats his scalp beneath his white hair. It is so deeply etched into him that the skin is raised and purplish, like a fresh scar. His dark eyes are nearly indiscernible as they trace over Rian and then turn to me. Flitt and Shush have ducked behind my shoulder, and I angle myself protectively between them and the Sorcerer as he glares at us with pure hatred.

"Leave the young ones," Iren booms from outside. "It is not too late, Emris of Devniban. Begone to Sunteri, never to return, and your misdeeds here shall be forgotten."

Emris doesn't acknowledge Iren. He takes in my armor, the braid at my shoulder, the empty harness that once held my sword. His mouth curves up into a wicked smile. "Azaeli the Protector," he laughs and moves closer. "So slight, so full of heart and yet," he pauses, his awful black eyes boring into me. "Yet not so pure as you were before you entered these walls." I recall my ice sword sliding into Gorgen and fight the shudder that threatens my disciplined stance.

"Bound by blood to a promise made by ancestors long dead," he hisses his disapproval. "Yet it is an oath easily broken, Azaeli. You need but to declare your defiance, and you shall be released." He tilts his head to the side sympathetically. "Oh, did no one tell you that? Secrets, secrets and deception. Even Rian kept what he knew from you, did he not?"

"You dare—" Rian growls, snapping Emris' attention away from me.

"And Rian Eldinae, Protégé of Gaethon, next in line for greatness at Cerion's pathetic Academy," Emris sneers. "Surely you see now that you are capable of so much more." He moves closer to Rian, examining him like some impressive artifact. "Power, stripped from one, given to another, amplified by the fae themselves. How," he laughs with slight amazement, "how are you managing to contain it? How have you not yet gone mad with the ecstasy of it?" Rian says nothing in reply, his expression a mix of defiance and distaste. "We can learn from each other, you and I," Emris offers gently. "Together, all of it could be ours."

"Do not heed him, Rian Eldinae," Iren's voice rumbles over us. "He would have you destroy all that you love. Emris of Devniban, twice I have warned you, and twice you have ignored my words. Hear me now. You shall be utterly destroyed, your threats against our lands ceased forever."

"Empty words," Emris laughs as he shouts his reply to Iren. "You are confined to the mountain, you great rock, and I am not within your precious borders now. You saw to that when you destroyed these walls. And so you are powerless to touch me." His eyes glint at Rian. "You and I," he whispers hungrily, "will have no such limitations on our power when Kythshire is ours."

"*When Rian says Cerion,*" Flitt's voice echoes in my mind, "*duck.*" I glance at Rian and note the familiar mischievous gleam in his eye. Something spectacular and most likely dangerous is about to happen. He doesn't want to give it away, though, and so his gaze remains locked with Emris'. The Sorcerer seems to take his expression to mean that Rian is actually considering his offer.

"Your callous pride will be your demise." Iren booms from the mountainside. "You will not survive this day, Emris of Devniban."

Emris leans closer to Rian. "Imagine the power you could unleash." Rian swallows, his fingers crackling with chaotic energy fighting to burst forth. Emris eyes his hands. "Imagine the sweet release. Have you ever fought against a mountain spirit, boy?" Rian, in response, risks a shake of his head.

"We don't have them in Cerion."

It happens in an instant. I duck down as Flitt instructed, and her colorful light bursts forth with a power so dazzling it makes my eyes sting. I squeeze them shut and brace myself as a commanding voice blasts across me from beside her. At first I'm stunned because I've only ever heard him whisper, but Shush's voice begins like a zephyr and slowly grows to a hurricane, all in the time it takes for my knees to hit the ground.

"You have been warned three times. You are not welcome here! I DELIVER YOU TO IREN OF THE MOUNTAIN TO MEET YOUR FATE!" Shush howls. Rian and I clap our hands to our ears and huddle together as the rubble blows around us, careening against the walls, swirling in a way that reminds me so much of the shadow cyclones. Flitt's blinding prisms dim as Emris is caught up in a mighty torrent, and I squint to watch the Sorcerer fight and struggle in vain within Shush's whirlwind. Dust and rock and rubble are kicked up violently as he's carried to the edge of the keep and across the border into Kythshire with Shush following behind, blowing great gusts ahead of him to guide the swirling force.

"Take cover!" Ember's command from outside is barely audible over the rush of the wind, and as Flitt's light fades, Rian and I clamber through the ruins together to the edge of the keep. Just outside, fairies and their golems scatter away from the windswept Sorcerer. He's merely a blur within the cyclone among the swirling mass of rubble, but occasionally there is a burst of lightning, fire, or ice that escapes the wind. Rian and I cling to each other at the precarious edge of the rubble, watching.

"He's trying everything to get out," Rian calls over the deafening wind, "but he doesn't realize it's only fueling the wind. Impressive, isn't it? I had no idea Shush had it in him."

"No wonder he's always whispering," I shout over the gale. Rian and I hold tight to steady each other as Iren rumbles to its knees before us. One hand remains cupped to its broad chest, and I note a thin stream of crimson trailing down its arm. With its free hand, Iren reaches out to Shush's cyclone and plucks the Sorcerer from it. As soon as he does so, the torrent of wind dies to a squall, then a rustle, and then a soft breeze. After a brief a nod of satisfaction, Shush darts back to us to join Flitt, who has perched on a broken bit of wall beside me. She grins at him a little shyly.

"That was brilliant," she whispers to him. Beside her, with little warning, Twig emerges slowly.

"Sorry I'm late," he says as he peers around the ruins warily. "Palace business. Did I miss anything?"

"Only everything," Flitt giggles.

"Shhh," Shush points and everyone's attention is drawn back to Iren, who holds the limp Sorcerer in his palm, level with its enormous, perfect stone lips.

"Amazing," Rian breathes as Iren parts its lips and, as though drawing a breath, takes in a stream of twisting blackened energy from the broken sorcerer. The stream goes on for a long while and we watch in silence, mesmerized by the way the energy changes from black, to red, to orange, to gold.

"It's stripping him," Rian whispers with a mix of awe and horror.

"Recovering that which was stolen," Ember corrects him as she drifts up the mountainside to join us.

"Will Iren keep it?" Rian asks, flexing his own fingers as if to quell the pent-up energy that still crackles from them. Ember shakes her head.

"Of course not. It doesn't belong here. It's Sunteri magic," Ember scoffs. "Isn't that obvious?" She rolls her eyes and Rian shrugs apologetically. Above us the stream of magic thins. Lifeless in Iren's hand, the Sorcerer's body seems slighter now. Faded, like a swatch of threadbare fabric.

"You'll be next, Mage," Ember says to Rian with a satisfied grin.

"What?" I gasp as my heart begins to race at the implied threat. The Sorcerer's frail form grows even more sunken and faded, and with the pounding of my heart comes the ache in my chest again. I reach up instinctively to rub it, my gloved hand clunking softly against the stony scales of my breastplate.

"I know," Rian says softly as he watches the final stream of energy leave the Sorcerer's body. "I'm ready." The air around Emris' body shifts slightly, his skin and robes fade to gray, and then he crumbles to tiny pebbles which Iren tips out of its hand like grains of sand.

"Rian," I hug his arm to me tightly as I watch the pebbles bounce gently down the jagged mountain slope. "No..."

"It won't be like that for me," Rian says. "Don't worry."

"Flitt," Iren rumbles, and as Flitt rises up to the eye, Iren blows a stream of golden energy into one remaining pebble. "When we are through here, take this stone," it holds out its hand, "to my son."

"All right, I will!" Flitt dives to retrieve it, tucks the glowing pebble into a belt pouch, and then darts back to us again.

"Azaeli, Rian," Iren shifts toward us, lowering the hand that has been clutched to its chest. As Rian and I inch forward together, its fingers uncurl to reveal Viala, her body broken and bruised, lying in a pool of blood which spills down its wrist. "I know of your history," Iren says, mostly addressing Rian, "and so I leave her fate to you." As its words softly rustle her tangled black hair, Viala takes a shallow, rattling breath.

"Choose to end her suffering, or choose a new life for her with us. One in which she will have no memories of her time before this moment." The eye moves from Rian to me. "If you choose death for her, then you yourself must deal the killing blow." Rian and I exchange looks. Neither of the possibilities seems ideal. The fairies in Ember's command line the base of the mountain, milling in silence as they watch our exchange. "Choose quickly, for the battle is not yet won. One Sorcerer remains, locked in battle with the king's men, just through the keep."

"You're sure she'll have no memory of her past?" Rian asks, staring at Viala's broken form as she takes another weak gasp for breath. "No way at all to cause this sort of mess again? What will you do with her?"

"You ask your questions without ceremony, Rian Eldinae." Iren smiles. "I am certain. She will begin a new life, a life of service to the Northern Border." Rian turns to me, his eyes searching mine.

"I don't know," he whispers, pulling me close. "She tried to kill you. She's been horrible."

"But it wasn't all her, Rian. She was being manipulated and controlled. They had her family..." I stare at her pale face, now free of the Mark. She looks so innocent.

"Still," Rian sighs. "We're taught to be guardians of the magic the fae allow us, and she squandered that trust. She shared secrets she vowed to keep. Ancient secrets. She held the prince with Sorcery. Her actions could have destroyed Cerion from the inside out. Kythshire, too."

I don't say anything. I know he's right. If she was in the hands of the Academy, she'd be stripped, imprisoned or banished, and left to

319

die. In their eyes, what she did would be deemed unforgivable.

"Yet," Rian shakes his head. "To kill someone knowing there's a chance they can be spared? To offer a second chance?"

"I know," I nod and reach up to brush a bit of splintered wood from his hair. "I trust Iren. But," I glance behind me. "Flitt?" She drifts up into the small space between us and crosses her arms.

"You're going to spare her, aren't you?" She purses her lips, and I can't tell by her tone whether she's for or against it.

"I am aware that she has wronged you, Flitt. But this choice is left to the humans. The fae cannot intervene." Iren says quietly.

"All right." Flitt glances at me with a hint of disappointment and then turns to Rian. To my shock, she floats up to his shoulder and perches herself there. Rian turns his head in her direction, wide-eyed. It's a simple act that might not mean a thing to anyone else here, but to us it means a great deal. With that one, simple movement, she has shown she supports his choice, no matter what he decides.

"We leave her to you, then, if you're sure she'll never be a threat again." Rian reaches up and rakes his fingers through his hair, his shaking hands still crackling and bursting with excess magic. Iren covers her over with its other hand and closes its great eye as it sits back onto its heels. "And this," Rian says, holding up his hands as he turns to Ember and Shush. "This I want to return to the Wellspring. Please." There's a hint of desperation in his tone that makes me press myself nearer to him and hold him closer.

"Don't you want to go out there and use it?" Ember chides. "Iren said the battle isn't over yet. Think of how impressed your people would be with you." She smirks. All around us, the fae seem to lean in closer, watching Rian with a mix of fear and awe in anticipation of his reply.

"No, I don't," he answers firmly. "It isn't mine. It belongs here, with you." He holds his hands out past me, reaching toward Shush. "Please."

"So honorable. These two have to be the ones," Shush whispers from behind me, and some of the fairies whip their attention to him, issuing a collective "shush!"

"As you wish," Iren booms. Gently, it tucks Viala onto a ledge nearby. "Give it to me, and I shall return it to the Wellspring." Its stony hand lowers to our level, and Rian kisses me softly and offers me reassurances before climbing up into it. Flitt leaves his shoulder to settle onto mine as Shush and Ember join him. When I start to follow, Iren shakes its head and raises his hand away carefully. "Rest now, Azaeli, and take comfort. It will not be long, and he will not be harmed."

"Don't worry. Wait for me, and we'll go together to join the others," Rian offers me a half-assured smile before he disappears behind Iren's stony fingers.

Though Iren insisted the process would be short, it seems like ages to me. Flitt, Twig and I try to watch, but from our angle I can't see anything at all except for the occasional flash of light behind Iren's bent fingers. A couple of times I feel myself start drifting off, and I'm reminded it's been nearly a full day since I've had any sleep. That's a dangerous train of thought, though, with a battle still raging on and our guild in need of us. Restlessly, I push myself to my feet and pick my way back inside to the ruins of the keep.

There's little that remains of them, now. Bits of tattered velvet drapes, a torn crest. I pause at the crushed settee where Ornis lounged, as a golden glow catches my eye from beneath a torn pillow. Moving it aside, I find the stone tablet, its golden script glowing and fading so quickly that I can barely read it. When I do catch a glimpse, I realize it's coming through in the Mage's language. I watch the curling lines ebb and flow as Flitt and Twig join me to peer over my shoulder.

"It's going so fast," Flitt whispers. "What are they saying?"

"Not yet sunset," Twig reads aloud, "but we cannot hold them much longer. The effort drains us. We lost another of our number just now. The well is nearly dry. Please, let us release them. We cannot hold on. Please."

"Who is it?" Flitt hovers close to the slab. "They sound desperate."

"It's the Sunteri fae," I whisper. I see them clearly in my memory, huddling around the roots of the trees, hunched over their own slab, hissing over their shoulders at Elliot and me as we near them.

"We cannot hold much longer," Twig reads aloud. I'm so drawn in by the golden lines that I don't notice Rian until he settles onto the settee and leans against me to reach across to the shining surface of the slab. I wonder at the now smooth, unmarked skin of his neck and face as he uses his finger to scrawl upon it. Twig reads his writing as the words form and fall away into the polished red surface:

"We have no need of the humans now. Release them and restore yourselves. Guard the Wellspring with your lives. It is yours to protect." We watch his script fall away into the depths and the reply rise to the surface. "Thank you! Yes! Masters, we will guard it!"

"Masters!" Ember barks over Rian's shoulder. "Masters! What have the southern fae reduced themselves to, addressing Mages as Masters? Answering to humans?"

"Careful, Ember," Shush whispers.

"Well!" Flitt says loudly, sending a burst of rainbow prisms dancing over the walls to divert our attention from Shush and Ember's exchange. "Will you look at that?" She points outside, where Iren sits with its head tipped back. A thick, steady stream of golden energy rises from its mouth up into the bright blue sky. "All of that was in you, Rian, and now it's going back to the Wellspring!" I turn to Rian, who looks as exhausted as I feel.

"I'm glad to be rid of it," he laughs with relief. "I don't wish that on my worst enemy, having to own so much power. I'm content to stay in the Sixteenth Circle for now." I graze my fingers along his pale jawline where the Mark once swirled, and he leans forward and kisses me. "You were brilliant," he murmurs in my ear, warming my cheeks.

"We're not done yet," I say, remembering the battle still being fought outside. Flitt settles on my shoulder as I push myself wearily to my feet and Rian tucks the slab into his bag.

"Azi?" My mother's voice echoes into the ruined keep amid a sudden uproar of cheers and applause from the fairies gathered outside. I lunge toward the edge of the keep ruins to see her making her way up the mountain slope among them, her silver plate mail gleaming bright in the midday sun. She pauses when she sees me, her hand reaching instinctively to her sword. At first I'm confused, but then I imagine how I must look to her in the strange, shimmering blue armor gifted to me by Iren, standing in the rubble with my white cloak whipping around me. It's only when Rian comes to stand beside me that she seems to realize who I am.

"Mum!" I cry as I stumble down the slope to her. We meet halfway and crash together in a tight embrace as the cheers rise to a deafening roar. Through my tears I watch the crowd of countless fairies in every color and shape gather. The mass of them stretches far up into the sky and deep along the golden wheat field all the way to the forest's edge. I stare in disbelief at the sheer number of them. I had no idea that Kythshire was home to so many. The sight is dazzling, and the sudden realization of how many creatures we fought to protect today overwhelms me. My knees wobble, and my chest aches with the pounding of my heart. Beside us on the slope of the Crag, Iren's great mouth closes as the stream of energy ends. It tips its head forward again and surveys us all.

"Iren! Iren! Iren!" The mass of fairies chants and cheers and dances wildly. Their energy is infectious, and I find myself grinning and laughing in my mother's arms as Rian comes to join us with Flitt and the others trailing close behind.

"Six there were, and none remain," Iren bows to us. "The battle is won." Its great eye slides past us to the keep above. Rian, Mum and I turn, and the first thing I see is a flash of red hair and the swish of a blue cloak. Slowly, other figures begin to emerge from the darkness and appear at the crumbled edge of the keep wall. Bryse is easiest to spot in his now badly dented plate, and Cort is at his side, his twin swords drawn and ready. Brother Donal is next with Dacva peering out from behind him. Then comes Uncle Gaethon, his tattered robes whipping around him as he stares at the gathering with an expression of wonder and disbelief.

Mya's voice carries over us before we see her, her fingers idly strumming her lute as the fox comes to sit at her side. Her song lifts me up, its power energizing and healing me. I search the darkness desperately as they arrive one by one, and I know my mother sees him before I do when she slips from my arms and starts clambering up the rocky slope, crying his name.

"Benen! Benen!" She struggles in her heavy armor, and Flitt, Twig, Ember, and Shush rush to lift her up to where my father stands with his arms outstretched.

"Lisabella!" His voice cracks as she falls into his arms. In unison they slide each other's helms off and drop them to the ground. My father holds her close, and they stare deep into one another's eyes in a way that plainly shows a hundred words silently spoken between them in an instant. Then he bends his head to hers, and they lose themselves in a sweet, deep kiss.

Chapter Thirty

HOME

Mya suggests that we set up temporary quarters in some of the lower, intact rooms of the keep and get a good night's sleep after the hard-fought battle. We settle easily back into our usual routine. Rian and Uncle go off together to whisper secretly while Mum, Da, and I prepare the room we'll sleep in with Mya, Elliot and Rian. I smile to myself as I help Mum off with her armor and she does the same for me. The quilted gambeson and trousers beneath the suit that Iren gifted me is just as finely made, and quite comfortable. We make up our beds and build a fire in the small hearth. When the work is done, Da settles beside my armor to admire its craftsmanship while Mum brushes the dust and knots from my hair. Bryse's laugh booms from the room beside ours followed by Donal and Cort's. Further away, Mya's song drifts along as she and Elliot scout the remains of the keep.

My heart sings with joy to know we're all together and safe again, and as its beat quickens, the pain I've come to expect follows. I press my hand to my chest and Mum pauses the brush mid-stroke.

"Sweeting? Are you hurt?" She rests a gentle hand on my shoulder and Da looks up with concern.

"Last night," I pause. Was it really just last night that Viala was stripped? No wonder I'm so exhausted. So much has happened. "Last night Viala struck me with a spell. I was healed, I thought, but I still have pain from time to time." Mum rubs my shoulder and exchanges a look with Da.

"I'll get Donal," Da says as he sets down my glove.

Brother Donal is of course trailed closely by Dacva. He does his best to avoid me while Donal looks me over, which is just fine by me. While we were making up the room, Da recounted some of their battle against Redemption and the Sorcerer and his skeletons. He laid on the praise of Dacva's newfound healing talents thickly for my benefit, even describing a moment when Dacva saved him from bleeding out by healing a deep gash while Da and Bryse were locked in battle with Dar. Still, it's going to be awhile before I can accept his change in allegiance.

Bryse and Cort mill just outside of the door and a hush falls over us as Donal administers to me. He describes the wound in detail to Dacva, who listens like a dedicated student.

"The spell was meant to kill," he says. "But it was stopped by some ward so it only affected the heart. It's been healed but not completely. Imagine a fist of energy clamped around the heart, squeezing. Of course one would notice it more during moments of fear or joy. Any time the heart would beat faster. See here." He takes Dacva's hand and moves to place it on my chest, but I roll away quickly in protest. Accepting him is one thing, but allowing him to touch me is quite another. Outside in the hall, Bryce growls.

"Right," Donal says with a sigh. "Very well, I'll do it myself, Azi. Come, now." He pats my shoulder and I roll back, and it's not long after he places a gentle hand over my heart that I drift to sleep.

I wake just after dawn to a room empty of all but Rian, who is snoring next to his parents' unoccupied bedrolls. Careful not to wake him, I pad across the room to sit at his side and take his hand. The conversation next door drifts into the room, and I listen quietly as I settle back against the wall.

"We can split the troops in the meantime," Da says. "Half here, half to guard the Pass."

"All of 'em should guard the Pass, and even that won't be enough," Bryse replies. "No reason to leave anyone here. That stone guard can handle any threat."

"Right," Cort says. "The main concern is keeping the banished at bay."

"But with the Keep unguarded and the border of the Outlands open... the banished could easily rally, win against the small number of guard posted, and then claim the keep in the time it takes us to petition the king for more coverage."

"What are they talking about?" Flitt whispers in my ear and I yelp, startled. "Sorry, jumpy!" She giggles and crunches into a sugar cube as she settles onto my shoulder.

"This keep used to guard the border to the Outlands, where Cerion sends its banished. But the Sorcerers moved it, and now there's no protection to keep the criminals where they belong." I tilt my head and smile at her. "Where have you been?"

"Sleeping," she takes another bite and my own stomach growls as she chews. "So if the keep stays here, then the bad people might come, too?" she asks, reaching into her pouch to pull out a dingy looking cube and offer it to me. I'm so hungry I accept it and pop it into my mouth.

"Possibly," I reply as the sweet sugar melts on my tongue. "We're not really sure how many of them are left. The Outlands are a harsh place. But that means anyone who does survive it is smart, strong, and very dangerous. How are the others? Twig, Shush, Ember?"

"Fine. Dancing at the Ring. Scree wants to see you and Stinky." I give her a look and she ducks and grins. "All right, Rian. And your Mum, too. Will you come?"

"Rian needs to sleep. He's been through a lot. Can it wait a little while?"

"Uh huh. They'll be dancing 'til midday, anyway." She takes another bite of her cube and Mya's voice drifts in over her crunching.

"We're talking in circles," she sighs. "It might be best if we remain here and station the troops at the border while we send a report to His Majesty and wait for instructions."

"You're staying here? We'll be neighbors!" Flitt pats my neck excitedly. I sigh and look down at Rian. As much as I would love to remain so close to Kythshire, I was really looking forward to going home with my family and getting back to our lives. I miss Mouli's cooking and Luca's warm smile, and the smell of the salty air through my open window. I miss waking in the morning and chatting with Rian through the circle hatch, and sparring with Bryse and Cort in the training square. If we stay here in the keep, it could be for weeks.

"I don't see any way around it. The Outlands are too much of a threat." I sigh. "The others are right, we can't just leave the border unguarded. Unless..." I turn to her. "If the keep was moved with magic, it can be moved back again the same way, can't it?" Flitt's eyes go wide.

"It would take a lot of magic," she replies. "Since it was done by

Mages, no, Sorcerers, we couldn't do it ourselves without almost draining the," she whispers almost inaudibly, "you know. That's what the dancing is about. Lots of arguing at the circle today about how to get rid of the keep. But there might be another way. Can you think of one?" It takes me a moment before I remember the promise made to me by Scree.

"Flitt, do wishes drain the Wellspring? True Wishes?" I watch her light sparkle brightly as our eyes meet, and she shakes her head with a grin.

"No, Azi. They don't." Her gossamer wings flutter as she hops up to hug my face and give me a sticky, sloppy kiss right on the cheek.

I wash up and breakfast on some stale nut bread and dried fruit while we wait for Rian to wake. The small window in our room is more of an arrow slit, and I stand on tiptoe as I chew and peer out of it. Our room faces the north side of the keep, where our guild's battle took place. Little evidence of the fight remains. Da said that Brother Donal and Dacva worked hard to heal everyone during the fight. Only three of the King's Guard were lost. They'll be given a heroes' burial at home.

The rest of the king's men are working at disposing of the bones of the sentries by way of an enormous pyre.

"Burning death itself," Flitt sneezes. "How revolting."

"What else can they do with them, though?" I argue as I take in the rest of the scene. Further to the east, another group of soldiers guards bundles of sleeping men wrapped in their own orange and red cloaks. I count four all together, one of them as massive as Bryse. "Retribution," I whisper to Flitt. "That's our rival guild, the ones who betrayed us. Uncle must have sent them to sleep."

"Will they burn them, too?" Flitt asks as she peers out curiously.

"No, they'll most likely have a trial." I look for evidence of the necromancers, but the battleground is already swept clean. Rian wakes and comes to join us, hugging me from behind and resting his chin on my unoccupied shoulder to watch out the window.

"Cleanup day," he murmurs. "Those are the unsung heroes of battle. Imagine having that job." He rubs his eyes and kisses me just below my ear. "I'll be back." As he leaves, Mum slips in, looking exasperated.

"They're never going to come to an agreement. Oh, good morning, Flitt," she smiles and Flitt sparkles brightly in reply. "Good morning, my darling. Are you feeling better?" She asks me with a hug.

"I am," I lean into her. "Mum, they want to see us at the Ring. You, me, and Rian."

"Yes, I wanted to go there anyway, to say goodbye. Now that they have the North Guardian back, they won't be needing me. But I do wish I knew a way to fix this mess with the keep."

"Don't worry about that," I say, turning back to the window. "I think I have it figured out. But we'll need to have everyone cleared out of here before we go back to Kythshire."

"Would you just listen to me?" Bryse booms from next door, stirring up another round of shouting.

"If that's the case, then you'd better tell them," Mum says. "Before it comes to blows."

It takes a moment for them to stop shouting long enough to notice me standing in the doorway of the makeshift meeting room. Rian joins us again as they settle down, and I clear my throat nervously.

"Do you have something to say, Azi?" Mya's usually peaceful voice sounds ragged and tired as she folds her hands on the table. Beside her, Elliot sits with his arms crossed and his head tipped against the back of the chair, sound asleep. It's strange to see him in human form again, but now that I know his secret I can certainly pick out the obvious foxlike qualities in his hair and in the shape of his face. I wonder if he's on a journey right now, as he sleeps among his arguing guild mates.

"Can you have the area cleared out by noon?" I ask. "I have a way to move the keep back to the Pass." I look from one of them to the other, expecting an argument.

"How?" Bryse is the first to ask. A dozen replies formulate in my mind and I try to speak each of them in turn, but I can't. Finally, I simply shake my head.

"I just have a way," I say. I want to tell them everything, but I honestly can't. It bothers me. Secrets still feel like lies to me, but I do understand the importance of keeping the fairies safe. To my surprise, it's Uncle who stands first.

"If Azaeli has a way, then let her do it." Around the table, one by one, the others stand in agreement. There's an underlying air of reverence about them as they look at me that makes me a little uneasy.

"I agree," Mya sighs with relief as she rises. "I was about to start pulling my hair out." She pats me on the shoulder. "Thank you, Azi. We'll have it cleared out by noon."

As soon as we reach the Ring, we're swept up in the dancing which is just as chaotic and wonderful as it has ever been. It seems as though so many more have come to join in once we arrive, it's a wonder we can maneuver at all around the edge of the mushrooms. The music is lively and upbeat, and I catch a bit of Mya's melody from yesterday woven through it as I go around and around with Mum's hand in my left one and Rian's in my right.

Flitt's light plays around us as the breeze blows my hair loose from its braid, and I can't remember the last time I laughed so hard for so long. Gradually the music slows, and with it the dancing. In the soft, grassy center of the Ring, Crocus's blossom falls open, this time to reveal shades of deep blue fringed with gold. A hush falls over the massive crowd of fairies as she smiles at the gathering.

Above us on the mushrooms, Ember is seated to our left and Shush rests on his own cap to our right. Beneath him, I recognize several of the wind fairies we rescued from the keep. In fact, many of them have clustered around Rian to pat his back and shake his hand and offer their thanks in the form of tiny gifts. As Crocus begins to speak, he turns to me and raises his present-laden arms with a bemused grin.

"We call forth Lisabella Hammerfel of Cerion." Crocus gestures gracefully to Mum, and I turn my attention back to the center of the Ring as my mother goes to stand before her. "Lisabella," Crocus smiles. "To you we bequeath first the title Scourge of the Shadow Twists, and second the title Protector of the North."

"Thank you," Mum smiles. Crocus nods and continues.

"Do you wish to remain with us in Kythshire, or return to your own in Cerion?"

"As fond as I have grown of your people and your lands," Mum gestures warmly to the assembly. "I long to return to my own home. If you are ever in need of me again, though, I shall honor my family's vow." Crocus nods again, and Mum steps back to join us.

"Rian Eldinae of the Academy of Cerion, we call you now." Rian squeezes my hand before he lets go to step into the Ring. "Our muses will sing of your strength, honor, and selflessness forever more. You held strong when the power proved too much, and you did not allow it to consume you or lead you astray. In the face of great evil, you turned away from temptation and helped those who were too weak to help themselves. You have shown us through your actions that some Mages can, in fact, be trusted. To you, we bestow the titles Windsaver, Oathkeeper, Arcane Guardian, and Steward of the Wellspring. You remain ever welcome within our borders, and we thank you." She dips into a bow and Rian does the same, and then the ground rumbles loudly as Scree pushes through the soil.

"Rian Eldinae: Windsaver, Oathkeeper, Arcane Guardian, Steward of the Wellspring," he booms as cheers erupt from the crowd of fae surrounding us. "You may now collect your debt and be restored from the Half-Realm." Rian shifts slightly and then turns to look at me as he rubs the back of his neck. I had forgotten about our request to be restored in exchange for stripping Viala, and I'm a little disappointed. Having the ability to move unseen and stay out of harm's way was quite helpful to us in our quest. By the look on Rian's face, I can tell he feels the same way. Now that we've learned how to work around it, it'd be a useful skill to keep. I hesitate and then step forward.

"We recognize Azaeli Hammerfel of Cerion," Crocus says with a hint of caution, as if expecting the reaction that follows. At once the gathered fairies erupt into deafening cheers, even louder than they had for Scree, and then the dancing starts again, livelier even than before, and we are swept away with it. It doesn't stop again until the sun is low in the sky, spilling splashes of pink through the deep green canopy above. Rian and I tumble back to the center of the Ring again, breathless.

"What have you to add, Ah?" Scree booms.

"If you please... I think Rian and I would like to remain in the Half-Realm, for now. If that's what you were thinking, Rian?" He nods.

"It's useful," he smiles at Crocus, who blushes and fans herself with a bit of her skirt.

"Very well," Scree booms. "But know that you may collect on this debt at any time. We forever honor our bargains." With that, Crocus turns to me.

"Azaeli Hammerfel of Cerion," she starts, and the crowd goes up in cheers again, but this time when she raises her hand there is a hush. "You have protected our kind through countless dangers, putting yourself in harm's way. Your actions have been brave, selfless, level-headed, kind, nurturing, loyal, just, and pure of heart. You have restored our Esteemed Guardian of the Northern Border, Iren, that we would no longer be plagued by the Shadow Twists. You stood beside your friends in the battle against the Sorcerers of Zhaghen and fought valiantly. We bequeath unto you the titles: The Temperate, Pure of Heart, Reviver of Iren, The Great Protector, and most importantly, if you will agree to it, Cerion's Ambassador to Kythshire."

As the colorful assembly erupts into a chaos of cheering and dancing again, I stand in the center of the blur, stunned. Rian nudges me and I stare up at him in disbelief. Over his shoulder, my mother wipes a tear from her eye just before she's caught up in the dancing. Flitt breaks free from the celebration and dives at me to hug me. The dancing goes on and on as the sunlight wanes, and Crocus yawns and stretches and finally beckons me closer with a bemused smile. I step forward, and Rian and Flitt join me.

"They are likely to dance to the moon this night," she says, her eyes sparkling. "You may think on this honor, Ah, and accept it later if you so choose. Accepting it would mean that you shall offer your aid to any of our kind who find themselves in trouble in Cerion. In addition you would assist in strengthening our relationship and trust with your country and its men." She smiles sweetly.

"We have grown fond of you. We should like to remind you of your status. You have been bestowed with a gift of armor by Scree's parentage, a mark of Iren's confidence in you. You also carry with you a token of great trust from Cerion's Academy. Have you forgotten?"

I remember Uncle's ring, which I retrieve from my belt pouch. Beside me, Rian's eyes widen as he recognizes it. I turn the signet in my hand, looking over the strong symbol that represents the Headmaster of Cerion's only school of magic. My uncle, who trusted me enough to offer me this token, which shows anyone who might question me that my word is as good as his. I tuck the ring safely away again and slip my hand into Rian's.

"Most impressive of all," Crocus says softly, "Is how much you accomplished on your own, without making use of that.""

"Not on my own," I tug Rian's hand so he steps closer, and take Flitt's hand on my other side. "Ember, Shush," I gesture to their mushroom tops, which they've left behind to join the dance. "Flitt, Twig, Rian, all of us worked together." I look around for Twig, who seems to be absent.

"Indeed," Crocus giggles. "Which reminds us," she looks down at Scree, whose voice booms across the ring.

"We offer you your True Wish, Azaeli, for returning the Oculus and restoring Iren, The Shadow Crag embodied, The Mountain Keeper, Esteemed Guardian of the Northern Border. What do you wish?" Some of the dancing fairies settle down as his voice rumbles over the din, but many remain dancing in a colorful blur around the outside of the Ring.

"What do you wish, what do you wish?" The gathering of fae repeats his words over and over in a hypnotizing rhythm. I glance at Flitt and go over in my mind one more time the wish that we rehearsed together as we made our way here earlier. True wishes are tricky, she warned me. They must be worded perfectly in order to be sure you get exactly what you want.

"My True Wish," I start, and suddenly everything is silent and still. The dancing fairies stop abruptly, and all eyes are on me.

"Ow," Flitt whispers and pulls her hand free from mine, flexing her fingers. I offer her an apologetic glance and loosen my other hand's grip on Rian's as I focus on my wish.

"What did I miss?" I recognize Twig's voice among the crowd, followed by a hiss for him to be quiet as the mass of fairies leans forward collectively, waiting to hear what I'll wish for. I close my eyes and recall the words one more time before I speak.

"My True Wish is for Bane's Pass Keep to be restored to its former strength and returned to its rightful place at the border between the country of Cerion and the land known to my people as the Outlands, that the North border of Kythshire remain undisturbed by my people now and always."

Crocus gazes northward, her flawless porcelain skin glowing bright against the deep blue of her petals as the ground beneath us trembles. In the distance I hear strange noises, loud cracks, muffled rumbles, thunderous sounds. The fairies around the Ring cling to one another and murmur quietly amongst themselves. I'm vaguely aware of Flitt's hand slipping back into mine as Crocus returns her attention to us. She speaks in unison with Scree this time.

"It is done," they declare together. "We are immensely grateful for your selfless use of this wish. Azaeli Hammerfel, Rian Eldenae, Lisabella Hammerfel, if there is nothing further, then we wish you a safe return to Cerion. Shall we send you there now?" Crocus asks.

Flitt watches us with interest, her eyes changing quickly from magenta to purple, from blue to gold.

"No thank you," I smile up at Rian, who pulls me close as the fairies start their dance again. "I think we'd prefer to ride home." I reach for Mum's hand. "All of us, together."

Thank you so much for reading Call of Kythshire. I hope you loved reading it as much as I enjoyed writing it. If you did, please be sure to write me a review on Amazon. I'd love to hear from you!

Visit my website to join my mailing list and be the first to hear about my newest releases.

www.missysheldrake.com

Read on for a sneak peak of the
Keepers of the Wellsprings:
Call of Sunteri

Book Two Preview: Call of Sunteri

Chapter One

FLAME AND SEA
Tib

Filth and grunge. Rats. Rot. Bones. Cobbles. Stench. Sobbing. Striking. Silence.

"Climb the wall."

Yes, climb. My feet are swift and sure in the darkness as I leap and cling to the rough stone. They find each crevice perfectly, anchoring me as I push myself up. Climbing feels good. Free. The higher I go, the better I can see the city stretched out before me. In the dye fields, they tell stories of Zhaghen with eyes full of awe. How beautiful it is, how majestic. For me, it's the place that breeds greed. Cruel. Twisted. Soiled.

"Higher."

Yes, higher. The towers are dark tonight, unprotected. Not as scary as I thought they'd be, reaching up into the sky. I creep closer to a slotted window and pause. Sniff. The air here is thick with the scent of old paper. Books. A fan of shining black hair flicks into my memory as my fingers grip the stone through soft leather gloves.

"Inside."

Yes, inside. My feet find the ledge and I crouch on the sill. Tucked safely into the shadows, I peer below into the darkness. It was a good climb, a long climb. Now I'm high, higher than any city boy could climb. Higher than I've ever climbed. Far up above the city. So easy here to ignore the suffering below. To live unaware of it. The cries of the starving, the stench of the gutters, they could never reach this high. Only the Mages. Mages and students. Worse. Sorcerers. My hatred for them pushes me forward.

"The hearth."

Yes, the hearth. I slide from the sill and land lightly on my feet. My new boots are silent on the plush carpet. The room is still. Huge.

Dark except for dying embers crackling far beyond tables piled with pages and books. Shelves. Scrolls. Bottles and jars. The ceiling is high. Domed. Glass. Stars shine above. No one is here this late. The tower is asleep. Empty, except for books. Hundreds. Thousands. Ancient. Irreplaceable. Sacred. Neatly arranged on dozens of shelves. Good to hide behind. To sneak behind.

"Start it."

I take a sheaf of parchment from the shelf as I pass through the last row and creep forward. The crackle of coals lures me. It's dying, but soon it won't be. Soon it will grow. I light the sheaf, watch the edges flare and curl black. I move away through the room. One by one I tuck the burning pages into place on shelves and tables. Everything is so dry and old, it catches quickly. I back toward the window, my escape. Watch the glow of flame that crawls up shelves and across tabletops. I did this. I alone. This is my revenge. Their precious knowledge, turning to char. Ashes. Dust.

"Outside."

Yes, outside. I slip through the window. My fingers find the crevices and I start my descent. Watch the smoke pour from the window. Hear the cries from inside. Fire! Fire! My feet are swift. My hands are steady. I land lightly on the cobbles and stroll away from the smoking tower. The gloves come off, tuck into my tattered bag. They're too fine for the rest of me. They'd give me away.

"On to the next."

Yes, on to the next. I step around the corner, into the gathering crowd. Necks craned up, watching smoke billowing. Some rush the doors with buckets of water, but even in this crisis they're turned away. No one notices me, the whelp in field clothes, older than a boy but not yet a man. I'm nothing to them. Unimportant. Unnoticed. I disappear as the crowd thickens around the base of the tower. On to the next.

Six pillars of black smoke rise into the night sky. Six towers burn. My work is done. The city is awake now. Watching, Screaming. Crying. Cheering. I don't need to run. Nobody suspects me. Nobody notices the poor boy in field clothes.

"Into the sea."

Yes, into the sea. I tuck my new boots safely into my bag and jump from the harbor wall into the deep. The water is warm and calm. I go under. Scrub the soot from my hands, face, and hair. Masts of tall ships loom before me, dark shapes against the darker sky, anchored in the inky water. I'm a fair swimmer. I find the ship with the crest I need: purple chevron under a blue ring. I reach it and pull myself into a skiff lashed beside. Rest a moment. Listen. On deck, men are talking. Watching the smoke rise. Wondering if it will delay their departure.

"Say something."

Yes, I ought to.

"Ho there, sirs!" I call up. Footsteps. Faces peering down at me. Men with trimmed beards. Hair tied neatly. Uniforms. Swords.

"Who goes?" one says.

"It's just a boy," the other answers.

"You swim all that way, boy?"

"Yes, sir. I'm a fair swimmer, sir."

"What for?"

"I need passage to Cerion, sir."

"Passage to Cerion!" Scoffing. Laughter. "We're no charter, boy! Find yourself another ship."

"I have no money for a charter, sir. I mean to work for it."

"Work for it!" More laughter. Footsteps. A deep voice growls about the racket. The men go quiet. Hushed discussion of the boy in the skiff. A broad man with a pitted face and squinted eyes leers down at me. Looks me over. Calls out an order for the rope ladder.

"Climb it," he says. I do, as quickly as the flames that licked the shelves. I stand before him. Bow respectfully. "You want to work, eh?" He eyes me. "Why should I let you?"

"I'm a fast learner, sir. A hard worker. I don't complain. I'll do any task. I'm not squeamish. I'm quick. I can climb. I can swim." I say. He grabs my wrists, inspects my hands. Looks at my fingers stained red.

"From the dye fields," he grunts and lets go. "Hard working, I'm sure of it. Ever been on a ship before?"

"No, sir."

"You'll get seasick."

"I've been on a carriage before, sir. A bumpy one. Never got sick, sir."

"A carriage!" Laughter again.

"A carriage is a far cry from a ship tossed by the waves of a storm.

We've got a crowd in the rows ashore, boy. Men. Strong men. All waiting to work for passage. Seafaring men. Men who know what they're doing."

"I know. That's why I swum out. I could have stowed away, but I want to work. I'll work harder than them. I'm honest. I won't argue. I don't eat much. I don't like to sleep. I'm respectful. I don't steal. I'm not afraid of anything. I'll do my work, you won't even notice me. None of them swum out. They don't want it as much, sir."

"Look at him, Cap, sir. Somethin's not right," one of the uniformed men murmurs. I cast my eyes down. Don't let them look too hard. Feel Cap's eyes on me.

"Climb the foremast. Untie the lashing on the fore moonraker. Stow it back proper again." He crosses his arms. Smirks. I don't question. I run to the ratlines and climb all the way to the top. Even anchored in the calm, the mast rocks. I grip hard with my legs. Work the knots. Drop the edge of the highest sail. Bind it up again. Tie it. They watch from below. I'm sure they're impressed. A boy from the dye fields shouldn't know knots, rigging, and sails. I don't know it, but it comes to me anyway. I lash it up again, exactly as it was. Make perfect knots. Slide down the ratlines. Land light and sure at the captain's feet. Salute.

"Well done." He's impressed. Pleasantly surprised. I nod once, but don't smile. Don't want to look too proud. Powerful men don't like that. "You can stay on. Do as you're told. One wrong move and we cast you over. Agreed?" He offers his hand, and I shake it. "What're you called, boy?"

"Tib, sir."

"Welcome aboard, then, Tib."

The journey is long. Days into weeks. I sleep anywhere but below, where the wood encases me, reminding me of the trees, the roots, the past. The crow's nest is my favorite. Here I can see all around me. Watch passing ships grow and shrink. See ocean stretch to a thin curve, all the way out on the horizon. I'm talented with the lamplight, and I learn how to send signals to the navy ships that follow us, too slow to keep our pace. We are their scout ship. We watch for danger.

Soon, I am invisible to those more important to me. I can lurk. Pick up conversations. Learn things. One of those navy ships carries

Prince Vorance. The only prince of Sunteri. He courts the eldest daughter of the king of Cerion. Her name is Sarabel. She is smitten with him. Six ships come with him including ours. Six is an auspicious number, they say. A circle number. I'm not sure what it means, but I can't ask. If I do, they'll know that I've been listening.

One month. We sail into the mouth of the river they call Jairun. I don't like it. We move slower here, through the center of Elespen, where the jungle creeps into the water on both sides of us. Days more of this. Days of watching jungle become village and jungle again, and then sand and only sand as far as I can see. An ocean of sand. Too much like Sunteri. Too much like the home I never wanted to see again. I feel the panic rise in me. I don't want to be in the desert.

"Sleep."

Yes, sleep. I curl up in the safety of the fore nest, and when I wake the stars stretch out endlessly above me. Noise. Lapping and chatting. Laughing and shouting. Bargaining. Unloading. The scrape of the hull against the pier.

"Boy!" Cap shouts, and I slip down the ratlines and drop to his side. The deck is deserted except for the pair of watch guards at the gangway. I stand straight and look Cap in the eye, as he has told me to do. It keeps a man honest, he says, to meet his crew's eyes.

"Sir!" I shout. He taught me to do that, too.

He tells me I'm a hard worker. I have earned five copper, which he jingles in a pouch. I like the sound of it. I have never held coin before. It has more weight than I expected. He tells me I can go ashore if I want to, and then he goes back below. I peer out at the city. Cresten. Capital of Elespen. It's different from Zhaghen. Cleaner. Brighter, even in the starlight. Noisy, but the noise is happier. No towers here, to watch and rule over them. Just a castle, low and sprawling. Music leaks out from the taverns into the street. People in beautiful colors dance in the glow of torchlight. Others toss coin at them. Even in the night, merchants in booths cook and sell. The aroma is exotic and flavorful. My mouth waters.

"Stay aboard."

Yes, stay aboard. I tie the coin to my belt and wrap the sash around it three times to secure it. Then I climb back into the nest and sleep again.

I wake to the signal. The air is cooler, even with the sun bearing down. We're sailing again, flying across the water. North still, but more west now. The jungle is far behind us, just a line of deep green between the sea and sky. I train the scope behind, find the trailing ship. Read the message. Flash the mirror to acknowledge.

Two months now at sea, since we left Zhaghen. Sea and days of messages filled with nothing. All is well. All is well. Back and forth. Over and again. Still, the work is easy. Not like the fields. Freer, even confined to a ship. I keep to myself way up here, and nobody bothers with me. The main nest collects the same messages as mine. Cap tells me I'm the backup. My keen eye is valuable. I could do the main nest one day, if I stay on. He thinks I want a life of this. He doesn't know.

When they appear, Cerion's cliffs are unmistakable. A white slash between the cloudless blue sky and the crisp blue-green sea. They grow impossibly high as we approach, so high that it would take ten of our ship's highest masts to reach the top. As we dock I'm paid again, and told that I'm welcome back. I say little in the way of farewells. I know I'll never return to the sea.

The climb up the cliff seems as long as the sailing itself. Stairs and more stairs. My legs are strong, though, from climbing the ratlines. I scurry past others who trudge more slowly. The stone glints wet beneath my feet, catching the sun. Wet, but not icy, which I find strange. The wind is threatens to carry me off, and I keep close to the wall as it lashes at me. I have never felt cold like this before. Winter. Sunteri has no winter. The chill is painful. I am not dressed for it. I have my gloves. I have my new boots. No cloak, though. No sleeves to cover my arms.

"*Climb faster.*"

Yes, climb faster. The work keeps me warm. Up and up I go, until I reach the top and the city stretches out before me. Low. Plain. Clean. Kind. Someone stops me. Offers me a clay mug filled with a sweet, hot drink. Tells me I should visit their tavern. Moves on to those behind me without asking for payment. I sip it and it warms me to the toes. Children run past, laughing, cloaks of fur flapping behind them.

"*Follow them.*"

Yes, follow them. I leave my empty cup at the stall and trot after them, ignoring the numbness in my toes and the sting of cold that pinches my fingertips through my gloves. I hug myself tightly as I pass booths selling fresh fish, or baubles, or fine clothes. I slow at one that boasts barrels of ground dye powders, heaping with red and blue and orange dust.

"Ten silver a scoop," a pretty lady smiles at me. I wonder if she knows the work that goes into one scoop. Thousands of blooms. The picking, the hauling, the drying, the grinding. The dozens who break their backs in the field for a loaf to feed their family and a roof over their heads.

"The children."

Yes, the children. I tear myself from the booth and chase after the laughter. When I catch up, I find them standing in a crowd that lines the streets. One of them, a girl just a little younger than I am with bright red curls that poke out from beneath her hat, bumps my shoulder.

"Aren't you cold?" she asks, eyeing my bare arms. Her eyes are green. Jungle green. Prettier, though. I shrug. "Raefe." She tugs the cloak of the boy beside her. He's an older boy, with his own spyglass. He cranes his neck to peer over the crowd through it. He's bundled. All of them are, in fur wraps and thick woven hats and strips of weaving that wind round their necks up to their noses. The girls have soft, round, pillow-like tubes which they slip their hands into to keep them warm. The colorful ribbons that trail from them flutter in the wind.

"The carriage is coming. It's going slow," he says on tiptoe. "Wish we could climb up on something."

"Nessa said no climbing, Raefe," says another girl with a bossy tone. "It's too icy." This girl is older than the first, and very prim-looking.

"Can you see the prince? Or the princess? Can you see her round belly?" An even younger boy hops, trying to see over the crowd. "Let me look!"

"Ruben!" The prim girl scowls and pokes the boy. "Don't be disrespectful!"

"Rae." The first girl tugs the older boy again. "I need a cloak."

"In my bag, Saesa." Raefe leans toward her, still watching. "No, can't see inside the carriage. The curtains are closed. They might open them when they get closer."

"I want to see!" The youngest of them tugs at Raefe while Saesa rummages through his shoulder bag.

"Here." She pulls out a thick woolen cloak, dyed green, and hands it to me. I eye it. "Don't be so suspicious," she says. "It used to be Raefe's but it's too small now. It's still good, though. Rube didn't want it, so Nessa said find someone who could use it. It has a hood and everything." She nudges me with it. My teeth chatter, but I don't accept. A drink is one thing, but this cloak is expensive. A gift is a trick, my Nan would say. Don't trust it. Anyone who gives freely just wants power over you. It's true. I've seen it happen.

"Here they come. They've opened the curtain, too!"

"Let me up, Rae-rae," the youngest girl whines.

"Hold on tight, Emmie," Raefe says as he hefts her to his shoulders. She squeals and waves to the carriage. I feel the cloak drape my shoulders and wrap snug round my arms. Sae smiles at me as she ties the laces closed. Then she ducks to peek through the mass of the crowd in front of us. I should protest, but I don't. It's warm. Nice.

"Stay with them."

Yes, I should stay with them. The crowd around us cheers, and the carriage glints golden and purple and burnished wood in flashes as it moves past. Those before us bow, and so do I as it passes. But I'm one of the first to look up.

"Hail, Prince Eron! Hail Princess Amei!" The crowd calls out. Inside the carriage, the princess waves happily. She is wrapped in clouds of lavender. Her skin is a dark color I haven't seen before. Rich and brown. Beside her, the prince looks pale but strong. He smiles and nods to those who call his name. His eyes are distant, though. Troubled. I wonder if anyone else notices. The crowd throws favors. Beside me, Saesa gasps.

"Oh, there she is! There she is, Rae!" She bounces with excitement and points to a rider far back in the escort. "Azaeli!" she cries.

The knight is shorter than the other riders around her, but different. Her armor is blue like midnight with stars that flash and dazzle in the sunlight reflected off of her white cloak. The flag she waves is blue and gold check. A great two-handed sword is strapped to her saddle. Her face is covered to her cheeks with her helm. She grins and waves at Saesa, who squeals with delight.

"Azaeli."

Yes, Azaeli. I watch carefully. Others in blue and gold ride beside her. Proud. Tall. Each one more different than the next. I try to pick out their professions. Five warriors, one a giant of a man. An archer with pointed ears. Two Mages. Two healers, but one of them might not be part of the group. He's got no gold or blue.

A score of royal guard follow those, and behind them trail a group of subjects who have chosen to walk behind the procession to the gates.

"Will they escort him all the way to Highcastle?" Ruben, the younger boy, asks.

"Just to the crossroads," Saesa answers. "Then the Lake Guard will take them the rest of the way. Oh, imagine it! They could meet any kind of adventure out there! Bandits and bandywilgits. Or trolls! I'll bet Sir Azaeli could take out twenty trolls."

"Oh, honestly, Saesa!" the bossy girl chides. "Only you would dream of being the knight. Imagine being the princess, whisked off to a romantic castle to be pampered and served while waiting for the royal heir to arrive. Strolling by the lake with Prince Eron..." she sighs dreamily. "I heard it's warmer there. Better for the baby."

"What does a princess do but sit around all day? I'd rather have adventure! Azi is the first knight her age in decades! Imagine that!"

"Well, I heard," Ruben pipes up, "that the real reason is they're sending the prince away—"

"Ruben." Raefe warns as the people in front of us turn curiously. He lowers Emmie to the street and stretches his neck from side to side. "Time to go home," he says. "Take Lilen's hand, Emmie."

"Yes, don't gossip in the streets like a louse, Ruben." Lilen grabs Emmie's hand and gives the boy a disapproving look. Beside her, Saesa rolls her eyes and turns to me.

"You have a place to go?" she asks. I shake my head. "Come on, then." She pulls me along with them, and I let her.

Ice. Ribbons fluttering. Red curls bouncing. Sweets. Running. Sliding. Laughter. Warmth.

"We're home!" everyone calls out as we tumble through the door out of the cold. Inside is bright and grand. Rich. Like a palace. They all

344

sit. Pull off their boots. Line them neatly on the side of the carpet. Fold their wrappings and stow them in the carved cupboard. I don't. My boots are new. My gloves are new. I won't lose them.

"Stay here."

Yes, stay here. A woman with a baby on her hip appears at the top of the twisting staircase. She smiles and presses a finger to her lips.

"Garsi just went down," she says in a hushed voice. "Into the sitting room with you. Luncheon soon." Her feet are light on the polished stone stairs even holding the baby. Her dress is fine. It shimmers in the light from the high windows. "Oh, and you've brought a friend." Her smile is bright. Kind. I look away from it.

"Yes, can he stay?" Saesa pleads. Lilen rolls her eyes. Raefe ushers the others to the sitting room. How strange, I think, to have a room just for sitting.

"Well, it isn't my place to say, is it? You'll have to ask Nessa. Go on, then. Take Errie with you." She gives the wiggling baby to Saesa. Goes through another door, letting out the mouthwatering aroma of fresh baked bread and stew. Saesa adjusts the baby. Tugs my arm.

"Come on," she says. "Meet Nessa."

She doesn't tell me to take off my boots, so I don't. I walk on the thick carpet with them. I wonder what it would feel like on my toes. Soft. Like sand, maybe. The sitting room is fine. Elegant. Lots of fancy furniture and thick draperies and baubles. Expensive things. Sparkling things. Things that serve no purpose but to be looked at and not touched. The lady on the sofa fits right in. Her skirts are all ruffles that take up most of the seat and spill to the floor. Bright green, like the cloak. Enough fabric to clothe all of the girls. But they are dressed prettily enough on their own.

Emmie runs to the sofa and climbs up, trampling the gown. The lady beams. Hugs her. Kisses her face, still sticky with sweets. Sets her book on the side table as she lovingly takes the baby from Saesa. Her eyes twinkle as the rest swarm to hug and kiss and pile together onto her skirts.

"So, did you see the prince, then?" Her voice is filled with affection and amusement.

"Oh, yes, and the princess," Emmie kneels on her lap, facing her. Reaches to Nessa's perfectly done hair. Twirls a lock around her finger.

It's black, not red like Saesa's or blonde like Lilen's.

"And Azaeli." Saesa says with excitement.

"All of His Majesty's Elite were there. And a score of High Guard, just like you thought," Raefe says as he leans against the grand hearth. I edge closer to its warmth, listening as the rest recount every detail of the procession. Details I didn't notice, but that seem to interest Nessa very much. The crackling fire reminds me of the towers. The flames. The smoke as it rose into the night sky. My task accomplished. My new life begun.

"Stay here."

Yes, I'll stay here. Here, where they'll never suspect me. Here, where I'll be safe.

Call of Sunteri

Available on Amazon.com
Be sure to sign up for my mailing list for updates on this and other upcoming titles!
www.missysheldrake.com

ACKNOWLEDGMENTS

When I began writing this book, I wanted to tell a story that would entice its readers and take them away to a place of beauty, wonder, and love. I wanted to create something that could be enjoyed by both the young and the young at heart. I'm so grateful to God for the inspiration that came to me while I was writing. I'm thankful to my husband James and my son Wesley, who were both so supportive and encouraging during the writing process.

I'm also very grateful to the following readers who were kind enough to take the time to explore Call of Kythshire before it was published: Emily Derrick, Mckayla Ford, Bonnie Hatch, Abby Venetsanos, Angie Venetsanos, and Debra White. Your encouragement in my writing ability and your advice has always been invaluable to me, and I will always be grateful to you.

To Stacy Marans and Karri Klawiter, I am indebted to you both for your expert advice on the design of my book cover. I am many things, but a graphic designer is definitely not one of them. I'm sure the look of my cover would have suffered greatly if not for your help. Thank you so much.

Finally to Ellisa Barr, who helped me with too many things to list here: Thank you for inspiring me to start, and for seeing me through to the end.

Thank you all!

About the Author

Missy Sheldrake lives in Northern Virginia with her amazingly supportive husband, brilliant son, and very energetic dog. Aside from filling the role of mom and wife, Missy is a mural painter, sculptor, and illustrator. She has always had a fascination with fairies and a great love of fairy tales and fantasy stories.

Call of Kythshire is her first novel.

You can see more of her work including color illustrations on her website: www.missysheldrake.com

CPSIA information can be obtained
at www.ICGtesting.com
Printed in the USA
LVHW091948211220
674833LV00020B/263